## Also by Reese Ryan

### The Bourbon Brothers
*Savannah's Secrets*
*The Billionaire's Legacy*
*Engaging the Enemy*
*A Reunion of Rivals*
*Waking Up Married*
*The Bad Boy Experiment*

## Also by Nicki Night

### Blackwells of New York
*Intimate Negotiations*
*One More Second Chance*

### The Barrington Brothers
*Her Chance at Love*
*His Love Lesson*
*Riding into Love*

Discover more at millsandboon.co.uk

# A VALENTINE FOR CHRISTMAS

## REESE RYAN

# WORK-LOVE BALANCE

## NICKI NIGHT

# MILLS & BOON

First Published in Great Britain 2022
by Mills & Boon, an imprint of HarperCollins*Publishers* Ltd
1 London Bridge Street, London, SE1 9GF

www.harpercollins.co.uk

HarperCollins*Publishers*
1st Floor, Watermarque Building,
Ringsend Road, Dublin 4, Ireland

*A Valentine for Christmas* © 2022 Roxanne Ravenel
*Work-Love Balance* © 2022 Renee Daniel Flagler

ISBN: 978-0-263-30392-6

# A VALENTINE FOR CHRISTMAS

## REESE RYAN

My new Valentine Vineyards series is dedicated to everyone who has read my Bourbon Brothers series and taken the Abbott family into their hearts. Because you weren't quite ready to let go of Joe, Duke, Iris, Blake, Parker, Max, Cole and Zora Abbott or end our adventures in Magnolia Lake, neither was I.

I hope you'll enjoy getting to know the Valentines and their regular interactions with the growing Abbott family.

# One

Chandra Valentine gripped the handle of her rolling carry-on luggage as she watched the tiny regional plane taxi toward her gate at the Charlotte Douglas International Airport. She honestly wished she hadn't seen it. Then she could pretend it was a larger plane. A stable plane. The kind she'd become accustomed to flying in over her past thirty-nine years of life. Not one of those little puddle jumpers she'd always taken great pains to avoid.

She loosened her grip when she realized her nails were stabbing her palms. She opened her hand, studying the row of angry semicircles that trailed across her skin. Chandra took a deep breath, her eyes drifting closed momentarily. When she opened them, she was greeted by a penetrating dark gaze.

The incredibly handsome man tipped his chin in greeting as he rubbed his full beard. Typically, she'd considered a full-grown beard a turnoff. Who knew exactly what might be lurking in that thing? But for this brother, she'd make an exception.

He was dressed in an unbuttoned, green-and-black plaid shirt over a black Henley shirt, distressed jeans and brown Timberland boots. His lopsided smile made her belly flip in ways it hadn't in longer than she cared to admit.

Chandra gave him a quick nod and an awkward wave before sauntering away.

The man was *fine*. In ways she could wax poetically about for days. But this wasn't a girls' trip to Vegas. She was about to board a tuna can with wings so she could meet her dad in some small mountain town in Tennessee.

If she didn't feel a sense of urgency to get to the little town of Magnolia Lake, where her dad had summoned her and her five younger siblings, she would've flown to the closest major airport, then driven the remainder of the way through the mountains. But she was worried about her dad.

Abbott Raymond Valentine had turned sixty-nine on his last birthday—which she'd missed because she was at a company retreat in Utah. Her father had been in sort of a funk since his mother had died a few years ago. It didn't feel quite like mourning, but something deeper. She hadn't been able to figure out what it was, and her dad wouldn't open up about what he was feeling. He'd been grumpy and evasive whenever she tried to broach the topic, which ruined the mood of their weekly calls. So she'd stopped asking, hoping he'd eventually be ready to confide in her.

But two weeks ago, her father had called a big family meeting via teleconference to inform them he needed to see all of them in person. Despite their pleading and threatening, her father wouldn't offer the slightest hint of what this was about. Chandra was terrified about what might prompt her father to gather them together like this for the first time since her grandmother's funeral.

It'd taken three days and an online calendar for the six

siblings to figure out when their schedules would permit all of them to take time off their jobs and get together for at least a week, preferably two—as her father had requested. But here she was, on her way to some tiny town in the Smoky Mountains where she only hoped they had internet, cell phone service and indoor plumbing, because hiking in the woods was the limit of her outdoorsyness.

Chandra settled into a seat as far away as she could get from the handsome man with the gorgeous dark eyes who was making her rethink her stance on beards. Because as much as she'd like to get to know him up close and personal, she didn't have time for extracurricular activities on this trip.

She was a problem solver. Had been since she was eight years old and returned from school to discover the *Dear Abbott* letter her mother had left on the kitchen counter.

Her father had been gutted. She, Nolan, Sebastian and Alonzo had been devastated. Just like that, she'd become the adult in the house as her father struggled to deal with her mother's abandonment. In some ways, she'd felt like the only adult in the room with her family ever since.

Chandra rubbed her arms against the chill in the airport, still devastated by the painful memory.

Mr. Handsome stared at her from across the wide expanse.

Chandra pulled the book on teambuilding she'd been reading from her purse and opened it. She couldn't afford to be distracted by the man. She needed to get to the bottom of whatever was going on with her father, solve whatever problem needed to be solved, then return to San Diego.

Julian Brandon returned to his airplane gate clutching a grease-stained bag with a piping hot panini sandwich and fries in one hand and pulling his rolling luggage behind him with the other.

His flight had already boarded.

The woman taking tickets at the door narrowed her gaze and gestured for him to hurry.

"I thought the plane didn't board for another five minutes." He produced his phone so she could scan his boarding pass.

"Everyone was here, so the captain wants to leave as soon as possible. Enjoy your flight."

Julian shoved his phone into his back pocket and made his way through the tunnel. Then he made his way to his seat. At six foot two, being folded into a cramped seat on one of these smaller planes was never a picnic. So while he preferred a window seat, he'd booked an aisle seat so he could stretch his legs. But it appeared he was in luck. The window seat beside him was empty. So he'd have the entire row to himself.

He put his bag in the overhead bin and settled into his seat, prepared to watch an episode or two of a sci-fi show while giving himself a reprieve from thinking about his reluctant return to the little town where he was raised. The town he'd be moving back to for the next four years—and not a day more. Not because he wanted to but because it was part of an obligation he'd made as a fourteen-year-old kid when a local philanthropist offered to sponsor his full ride to college and then med school.

They sealed the door of the plane and the captain announced they would be leaving soon, so everyone should take their seats. Julian breathed a sigh of relief; grateful he'd gotten lucky. He slid over to the window seat.

"Excuse me, but you're sitting in my spot."

Julian looked up and locked eyes with the stunning woman he'd been checking out in the airport terminal. Her black T-shirt said Wake Up, Kick Ass, Repeat in bold white letters. Slim black pants hugged her curves. Her dark brown hair was pushed back with a pricey pair of sunglasses. Her dark brown skin looked flawless and her pursed lips were punctuated with a deep purple lipstick.

Julian sat there, blinking, as if he'd never seen a beautiful woman before.

He was usually much more suave than this. But something about this woman threw him off his game. He was at a loss for words.

"Ma'am, you'll need to take your seat." The flight attendant's bright smile did little to mask her irritation.

"I will." The woman propped a hand on her hip. "As soon as this gentleman gets out of my seat."

"Sorry. Thought I had the row to myself." Julian unbuckled his seat belt and stepped into the aisle, so the woman could get to her seat.

The flight attendant gave him the evil eye, then moved to help an older couple searching for space in the overhead bins.

"Sorry," Julian said to the woman who was buckling her seat belt as she stared out onto the tarmac. "When they shut the door and no one was here, I assumed—"

"That you'd hit the air travel lottery and had the row to yourself?" Her lips twitched with a hint of a smile. She tucked loose strands of hair behind her ear. "Given the situation, I would've made the same assumption. But I was here...just in the restroom." She dropped her gaze, and he wondered if beneath her rich dark brown skin her cheeks were flushed. "When I'm traveling alone, I don't like leaving my things on the seat unattended."

"Understandable." He nodded. After an awkward bit of silence, he extended his hand. "I'm JB, by the way. And I'm not usually a seat stealer."

Her smile broadened. She shook his hand. "Chandra."

"Pleasure to meet you, Chandra." He realized he was smiling like a goober and still holding her hand when she gently tugged it free.

He cleared his throat and focused intently on sticking his phone and tablet into the pocket on the back of the seat in front of him.

Chandra reached into her bag and dug out a pair of premium over-the-ear headphones. A clear sign, if ever he'd seen one, that she had no intention of engaging in conversation.

*Message received.*

He'd go back to Plan A: catching up on episodes of television shows he never had time to watch. Up until today, he'd been too slammed with residency at a busy hospital in Philadelphia and volunteer work at clinics in both the inner city and rural Pennsylvania to make time for sci-fi escapism…but his life was going to be very different now.

During his going-away party in the hospital cafeteria the night before, his friends had said he should be glad to have a normal schedule and free time. They were jealous that he'd get to have a life now that he was going to be a small-town doctor.

He'd smiled politely and pretended to agree, but truthfully, he knew he'd miss being so busy he barely had time to dwell on his past mistakes—like the fractured relationship with his mother. Now that he was returning to the town where he'd grown up and where his mother still resided, there would be little chance of avoiding those uncomfortable feelings. This plane ride might be his last opportunity *not* to ruminate on what an awful son he was.

As the plane sped along the runway in preparation for their ascent, the woman gripped the armrest between them, her fancy high-heel boots dug into the floor, and she squeezed her eyes shut.

Julian wanted to ask if she was all right. But it would be a stupid question. Clearly, she wasn't. It was also clear Chandra didn't want to be bothered, so he'd respect that.

He just hoped to God this woman wouldn't get sick during the flight.

Before long, they were given the okay to turn on electronics. But the pilot warned that it would likely be a bumpy ride and kept the sign on admonishing them to remain seated with their seat belts fastened.

No air traveler liked turbulence, but it didn't particularly bother him…except when he was trying to watch a show on his tablet and eat his no-longer-hot panini and fries. He stuffed a few of the delicious, lukewarm fries into his mouth, then bit into his sandwich. When he opened his bottle of soda, the woman beside him nearly jumped out of her skin.

Chandra's arms tensed as she white-knuckled her grip on the end of the armrest. She pointed at his iPad screen.

"Is that *Orphan Black*?"

Julian slid one earbud out of his ear and nodded. "Yeah. A couple friends of mine are science fiction geeks. They've been urging me to try the show for years, but they recently gifted me all the seasons. Figured I'd finally give it a try."

"My sister raved about the show when it was on, but I never got around to watching it." Chandra's jaw tightened in response to the dip and sway of the plane. "I'd planned to read, but with all this turbulence, I can't focus."

"Nervous flyer?"

"Not on larger aircraft. Which is why I usually avoid smaller, regional planes." Chandra squeezed her eyes shut momentarily, taking a deep breath before opening them again. "Let's just say I'll be glad when we land."

"You're welcome to watch the show with me," he suggested, surprising himself. "I'm just starting Episode One. It'll distract you from the bumpy ride and give you something else to focus on."

"I don't want to disturb the other passengers."

"I can share my audio with you." Julian was glad he'd

paid attention when his tech geek roommate had shown him this trick. "Just tap the power button on your headset."

She did and he shared his audio with her.

Chandra seemed surprised when the show began playing in her headset. "Thank you, JB."

"My pleasure." He extended the greasy cardboard box toward her. "French fry?"

Chandra stared at them apprehensively, her brows scrunched. Then she thanked him and grabbed two fries. She nibbled thoughtfully while watching the screen where he'd restarted the first episode. Chandra was completely engaged with the show from the opening scene, and he was mesmerized by her.

She was even more beautiful up close. Her sweet, subtle scent reminded him of the honeysuckle that grew along the fence in the backyard of his childhood home. They shared the armrest she'd been clutching for dear life minutes earlier. And the tension in her shoulders seemed to have eased as she focused on the screen of his tablet, propped on his tray.

When he offered her the fries again, she gladly accepted the box. Chandra nibbled quietly on the fries—which she apparently had no plans of relinquishing—as she reacted to each scene. The tense, action-packed show was doing its job—distracting her from the movement of the plane. But as exciting as the show was, he'd rather be spending their time together getting to know her.

There were a dozen questions he wanted to ask: Where was she traveling to? Where was she from? Was this a business or pleasure trip? Would she like to go out for coffee? What would she like for breakfast?

Instead, they watched the screen in silence. Her arm leaned against his, and her warmth seeped into his skin, despite the layers of fabric between them.

Suddenly the turbulence became far more noticeable as

the plane dipped and then swayed. The captain requested that everyone take their seats and put away any trays. He complied. And after a particularly violent rumble, Chandra gripped his forearm, her heels pressed into the floor.

Julian placed his hand atop hers and forced a smile, even as his own stomach dipped. "I know it feels scary, Chandra. But everything is going to be fine—I promise."

Chandra jerked her attention toward him, her forehead furrowed by a deep frown. Her mesmerizing eyes were a gorgeous deep shade of chocolate brown, rimmed by a slightly darker hue. Her smoky purple eye shadow made her brown eyes pop, and he honestly couldn't help staring.

Chandra studied him; one perfectly arched brow hiked toward her hairline. She heaved a quiet sigh, and her shoulders slid back into place. She loosened her grip on his forearm but didn't remove her hand. Nor did he remove his hand from hers.

"My brain realizes that, logically, you're in no position to make such a promise. You don't have any control over what the plane does, and for all we know, the pilot and co-pilot were in the lounge drinking body shots off the flight attendants and smoking J's." She shrugged. "But hearing you promise everything will be fine, like you truly believe it, really does help. So thank you."

Julian's mouth curved in a smile. He had that unsettling feeling in his gut again. Like he was at the top of a roller coaster, counting down the milliseconds until the car would careen down the hill.

What was it about Chandra…he didn't even know her last name…that ignited that kind of reaction?

"Glad I could help." Julian reluctantly removed his hand from atop hers and settled back against his seat.

Chandra released his arm, then frowned when the plane dipped and the cabin rumbled, causing several of the passengers around them to gasp and murmur.

Chandra closed her eyes. "Everything is going to be fine. Everything is going to be fine. Everything is going to be…"

Another bout of rough turbulence hit. Chandra slapped a hand over her mouth, as if to stifle a scream. She was shaking.

"I need you to make good on that promise, JB," she said.

"Did you roller-skate on the sidewalk as a kid?" he asked.

Chandra furrowed her brows. "Sure. Why?"

"Remember how bumpy it was versus skating on a smooth surface, like at the rink? This is like that. Or like driving on a road filled with potholes. It's uncomfortable and creates a bit of drama, but in the end, it's always okay. It will be today, too." Julian winked. "All right?"

Chandra blew out a breath and nodded.

"In the meantime, maybe this will help…"

He switched to a calming Zen playlist he listened to while meditating each morning. It was his way of chilling out despite the stress of medical school and his residency. Since their audio was still linked, the music played through Chandra's headphones, too.

Julian perched his elbow on the armrest between them and opened his palm. "If you get really nervous, you can hold my—"

There was another dip and rumble, and Chandra pressed her palm to his and threaded their fingers. She squeezed tightly, her nails digging into the back of his hand.

Julian squeezed her hand reassuringly, hoping like hell everything would, in fact, be just fine.

# Two

Chandra was grateful the plane had finally landed. Her fellow passenger's calm reassurance and the Zen playlist he pumped through her headset had helped her get through the worst bout of turbulence she'd ever experienced.

She released his hand, which she'd been clutching for dear life for the past forty minutes. "I guess I should give that back now." Her cheeks heated with embarrassment. "You'll probably be needing it."

"Once the feeling returns." The man's broad smile as he shook his presumably numb hand put her at ease.

Still, she couldn't help being embarrassed. She'd behaved like a child frightened by a thunderstorm. It was unlike her. She'd always been the one who'd comforted her younger siblings and reassured her father through whatever storms life brought.

And she was the take-charge director of supply chain, logistics and workplace whose claim to fame was her ability to get shit done with an unshakable smile while stepping on the fewest toes possible. She made the hard decisions that needed to be made: budget cuts, department closures, staff reassignments. Whatever it took to keep the company lean and efficient. Even if it meant crying over a bottle of wine that night because she'd been forced to cut someone's job.

When she'd been sent to San Diego with the assignment to "clean house," she'd been dubbed the Smiling Assassin. But she'd established a new company culture and earned the respect of the frontline employees.

Her Achilles' heel, in a position that frequently required travel, was that she didn't much enjoy flying. Thus today's embarrassing display.

She was grateful JB had been seated beside her and that he'd been genuinely sweet, patient and kind. She doubted that coddling a grown woman through a bumpy flight was how he'd planned to spend his day.

"Here's your carry-on." The man's deep, soothing voice stirred her from her daze. He took her black designer bag with hot-pink-and-white flowers printed on it down from the overhead bin and pulled up the handle.

"Thank you again, JB. It was nice meeting you." Chandra extended a hand.

His large, warm hand enveloped hers. He held it for a moment before shaking it.

"The pleasure was definitely *mine*," he said, still holding her hand. His eyes crinkled with a smile, his full, sensuous lips peeking out from beneath his beard.

Her belly did somersaults and her pulse raced.

Chandra tugged her hand from his. Not because she was offended by his flirtation. Because she liked the feel of her hand in his a little too much. For the briefest moment, she'd imagined lifting onto her toes and pressing her mouth to the lush, full lips that taunted her with a sexy little smirk.

"Take care." Chandra lifted the strap of her bag higher on her shoulder.

As she turned to walk away, she could practically feel the heat of his stare warming her skin.

She'd come to town to find out what was going on with her father and to reconnect with her siblings. She hadn't risked her life on a tiny plane to hook up with some ultra-hot, lumberjack-looking brother who'd probably developed those muscled biceps and broad shoulders while swinging an axe in the forest.

Still, a tiny part of her was disappointed the handsome man hadn't at least inquired about seeing her again. She would've politely rejected his advance, of course. But it was nice to at least be asked.

Chandra rolled her bag through the tunnel and onto the concourse of the airport in search of strong coffee. Then she headed to the car rental desk so she could make the hour drive to the little town of Magnolia Lake, where she'd been summoned.

According to her GPS app, Chandra was halfway to her destination. She hadn't expected long stretches of lonely country road threaded through wooded areas and vast farms, with not another person in view for miles.

What if she blew a tire or worse?

*Stop being so melodramatic.*

Everything would be fine. Fretting over worst-case scenarios was just her brain's way of avoiding the issue at hand. Namely, whatever was going on with her father.

Whenever she permitted her mind to wonder about the possibilities, they frightened her. Chandra gripped the steering wheel of the midsize import she'd rented.

"Please be okay, Dad. *Please.*" She whispered the words in the emptiness of the car, her heart racing.

No one lived forever; she realized that. Still, she was nearly forty and she would be a daddy's girl until the day she died. Maybe she lived two thousand miles from her father.

But across that distance, she still needed to know he was okay and that he would be there whenever she needed him.

Chandra's phone rang. She had been in too much of a hurry to bother syncing it to the rental vehicle. So she reached for the phone, sitting in the cup holder. The name and photo of her youngest sibling, Naya, flashed across the screen.

Nyles and Naya, her father's late-in-life fraternal twins from his second marriage, were the babies of the family and acted the part. Nyles had a different job every time she talked to him. And at nearly twenty-eight, he seemed to be in a perpetual state of finding himself. Meanwhile, Naya had stumbled into being an Instagram influencer. Her little sister made a very comfortable living. She was based in LA, but often took sponsored trips all over the globe. They spoke often and got together once or twice a month.

Chandra had been calling her sister since her plane landed an hour ago. She was in no hurry to respond to Naya now.

She glanced up at the stretch of road in front of her and was startled by the sight of a large black bear and two cubs crossing the road. Chandra dropped her phone and gripped the wheel so tightly that her knuckles ached. She jammed her foot on the brake but didn't floor it. The last thing she wanted was to come to a complete stop with three angry black bears lurking around her.

But as the car hurtled toward the family of bears, the mother bear stood tall and Chandra screamed, swerving the car hard to the right and jamming her foot on the gas this time, hoping she could drive around the bears and get the hell out of there.

Suddenly, the front right wheel of the import spun out on the muddy shoulder. Without traction, the car slid down an embankment.

"No, no, no!" Chandra tried to yank the wheel to the

left—back toward the bears who watched her dilemma with mild interest. She tried her best to avoid sliding down the embankment and into a ditch. But the car continued to careen off the edge of the road until the vehicle tipped over, tossing her cell phone, purse and lukewarm coffee into the air right before everything came crashing down.

It all happened so fast, she barely had time to think, let alone react. Chandra felt dazed and disoriented. Her wrist and head throbbed, and she was wet and sticky, courtesy of the remnants of her latte. Her chest ached as the seat belt cut into it. Chandra's breathing was labored, and her eyes were still wrenched shut. She didn't dare move. And she hoped to God the bears had continued on their merry way across the road and wouldn't make an awful situation even worse by trying to pry her out of this glorified aluminum can.

After several moments passed without another sound, Chandra pried open one eye, then the other.

Her world had *literally* turned upside down.

Chandra was suspended by the seat belt that cut across her chest uncomfortably as she hung upside down. Blood rushed to her head and her hair hung in her face.

*But at least I'm alive... I think.*

Her wrist ached, but nothing appeared to be broken or bleeding. Suddenly, the ring of her phone cut through the eerie quietness. She could hear the phone ringing but had no idea where the sound was coming from. And she definitely couldn't reach it.

She tried to unlatch her seat belt, but it was jammed. Both her wrists were sore, and she didn't have the strength to wrench the seat belt loose.

Chandra's eyes flooded with tears and her body ached.

Correction: she wasn't dead *yet*.

Was this the way her story would end?

# Three

Julian had opted to take the scenic route to Magnolia Lake. He was driving a vintage tan-and-white 1970 Ford F-100. He'd needed a way to get to town from the airport in Knoxville and his cousin Elias, who owned body shops in Knoxville and Gatlinburg, needed a truck transported to Magnolia Lake. So he was delivering the iconic old truck, which had been completely refurbished.

He hadn't been back home to Magnolia Lake in the last three years. And in the five years preceding that, his visits home had become less and less frequent.

It had been better that way. Each visit home to spend time with his mother had become more painful and awkward than the last. So one year, when his roommate and a few of their friends had invited him to join them in Cancún for Thanksgiving, he'd said yes. His mother had almost sounded relieved when he'd said he wouldn't be home for the holiday.

So when another friend had invited him on a ski trip to

Colorado Springs for Christmas, he'd said yes to that, too. Since then, going on some adventure over the holidays had become his tradition. But now, heading back to Magnolia Lake for four years, he could no longer evade the hurt and painful memories each visit home plagued him with.

He could deal with the temporary loss of the things he loved about living in a major East Coast city. Sporting events. Nights out with friends. Being an easy drive from New York and Broadway. What caused an unbearable knot in his gut was being back in the town where his father had died, knowing he was the reason his dad wasn't there. And seeing the resentment in his mother's eyes. Because she, too, blamed him for his father's death.

Julian scratched at his beard, well overdue for a trim.

He'd grown the beard two years ago, at the request of the woman he was seeing. The beard had lasted far longer than the relationship. He'd kept it because it made him look five or ten years older than his thirty years. That put a lot of the older patients he'd seen during his residency at ease. Now that he was returning home to serve as the local GP to people who'd known him since birth, keeping the beard seemed like a good idea. Maybe it would help them take him seriously and realize that he wasn't a kid anymore.

Knowing his mother would hate it gave him a perverse sense of joy.

Julian slowed the old truck when he saw some tire tracks ahead that veered off the road.

What had happened? Was someone hurt?

Julian pulled to the side of the road and turned on the caution lights. Then he hopped out of the truck and went to take a look.

"Shit."

There was a car turned over in the ditch. He'd treated lots of patients who'd been in car accidents. Not all of them had survived—despite his best efforts. He only hoped the occupants of the car had been wearing their seat belts.

Julian slid down the embankment, not caring about the mud soaking his designer jeans and ruining his expensive boots. He approached the car, where a woman hung upside down, unmoving. His stomach knotted.

"Ma'am, are you all right?" He pressed a hand to the window. "Can you hear me?"

She moved the slightest bit, then bobbed her head. "The seat belt is jammed. I can't get out," she mumbled.

He could barely hear her through the glass, but his shoulders sagged with relief at the sound of her voice. She was alive and conscious. He tried opening the door, but it wouldn't budge. "Sit tight. I'm going to get you out of here, all right?"

"I don't expect I'll be going anywhere soon," she said.

Julian couldn't help chuckling, impressed that she didn't seem panicked. And despite needing his help, she was a little bit of a smart-ass. He couldn't help admiring her fight and spirit.

He took a less steep hill to climb back up the embankment and called Elias to request a tow truck. He retrieved his luggage and dug out one of his going-away gifts: a car safety hammer with a built-in seat belt cutter.

Julian shoved his phone into his back pocket and hurried back down the hill, trying hard to ignore the chilly mud that had soaked through his jeans, making them feel five pounds heavier.

"Turn your head and close your eyes," he instructed. "I'm going to break the glass."

When the woman turned her head away and shielded her face with her arms, Julian removed the safety cap from the pointed end of the hammer and looked away as he tapped on the glass. The window shattered, but the safety glass stayed in place. He used the flat hammerhead to knock the glass out of the window, some of the pieces landing in her hair.

"You're doing great. We're almost there." He employed the calm voice he used to put his patients at ease. "Are you injured? Is anything hurting?"

"Just my pride," she muttered. "And my head because the blood is rushing to it."

"Then let's get you down. Brace your hands on my shoulders while I cut you out of this seat belt. I won't let you fall," he promised before she could object.

The woman, who wore a tan jacket, nodded. Her long hair shielded her face. She gripped his shoulders, and he placed a hand on her waist to stabilize her as he sliced through the seat belt.

He held on to her when the seat belt snapped, then eased her out of the car window, legs and bottom first. It was inelegant, but it got the job done and she was out of the car safely.

Julian set her on her feet, a hand on either side of her waist. She wavered slightly and clutched her head.

"Ma'am, are you sure you're all—"

The woman flipped her hair out of her face.

"Chandra?" He was stunned. With the adrenaline rushing through his veins and the scent of coffee splattered throughout the car, Julian hadn't recognized her alluring scent or her voice.

"JB?" Chandra pressed a hand to her forehead, as if she was feeling a bit woozy. She glanced at the cows grazing in the distant pasture. "Am I dreaming?"

"Afraid not. Seems you were in a single-car accident. I was driving along this road and noticed the skid marks veering down the hill, so I stopped to help."

"You're a regular Black Superman, aren't you?" Her voice was filled with more quiet amusement than mockery. "Did you just pop out of a phone booth around here?"

"I prefer to think of myself as Falcon with a dash of Luke Cage." He chuckled, glad she was lucid enough to make jokes.

She cocked her head and studied him for a moment. "Yeah, I guess I can see that. Now, I need to find my phone." When she turned toward the car, she swayed. He reached out to steady her.

"Are you sure you're okay? Maybe I should call an ambulance. You might've sustained a concussion or—"

"I'm fine." She pressed a hand to her forehead. "I didn't hit my head. I'm just not sure how long I was hanging upside down." Chandra ran her fingers through her hair, which was still a little wild. Pieces of glass fell from it. "I just need to get my things and call my family."

"My cousin owns a couple body shops. He's got a guy in the area. The tow truck should be here any minute." Julian placed a hand on her arm, hoping to calm her. She seemed panicked about not being able to locate her phone. "But if you need to call your family, you can use my phone."

"Thanks. I—" Chandra frowned midsentence. "I... I don't remember any of their numbers."

"Are you experiencing any nausea, double vision or ringing in your ears?" Julian pulled out his phone, his heart rate accelerating. "If so, I'm calling an ambulance right now."

"I don't remember their numbers because I *never* dial them. They're saved in my cell phone." Chandra placed a hand over his to prevent him from making the call. "*Please* don't make a fuss—this is embarrassing enough."

"What happened exactly?"

Chandra's eyes widened and she glanced around at the open fields. "Did you see that mother bear and her two cubs?"

"I didn't." He still wasn't convinced she wasn't suffering from a head injury.

"They were there—I assure you. My phone rang and I

glanced down to see who it was. When I looked up again, there were *freaking bears* crossing the road. I tried to go around them, but I lost traction on the shoulder and ended upside down in this ditch." Chandra folded her arms. "Those damn bears owe me a rental car."

"Yeah? Well, good luck with getting them to pay up." Julian was dirty, tired and hungry. He needed a steaming shower, a hot meal and a warm bed. Yet he couldn't help being amused by this woman who was gorgeous, even if she was a little worse for wear after her tumble down the hill. "I'll help you up to the road. We can wait in the truck until the tow truck arrives. Once your rental car is out of the ditch, we'll retrieve your things."

"I'm sorry if I'm grouchy right now. I just can't believe this happened. I'm usually so careful when I drive."

"The important thing is you're all right." Julian held his hand out to her. "Come on. The hill is less steep up there. It'll be easier for you to climb up it in those boots." He regarded her feet, clad in a pair of sexy black leather boots that had done things to him the moment he'd seen her prancing through the airport in them.

Chandra took his hand and they climbed back up the hill. She stomped the mud from her boots, and he helped her inside the truck, thankful his cousin had been overly cautious and had covered the floor and seats in several layers of heavy plastic.

But his clothing was soaked through with mud. He doubted the plastic would be enough to protect the newly recovered leather seats.

"This is a customer's truck. I'm transporting it for my cousin, so I can't get it all muddy," Julian said. "I'm going to grab my luggage and change into some dry clothes."

"Of course." Chandra raked her fingers through her damp hair and fanned her shirt, stained with coffee. "I promise not to look." One corner of her mouth curved in a sexy smirk.

It was the most Chandra had flirted with him since they'd met, but he tried not to read too much into it. He cleaned his hands on a rag, then dug into his bag for clean T-shirts and sweats.

He opened the truck door and handed her a long-sleeve gray shirt bearing a blue bison and the name of his alma mater—Howard University—in bold red. "In case you'd like to get out of that sticky shirt. I won't look either. Promise."

"Thanks, JB."

Julian stripped down to his boxers and kicked off his muddy shoes and socks. He dropped the wet, dirty clothing and shoes in a plastic bag. Then he tugged a long-sleeve navy blue Howard T-shirt over his head. He pulled on gray sweats, then slipped on his Adidas running shoes.

"You good?" he called before approaching the driver's side.

"All changed," Chandra replied.

Julian climbed into the driver's seat and couldn't help smiling. She looked great in his old college T-shirt, despite it being too big for her.

Chandra shoved the sleeves up. "Much better. Thanks."

"And you're sure you're—"

"I'm fine. *Really*," Chandra insisted. "Like I said, my pride is more hurt than anything else."

"Could've happened to anyone." He nodded toward the rearview mirror. "Here comes the tow truck driver now."

Julian turned the idling truck off and they both hopped out. Once the rental car was out of the ditch, they retrieved her belongings. She called the rental company and they arranged for the tow driver to return the car to Knoxville.

"I know you're probably tired and your family is expecting you," Julian said while Chandra was on hold with the rental company. "I'd be happy to drop you wherever you need to go. You can arrange to have them deliver a car to you later."

Chandra frowned, her adorable nose scrunching. "You've already done so much for me. I don't want to impose any further."

"I'm headed to Magnolia Lake, about half an hour up the road. How far do you need to go?" he asked.

"I'm headed there, too. To this address." She held up her phone.

"I know the area. It's on the way into town." Julian rubbed his beard. "There are mostly farms and ranches out there, on the outskirts. It's on the way."

Chandra's dark brown eyes flickered with amusement. "I don't mean to sound ungrateful, but haven't I caused you enough trouble for one day?"

"Maybe I needed a little adventure." Julian shrugged, his hands shoved into the pockets of his gray sweats.

Chandra gave him a reluctant smile. But when the operator returned, she made arrangements for a car to be delivered to her in Magnolia Lake.

Julian grinned. He hadn't asked Chandra for her number when they'd parted on the plane. But fate had given him another chance. This time, he'd definitely shoot his shot.

# Four

There was something inherently calming about JB. He'd settled her nerves on the plane and reassured her as he'd rescued her from her vehicle.

The warm tenor of his deep voice had sluiced over her skin like warm honey while he'd graciously made her feel less bad about wrecking her rental car on an open country road.

As they drove past a sign welcoming them to Magnolia Lake, home of the King's Finest Distillery, JB had asked whom she was visiting. Chandra had reluctantly explained.

"I keep thinking of all the possible reasons my father would call us out to a tiny town in the middle of nowhere. None of them are good." Chandra rubbed her arms as she scanned the road in search of more migratory bears.

Julian cranked up the heat. "I can understand why you'd be worried. But let's hope your dad has a positive reason for bringing you all here. Like maybe he's planning to move to Magnolia Lake."

"Why would he move here? Not that Magnolia Lake isn't a perfectly lovely place to live," she added quickly.

"It is," he said, only slightly defensive.

"Yet you couldn't wait to escape and haven't been back in three years?" Chandra's smile widened when JB's did.

"The urge to put as much mileage as you can between yourself and the small town you grew up in is a rite of passage for two-thirds of the kids who grow up in them," he said with a slight chuckle. "But in the end, a lot of folks develop appreciation for home and return."

"Like you?" she asked.

On the plane, JB had mentioned that he was returning home after being away for several years. He hadn't seemed thrilled about it. Chandra was curious as to why he'd chosen to return, but it seemed like an intrusive question to ask a complete stranger. She hoped her current prompt would elicit more details.

"My dad died in a traffic accident when I was a kid. Being home reminds me of that." Deep lines spanned his forehead as his brows furrowed. "Probably not the healthiest approach, but I've avoided returning home as much as possible."

"I'm sorry. I didn't realize—"

"Not a big deal." He stared ahead as they hugged a curve in the road. "Besides, it was a long time ago."

"When it comes to losing a parent, it always feels like it happened yesterday." Chandra sighed.

"How'd you lose your mom?" He glanced at her momentarily.

"She walked out when I was eight." Chandra shrugged. "Raising four kids under the age of ten while her husband worked sixty-plus-hour weeks in the family business apparently wasn't her thing. Haven't seen her since."

It'd been thirty-one years since Mary Valentine had

walked away. Yet a hole practically burned through her chest every time Chandra talked about it.

"I'm sorry, Chandra." JB squeezed the hand that gripped the edge of the seat. "I lost my dad when I was ten. But something about being back here... It feels like it happened yesterday."

The heat from JB's large hand enveloped hers. Warmth trailed up her arm, her skin tingling in its wake. When she'd held his hand on the plane, she'd been so nervous about the flight that she hadn't been able to take in anything else. She'd been simply clinging to him like a lifeline. But now she was distinctly aware of the strength of his hand, the warmth of his skin pressed against hers. And she was reminded of how attracted she'd been to JB the moment she'd laid eyes on him in that airport. A distraction she couldn't afford.

Chandra discreetly tugged her hand from his. She raked her fingers through her hair. She could only imagine what a mess she must be. Thankfully, JB had been kind enough not to mention it.

"My family has owned a very successful textile firm in Nashville for several generations. My father has been devoted to the place his entire life. In fact, his dedication to work was a point of contention between him and my mom," Chandra explained. "We have a sizable family estate in Nashville. So why would he suddenly want to own property here?"

"Lots of people own cabins around here for fishing and hunting or just to get away from the hustle and bustle of city life."

Her father and brothers did like to fish. But even if her dad had purchased a cabin here, what about that would be so urgent that he'd insist they all needed to come see it?

"I don't know. It just doesn't make sense." Chandra

rubbed the chill bumps that suddenly formed on her arms, despite the heat pumping in the truck.

"Guess you won't have to wait long to find out." JB nodded toward a sign that said Richardson Vineyards. "We're here."

"Are you sure this is the address I gave you?" She studied the sign and the vast property surrounding it.

He read off the address and she checked it against the one in her dad's text message. The address was the same, but maybe it was a typo. Why would her father want them all to converge on a broken-down old winery? "This has to be a mistake."

Another car whipped into the driveway and pulled around them. It was a black convertible with the top down, despite the chilly fall weather. A song by Doja Cat blared from the speakers and her baby sister was behind the wheel wearing a dark pair of designer shades. Likely a gift from one of her high-end sponsors. A hot-pink wig shaped in an adorable bob framed Naya's gorgeous face.

She whipped into a space in the small paved lot near cars Chandra recognized as her father's and younger brothers'.

"I guess it is the right place. That's my sister." Chandra studied the large old house sorely in need of a paint job, a new roof and several other repairs. She stepped down from the truck carefully. There were more potholes than pavement in the parking lot. "Sorry in advance for anything uncouth my baby sister is about to say."

"Duly noted." JB chuckled as he stepped out of the truck. "I'll grab your bags from the back."

"Hey, sis." Naya waved as she slid her sunglasses atop her head. "I was on the phone with Erica when you called the first few times. I tried to call you back, but I can see you've been…*busy*." Naya lifted her eyebrows mischievously as she studied JB letting down the tailgate and bending over to reach for Chandra's luggage.

It was the first time she'd seen JB from behind. And to be fair, the man was in possession of an incredibly impressive set of glutes, spotlighted by ass-hugging gray sweats.

Chandra's cheeks heated and there was a fluttering low in her belly. A man with a traffic-stopping ass was *definitely* her weakness. Not that she'd dated much in the five years since her engagement had ended.

"You're blushing," Naya whispered loudly as she poked her in the side and giggled.

"First of all, you couldn't tell if I was blushing." Chandra held up a finger, thankful for her deep brown skin. "Second, did no one ever teach you how to whisper? Because the point of it is to *not* be overheard by other people."

JB snorted, glancing away when they turned toward him.

"See what I mean?" Chandra gestured toward JB.

"Hi, I'm Naya Valentine." Her sister extended a hand and batted the ultralong mink eyelashes nature definitely hadn't gifted her with. She nodded her head toward Chandra. "I'm this one's baby sister. And you are?"

"This is JB," Chandra said quickly. "We met on the plane. The rest I'll tell you later."

She'd opted not to call her family once she'd finally located her phone. Her car was being taken care of, and she already had a ride to the house. There was no point in alarming them for nothing. Thanks to JB, she was fine.

"I'll see you inside in a few. But in the meantime, could you pop your trunk? That way, JB can put my bags inside until we figure out where we'll be staying. Assuming there's room in there."

Her sister traveled heavy. She usually had a full suitcase just for her makeup and colorful wigs.

Naya popped the trunk, as requested.

"I'm surprised Erica didn't come with you," Chandra said.

Naya frowned at the mention of her current love interest. The two had been together a little more than a year. They'd met at an Instagram influencer convention.

"We'll talk about that later, too." There was a hint of sadness in Naya's dark brown eyes, though she turned up the wattage on her ever-present smile. "Nice to meet you, JB. I hope we'll be seeing you again soon."

Chandra turned to the handsome man whose warm gaze made her temperature rise and her stomach do flips. "Thanks for everything, JB. I don't know what I would've done without you today."

"You would've managed fine. I have no doubt of that." He scratched at his beard and flashed a devilish smile that sent heat rocketing up her spine and left her wondering about the taste of his full lips.

She shuddered, ignoring the beading of her nipples and the steady pulse between her thighs.

"Well, I'm really glad I didn't have to find out."

"Let me put these bags in your sister's trunk." He grabbed her bags and moved toward the open deck lid of her sister's rented convertible. She walked over with him, impressed when he managed to squeeze her two bags inside the space overflowing with her sister's Gucci luggage, stamped with the company's iconic logo.

When Chandra closed the trunk, she winced in pain.

"You *did* hurt yourself." JB's eyebrows furrowed with concern as he examined her wrist. An angry bruise had become visible and her wrist was much sorer than it'd been before. "That's a nasty bruise, Chandra. Can you move your wrist?"

"Yes, it's... *Ow*," she muttered as the pain shot up her arm when she tried to move her wrist in a circle. "It's fine. Just a little sore."

"You have complete range of motion, but still, it could

be a bad·sprain. If the pain persists or if that headache doesn't go away—"

"The headache is already gone, and my wrist is fine. But I promise to see someone about it if it's still hurting in a couple of days," she said.

"All right, then." JB let go of her hand and she couldn't help feeling a bit disappointed.

*You are not here to hook up with the sweet, sexy lumberjack with the perfect ass. You're here to see about Dad.*

"Well, thanks again." Chandra hugged JB, trying to ignore how wonderful it felt as he wrapped her in his solid arms and squeezed her to his chest. She reluctantly pulled free of his embrace. "It was really nice meeting you, JB."

She shoved the too-long sleeve back up her arm—then remembered where she'd gotten it. "Your shirt. I'll run inside and change so I can give it back to you."

"How long will you be in town?" JB asked.

"A week, maybe two." She shrugged.

"I'll get it next time we see each other." A flirtatious grin curved one side of his sexy mouth.

Electricity crackled down her spine. She folded her arms over her chest and tried to ignore her body's reaction to the possibility of them seeing each other again.

"I have no idea what I'm walking into here. So it doesn't feel right making plans."

"Fair." He nodded sagely, folding his arms and widening his stance. "But I'm betting your dad invited you here for a happy reason. If I'm right, you call me and then we can meet for coffee maybe. You can bring the shirt then." His dark eyes glinted in the sunlight. "Deal?"

She pushed her hair, still sticky with coffee, behind her ear and nodded. "Sure. Why not?"

He grinned. "Pen?" He nodded toward her purse.

Chandra produced a pen from her handbag and JB scribbled his name and a phone number on the white plastic bag she'd put her coffee-stained shirt in. He returned the pen and headed toward the truck.

"Hey, what if...? I mean...what if I can't go out with you?"

"Then you can keep it." JB winked, then hopped into the truck and drove off.

Chandra watched him drive off, wishing they'd met under different circumstances. Then she turned and surveyed the old house more closely.

With its deep gold stucco, terra-cotta roof and antique arched double doors, it looked like a Tuscan villa that had been transported to the Smoky Mountains from another place and time.

Rather than the typical front porch she was accustomed to seeing on Southern homes, the house had a bona fide loggia. The Italian-style porch ran the length of the front of the house. Its stucco-covered columns formed arches that ran across the entire structure. Black wrought iron lanterns and sconces—in desperate need of refinishing or replacement—dotted the walls and hung from the ceiling.

The stucco exterior was stained and discolored. In some places, there were substantial cracks. Still, the place had enormous potential. If the owners would put some money into it, the building would make a great space for wine tastings and small events. Maybe even small wedding receptions. But in its current state, it felt as if she was risking her life just climbing the three cracked stucco stairs.

Chandra pushed open the heavy antique wooden door her sister had disappeared through earlier. She stepped inside and scanned the dark, dated decor. A beautiful young woman stood behind the large front desk made of dark wood. Behind her, the words *Richardson Vineyards* were burned into a wooden wall.

"Welcome, Ms. Valentine." The woman offered a

guarded smile that revealed none of her teeth and didn't reach her eyes. "I'm Dejah Richardson, the vineyard manager. Your family is waiting for you in the game room. If you'll follow me."

Chandra followed the woman through a large, sunny great room with dated decor and a few gorgeous antiques. They walked down a long narrow hall past the dining room with a large table. Finally, Dejah opened another antique door and Chandra heard the voices of her siblings.

Chandra stepped inside. "Hello, everyone."

The space went quiet.

Her brothers—Nolan, Sebastian, Alonzo and Nyles—had tentative expressions that matched her own. Her sister, Naya, had been chatting happily with their father, who appeared to be in an equally cheerful mood.

Given the gravity with which he'd impelled their presence here and his generally bleak mood for the past few years, Chandra was surprised to see her father so upbeat.

Maybe JB was right. Perhaps her father had summoned them all to this place for a happy reason. The family equivalent of a company retreat, perhaps? After all, they'd grown apart over the past five years or so. And she was likely to blame for that.

After her mother's unexpected departure, Chandra had made it her mission to be the single thread holding their family together. But following her failed engagement, she'd needed a change.

A part of her had grown resentful that she was still the one always cleaning up the family messes. So she'd done something unexpected. She'd left their family's textile firm and taken a job in San Diego with Phillips Athletic Wear.

Her father had been hurt but understood that she needed some space. Naya, who had an inherent gift for rolling with the punches, easily adapted. Her four brothers had been decidedly less understanding.

Nolan, the CFO of Valentine Textiles, a company started by her paternal great-grandfather and run by her father, had said it felt like she'd pulled the rug out from under them.

Maybe she had. But it had forced all of her siblings to become less dependent on her. Alonzo, Nyles and Naya—the three youngest—were forced to finally grow up, handle their business and clean up their own messes.

Chandra had spent the past five years consumed with her work. Her relationships with Nolan, Sebastian and Alonzo had become distant. And without her there to coordinate family vacations, holidays and general family get-togethers, they'd become like individual satellites circling their father but rarely connecting.

She felt bad about that. So maybe a family retreat was *exactly* what they needed.

"Glad you could make it." Nolan hugged her.

Chandra hugged Nolan back, ignoring the hidden jab referencing all the times she hadn't been able to make it home for birthdays, company celebrations and a few major holidays. "Good to see you, Nole."

Nolan adjusted his ever-smudged glasses, his smile shifting to a more genuine one. "You too, Chandra."

She exchanged similar greetings with Sebastian, Valentine Textiles' VP of operations, and Alonzo, who worked for an advertising firm in New York.

Nyles, whom she still spoke to regularly, gave her a warm hug. "Good to see you, sis."

"Now that your hot new *friend* is gone, maybe I can finally get a hug." Naya approached her with a mock pout.

"You brought some dude to the family meeting?" Alonzo raised one of his thick brows and frowned.

"No, I didn't." Chandra gave Naya the evil eye, then

hugged her little sister, getting a whiff of her delicate perfume. Chandra released Naya and pointed a finger at her. *"Snitch."*

"Guess some things never change." Alonzo chuckled. Naya gave his arm a playful punch.

"That perfume smells amazing and insanely expensive," Chandra noted.

"It is." Naya smiled proudly. "A gift from my latest sponsor. I'm doing a photo shoot in France with them in February."

"Good for you." Chandra squeezed her sister's arm.

They'd all been a little worried when Naya had graduated college, spent two years traveling the world, then declared that she was going to become a full-time Instagram influencer rather than joining the family textile firm. But in the past four years she'd continued to increase both her income and her follower count while working on her own terms.

Chandra envied her little sister for that.

"Guess I'll just stand over here and be ignored." Her father folded his arms and tried to look serious, but a slow grin spread across his handsome face.

"I always save the best for last." Chandra smiled.

"Am I the only one who feels insulted by that?" Sebastian's dark eyes flickered.

"Hush, Bas." Chandra crossed the room and hugged her father. She settled into her dad's lingering embrace and inhaled his familiar scent. Abbott Raymond Valentine gave the best hugs. They made everything better. "Missed you, Dad."

"Missed you too, pumpkin." He hadn't called her that in years.

A knot tightened in Chandra's stomach. She searched her father's dark eyes. "What's going on, Dad?"

"Have a seat, and I'll tell you everything. Promise."

Chandra sank onto the love seat beside Naya. Tension rolled off her sister's slim shoulders and marred the handsome faces of her four brothers.

Clearly, she wasn't the only one worried about their dad.

# Five

$R$ay Valentine adjusted his glasses as he surveyed the faces of his children. They were worried by this cryptic meeting he'd called, and they'd probably think he was losing it once he shared his big news. A valid concern, given that his own mother had battled dementia the last several years of her life. Still, he hoped they'd see things his way in the end.

"Thank you all for coming. I know it wasn't easy to re-arrange your schedules on such short notice. But I thought it best if I told you all this in person and all at once."

"Told us *what*, Dad?" Chandra gripped her younger sister's hand as the two of them huddled together on the love seat. "Are you not feeling well?"

"I'm fine, sweetheart." He felt guilty about the pained look on his eldest daughter's face.

She wore her heart on her sleeve and believed it her job to take care of everyone in her life. She'd taken the abandonment by her mother, then stepmother, particularly hard.

And when her fiancé had suddenly called off their wedding, it had been more than his sweet girl could take.

When Chandra had pulled away, he hadn't tried to stop her. After she'd practically raised her siblings, he couldn't blame her for finally putting her needs first.

"A few months before your gram passed, she said to me, 'I love you, son. You've always been such a good boy. But you're just not...*him*.'"

"You're just not *whom*?" Sebastian furrowed his brows.

"She probably didn't realize who you were. It's the nature of the disease." Nyles shifted to the edge of his seat.

"She knew *exactly* who I was." Ray sank onto the broken-in leather chair. "It was the most lucid she'd been in years."

"Then what do you think she meant?" Alonzo rubbed his chin.

"I didn't know, but it felt important, like something that could explain the disconnect I've always felt between us." He glided a hand over his thinning hair. "After she passed, I was going through her papers and found my real birth certificate and the birth and death certificates for a son I never knew my parents had."

"You had a brother?" Sebastian asked. "What happened to him?"

"His name was Charles, and he drowned in the pond on the family estate when he was three—five years before I was born."

"And neither of your parents ever mentioned him?" Alonzo was on the edge of his seat now, too. "There were no photos in the family albums...nothing?"

"There were two photo albums in her safe-deposit box along with the vital certificates and a few other items," he confirmed. "Those two there."

Ray nodded toward the albums he'd left on the table.

"That's...wild." Sebastian picked up one of the albums and thumbed through it so his brothers could see its contents.

Naya picked up the other and flipped through it as Chandra looked on.

"So when Nana said, 'You're just not him,' she was referring to Charles. The child she lost before you were born." Chandra's eyes filled with tears.

"Correct."

"That's messed up." Nyles handed the album to Alonzo. "Gram was comparing you to a brother you didn't even know you had."

"No." The word caught in Ray's throat. "She was comparing me to their son."

His children, except Nolan, exchanged confused glances.

"But if Charles was their son, that would make him your brother." Sebastian cocked his head. "Unless..."

"What did you mean when you said you found your *real* birth certificate?" Chandra stood. "Are you saying—"

"Eugene and Melba Valentine were not my biological parents. They adopted me when I was two months old, after my mother died."

Chandra moved behind his chair and leaned down to wrap her arms around his neck. "I'm so sorry, Daddy."

"It's okay, baby girl." He patted her arm. "Part of me was relieved to learn the truth. After that, it all finally made sense."

"What made sense?" Nyles asked.

"Why I felt like a disappointment to her. Why it seemed as if looking at me brought her pain. It did—but not because of anything I'd done wrong. I just reminded her of the child she'd lost."

Ray shifted in his seat, making room for Chandra to perch on the edge, her head against his shoulder.

"After I discovered the birth certificates, I went to my mother's sister—your great-aunt Imogene. When I told her I knew the truth, she filled in the missing pieces. My mother didn't want to adopt. She wanted to keep trying to have a child of their own. But my father was an only child and had a heart condition. He was afraid they wouldn't have an heir to leave the company to. And he wanted the textile company to stay in the family and be run the way he'd run it."

"You were their replacement kid." Naya's voice ached with sadness.

"Yes." The truth of that statement hit him in the chest with the weight of a two-ton wrecking ball. "Which explains why my father was so desperate to teach me all there was to know about Valentine Textiles. He started taking me to the office when I was five. He wasn't unkind, mind you, but he was laser focused on me learning the family business inside out."

"*Their* family business." Nyles frowned.

"*Our* family business. They're still my parents. They raised me the best they knew how and gave me a good life," Ray said. It was a line he'd repeated to himself whenever the anger started to build in his chest, like a volcano threatening to explode. "But my father was too focused on the legacy of his company to realize I needed him to be my dad first. And my mother was struggling with the death of her child and the guilt she felt over it. Maybe that's why she seemed incapable of bonding with me. She was never harsh, but she was distant." He shrugged. "Maybe she was afraid to get too close to another child she could lose."

Chandra squeezed his hand, her touch filled with warmth and comfort. She had always managed to bring him a sense of peace when he was at his lowest.

"That's no excuse for how they treated you." Naya's big brown eyes filled with unshed tears.

"Maybe. But I don't want you to think ill of your grandparents. That isn't why I invited you here."

"Why *are* we here?" Sebastian frowned more than any of his children. He wished his son would learn to relax.

"And don't you want to know about your biological family?" Alonzo asked.

"Yes." Ray nodded. "I spent the past couple of years trying to locate them. My birth certificate revealed the identity of my mother, but the line for my father's name had been left blank. Now I know why. He died a few hours after my birth on a road between the hospital where I was born and his house. I believe he came to the hospital to see me or maybe he was there for the birth. I don't know." Ray shrugged. "But he didn't make it back home to his family."

"He was married?" Chandra asked.

"Yes."

"So who was this philandering grandfather of ours?" Alonzo topped off his glass with the bottle of King's Finest Bourbon on the table in front of him.

Ray indicated the glass in his son's hand. "King Abbott."

Alonzo froze, the glass perched inches from his lips. "As in *the* King Abbott? The founder of the distillery?"

"King didn't start the distillery. He was a bootlegger who ran moonshine in the hollers in these mountains. It was his son Joseph who founded King's Finest as a legitimate distillery long after his father's death."

"Joseph Abbott is your half brother?" Chandra's eyes widened. "Is that why we're here? You're planning to... what? Confront him with this?"

"That's *part* of the reason you're here," Ray clarified. "But there won't be any messy confrontations. I met Joe and his family a couple weeks ago, when they opened that new restaurant of theirs. He was as stunned as I was to learn the news. It took a DNA test to convince him, and it's something we're both still trying to wrap our heads around. But we've chatted quite a bit since then."

The room was dead silent as each of his children absorbed this new information.

"Does that mean we get free liquor?" Nyles asked. "Because their top-shelf bourbon is *banging*. I could definitely use a case of that."

"What the hell is wrong with you?" Sebastian asked. "You are *not* going to embarrass us by asking for free liquor."

"Relax, dude. I was kidding." Nyles poured bourbon into his glass, looking like a puppy that had just gotten scolded for whizzing on the carpet.

"We're doing just fine. We certainly don't need any handouts." Ray gave his youngest son a pointed look. That boy was going to be the death of him. He was sure of it. "But I would like you all to meet your uncle and cousins. They're not just successful. They're good people. And despite the awkwardness of the situation, they're eager to meet you all. They're throwing a party for the entire town this weekend and we're the guests of honor."

"Joseph Abbott is throwing a party to introduce the entire town to his long-lost illegitimate brother and his six brats?" Sebastian cranked up an eyebrow. "I find it hard to believe he'd want to publicize his family's dirty laundry."

Ray cringed at Sebastian's reference to him as the Abbott family's "dirty laundry." But he understood what his son was getting at.

"It doesn't feel like something that would benefit their company image," Chandra agreed.

"That brings me to the other reason you're all here." Ray stood, retrieving his bourbon and soda from the table.

He walked to the window and regarded the rows of grapevines, already preparing themselves for the next harvest. Then he turned back toward the six faces staring at him expectantly.

"Discovering that King Abbott was my biological father

gave me a renewed sense of purpose. I needed to learn *everything* I could about him. I hired an award-winning genealogist who was able to discover a lot, including that he'd experimented with wine-making."

"It must've stunned you to learn you two have that in common," Chandra said.

Wine-making was a hobby he and his oldest son, Nolan, shared. They worked in an old greenhouse on their family estate in Nashville and had gotten good at making small batches of wine.

"I was. King ran moonshine because there was good money in it, but he had a passion for making wine. He'd hoped to branch out into wine-making professionally. I believe that's how he met my mother. Her family owned a small vineyard. *This* one." Ray held up his palms and glanced around the space.

"We're related to the Richardsons, too?" Nyles seemed panicked by this. Undoubtedly because he'd been flirting shamelessly with Dejah Richardson since he'd arrived.

"Dejah isn't a relative—relax, son." Ray chuckled and so did Nolan and Alonzo. "The property has been sold three times since my biological mother's death. First to an Italian family who bought a neighboring property and built this incredible house and the outlying villas. They even had much of the material imported from Italy. When the family decided to move back to Italy, they sold the property to the Richardsons, who expanded the vineyard to its current size. They produced a phenomenal product, but they weren't the best businesspeople." He lowered his voice. "And, as you can see, they haven't invested much money into keeping up the place."

"So we're here to meet the Abbotts and to connect with our grandmother's history?" Alonzo set his glass down.

"Wait... You said that the property has been sold *three*

times since your mother's death." Sebastian held up three fingers. "Who owns the property now?"

"We're the new owners."

"What?" five of his children said simultaneously. There was a brief moment of silence followed by the chaos of everyone speaking at once.

"Dad, please tell me you didn't impulse buy this vineyard," Chandra pleaded.

"When you say *we* own it…who exactly do you mean by *we*?" Alonzo frowned.

"How could you make a decision like this without consulting any of us?" Sebastian demanded.

"I don't know that none of us were consulted." Naya folded her arms and nodded toward Nolan. "Because Dad's wine-making buddy over there is suspiciously quiet, and he doesn't seem nearly as shocked by this revelation as the rest of us."

Every head in the room swiveled toward Nolan. His oldest son adjusted his smudged glasses and shifted in his seat. He shrugged. "I'm the CFO of Valentine Textiles."

"What has that got to do with Dad purchasing this place?" Chandra cocked her head. Then everyone's attention shifted back to Ray.

He downed the rest of his bourbon and soda and set his glass down. He stood tall, tipped his chin and spoke with conviction. "Because I'm selling Valentine Textiles."

He ignored the audible gasps in the room and continued.

"We received an offer from a California conglomerate that's been trying to buy the place for years. I was going to turn them down again, but then I realized that I've always resented the firm. It's never been my passion. My parents *acquired* me for the purpose of taking over the business. That's why it's always felt like an albatross around my neck. I don't want any part of it anymore. I want to build

something *I'm* passionate about. Create my own legacy...
like Joseph has."

"Dad, I understand how you must feel." Chandra's eyes
were filled with concern. "But buying this old vineyard on
a nostalgic whim with the hopes of turning it into something comparable to what the Abbotts have built... Dad,
that's unreasonable. It's taken them fifty-plus years and
three generations to build their empire."

"That's why I said *we* own this place." He gestured
around the room with a soft smile. "I want this to be *our*
legacy. Something we can build *together*. Something we
can all be truly passionate about."

Sebastian stood, his eyes filled with hurt and anger. "So
just like that, you're selling the textile firm? Without consulting anyone except Nole?" Sebastian gestured toward his
brother. "You made this decision with *zero* consideration
for the fact that I've dedicated my *entire* career to running
and growing the firm. Maybe that doesn't matter to Nolan.
But did you even, for a second, consider how that would
make me feel?"

Except for the twins, all of his children had worked for
Valentine Textiles—though Alonzo and Chandra had eventually ventured elsewhere. But Nolan and Sebastian had
spent their entire careers with the family firm, serving as
the CFO and VP of operations, respectively. He regretted
that they'd followed his example and made Valentine Textiles their lives. And like him, they both had brief, failed
marriages because of it.

Ray drew in a pained breath. He'd known that Sebastian
would be most upset by his sale of the firm. But he couldn't
regret *finally* making a choice that felt right for him. He just
wished Sebastian hadn't been hurt by his decision.

"Of course I did, son. And I'm sorry to disappoint you.
I appreciate everything you and your brother have done to
increase the value of Valentine Textiles. That's why I in-

sisted that you and Nolan be kept on by the new owners, if you choose to stay. I've already talked to Nolan about it. He's all in with building this new business. But there will always be a place at the textile firm for you, if you want it. They'd be thrilled to keep a Valentine as the face of the company. Even asked if I thought you'd make a good fit for the role of CEO."

Sebastian seemed stunned. "You recommended me as CEO?"

"Why not? You're passionate. Knowledgeable. Qualified. And you're ready, if that's what you really want." Ray placed a hand on his son's shoulder. "But I'd prefer to have you here with me. Building our own legacy on land once owned by my mother's people. Doing the work my father once hoped to do. Not because I feel obligated to, but because it's my passion, too. I've never felt as at peace or at home as I've felt since the day I walked onto this property."

"Dad, I appreciate why you bought this place. I can even understand why you'd take the deal to sell the firm. But we all have lives of our own," Chandra said. "I'm in San Diego. Naya is in L.A. Alonzo is in New York. Nyles is in Atlanta. You don't honestly expect us to drop the careers we've been building because you've suddenly decided to try your hand at creating an empire as a vintner," Chandra continued. "This dream of yours…what if you change your mind in a few months? Or what if it just doesn't work?"

"The textile company might not be exciting, but the market is steady and so is the income it produces," Alonzo added. "What you're asking, Dad…we'd be taking one hell of a risk."

Alonzo wasn't wrong. Each of his children owned stock in the textile firm. Shares gifted to them at birth and then on their twenty-first birthdays. Shares that helped fund their current lifestyles. Nyles, in particular. Asking them to leave their high-paying careers and lose their quarterly stock payouts was a huge gamble. But he had a plan to make it worth the risk.

"I'm not asking any of you to step out on a wing and a prayer. If you decide to join Valentine Vineyards—" his soul surged just saying the words aloud to his children for the first time "—it will be in a generously paid role—comparable to your current salaries."

*Now I've got their attention.*

"And if you'll give me three years here at the vineyard, helping me turn this into the empire I believe it can be, you'll receive one-seventh of the sale price of the textile firm *plus* the interest that will have accrued during that time."

"It's a generous offer, Dad," Chandra said after a few minutes. "But this is a lot to take in. Mind if we take some time to think about it?"

Ray hadn't expected this to come easily. And he still expected a fight from Sebastian and Alonzo. They'd probably try to convince their siblings that he needed a conservatorship.

"Fair enough, sweetheart." He gripped Chandra's left hand and was startled when she yelped. "What's wrong, honey?"

"I had a run-in with a bear and got into an accident on my way into town." Chandra cradled her wrist.

The room was in commotion as everyone inquired about what had happened. Ray wrapped ice in a cloth napkin and placed it on Chandra's wrist as she told them about the man she'd met on the plane who'd apparently saved his daughter's life.

"So this dude steals your seat on the plane, comes off all knight in shining armor during your flight, then just happens to be the guy who comes to your rescue when your car ends up in a ditch?" Sebastian rubbed his chin suspiciously and shook his head. "That's too much of a coincidence. I don't like it."

"Which part is it exactly that you don't like, Sebastian?" Chandra narrowed her gaze at her always cynical brother. "The part where JB kept me from having a panic attack on the plane or the part where he saved me from dying alone in a ditch?"

Nyles chuckled and put a hand on Sebastian's shoulder. "Trust me, bro. You're not gonna win this one. I suggest you let it go."

"And I suggest you be grateful to this JB." Naya folded her arms. "Otherwise, we'd be sitting here wondering where Chandra was right now."

"You're right. We should be grateful to this guy," Sebastian conceded with a nod. "I'm really glad you're okay, sis."

"Thank you, Sebastian." Chandra gave her wrist a reprieve from the ice.

"The fact that the guy is a tall, dark and handsome drink of water that sis is totally into..." Naya shrugged with a grin. "That's just a happy bonus."

His youngest daughter's comment drew various responses from her older brothers and a whispered "Snitch" from her sister. Ray chuckled. He missed having all of his children together like this. Even missed their petty bickering. Because they only did it because they loved each other.

Ray draped an arm around Chandra and lowered his voice. "So you really like this fella, hmm?"

"He was nice. Sweet even. And yes, he was handsome. So yeah, I guess I do like him a little in a passing fancy sort of way." Chandra shrugged.

"You do realize that no one says 'passing fancy' anymore, right?" Naya leaned over the seat, poking her head of pink hair between his and Chandra's, just like when she was a little girl and would eavesdrop on their conversations.

"And you do realize this was a private conversation?" Chandra shot back.

Naya shrugged, then sauntered off.

Ray shook his head and laughed.

"As I was saying, yeah, maybe I have a crush on the guy. But it's nothing serious. Besides, he lives here, and I don't." Chandra shrugged her shoulders. "End of story." She dropped the ice wrap on the table and stood. "I'm starving. I'm gonna grab something to eat." She indicated the platters of sandwich fixings her brothers were already attacking. Dejah had just set them on the sideboard. "Want anything?"

Ray waved a hand and sighed quietly. He topped off his drink and took a sip.

Maybe this town could deliver the two things he wanted most. To build a legacy of his own for his family and to see his children find the happily-ever-after that had always eluded him.

# Six

Julian pulled the borrowed truck into the gravel driveway of his mother's house and turned off the engine. Her small red import was parked near the entrance to her prized garden beds. Gardening was the one thing that still seemed to bring his mother joy since his father's death twenty years ago.

He stepped out of the truck, not bothering to grab his luggage. He wouldn't be staying here. The deal to return home to Magnolia Lake as the local doctor included accommodations and the use of a vehicle.

Julian shielded his eyes from the glaring afternoon sun as he surveyed the unassuming little white cottage. The house and the white picket fence surrounding it had recently been painted.

Fall flowering bushes and late-blooming perennials added pops of color to the stark white structure and lent warmth and curb appeal to the one-hundred-year-old house.

His father had purchased the dilapidated, abandoned structure before Julian was born and remodeled it bit by bit.

Julian sometimes wondered how his mother had managed to stay in the old house all these years. Every room, every surface echoed with memories of his father—a large, amiable man with dark gleaming eyes, a contagious smile and a deep, rumbling laugh.

"Plan on coming inside?"

Julian's gaze met the dark eyes that were a carbon copy of his own. His eyes and nose he'd gotten from Luetta Brandon. Yet in all the essential ways he'd been the spitting image of his dad.

It was undoubtedly why there was so much pain in his mother's eyes whenever she'd looked at him. It must've been like seeing the ghost of his dad plastered on the face of the person she blamed for his death.

"Hey, Ma." Julian crept forward. "The house looks great. When'd you have it painted?"

"Earlier this year. Also had the kitchen and bathrooms updated." His mother pulled off her gardening gloves and shoved them in the pocket of her apron.

They shared their obligatory hug. Only, this time his mother held on to him a little longer. It reminded him of the warm hugs she'd given him as a kid.

"You didn't mention that you were having work done. I could've painted the place for you." He'd done it twice before in the twelve years since he'd moved away.

"I know you would've. But you're a busy doctor now, Jules. You barely have time to spend with your mother as it is."

*First shot fired.*

But to be honest, he'd had it coming.

Julian communicated with his mother regularly but avoided coming home, convinced neither of them enjoyed suffering through awkward holiday weekends together.

Had he simply been projecting his own feelings onto her so he'd feel less guilty about staying away?

"Sorry I haven't been home in a while, Ma. I guess I was trying to—"

"Get in all the adventures you could before you had to come back here?" She studied him. "Magnolia Lake isn't a prison."

"I know. But I'd be lying if I said I wasn't going to miss the conveniences of city life."

"Conveniences?" She tugged on his beard. "Like a good barber? Because we have those here, mountain man." She chuckled. "Almost didn't recognize who it was out here lurking in my yard. I was about five seconds away from loading my rifle."

*Welcome to the "Julian Brandon can't do shit right" show.*

"I've been here like five minutes, Ma. Can we save the discussion of my questionable life choices for the hour mark?" he suggested, only half teasing.

"Unfortunately, an hour is all I have." She glanced at her watch—a tenth anniversary gift from his father. She was hardly ever without it. "I volunteered to take the evening shift. Everyone else has children or grandchildren to see about."

She made the statement matter-of-factly. Still, guilt churned in his gut.

His mother was a nurse in the maternity ward of a premier hospital in Gatlinburg. When he was a kid, she'd wanted him to grow up to be a doctor. At the time, his only interest was in being a superhero or a firefighter. But the day Joseph Abbott had asked him what he wanted to be when he grew up, his response had been immediate. He wanted to be a doctor.

It felt like his best shot at getting his mother to forgive him for destroying their lives.

Somewhere along the way, he'd come to enjoy being a doctor. He found recompense in being there for people on what was often the worst day of their lives.

"Sorry, I'd planned to get here earlier, but…" Chandra's lovely face flashed in his brain and his mouth curved in an involuntary smile. "I stumbled across an accident and stopped to help. Turned out it was the passenger I sat beside on the plane."

"It's the same thing your father would've done." There was a hint of pride in her dark eyes. "Probably didn't hurt that she was pretty either."

"How'd you know…?"

"I'm still your mother, Julian Aurelius Brandon," she reminded him. "The twinkle in your eyes and that sly little smile were a dead giveaway. She local?"

"No, she's in town because her father asked her and her siblings to meet him at the Richardson Winery. He was kind of mysterious about it, so she was worried."

"The Richardson Vineyards is now the Valentine Vineyards. The Richardsons sold the place a few weeks ago," his mother informed him. "The woman you helped…was she a Valentine?" Luetta Brandon propped a fist on her hip.

"Possibly." Julian shrugged.

"Well, ain't that something." She glanced at her watch again. "You hungry? Got leftover pot roast and mashed potatoes from last night, if you've got time for a late lunch."

"Yes, ma'am. Of course."

His mother heated up the leftovers while he took a quick tour of the renovation that had breathed new life into the place. Then they sat down and ate, catching each other up on the basics of their lives. The conversation was superficial—the kind of things one might share with a stranger.

"I realize fancy accommodations are part of the deal," his mother said. "But this is still your home and there's plenty of space for you here."

Was she offering because she felt she should or because she genuinely wanted him there?

"Thanks, but coming home is already a big adjustment for me. Thought it'd be best if we each had our own space," Julian said.

"You're probably right." Her tight smile was unconvincing. She collected their plates.

The sadness in her voice gnawed at his gut. Maybe the offer was an olive branch—her way of making amends for her resentment of him in the past. A few years ago, that might've been enough. But he'd gone from that broken-hearted little boy desperate for his mother's approval to a man harboring resentments of his own. He wouldn't let her off that easily.

Julian stood. "I'd better go. I have to meet Joe and Duke Abbott at my new office in about fifteen minutes. But I'll see you soon."

"In case that fancy new place of yours doesn't come with groceries." His mother handed him a bento box filled with leftovers.

Julian thanked his mother, then headed out to the truck. He drove into town and met Joseph Abbott, founder of the world-famous King's Finest Distillery, and his son Duke, the company's current CEO. He hadn't expected the brand-new, state-of-the-art office building. The Abbott family's gift to the town of Magnolia Lake.

Julian's new office was located on the second floor of the Abbott Medical Center. The building would eventually house dental offices and a pharmacy. *Dr. J. Brandon* was printed on the board in the lobby and on the door of his practice.

He'd been dreading his return home, but seeing his name on that door felt gratifying. He'd accomplished his goal, and the Abbotts were welcoming him back with open arms.

Which made the request he was about to make of Joseph that much more difficult.

After a quick tour, Duke took off, saying he was on grandpa duty. As soon as he'd left, Joseph looked at Julian warily. Father Time and the stroke the old man had suffered a few years ago had aged him considerably. Made him look almost frail.

Joseph narrowed his dark eyes, framed by wiry gray brows. "Something is obviously weighing on you, son. Let's hear it."

*The old man is still as sharp as ever.*

Julian cleared his throat and stood taller. "Mr. Abbott... I appreciate everything you've done for me. And I'm prepared to fulfill my part of our agreement."

"But?" Joseph sat in one of the office chairs, his arms folded over his chest.

Julian sat beside the older man. "You made a financial investment in me, sir. I'd like to repay that debt...with interest." Julian pulled a check from his wallet and handed it to him.

Joseph Abbott rubbed his chin as he studied the six-figure check. "You want to repay me in lieu of serving your four years as town doctor?"

"Yes, sir."

"No." The old man handed the check back to him. "I don't need the money, son. But this town does need you. And maybe you need it, too."

Julian had hoped that Abbott would be tempted by the offer. But knowing what he did about the old man, his answer didn't surprise him.

"Should I be worried about where you got that kind of money?" Joseph asked.

"No. I worked for every penny. Started off flipping properties with a few buddies. Then I got into real estate investment and stock market investment."

"You've been busy." Joseph sounded like a proud father. But then he grimaced. "Being able to buy your way out of this agreement must've been pretty damn important to you."

"Yes, sir. It was."

"Why, son?" Joseph asked.

"I've built a good life in Philly," Julian said.

"And what about Lue?" the old man asked.

Julian sighed heavily, the guilt over his relationship with his mother weighing on him. He ran a hand over his head. "I love my mother. But you know how things have been between us." He shrugged. "Me coming back here... It'll only churn up painful memories for both of us."

"Your mother loves you very much, and folks around here are awful glad you're back. As for those memories... I think you'll find that facing them head-on is far more effective than trying to outrun them."

The old man's words hit Julian squarely in the chest. Outrunning painful memories was exactly what he'd tried to do for years now. Yet they haunted him at every turn. So maybe Joseph was right.

"I've been a man of my word—now I expect you to be the same." Joe climbed to his feet. He pulled an envelope from his inside jacket pocket. "Inside you'll find the address to your cabin and three sets of keys. One to this office. One to the cabin. One for the vehicle parked in the drive. The cabin is fully stocked, and your staff is all set and eager to work with you. Need anything else? Don't hesitate to give me a call."

Julian accepted the envelope and nodded. "Thank you, Mr. Abbott. For everything."

The old man patted Julian's arm and smiled. Then he took off.

Julian surveyed his fancy new office, hoping the old man was right about his coming back home being a good move.

He locked up the office and headed for Old Man Simpson's farm to deliver the truck. But he couldn't help thinking about Chandra—the intriguing woman he'd met on the plane.

Julian hoped things had gone well in her meeting with her dad and siblings. But most of all, he hoped he'd get to see Chandra again before she left town with his favorite shirt.

If he was lucky, he'd get to see Chandra in that shirt again—and not much else.

# Seven

It'd been two days since her father had stunned Chandra and her siblings with the news of his true paternity, the fact that they were cousins of the Abbotts—owners of the world-renowned King's Finest Distillery—and also apparently the owners of the run-down old Richardson Winery.

Chandra flexed her wrist, which was still sore and incapable of bearing weight. She figured it would be fine, but her dad insisted someone look at it. Then he'd tasked Dejah with making an appointment with the town doctor. Chandra glanced over at the younger woman who was transporting her into town for her appointment. They rode mostly in silence in the woman's beat-up old Jeep that was probably as old as she was.

Dejah Richardson—the youngest daughter of the vineyard's former owners—had agreed to stay on and work for Chandra's father. It explained Dejah's reserved demeanor. It couldn't have been easy watching someone else take over her family's business.

Chandra's father felt Dejah's help was invaluable, but she couldn't help being wary of Dejah's true motives for staying on at the vineyard.

"What made you decide to stay on at the winery when your family decided to sell?" Chandra asked.

Dejah's nostrils flared, her eyes not leaving the road. "I've been harvesting grapes and learning about wine-making since I was four. That winery has been my entire life." She shrugged. "Where else was I supposed to go?"

*Anywhere.*

Family businesses could be a blessing and a curse. Her father's situation was proof of that. Without the weight of family expectations, there were undoubtedly several options open to a smart, resourceful woman like Dejah. But she didn't know the woman or what she was looking for in life. Maybe there was something or someone keeping her in town.

Chandra wanted to ask, but the finality of the younger woman's answer made it clear she didn't want to discuss it further.

"Well, thank you for staying. My dad's heart is in the right place. I'm just not sure if he realizes exactly what he's gotten himself into." Chandra stared out the window as they passed over a river on a narrow one-car bridge. Then the colorful buildings of the quaint little town came into view.

"Here we are." Dejah parked in front of a building more modern than the quaint, colorful storefronts surrounding it. "The medical office is on the second floor. Doc Jules will get you all fixed up. I'll be back through here in about an hour and a half. I'll meet you at the Magnolia Lake Bakery across the street. If you get lost, call me."

Chandra thanked Dejah, then made her way to the second floor of the Abbott Medical Center and entered the offices of Dr. J. Brandon.

"Hello, I'm here to see Dr. Brandon about my wrist." Chandra held up her arm.

"The car accident." A pretty brunette woman shoved her fashionably colorful eyeglasses up her nose and nodded. "I'm glad that wrist is the only thing you hurt."

"Me, too." Chandra felt silly every time she had to recount running her rental into a ditch. She glanced around. Several pretty young women wielding some sort of basket or container occupied seats in the waiting room. "Is the doctor running behind schedule?"

"Not at all." The receptionist sounded offended. "Don't worry—Dr. Jules will get you all fixed up and out of here in no time." The woman handed Chandra a clipboard and pen. "*After* you finish your paperwork."

She accepted the clipboard, and once her paperwork was complete, a nurse called her name, right on time. After getting her vitals and following up on a few items, the older woman left her in the exam room to wait for Dr. Jules.

Chandra adjusted her position on the exam table, the paper crinkling in protest. Then she scanned her emails while she waited for the doctor.

A knock at the door startled Chandra.

"Come in," she said. But when she gazed up from her phone, the face staring back at her didn't belong to the matronly physician she'd expected.

The baby-face doctor in a white coat with a stethoscope draped around his neck was incredibly handsome and surprisingly familiar. The sexy beard she'd admired on the plane was gone. But she'd recognize those dark eyes and devilish grin anywhere.

"Ms. Valentine. I see that wrist is still giving you trouble."

"JB?" She stared at him, blinking. "*You're* Dr. Jules?"

"Not the middle-aged white woman you were expecting, huh?" JB chuckled, his dark eyes twinkling. "Jules is a childhood nickname which has been unbelievably hard to shake. One of the hazards of returning to the little town you grew up in, I guess. I've been away for more than a decade, became a whole-ass doctor, and most of them still see me as Little Jules who got chased down Main Street by a baby goat."

Chandra's deep belly laugh alleviated the knot that had formed in her gut once she'd realized she'd been lusting over the town's child doctor. "You look...*different* without the beard."

"I know." JB rubbed his chin and sighed. "Did it as a favor to my mother. But I'm regretting that decision. The crotchety old mountain man look works for me, and it reminds folks around here that I'm not a mischievous kid anymore."

"No, of course not." She slipped her phone back into her purse and ran her fingers through her hair. "You're a mischievous adult now."

"Guilty." JB chuckled as he scrubbed his hands at the sink. The scent of the antiseptic soap filled the air.

Chandra couldn't help watching him. Even from behind, bent over a sink, this man was an absolute thing of beauty.

Her cheeks burned. For the past two days, she'd been daydreaming about her handsome, mysterious, bearded knight bending her over and taking her from behind. And now she just felt...*wrong*. And a little dirty. No, *a lot* dirty. Because he might technically be a grown-up and even a doctor. But he looked...*young*. Way too young for a woman who was nearly forty.

Thank God she hadn't taken him up on his offer to call her if she needed...*anything*. So maybe she'd had a few erotic thoughts about the handsome doctor. They hadn't actually done anything, so she had nothing to feel guilty about.

"All right, Ms. Valentine. Let's take a look at that wrist."

The rest of the appointment went as expected. He called her Ms. Valentine. She called him Dr. Brandon. Chandra tried to ignore the spread of warmth through her skin as he gently handled her wrist to examine it. She managed to restrain herself from sliding off the exam table and straddling his lap as he sat on the rolling leather stool.

After all, she wasn't some sex-starved vamp who was desperate for the man.

Okay, maybe she was sex starved...and kind of desperate for this man—but she was certainly not a vamp.

"Ms. Valentine?" JB looked slightly amused, and she had the feeling he'd had to call her name more than once.

Chandra's face heated. "Yes, Doctor?"

"I asked if your rental car has been replaced." He washed his hands again.

"There are several cars between my dad and siblings. So I don't really need one. Besides, with my wrist being sore, I'd rather not drive."

"How'd you get into town?"

"Dejah Richardson dropped me off on her way to get some supplies. She's meeting me at the café across the way in—" Chandra glanced down at her watch "—about an hour."

"Then you're in good hands. Say hello to Dejah for me." His eyes lingered on hers. Warmth spread through her skin. Her belly fluttered.

What was it about Dr. Julian Brandon that made her feel like a teenager with a crush?

"We'll do a quick X-ray, just to make sure none of the small bones in your wrist have been damaged." He folded his arms and leaned against the counter. "If this is a mild sprain, as I suspect, the ligaments in your wrist probably got stretched while you were gripping the wheel during your accident. We'll wrap your wrist and have you follow the RICE protocol—rest, ice, compression, elevation. A little ibuprofen, when needed. Follow those guidelines and you'll be good as new in no time."

"Thank you, Doctor," she called to his retreating back. He gave her a brief nod and exited the room.

Chandra hadn't wanted JB to flirt with her now that she realized he was far too young for her. Still, she couldn't help feeling a little insulted. His all-business demeanor and sudden lack of interest likely had everything to do with him seeing her age on her chart.

After her X-rays, the doctor wrapped her wrist, said his goodbyes, and then his nurse went over the care protocol with Chandra before directing her back to the reception desk.

A pretty redhead approached the receptionist while Chandra was digging for her credit card.

"I've been sitting here *forever*," the redhead complained, clutching her small wicker basket. "How is it that everyone else manages to get seen?" The woman cast an angry gaze at Chandra.

"Because they made appointments for actual medical issues. They didn't just pop in for an unscheduled social call with the doctor. And as I said, I can understand if you don't have time to wait until he's free. I'd be happy to deliver the—"

"No." The woman shifted the basket away from the receptionist's outstretched arms. "I'd like to deliver this to Jules myself, if you don't mind."

"Up to you." The receptionist—Lindee, according to her name tag—shrugged. "But you'll need to wait a bit longer while he sees actual patients. If you don't mind," Lindee said with a smirk.

The redhead huffed off, her heels clicking against the tile floor.

"Sorry about that." Lindee turned back to Chandra. "Dr. Jules has become Magnolia Lake's most eligible bachelor since his return." She indicated the women seated in the waiting room clutching various gifts.

"Who did he displace?" Chandra asked.

"The previous reigning champion, Cole Abbott, who surprised us all and got engaged a few months ago."

*Of course.*

Chandra glanced at the door that led to the doctor's office. So much for her fantasies about her knight in shining armor.

Julian slipped into his office to check his messages. He peered out the window as Chandra crossed the street. He'd wanted to greet her with a hug, as they had when they'd parted at the winery. But she was there to see him in his official capacity as the town's doctor, so it didn't feel appropriate.

He was startled by a gentle knock on his open door. Lindee—his receptionist and a childhood friend—stepped forward, a wide smile on her face. "Hey, Jules. We had two last-minute cancellations. Your next patient isn't until after lunch. Would you like to start seeing the ladies waiting for you in the lobby?"

No, he wouldn't. He'd much prefer to be sipping coffee with the intriguing Ms. Valentine.

He glanced out the window again. "Actually, I need to step out. I won't be more than an hour. Please offer again to accept the baskets on my behalf. If they'd prefer to wait, I'll see them when I get back."

"But I—"

"I'll bring back a box of those bear claws you like so much." Julian stripped off the white coat and hung it on the back of the door. Then he hurried out the back door, rather than going through the waiting room.

Julian jogged over to the Magnolia Lake Bakery. He

paused for a moment to catch his breath, then approached the counter as Chandra placed her order.

Chandra was wearing a simple short flared black skirt, a white blouse and a gray wool coat. Her dark brown hair fell in soft curls over one shoulder. The smooth brown skin of her legs shimmered. And that subtle honeysuckle scent that had grabbed him the moment he'd sat beside her on the plane seemed to drift in the air, reminding him of playing in the backyard with his dad when he was a kid.

"You can add that to my order," Julian said, when Chandra reached inside her purse for her wallet.

The cashier looked to Chandra for confirmation. She gave the younger woman a reluctant nod, then turned to him, her arms folded.

"I feel like we need to start over again here," Julian said, taking in Chandra's cocked hip and skeptical expression. He extended a hand. "I'm Dr. Julian Brandon, hometown boy slash prodigal son. JB is what most people outside this town have called me since college."

"Chandra Valentine." She shook his offered hand, still regarding him suspiciously. "Tell me, do you treat all of your patients to lunch, Dr. Jules?"

Damn, he really wished she hadn't gotten wind of that nickname. He'd been trying to ditch it since he was ten. Slapping *Doctor* on the front of it didn't do much to make it better.

"Just the really beautiful ones who sustain wrist injuries while trying to avoid a bear."

And just like that, her determined frown turned into an adorable smirk.

He ordered a sandwich and coffee. When the cashier asked if it was for there or to go, Julian turned to Chandra.

"Here," Chandra said. Once they were seated in a booth, she folded her hands on the table. "Thank you for lunch."

"Thank you for accepting my invitation."

"Is that what that was?" Her eyes flickered.

"Okay, it was an *implied* invitation." He leaned forward, his arms folded on the table as he drank her in.

Chandra was more gorgeous every time he saw her.

She dropped her gaze, as if embarrassed by his stare. "Isn't there some rule about doctors and their patients—"

"Having lunch?" Julian shrugged, barely able to hold back a grin. "None that I recall."

"You know what I mean, *Doogie Howser*." Chandra pointed a finger. "You must be all of...what? Twenty-five?"

"*Et tu*, Chandra?" He'd been in town a few days and had heard his fair share of references to the fictional child doctor. Otherwise, he wouldn't have known who Doogie Howser was. "I'm thirty. Thirty-one on my birthday in a few months."

"I'm nearly old enough to be your mother," she muttered.

Julian tried his best to hide his amusement.

"You're nowhere close to my mother's age. Besides, I've dated women older than you." He shrugged. "The age difference doesn't bother me. As for your question about the doctor-patient relationship... If we'd met in my exam room, I wouldn't be sitting here. But our relationship clearly predates any doctor-patient connection."

"I wasn't aware we had a *relationship*." Chandra leaned forward, her elbow on the table and her chin propped on the fist of her uninjured hand. Her rich brown eyes studied him.

"Well, you did hold my hand on the plane," he reminded her. "In some cultures, that's practically a marriage proposal."

"True. But neither of us is from such a culture." Her full lips curved in a reluctant smile.

Julian had the sudden urge to glide his fingers into the nape of Chandra's neck and tug her forward, so he could sample the berry-tinted gloss on her lips.

"Then there's that hug you gave me," he continued, ignoring her earlier objection.

"That was a show of gratitude. You saved my life."

Someone would've come along and extracted her from the vehicle, and she certainly wasn't in danger of death. But now, while he was trying to convince her to go out with him, probably wasn't the best time to bring that up.

"I'm just saying…after the thirty-second mark, I'm pretty sure the hug went from gratitude to something… *more*." Julian chuckled when she huffed indignantly. "What? Is it so terrible to admit you're attracted to me?"

"No. I mean…yes." Chandra looked adorably flustered. "Maybe I was attracted to you. But—"

"Great. Because the attraction is mutual." Julian leaned in slightly and lowered his voice. "The Universe keeps throwing us together, Chandra. Seems like a glaring sign it's best not to ignore."

"So now our meeting was destiny or something?" Chandra furrowed her brows.

"Or something." He grinned.

The server brought a chicken club for her and hot pastrami for him.

"This sandwich is delicious," Chandra declared after a few minutes of eating in awkward silence.

"The food here is always amazing."

"What about at the King's Finest Family Restaurant?" Chandra asked.

"The place just opened a few weeks ago. I ate there for the first time last night. The Blake's Steak was phenomenal. Not surprising though." He shrugged. "The Abbotts don't do anything half-assed."

"You know them?" Something shifted in her demeanor at the mention of Magnolia Lake's first family.

"Around here, they're practically royalty." Julian chuckled.

"But what you said speaks to a closer relationship with the family. You don't just know them by reputation," Chandra noted.

"You could say that." He set down the remainder of his sandwich and wiped his hands. "Joseph Abbott paid for my education."

"That was generous." Chandra took another bite of her sandwich. "Was it a town scholarship?"

"It was sort of my personal deal with the Devil." Julian laughed when Chandra's eyes went wide. "Don't get me wrong—Joseph Abbott is a great guy. But he's used to getting his way. He didn't get where he is in life without knowing how to turn a few screws to get people to do exactly what he wants."

"And what did he want from you?" Chandra asked.

He studied her brown eyes, brimming with curiosity. He was glad she was interested but couldn't help wondering why.

"He wanted me to come back here and become the town's doctor once Doc Johnson was ready to retire."

"For the rest of your life?"

"He's not *that* persuasive," Julian said. "He asked for an eight-year commitment. We settled on four."

"You proposed the deal?"

"No." Julian rubbed his neck. "Let's just say he made me an offer I couldn't refuse, so I made the most of it."

Chandra leaned in closer. "Did they threaten you?"

"Yes. Joe Abbott threatened my bad ass with jail for stealing his Mercedes and taking it for a joyride."

"You *stole* his car?" She whispered the offending word. "How old were you?"

Julian sighed, abandoning his sandwich again. He licked honey Dijon mustard from his thumb and Chandra's eyes darkened. His body responded and he was more than a little glad they were seated at a table.

"I was fourteen and not at the best place in my life." He frowned, thinking about his life then.

"Why?" Chandra's warm hand covered his.

"Why did I steal his car or why was I at a bad place in my life?"

"Both," she said, without hesitation.

He'd already divulged more of his personal history to Chandra than he had with any woman he'd been interested in. Normally, he pulled away or simply changed the subject when a topic came up he didn't want to discuss. A few relationships had ended because he hadn't been willing to open up about his past.

So why was he telling Chandra Valentine, whom he barely knew, his pitiful life story?

Maybe because he was back in Magnolia Lake, where his story was common knowledge. Chandra was bound to find out if she asked the right person, and he'd rather she hear it from him. Or maybe it was because he'd do just about anything to keep her there with him, her warm skin covering his.

"I told you my dad died in a car crash when I was a kid." His mouth suddenly felt dry. The words just wouldn't seem to come. This was something he hadn't talked about in ages. Since he stopped going to therapy years ago.

His hands involuntarily tensed. But rather than withdrawing her hand from his, Chandra slid her fingers into his palm, comforting him the way he'd comforted her on the plane.

It was always embarrassing to tell this story. But there was something about Chandra that put him at ease. Like he could trust her with his truth—no matter how ugly it was.

"My mom and I…neither of us handled my dad's death well. She kind of checked out, and my bright idea to get her attention was to act out. I did an escalating variety of stupid things to get into trouble, hoping she'd snap out of it."

Chandra stroked the back of his closed fist with her thumb. His grip loosened and his shoulders relaxed.

"That must've been really tough for both of you." Her gaze lowered to their connected hands. "My mother walked away when I was eight. My stepmother ditched us when I was fourteen. Both times, I spiraled into this dark place, believing there must be something wrong with me because neither of them stuck around. I felt lost and didn't always make the best decisions. It didn't mean I was a bad person." She met his gaze and smiled softly. "And Joseph Abbott evidently saw the good in you."

"I guess he did." Julian sighed. "He gave me a choice. If I planned to continue on the 'road to ruin,' he'd save me some time and make sure my ass ended up in juvie. Option two—if I was willing to work hard for it, he'd help me become anything I wanted to be. I told him fine, I wanted to be a doctor."

Julian chuckled recalling the old man's expression.

*You sure do swing for the fences, don't you, son?*

"That was quite a commitment." Chandra released his hand and picked up her sandwich. A soft smile lit her eyes. "Bet he wasn't expecting that."

"He definitely wasn't. But he kept his word. Gave me a free ride to college and then medical school. In return, I agreed to serve as the town's doctor for at least four years once old Doc Johnson retired. A week ago, he finally did. That's why I'm here."

"So then you'd consider Joe Abbott a pretty trustworthy guy, then?" Chandra asked.

"I would." Julian folded his hands on the table. "Now I have a question. Why are you so interested in the Abbotts?"

Chandra set down her sandwich and folded her hands, too. "I found out what's going on with my dad. He's been going through sort of an identity crisis. After his mother's death a few years ago, he learned that he was adopted. He hadn't told any of us, but he joined one of those DNA ancestry registries, hoping to find his real family."

"Your father is related to Joe Abbott?" Julian asked.

"He's my dad's half brother. King Abbott was both their fathers, but they had different mothers. Joseph didn't know about my dad until recently. And my biological grandmother died a couple months after giving birth to my father. She knew she was going to die and asked that the family who adopted him keep his given name… Abbott."

"Which took on a hell of a lot more meaning once he discovered who he was related to." Julian whistled. "That must have come as quite a shock to all of you."

"It did. But the bigger shock was that he's selling the family textile business and has purchased the Richardson Vineyards. He has aspirations of building a wine empire that will rival his brother's bourbon empire."

"That's a tall order. Joe's been at this half a century," Julian said as diplomatically as he could.

"My dad swears it isn't a competition. But he discovered that King Abbott had hoped to branch out into winemaking. My dad and my brother Nolan have been amateur winemakers for years. The rest of us consume our fair share of it." She laughed nervously. "Guess Dad considers that enough of a reason to start a family-owned winery."

"None of you had any idea your dad had bought the winery?"

"Just my brother Nolan. And now Dad is asking us to drop our entire lives and move here to Green Acres… No offense," she added quickly.

"None taken. But for the record, the sitcom was called *Green Acres*. The town was Hooterville."

"How on earth would you know that?" She seemed impressed. "That show was way before my time. It was definitely before yours."

"Syndication. Same as you." He grinned. "My mom always said I was an old soul."

"Which explains why you're asking me out when half a dozen beautiful women your age are probably still sitting in your waiting room bearing gifts."

"I'm not interested in any of them. I am *completely* taken with you. I have been since you nodded hello in that airport."

Why was there a weird fluttery feeling in his chest whenever he thought of that moment?

Her expression softened. She set down her sandwich. But before she could respond, her phone rang. "I'd better take this. It's Dejah."

He ate his sandwich while Chandra quickly chatted with Dejah Richardson.

"Dejah completed her errands quicker than expected. She's five minutes away. I have to go." Chandra stood.

Julian stood, too. "I know you won't be in town long, Chandra. But I'd love to see you again."

"Why?" She adjusted her purse strap on her shoulder. "Like you said, I won't be here long."

"I don't know." Maybe he was being too honest. It wasn't the most romantic appeal. "But I can't let go of the sense that you and I were meant to meet. I know that sounds—"

"Corny with a side of flower child?" She laughed.

"Something like that." Julian rubbed his chin.

"True. But it's also really sweet. It helps, of course, that you're cute, especially when you turn up the charm."

Julian grinned. "Is it working?"

"It would be," she said. "But my hands are pretty full right now. My dad is going through an identity crisis. It feels like each of my siblings is on the edge of some sort of personal crisis, too. And I'm this close to finally getting that corner office and the title and salary that go with it back in San Diego." She worried her lower lip with her teeth and frowned. "I can't afford any distractions right now, Julian. Not even one as handsome and charming as you."

He was interested. She wasn't. C'est la vie. He'd never be that asshole guy who wouldn't take no for an answer.

"Well, take care of that wrist, Ms. Valentine. And call me if you need…well…*anything*."

"Thank you, Dr. Brandon. And thank you for lunch. It was lovely getting to know you."

"You, too."

Julian groaned quietly as she turned and walked away.

He slipped back into the booth to finish his lunch, but he'd lost his appetite.

Maybe he should be more like Chandra and remain focused on his goal.

He'd committed to staying in Magnolia Lake for four years, and he'd do exactly that. Then his life would be his own, his obligation to the Abbotts and the town repaid.

Still, it was a shame she wouldn't be sticking around. Chandra Valentine was just the type of distraction that would make his time in Magnolia Lake go by more quickly.

# Eight

Chandra stood in the middle of the barn where the Abbott family would be hosting a party for a couple hundred Magnolia Lake locals. The previous night, she and her siblings had met their father's half brother Joseph Abbott; his son and daughter-in-law, Duke and Iris Abbott; and all five of his grandchildren—Blake, Parker, Max, Cole and Zora, as well as their significant others, children and various in-laws, during a meal Iris hosted there.

Chandra and her brothers had been tense and unsure of what to expect. But Naya had walked in and hugged each of the Abbotts, as if she'd known them her entire life. Naya's relaxed attitude coupled with Zora's and Iris's warm and welcoming demeanor had eased any tensions between the two families.

The food—catered by the King's Finest Family Restaurant—had been as amazing as Julian had said. They'd bonded over delicious food and classic soul: Marvin Gaye; Otis Redding; Aretha Franklin; Earth, Wind & Fire; Gladys

Knight; and The Isley Brothers. By the end of the evening, the Abbotts felt like old friends—if not quite yet family. Even Sebastian's ever-present frown had eased a bit. Chandra wasn't sure if it was because Bas was actually having a good time or because he seemed taken with Parker's sister-in-law: his wife Kayleigh's older sister Evelisse.

Either way, it was nice to see her father happy, smiling and more at peace than she'd seen him in years. Nolan and Sebastian had actually let their guard down and enjoyed themselves. And she couldn't remember the last time she'd heard Alonzo, Nyles and Naya laugh so much. Seeing her family together and happy—something they hadn't been in so long—made her heart swell.

"So what do you think?" Blake's wife, Savannah, stood beside Chandra. Her adorable one-year-old daughter, Remi, whose hazel eyes were carbon copies of her mother's, was perched on Savannah's hip. "We went a little overboard, I know."

"No, not at all." Chandra tweaked the little girl's nose, and Remi giggled. The sound was pure joy, and it made Chandra smile. "The barn is stunning. Elegant and ethereal. It's like a winter wonderland."

"I know mid-October is way too early for Christmas decorations," Savannah said. "But country music star Dade Willis filmed his upcoming holiday special here. His team let us have the decorations, so we decided to keep them up and just roll with it."

"Everyone is going to love it, the kids especially," Chandra assured Savannah.

"Thanks, Chandra. We're thrilled you all are here. It's great seeing Grandpa Joe so happy." Savannah nodded toward the two newly minted half brothers. They were deep in animated conversation and clearly enjoying each other's company.

"My dad hasn't been this happy in a while," Chandra admitted. "Maybe never."

Savannah's gaze followed Chandra's as the barn door opened and a handful of guests filtered in. "Nervous about meeting the entire town?"

"A little." Chandra's shoulders tensed. "Not really looking forward to becoming the town curiosity."

"Folks can be a bit...*inquisitive*," Savannah conceded. They both laughed at her diplomatic way of saying *nosy*. "But they're good people. Warm and open. I'm originally from a little town in West Virginia, and I've only been here about five years. But Magnolia Lake feels like home now. It's a great place to live and raise a family." Savannah kissed her daughter's forehead.

For the briefest moment, Chandra thought about the wedding and family that didn't materialize for her five years ago. Edward, her ex, she didn't miss. But in fleeting moments, like this, she missed the *ideals* of marriage and motherhood. The realities of a husband and children... maybe not.

"I'm afraid my siblings and I are more inclined toward living in the city," Chandra said. "But Magnolia Lake is a lovely place to visit. I haven't been this relaxed in ages."

"I didn't move here with the intention of staying either. But then, I never planned on falling for this incredible guy." Savannah flashed a flirty smile at her husband, Blake, who was approaching.

There was so much love in both of their expressions. It almost felt as if Chandra was intruding on a private moment.

Blake leaned down and kissed his wife. He took their daughter, whose arms were outstretched to her father. Then he slipped an arm around Savannah's waist. "You coming here changed my life and started a chain reaction that changed our family and the company for the better."

Iris had told the story of how after Blake and Savannah had gotten married, it had seemingly created a domino effect, with each of her children finding their perfect mate, one by one. Chandra's father had quipped that his children seemed *determined* not to produce any grandchildren for him to spoil. And while he'd been teasing them, they all knew her dad was only half joking. He'd hoped that one of them would've given him a grandchild by now.

Blake grinned. "Four weddings down, one to go." He nodded toward where Cole and his fiancée, Renee, stood with her young son, Mercer.

Chandra had been struck by just how much Cole and Mercer seemed to adore each other. The sweet little boy was autistic and nonverbal, but it was clear just how much he loved Cole.

"Please, don't give my dad any ideas." Chandra laughed. She turned toward a familiar voice.

*Dr. Julian Brandon.*

She'd seen him in casual attire on the plane, titillating gray sweats—the memory of which still made her body tingle—and his crisp white doctor's coat. But tonight's look was her favorite thus far.

Julian wore a handsome suit fitted perfectly to his athletic form. The suit, in an unexpected deep plum shade, looked good with the navy shirt he wore. The color of the suit was festive but not garish and popped nicely against his deep brown skin.

Chandra forced her attention back to Blake and Savannah, who both seemed to share a knowing smile.

"Anything I can do to help?" Chandra asked.

"Mingle and enjoy yourself." Savannah nodded in Julian's direction. "Your audience awaits."

Before she could think of a reply, Savannah and Blake were gone, leaving her there staring across the room at Julian. When their eyes met, his mouth curved in a lopsided smile, and he shoved one hand in his pocket, his gaze sliding down her body.

Chandra's face heated. She'd hoped that knowing Dr. Julian Brandon was too young for her would abate the deep attraction she felt for him. It hadn't. Now he wasn't just kind and devastatingly handsome. He was a tempting, forbidden morsel she couldn't stop thinking about.

As Julian moved in her direction, he was quickly cut off by three young women, one of whom was the redhead from his office the other day.

Chandra heaved a quiet sigh.

"Looks like your friend is the biggest thing to happen around these parts in a while." Naya approached her with a clear mug filled with what looked like hot apple cider. Her sister was wearing an adorable chin-length bob in a deep flame red. Her makeup—dramatic, yet tasteful—was festive and complemented her hair color nicely.

"It seems so." Chandra stared wistfully in Julian's direction, then indicated Naya's mug. "That smells good."

"It is." Naya handed her the mug.

Chandra sipped the heated beverage. The warmth and spicy sweetness washed over her tongue. The crisp taste of fall apples was followed by heat slowly building in her belly. She coughed a little. "There's liquor in this." She handed back the mug.

Naya laughed. "Lots of it. Cousin Zora was a little heavy-handed when she spiked the apple cider. But you won't hear me complaining about it."

"Duly warned." Chandra fanned her face.

Was the warmth surging through her from the unexpected shot of bourbon or seeing Julian in that suit that hugged his muscular body like a glove?

"Now, about your friend…" Naya gestured in his direction.

The crowd around him had gotten larger. Now there

was an older woman standing with a younger woman who looked like her daughter. Even from this distance, it was obvious the woman was angling for a son-in-law.

"I feel sorry for Julian," Chandra said. "An entire night of fending off husband-hunters can't be much fun."

"Then what do you plan to do about it?" Naya asked.

"Me? Why do I need to do anything about it? It's not like we're involved."

"They don't know that," Naya noted. "The dude came to your aid *twice*." Naya held up two fingers. "Here's your chance to return the favor."

"And what exactly do you expect me to do?" Chandra turned toward her sister.

"Strut your fine ass over there and stake a claim on your man. Or, you know…your *pretend* man." She sipped her cider.

How many of those spiked apple ciders had her sister had? "You're suggesting that I pretend to be his girlfriend, *unsolicited*? I don't know, Nay. I'd love to help Julian out, but it isn't like he asked me to run interference."

"Look at the poor man. His eyes are *pleading* for help." Naya gestured toward him. "He rescued you from a bear-induced car accident. We cannot let him spend the evening miserable."

When Chandra didn't respond, Naya handed Chandra her mug and stood taller. She propped up her already perky breasts, then fluffed her wig.

"Fine. If you won't do it, I guess I'll have to. I'm going to walk right up to the baby doc and stick my tongue down his throat. That should send a pretty clear message."

"No!" Chandra's objection came out louder than she'd intended. She handed the mug back to Naya. "I'm the one indebted to him. I'll do it." She raked her fingers through her hair and straightened her shoulders.

Naya sipped her drink and grinned maniacally.

*Manipulative little brat.*

Chandra cut her eyes at Naya. "I hate you sometimes, you know that?"

"Love you, too, sis." Naya giggled. "Now let's see you work it. Show those little girls what's up." Naya slapped Chandra on the bottom and she jumped.

If this thing went sideways, Chandra was going to strangle her sister.

Chandra sucked in a deep breath, then walked to the other side of the room. She made her way through the crowd of women and touched Julian's arm.

"There you are, babe. I didn't realize you'd arrived." Chandra smiled sweetly, hoping he wasn't about to out her as a lunatic feigning a relationship.

Surprise flashed in his dark eyes, followed by an appreciative smile. He slipped a strong arm around her waist. She was reminded of when he'd lifted her from her car. Julian kissed her cheek and whispered, "Thanks, I owe you one."

"I just arrived," he said for the benefit of the women around him whose faces displayed varying degrees of disappointment. The redhead looked completely undone. "I was catching up with a few old friends."

"You two are dating?" The older woman who was standing with her daughter gestured between them. "That's news."

"I certainly haven't heard anything about you having a girlfriend." The redhead's tone was accusatory, as if there was some official town registry for dating couples.

"We met recently." Julian pulled her closer, not acknowledging either of them directly. "But the moment I laid eyes on Chandra—" a warm smile lit up his handsome face "—I knew she was the woman for me. Made it my mission to make her mine." He kissed her temple.

Chandra's skin tingled where Julian's body pressed to hers.

"I'm always nervous on those small regional planes. When we hit severe turbulence, I was scared out of my mind. Julian was so sweet and such a gentleman. I don't know how I would've made it through that flight without him." Their eyes locked and Chandra's stomach fluttered. "Julian took such good care of me. He held my hand through the worst of it."

"I'll bet he did," the redhead muttered.

The redhead's friend elbowed her, then extended a hand. "I'm Olivia Henderson. Folks call me Livvy. My aunt and uncle run the general store. I'm Benji and Sloane Bennett's nanny. Welcome to town…"

"Chandra. Chandra Valentine." She shook the woman's hand. "Nice to meet you, Livvy."

The rest of the women in the group introduced themselves, one by one, including the reluctant redhead, Deanna Jasper.

Finally, the crowd dissipated.

"I can't thank you enough." Julian uttered the words through clenched teeth and a smile, so only she could hear them. "You saved my ass."

"Thank my sister." She indicated Naya, who held up what Chandra was pretty sure was a fresh mug of spiked apple cider. "She suggested that rescuing you from the circling piranhas was the least I could do after all you've done for me. Besides, if I didn't, she threatened to prance over here and introduce her tongue to your tonsils. I figured I'd save us both the embarrassment."

Julian's deep chuckle rumbled through his chest. He lowered his voice. "Remind me to thank little sis."

A shiver ran down her spine. The space between her thighs pulsed and ached. She needed to get it together.

"Like I said, I owed you. Hopefully that sent the message, and you won't be harassed the rest of the evening,"

Chandra said. "If there's someone here you are interested in, just tell them we broke up."

Julian rubbed the five-o'clock shadow on his strong jaw and smirked. "Sweetheart, you have no idea what you've just done, do you?"

"What do you mean?" Chandra glanced up at him.

"Ms. Adelaide—the older woman who was trying to marry off her daughter—is Magnolia Lake's walking, talking news bulletin."

"You mean the town gossip?" Chandra was beginning to feel like she was in Hooterville or perhaps Mayberry.

"Your words, not mine." Julian chuckled. "Ms. Adelaide will definitely spread the word about us. But if you think that little act alone will convince this crowd I'm off the market, you're mistaken." Julian's warm breath ghosted over her skin as he whispered in her ear. "Everyone here will be watching us all night."

Chandra glanced around the room. Several people were staring and whispering.

Why in the hell did she let Naya get her into these things?

*No good deed goes unpunished*

It'd been a favorite phrase of her late grandmother's.

Chandra huffed. "My college drama teacher always said, 'Commit to the role.' I started this, so I'm in. I'll only be here another week and a half. Then you can say we're in a long-distance relationship for as long as you need to."

"Thanks, babe." Julian's eyes twinkled with amusement. He extended his large hand and she slid hers into it. "Heads up…the pissed-off woman marching in our direction is my mother."

*What on earth have I gotten myself into?*

# Nine

Julian intertwined their fingers and glided his thumb over the back of Chandra's hand, hoping to ease the sudden tension rolling off her shoulders. "Just breathe."

Chandra sucked in a deep breath, her hand trembling. She pressed her lips—painted a deep, enticing shade of wine—into a tentative smile. "Commit to the role," she muttered quietly.

"Hey, Ma. Didn't realize you'd arrived." Julian kissed his mother's cheek but didn't release Chandra's hand. "There's someone I really want you to meet. This is—"

"You must be Chandra Valentine." His mother ignored him. She extended a hand to Chandra and offered a stiff smile. "I've heard so much about you…*in the last five minutes.*"

"It's a pleasure to meet you, Mrs. Brandon," Chandra said. "Julian has told me so much about you."

His mother's expression softened. She seemed to appreciate that Chandra had called her *Mrs.* Brandon. "Some of it good, I hope." His mother finally spared him a glance.

"All of it good," Chandra lied, which he appreciated. "He tells me you're a nurse in the maternity ward at a hospital in Gatlinburg."

"Yes, I am." His mother seemed puzzled as she glanced between them.

"He admires the work you've done. Even more so as a single mother. I was so moved to learn that your work as a nurse is what prompted Julian to become a doctor. You must be really proud of him and thrilled he's finally back home."

His mother blinked, seemingly stunned.

Chandra had defused the fire in Luetta Brandon's eyes and turned the woman into a puddle of goo. She'd have to teach him that trick.

"You never told me that me being a nurse is the reason you became a doctor," his mother said.

"I just assumed you knew."

Julian was glad his mother wasn't lighting into him—especially since he had it coming. She couldn't have been happy about Ms. Adelaide making her feel like she was the very last to know about his "relationship" with Chandra. But having this conversation about why he became a doctor was uncomfortable. As were the raw feelings and bitter memories the revelation invoked. Especially here in front of his fake girlfriend in whom he was *seriously* interested.

"I didn't." There was a hint of sadness in her voice. "I guess that's one more thing we need to talk about." His mother cleared her throat and returned her attention to the woman clutching his hand. "Well, it's nice to finally meet you, Chandra."

"And it was a pleasure to meet you, Mrs. Brandon." Chandra sounded more confident. "I'm sorry we didn't get a chance to meet before now, but the past few days have been a whirlwind, meeting my new cousins and learning about the winery."

"I can imagine." His mother pulled her black sequined cardigan tight around her shoulders. "And please, friends call me Lue." She turned to Julian. "I realize you're both busy, but I hope my son finds time to bring you by the house for lunch. How long are you staying in town?"

"A week and a half. Then I have to get back to San Diego."

"That's a shame." His mother frowned. "Folks around here are hoping that you'll all put down roots and become part of the community, like the Richardsons were."

"Magnolia Lake is a charming town, and everyone I've met has been really lovely. Now that my dad is moving here, you won't be able to keep us away," Chandra assured her.

"Good," his mother said. "Now, I should make the rounds. I'll see you two later."

"Of course," Julian said.

"Looking forward to it." Chandra smiled sweetly.

"You realize you defused a live bomb just now, right?" Julian slid his arm around Chandra's waist. "What is it you do for a living again? Because if what you just did isn't part of it, your gift is being wasted."

Chandra laughed, leaning into him. "Essentially? I baby-sit grown-ass folks who behave like toddlers and do whatever it takes to get them to either actually do their jobs or find somewhere that might be more suitable for them. Even if that's the couch in front of their TV at home."

"You're a hatchet woman. No wonder your job has you so tense." He turned her around and placed his hands on her tight shoulders, gently kneading the corded muscles there.

Chandra purred and the sound went directly below his belt. He couldn't stop imagining having this stunningly beautiful woman beneath him as she made the same sound, their fingers threaded above her head.

"Get a room, you two." Chandra's younger sister—*Maya? Or maybe Naya?*—grinned.

"*You're* the one who got us into this." Chandra pointed an accusatory finger.

Julian mouthed the words *thank you* and winked.

Chandra's sister laughed again. "Anyway, Savannah sent me over here to tell you she made room at our table for your new beau here and his mom."

Chandra sighed. "This just keeps getting better."

"Agreed," Julian said. Though he meant it literally, while she was clearly being sarcastic. "I'll let my mother know."

"You realize what this means?" Chandra turned to him after her sister walked away. "We're going to have to sit through a bunch of awkward questions about our relationship, which isn't a relationship, while…while…"

"Holding hands, cuddling and showing borderline inappropriate amounts of PDA?" Julian chuckled. "I'm *totally* down with that."

Chandra huffed, though there was a hint of amusement in her eyes. "You're getting a kick out of this, aren't you?"

"I am." Julian stepped closer and looped his arms around her waist as he gazed down into those dark brown eyes that had captured him the moment they'd locked on to his. "Aren't you?"

"You're beneath the mistletoe." Nannette Henderson, owner of the general store in town, pointed above their heads.

"So we are." Julian smiled at Chandra.

"But it's nowhere close to being Christmas," Chandra objected.

"I don't make the rules, sweetie." Mrs. H shrugged. "Didn't hang the mistletoe in the middle of October either."

Julian smiled at Chandra. He leaned down slowly, providing ample opportunity for her to object if she didn't want to be kissed. She erased the remaining space between them and pressed her mouth to his.

Chandra's lips were soft and supple. Her mouth tasted like apples and bourbon. And her warm curves molded to his body.

Julian forced himself to pull back, wishing they were somewhere more private.

"Well." Mrs. H fanned herself. "That was *some* kiss. Seems you two are the real deal…not that I ever doubted it," she added quickly. Mrs. H hurried over to Ms. Adelaide—who'd undoubtedly put her up to the stunt.

"You think that'll keep them at bay?" Chandra flashed Ms. Adelaide a cheeky smile.

"Maybe for about an hour." Julian chuckled, taking her hand again. "C'mon. There's a town full of people eager to meet you."

Julian leaned against one of the posts, a glass of mulled cider in his hand. He tried not to stare at Chandra, but whenever she wasn't by his side, her hand tucked in his, he found himself searching the room for her. He studied every delicious curve on her tantalizing frame.

Who knew a sweaterdress could be so damn sexy? The deep V-neck of the belted red dress offered a hint of cleavage. The hem fell an inch or two above her knees, and a side split exposed the smooth, deep brown skin of one mouthwatering thigh. Her dangling silver earrings matched her belt and the glittering silver stiletto heels made her legs look a mile long. He had an unhealthy obsession with the idea of those shoes dangling over his shoulders as he kissed his way up her inner thigh.

*Down, boy. Down.*

Chandra might've been amenable to a kiss for the sake of warding off the group of women who seemed fascinated with him since his return. But since she'd turned down his request for a date, taking her to bed probably wasn't in the cards for them.

Still, he was enjoying their little charade more than he should. Every touch of her hand. The warmth of her skin as they stood together with his arm around her waist. The taste of her soft, sweet lips when he'd kissed her beneath the mistletoe. Chandra Valentine had a gift for driving him wild.

Even as they sat beside each other at the table, their parents grilling them, he enjoyed being with Chandra and getting to know her and her family.

The twins—Naya and Nyles—were a hot mess but entertaining. Nolan was fairly quiet but seemed to be constantly observing everyone and everything. Sebastian had spent most of the night frowning at him, and Alonzo was definitely a ladies' man. Her father, Abbott—who went by his middle name, Ray—was warm and friendly, but clearly assessing him. Deciding whether he measured up to his daughter.

Still, he was enjoying every single moment with her.

"You're *really* into my cousin, aren't you?" Cole stood beside him, a beer bottle in his hand. "Don't even try to deny it." Cole chuckled before Julian could open his mouth to object. "Got that damn goofy grin on your face. You're in heaven."

"So, apparently, are you." Julian nodded toward Cole's fiancée, Renee, who was twirling her son on the dance floor, to the boy's delight.

"Yeah." Cole's eyes lit up. "I am."

"I'm surprised Milo Lockwood didn't object to Magnolia Lake's notorious bad boy dating his granddaughter." Julian nodded toward the older man who was dancing with his wife to "For the Love of You" by The Isley Brothers.

"Object? I'm pretty sure the old goat tricked us into it." Cole chuckled. "And I could kiss the old bastard for it."

Cole Abbott was a few years older than Julian. But he

was the Abbott sibling Julian was most familiar with. He'd gotten to know Cole while working as a laborer for Milo's construction company one summer. Who knew Cole would go on to start his own real estate development company and achieve all he had? He usually grabbed a beer with Cole whenever he returned to town and they'd met up a couple of times when Cole had come to Philly.

Julian had been stunned to learn his friend had settled down and was about to become a stepfather.

"Legendary badass Cole Abbott is putting down roots. Wow, I feel like I'm in the *Twilight Zone* right now. You'd tell me if we were in a parallel universe, right?"

"Shut up, *Jules*." Cole nudged Julian with his elbow but laughed. "Times change and people mature." He shrugged. "Ren and I found each other again at the right time. And I honestly couldn't be happier."

"I'm happy for you, man. Seriously. Congrats." Julian held up his mug of mulled cider and Cole tapped it with his half-finished bottle of beer. "When's the big day?"

"Next summer," Cole said, with a goofy grin of his own. He turned to him. "But enough about me. What's up with you and my cousin? I'm not gonna have to kick your ass, am I?"

"You two have been related for like five minutes," Julian noted. "We've been boys for over a decade, and it's like that?"

"Family is family. So don't do anything stupid," Cole warned.

*Like pretend dating?*

"I really like Chandra." Julian glanced at her wistfully. "So don't worry. I'm pretty sure I'm the one who'll end up with a broken heart."

"Then here's hoping it works out for both of you." Cole held up his fist and Julian bumped it with his own.

Cole joined his fiancée and her son on the dance floor.

Mercer could barely contain his excitement as Cole approached, and Julian couldn't help feeling the tiniest bit of envy.

Suddenly, the opening strains of McFadden & Whitehead's "Ain't No Stopping Us Now" began to play. The DJ encouraged everyone to form a Soul Train Line.

Julian went over to Chandra, who was chatting with Max Abbott and his wife, Quinn. After apologizing for the interruption, he slipped an arm around her waist and asked her to join him on the dance floor.

"I haven't done a Soul Train Line in years." Chandra gazed at the dance floor longingly.

It wasn't a no. She just needed some encouragement.

"Great idea," Quinn said. "C'mon, Max. Let's join them."

They went through the Soul Train Line twice. There was something about Chandra's genuine joy and laughter that made his chest swell. The sway of her generous hips in that sweaterdress made other parts of his anatomy swell, too.

When "Be Ever Wonderful" by Earth, Wind & Fire came on, he clutched her hand. "Dance with me?"

Chandra's eyes glittered beneath the twinkling lights strung along the overhead beams. She stepped into his arms as they swayed together.

"Have I told you how incredible you look?" Julian asked.

"A time or two. Not that I mind hearing it again." Chandra's bashful grin made his pulse race. "So thank you."

"Thank you for stepping in to save me earlier. It was an extremely pleasant surprise."

"It was the least I could do. Besides, there are worse things than spending the next seven days on the arm of a handsome doctor who rescues nervous flyers and accident victims." Her sweet smile lit up the entire room.

Why did his heart swell and his pulse race every time she looked at him like that?

"The night sky here is so gorgeous." Chandra nodded toward the barn door, which opened when someone stepped outside. "I miss how bright the stars appeared in the night sky when I was a kid. The city lights dim the brilliance of the stars."

"Light pollution." Julian nodded. "I love city life, but I did miss seeing the stars. When I was a kid, my dad bought me a telescope and he'd point out the constellations. It was our thing." Julian hadn't thought of those nights under the stars with his dad in so long.

When the song ended, he didn't release Chandra and she didn't pull away. He stared at her a moment.

"There's something you should see. Wanna get out of here?"

Chandra studied him a moment, then slid her hand in his.

# Ten

"This is quite an upgrade," Chandra noted, surveying the brilliant blue Audi e-tron Premium Plus quattro SUV the valet pulled up in. It was one of the models she'd considered before she'd purchased her black BMW X3.

"Part of the package." Julian helped her inside, then tipped the valet.

"What is it that you want to show me?" Chandra asked after they'd pulled onto the road.

"It's a surprise. But you'll like it. Promise."

Chandra had spent the evening dancing with Julian, holding his hand, even kissing him. She'd reminded herself time and again it was just an act and that he was too young for her. But that hadn't stopped her belly from fluttering or the sparks of electricity from dancing along her skin.

"How are you adjusting to meeting your new family and discovering that you're now part owner of a winery?" Julian's eyes didn't leave the road. "It's a lot to take in."

The concern in his voice reminded Chandra of why

she'd been so drawn to him when he'd comforted her on the plane.

"It's been a roller coaster of emotions. I'm still worried my dad made a rash, impulsive decision in buying the place. But I can't deny this is the happiest I've ever seen him. It's like he's finally found his place in the world."

"I understand your concern about whether buying the winery was a good business move," Julian said thoughtfully. "But there's something to be said for finding your place in the world. And if anyone can help your father elevate the winery to its full potential, it's the Abbotts. Even Cole—who isn't involved in running the distillery—has proven himself to be a brilliant businessman."

Julian chuckled before continuing. "Cole shocked the entire town, including his family, when he didn't go into the family business. They thought he'd fail and come crawling back to the distillery. But going into construction and development was right for him. I think they all appreciate that now."

Chandra couldn't help feeling bad for her father, knowing now that he'd felt trapped in his adopted family's business all those years. She'd also felt stifled by Valentine Textiles. The sudden end of her engagement had given her the courage to walk away, and it was what she'd needed to do at the time. But she'd also distanced herself from most of her family. That she regretted. Spending the past few days with her father and siblings made that abundantly clear.

"Do you ever regret becoming a doctor?" Chandra asked.

"No." His answer was immediate. "True, I made the decision hoping it would be a magic bullet that would fix things between me and my mom. And the deal I made with Joe Abbott forced me to return home when I would've preferred to stay in Philly. But I love helping people. Being there for them in life-changing ways." He glanced over at her. "Sounds sappy, right?"

"Sappy with a side of flower child." They both laughed. "But I like it, and I like you. You're a genuinely good guy, Dr. Julian Brandon. Magnolia Lake is lucky to have you for the next four years. You were well worth the investment."

"Thanks." Julian covered her hand, perched on the console between them, with his own. She thought about when he'd offered her his hand on the plane. "And thank you for defusing things with my mother. She was hurt and probably embarrassed to learn about us from town gossip. You handled the situation brilliantly. I'm not surprised your father wants to make you the company CEO."

Her father, who was doing his best to talk them all into joining the company, had mentioned during dinner that he was offering her the role of CEO. She was flattered, but she couldn't accept the position.

Maybe her current company wasn't the perfect fit. But she'd worked hard toward her goal of joining the management team. She was too close to walk away now. If she did, what had the past five years been for? She needed to prove she could succeed on her own. Not because her surname was on the company letterhead.

"I appreciate my dad's confidence in me," Chandra said. "But I'm so close to achieving a goal in my career. I'm not prepared to walk away."

"But are you happy?" Julian asked. "I only ask because the way you describe it…it sounds pretty rough."

"Not everyone gets to play the hero." Chandra realized she sounded defensive. "I honestly don't know a lot of people who'd say they love their job."

"True. But we spend so much time at work. Seems a shame to spend that much time doing something we don't actually enjoy." He shrugged. "But you obviously know what's best for you."

*Do I?*

Chandra looked out the window, unsure how to respond. She wanted to tell Julian he should mind his own business. After all, he'd been dragged back to Magnolia Lake to settle a debt with the Abbotts based on a commitment he'd made as a teen.

*Who is he to be doling out life and career advice?*

But a part of her recognized the truth in what he'd said.

Julian turned onto a paved road that ran through a wooded area. A few streetlights dotted the path as he turned down another road and a lake came into view. The gorgeous moon was reflected in the water.

"Julian, the sky here is absolutely stunning." Chandra craned her neck to take in the night sky. "The moon is so brilliant, and the stars are so vivid."

He parked the SUV. "You said you missed seeing the stars, and this is one of my favorite places in the world. My dad brought me here to fish when I was a kid. Sometimes, we'd pitch a tent by the lake and spend the night looking at the constellations with this telescope he bought for my eighth birthday. So I thought you'd—"

Chandra kissed his cheek. "This is perfect, Julian. Can we take a stroll around the lake?"

Julian seemed stunned by her kiss. "I didn't think you'd want to walk in those." He indicated her silver stilettos.

She slipped them off and pulled a pair of foldable black Italian leather ballet flats from her bag. "These things are lifesavers."

They both stepped out of the SUV and Julian pulled a heather-gray coat from the back seat. He held it up. "The temperature has dropped quite a bit. Better put this on."

She removed the red shawl that provided little warmth against the chill of the crisp fall night air. Then she slipped her arms into the coat that carried Julian's clean, woodsy, masculine scent. She pulled the fabric around her. "Thank you. But what about you? You'll freeze out here."

"I'm fine." Julian buttoned his suit jacket.

Julian locked the vehicle and extended his hand. Chandra slipped her hand into his and they set off toward the well-lit path that circled the lake. A chilly breeze rustled her hair, the strands whipping across her face.

"What was your life like in Philadelphia?"

"Busy, but good. I worked the ER at a suburban hospital. Volunteered at a clinic in an underserved community. Did some real estate investing."

"You weren't kidding about being busy." She laughed. "What part of the city did you live in?"

"Phoenixville. It's a great little artsy neighborhood with tons of restaurants. I felt at home there."

"It sounds nice, but I'd be tempted to try a different restaurant every night."

"When I first moved to the area, a fellow resident and I shared an apartment above an Italian restaurant. We could smell everything they were cooking. We both gained about twenty pounds." He chuckled.

Chandra could relate. Her freshman fifteen had been more of a freshman twenty-five. Most of which was still with her.

"And how is it being back here and living a slower, quieter life?" she asked.

"I'm slowly adjusting to having my own practice and to being back home," he admitted. "And getting to know you has been a pleasant surprise." His dark eyes flickered. "But enough about me. What made you leave the family business and move to San Diego?"

"A broken engagement weeks before my wedding day." Chandra's cheeks heated with embarrassment. "I needed a change and to prove to myself that I could make it in a company my family didn't own. So I accepted a position in San Diego."

"The separation from your family must've been tough."

"It was. I cried nearly every day for the first few months. I thought about going back home a lot in the beginning. But I felt like I had something to prove. I'd just had a failed relationship. I didn't want to admit that I'd failed in my career, too."

"Sounds like a lot of pressure." Julian threaded his fingers through hers and squeezed her hand.

"It was. Nolan, Sebastian and Alonzo felt like I'd abandoned them, like our mother. I missed my brothers, but I was too proud to admit I wanted to come home. So I pulled away. Threw myself into my work, so I didn't have time to feel homesick or wonder why I hadn't been enough for my fiancé, who'd been hooking up with an ex."

After all this time, knowing she hadn't been enough for Edward still hurt. "The further I advanced at work, the less time I had to connect with my dad and siblings. I was the one who'd always kept everyone connected by planning family meals and holiday get-togethers. Once I stopped doing that, we started to drift apart."

She hadn't talked about this with anyone. Not even her family. But everything about being with Julian felt comfortable. Easy.

*I can't let go of the sense that you and I were meant to meet.*

Julian's words to her at the café echoed in her head.

*Now who's being corny with a side of flower child?*

They each had their roles in the family. The bohemian who believed in the wonders of the Universe was strictly Naya's territory. Chandra was the sensible one tasked with playing devil's advocate and raining on her dad's and siblings' parades with a healthy dose of reality. She wasn't the one who chased sunshine and rainbows and believed everything would work out. In her experience, it rarely did.

They sat on a covered bench overlooking the lake.

"This is the perfect spot." Julian gestured toward the star-filled sky.

He'd pointed out various constellations as they'd walked the trail around the lake. But this was the best vantage point from which to study the moon and all of the stars.

"The moon is beautiful tonight," Chandra marveled. A deep sense of contentment washed over her.

"It's a waning gibbous moon, which follows the full moon. About seventy-five percent of it is illuminated by the sun tonight. Those dark splotches you see are large plains of basaltic rock caused by volcanic activity nearly four billion years ago. And the craters..." Julian glanced over at her, then dragged a hand down his face. "Sorry. I'm boring you to tears."

"No, you aren't." Chandra smiled. "This is fascinating. And so are you, Julian. Thank you for bringing me here. This place is obviously very special to you. It means a lot that you wanted to share it with me. It's the perfect end to our night."

Julian stared at her; his dark eyes filled with heat. "What if we didn't want our night to end just yet?"

"What did you have in mind, Dr. Brandon? Though I should warn you that I'm not the kind of girl who makes out in the woods...especially on a first date."

Julian chuckled, leaning in closer. His breath, visible in the chilly night air, warmed her face. "Fair. But this isn't our first date. It's our fifth."

"Is this about that hand-holding thing again?" She studied his handsome features beneath the moonlight.

"Hey, don't knock it." Julian's dark eyes glittered with amusement. But there was heat in them, too. "And since lunch at the café was our third date, you kissed me under the mistletoe on our fourth date. That makes this our fifth date."

Didn't quite hit her six-date rule…but close enough.

"Hmm…" She tried to hold back a grin. "Keep talking."

"And while I don't intend to make out with you in the woods—" he tipped her chin, his gaze locked with hers "—I would like very much to kiss you beneath the waning gibbous moon."

Julian captured her lips in a kiss as he cradled her cheek.

Chandra's eyes drifted closed as she sank into the lusciousness of Julian's kiss, his full lips pressed to hers. His large hand cradling her cheek.

Their earlier kiss had been good but tame compared to this. Here beneath the beautiful night sky, and away from prying eyes, Julian's kiss was hungry and eager. Her response needy and desperate. The intensity of the kiss growing with each moment beneath the stars.

Julian's tongue teased the seam of her lips, then slipped between them and glided against hers. Chandra relished the taste of apple crumb pie and the hints of the Zinfandel wine, supplied by her family's new winery. Julian slid his fingers into the nape of her hair as his thumbs grazed her cheeks.

Chandra sighed softly, leaning into him. Needing more contact with the hard body that had teased her earlier when they'd slow danced.

Julian's tongue ravished her mouth, the sensation filling her body with heat. Her nipples pebbled, and the space between her thighs grew damp and ached for his touch.

"So is this why you really brought me here?" she teased, when he finally broke their kiss. "To play doctor in the woods?"

Julian chuckled, those penetrating dark eyes glittering in the moonlight. "I really wanted you to see how incredible the night sky is here." He gazed reverently at the sky above them before meeting her eyes again. "But if you're asking if I'd hoped for another chance to kiss you—for real this time—the answer to that is an unapologetic *hell yes*."

Chandra nibbled on her lower lip, all of the reasons she shouldn't do this cycling through her brain.

Julian was too young for her. Even if he wasn't, she'd be leaving soon, negating the possibility of anything serious between them. And something purely casual could get messy. If she agreed to a one-night stand, they'd undoubtedly cross paths whenever she visited her dad. Which could be…awkward.

Chandra frowned, slowly pulling away. She could see the disappointment on Julian's handsome face. He knew she was going to say no. Which was the sensible choice. And wasn't that her role? The sensible, play-it-safe oldest daughter and surrogate mother to her siblings?

*But are you happy?*

Julian's earlier words echoed in her head. She sighed. Her father hadn't played it safe when he'd purchased the vineyard once owned by his biological mother's family. And look how much happier he was.

She wasn't expecting anything from Julian. But maybe she could permit herself the euphoria she felt whenever she was with him. Because it'd been more than five years since anyone had made her feel this way.

Didn't she at least deserve temporary bliss?

Chandra swallowed hard, her heart racing. "I assume we're going to your place. Mine isn't an option."

Julian's eyes widened with surprise. "Got the perfect spot in mind."

He gave her a quick kiss, then took her hand, before leading her back to his SUV. He took the road in the opposite direction from which they'd come. Up the road just a bit, he pulled into the driveway of an idyllic little cabin with a large front porch.

"This is your place?" Chandra slapped his arm, playfully.

"The cabin is part of the package, too."

"You brought me to stargaze at a spot that just happens to be about five feet from your bedroom, huh? Very crafty, Dr. Jules." Chandra shook a finger at him. "You'd better be glad you're a *really* good kisser."

"Noted." Julian winked.

The cabin was far more luxurious on the inside than its rustic outer appearance suggested. The decor was warm and modern, accented by lots of dark leather and warm, natural woods. Folding glass doors led to a well-lit patio out back.

"The cabin…it's really nice." Now that they were there, Chandra's stomach was doing somersaults. And she was sure Julian could hear the thud of her heartbeat.

This was why she'd essentially given up on dating. She wasn't good at dealing with the unfamiliar. Not knowing a potential lover's wants, expectations or predilections.

Would he be awful in bed? Would he ask her to do something that made her uncomfortable? When was the last time he'd vacuumed his room or changed his sheets?

Chandra heaved a quiet sigh, her eyes drifting closed. Suddenly, Julian was standing in front of her. One hand was planted on her hip; the other cupped her chin.

"Chandra, it's okay." His tone was reassuring, and a genuine smile lit his eyes. "We'll take this as fast or as slow as you'd like. If all you want to do is sit on that sofa and watch episodes of *Orphan Black* with me, then that's what we'll do." He dropped a soft kiss on her lips. "No pressure, all right?"

She nodded and her pulse slowed a little. "Are you always this sweet and considerate?" she asked. "I'm beginning to think you can't be real."

"I've been a selfish jerk plenty of times in my life. Hopefully, I'm a better person now."

"Undoubtedly." Chandra smoothed her hands down the lapels of the suit that hugged his athletic body so well.

"Can I get you a drink or maybe a snack?" Julian offered.

Chandra studied Julian's face and tried to summon a little of Naya's "I know what I want, and I'm not afraid to ask for it" courage.

"The only snack I'm interested in tonight is you." Chandra laughed when Julian's eyes darkened, and he licked his lower lip. "But first, can I use your restroom?"

"Absolutely." He held up a finger. "Just give me a sec."

Julian disappeared down a hallway, returning a minute or two later. Then he showed her the bathroom off the main bedroom.

Chandra stepped inside the restroom and closed the door, her back pressed to the wall.

*Last chance to chicken out.*

# Eleven

Julian opened a bottle of his favorite red Moscato and filled two glasses halfway. When he returned to his bedroom, Chandra was emerging from the bathroom. She stood still, as if frozen in place.

"Wine?" He lifted a glass.

"Please." Chandra dropped her handbag on the dresser and accepted the glass of wine.

She took a healthy sip, then sucked in a deep breath. She was reluctant at the least—terrified at worst.

Julian had dreamed of having Chandra Valentine in his bed since the day they'd met. But the night of mind-blowing pleasure he'd envisioned couldn't happen if she was as skittish as a cornered rabbit. He wanted them both to remember this night fondly.

So a literal Netflix and Chill night it would be.

"Why don't I give you the penny tour?" he asked. A subtle attempt to get them out of the bedroom, so she'd be more comfortable.

Chandra set down her glass roughly and stalked toward him, her eyes filled with heat. She ran her palms down his navy shirt. "Later?"

"You're sure? Because as much as I want this... I need you to know there's absolutely no press—"

Chandra's mouth was suddenly on his, her fingers pressed to his back.

Julian set down his glass of wine, too. He kissed her, eager to taste her mouth again. His hands glided down over her firm, round bottom as he tugged her against him, his hardened length pinned between them.

Chandra tugged his shirt from the waist of his pants and fumbled with the buttons, her hands trembling slightly. As the kiss escalated, they undressed each other with a growing sense of urgency. One garment after another drifted to the floor between frantic kisses. Finally, bare bodies pressed together, they tumbled into his bed and climbed beneath the covers. Julian trailed kisses down her neck and chest, his tongue teasing one of the beaded tips.

She arched into his touch, a soft murmur emanating from her lips. He'd wanted to taste every inch of her soft brown skin. To know what sounds she'd make as he swirled his tongue around her dark brown nipples. Had wondered how Chandra would react when he feasted on her—and he couldn't wait any longer to find out.

Julian kissed his way down her body. Over her soft rounded belly, which tensed as he sank lower. Over the neat tract of dark curls at the apex of the thick thighs that had teased him all night.

He pressed a kiss to the glistening swollen flesh between her thighs. Then another and another. Julian spread her with his thumbs, loving the shallow breaths and increasingly desperate murmurs each swipe of his tongue elicited.

Chandra moaned, her hips undulating and her fingers spiking into his hair as she rode his tongue until she shattered. Her body tensed and she dug her heels into the mattress as she muttered his name again and again.

As beautiful as Chandra was on any given day, she was even more beautiful sated. Her dewy skin glowed. Her chest rose and fell with each shallow breath.

If he got to see Chandra fall apart like that every day for the rest of his life, he'd never tire of it. Julian kissed the junction of her neck and shoulder.

Chandra's bashful smile made her even more beautiful.

"God, I love that smile." Julian stroked her cheek and her smile deepened.

"Do that again and I guarantee you'll see a lot more of it." Chandra flashed him a wicked grin as she stroked his stubbled chin.

Julian's tongue glided along his lower lip, salty with the taste of her, and he winked. "Is that a personal challenge? Because from the moment I saw you in those sparkly stilettos tonight, I've been imagining them dangling over my shoulders with my mouth on that—"

"You, Dr. Brandon, have a filthy mind and a deliciously dirty mouth." Her hands trailed up his chest. "And I'm definitely here for it."

He devoured her mouth with a hungry kiss as her hands moved down his back, her fingernails grazing his skin. Julian reached inside the nightstand and tore into the box of condoms. He ripped open a packet and sheathed himself.

He savored the sensation as he inched inside her, loving how snugly her body enveloped his. As if they were two pieces designed to fit together.

Chandra's lips parted on a soft gasp once he was fully seated, and he captured her mouth in a kiss. He moved his hips slowly, determined to appreciate every single moment of this. But as with every taste of her sweet lips, every delicious sensation of pleasure that rolled up his spine only made him desperate for more of her.

When he lifted her leg over his shoulder and ground his hips against hers, Chandra's murmurs turned to soft moans, then insistent pleas. Finally, she called his name, her muscles tensing and her back arching. Her inner walls clenched his heated flesh, pulling him in deeper as she reached her climax.

He kissed her hard, swallowing her cries. Her nails dug into his skin, as if she was marking him as hers. His hips moved until he, too, tumbled over the edge, Chandra's name on his lips. Julian heaved a sigh and collapsed onto the bed beside her. He gathered her in his arms, their labored breathing the only sounds in the room.

Julian kissed Chandra's temple. "Meeting you is the absolute best thing that's happened since I returned to town."

"We're supposed to say that seeing our families is the best thing that's happened since we've been here." Chandra grazed his nipple with her thumb and dropped a kiss on his chest. "But just between us…same."

Chandra was funny, smart and beautiful. He'd loved every moment he'd spent getting to know her. But he wanted to know more—everything there was to know about Chandra Valentine. Her history. Her hopes for the future. What she liked for breakfast. And all of the ways she liked to be pleased.

Chandra would return to San Diego in a week. A week with this amazing woman could never be enough. But if it was all he had, he'd enjoy every moment he got to spend with this goddess who made his spine tingle and his heart skip a beat.

Julian's eyes fluttered open to the sound of water running in the bathroom. Chandra stepped into the darkened bedroom fully dressed. She sifted her fingers through her disheveled hair.

He propped himself up on one elbow and rubbed the

sleep from his eyes. "You're leaving? I was hoping to impress you with my breakfast skills."

"You cook?" Chandra arched an eyebrow.

"My repertoire is limited, but the things I do cook are damn good. Like my variations on French toast."

"Such as?" Her interest was piqued, giving him the slightest hope that she'd crawl her fine ass back into bed with him.

"Crème brûlée French toast, churro French toast, banana bread French toast…"

"You're a regular French toast connoisseur, aren't you?" Her kiss-swollen lips, bearing only a hint of her lip gloss, formed a reluctant smile that tugged at something in his chest. "Would've figured you for a bacon guy."

She wasn't wrong. He had six pounds of bacon in his freezer. But she didn't need to know she'd read him right. *Again.*

"If you stay, I might surprise you in a few more ways." He grabbed her hand, tugging her closer.

"I didn't think you'd want me to stay. I mean, I assumed this was just—"

"A one-night stand?"

"Well, yes." She shrugged. "I'll be gone in a week."

"Then we should make the most of that time." He pulled her onto his lap, peppering her neck and shoulder with kisses.

Chandra made a purring sound that vibrated in his chest. He fought the urge to strip her naked and take her again. Remind her that he was a grown-ass man whose stroke game and tongue skills were on point, given how fervently she'd called his name each time he'd taken her over the edge.

"As tempting as that sounds, I really do need to get back. I came here to check on my dad and spend time with my siblings. It would be rude if I spent my entire vacation banging the town's baby doctor." She gave him a teasing smile, followed by a quick kiss. Then she retrieved her ballet flats and sat at the foot of the bed to put them on.

"Fair point." Julian groaned. "I'll drive you over to the winery."

"I'll call a car service."

"Sweetheart, this is Magnolia Lake, not San Diego. There won't be any car service available at—" he glanced at his watch "—one forty a.m."

"Right." Chandra furrowed her brows, and her mouth twisted as she assessed the situation, which only made her more adorable. "Then I'll just call my—"

"Chandra, I brought you here. And I'm going to deliver you home safe and sound. Just like I promised your dad." He got out of bed and pulled on his boxers.

"Thank you." The smile she flashed was almost shy. He could swear his heart did a somersault in his chest.

*What the hell is this woman doing to me?*

If he had good sense, he'd drop Chandra at home, thank her for a wonderful evening and wish her safe travels without any intentions of seeing her again. She didn't want to get serious, and the complications of a relationship that would tie him to Magnolia Lake were the last thing he needed.

But apparently, he lacked a sense of self-preservation.

When he pulled into the driveway of the old winery and turned off his engine, he kissed Chandra good-night. But the kiss didn't feel like a goodbye.

"I realize you came here to spend time with your family," he whispered between kisses to her full, lush lips. "And that you'll only be here a few more days. But I'd really like to see you again before you leave, Chandra."

Chandra nibbled on her lower lip, then nodded. She pressed a final kiss to his lips. "I'll try."

Julian got out and opened the door for Chandra. Her fancy heels were hooked over the strap of her purse.

"I'll walk you to the door."

"That isn't necessary. I texted Naya. She left the back light on and the door unlocked."

Julian forced a smile to mask his disappointment that their evening was officially at an end. "Then text me to let me know you got inside safe. Here..." He held out his hand.

When Chandra unlocked her phone and handed it to him, he scrolled to her contacts, added his cell phone number, then typed in his information. Julian handed the phone back.

"Text me once you're inside safe and sound, or I *will* knock on that door to make sure you're all right."

"I don't doubt it." Chandra slipped the phone into her bag.

"I look forward to seeing you again." He kissed her.

"Good night, Dr. Brandon."

"Good night, Ms. Valentine." Julian sighed quietly as he watched Chandra strut toward the back door of the winery.

He climbed back into his SUV and waited patiently until a message appeared on his phone.

I'm inside. Thank you for a lovely night under the waning gibbous moon.

He added her number to his contacts, then turned around and pulled out of the drive.

Maybe neither of them was looking for a relationship. But perhaps they'd stumbled into one just the same.

# Twelve

A smile spread across Chandra's face when she reviewed the contact information Julian had typed into her phone.

*Julian "Baby Doctor" Brandon.*

The man had a self-deprecating sense of humor that made him even more adorable. It was a refreshing change from the pompous, self-important assholes she was accustomed to dealing with.

Chandra was about to tiptoe up to bed, but there was a slamming sound, followed by a woot and raucous laughter.

She followed the voices to the game room.

"Hey there, sis. So… How was your night?" Naya asked in a singsong voice as she Groucho Marxed her perfectly arched eyebrows up and down.

"Don't answer that." Sebastian held up a hand. "I don't think any of us *really* want to hear the answer."

Her father and brothers agreed.

"Speak for yourselves. I want *all* the tea. The dirtier, the better." Her sister giggled. "You can tell me all about Dr. Brandon's *bedside manner* later." She winked.

"You're a mess." Chandra poked her sister's arm.

The room settled into an uncomfortable silence.

Chandra didn't miss this part of not being around her father and brothers as much anymore. She was a grown woman. Yet she felt like a teenager who'd been busted making out in a parked car with her boyfriend.

"What are you all still doing up? Please tell me you weren't waiting up for me," Chandra said.

"Not me," Nyles offered quickly. "Me and my partner here are whipping that collective ass." He tipped his chin toward Alonzo, who responded with a cocky grin and a head nod. "We're playing rise and fly Bid Whist and none of these chumps have been able to unseat us all night."

"That baby brother of yours has been talking shit for the past two hours." Her father went to the sideboard and poured himself a glass of King's Finest Bourbon and added a splash of soda. "I want someone else to win just to shut him up."

Chandra couldn't help thinking how surreal it was that her father had been drinking King's Finest Bourbon for decades, not realizing the company was owned by his half brother.

"He wasn't talking that mess when you and I ran through the lot of them a few years ago." Her father flashed a warm smile at Chandra and draped an arm over her shoulder.

The memory elicited a smile. It was the last time they'd all been together like this before coming to Magnolia Lake. After spending the past few days with her family, she realized how much she missed them. Even trash-talking Nyles.

Chandra leaned her head on her dad's shoulder. He didn't seem quite as tall as he once had. "Good memories."

They watched Alonzo and Nyles, who were well on their way to running a Boston on Nolan and Sebastian.

"Everything good, kiddo?" Her father's brows knitted with concern.

"Of course." Chandra ran her fingers through her hair, wondering if it looked like she'd just tumbled out of bed with the hot young doctor. "I'm an adult, Dad. And sometimes I do *adult* things."

"I realize that, sweetheart, and I'm not arguing. I just want to make sure my baby girl is okay. Been worried about you since you called off your engagement and took off for San Diego."

"That's a generous way to put it, Dad." Her father knew very well that Edward had been the one who'd ended things, taking her completely by surprise. She'd been foolish enough to think they were happy. Despite the signs that indicated otherwise. "Besides, I'm thirty-nine. I'd think you'd be over worrying about me."

"Never. You will *always* be my baby girl. I can still remember the first time I held you in my arms. And the way you used to love it when I lifted you onto my shoulders and trotted through our backyard. Those memories will always live here." He tapped the half-empty glass against his chest. "And worrying about your kids…that's something a parent does till the day they die."

"Maybe that's what *good* parents do." Chandra's eyes stung.

Her mother had walked away more than thirty years ago. Her stepmother—Nyles and Naya's mother—had walked away when the twins were just three years old. Chandra should be over the pain and anger of both women—whom she'd loved and adored—abandoning them. So why did discussing her mother's leaving still feel like a crushing weight on her chest?

"Not everyone is cut out to be a parent, sweetheart. Problem is, most folks don't figure that out until they actually have children." Her father drained the remainder of his bourbon, then turned to her. "I'm under no illusion that I was father-of-the-year material. But I loved you kids... and your mothers."

"So you weren't perfect. Who is?" Chandra shrugged. "But you were there for us then, and you're here for us now. We appreciate everything you've done and everything you're trying to do."

Her father's face brightened, and he pulled her into a bear hug. "I just need to know you're safe and that you're happy. That's all I want for all of you."

"That's what we want for you, too, Dad. So if buying this place and building your own empire is what makes you happy, I'll do whatever I can to support that. But I just can't—"

"I understand." He gave her a pained smile. "But the dream isn't just building an empire, sweetheart. It's building it *together*. With all of you by my side. I know you can't see my vision yet. But I'm not giving up." He winked.

"Well, I'm exhausted," Chandra said.

"I'll bet you are," Naya chimed in, her mouth twisted in a mischievous grin.

Chandra narrowed her gaze at her younger sister in a silent *behave*. A look Chandra had honed when she was young and had often been left in charge of her younger siblings.

Naya giggled, undaunted, and munched on a handful of tortilla chips.

"I'm going to bed. We've got a lot to do around here before I return to San Diego." Chandra kissed her father on the cheek and bade her siblings good-night. Then she showered and got ready for bed. But she tossed and turned, unable to fall asleep. She couldn't stop thinking about the amazing night she'd had with Julian and how much she liked him.

Her skin tingled as her mind replayed the visceral memory of how Julian had trailed kisses over her skin.

The sex had been phenomenal. But there was so much more to Dr. Julian Brandon.

He was caring and insightful. He'd known just what to say to calm and reassure her. He'd swooped in and extracted her from her car, turned over in that ditch, like a modern-day knight in shining armor. She hadn't been able to stop thinking about him long before she'd encountered him in that doctor's office.

Chandra couldn't deny that she really, *really* liked Julian. But the young doctor was an indulgence Chandra couldn't afford.

He didn't fit into her plan for a big promotion and a corner office back in San Diego. And the past few days had reminded her she needed to be a more engaged daughter and a better sister. Because despite what they all claimed, it was obvious that the kids *weren't* all right. Something was going on with each and every one of them, and as the family fixer, she couldn't let that go. So she didn't have time for a relationship with the pretty-boy, small-town doctor who lived two thousand miles from the place she called home.

Still, she couldn't help smiling whenever she thought about Julian. And she hadn't laughed this much in years.

A relationship was out of the question. But perhaps a tension-relieving, no-strings fling before she returned to the stress of her real life was *exactly* what the doctor ordered.

# Thirteen

Julian strolled out of the King's Finest Family Restaurant with Chandra's hand tucked firmly in his. He was grinning like an idiot, but he couldn't care less. He was beyond happy.

He and Chandra had managed to spend time together nearly every day for the past week. Julian had been pleasantly surprised when she'd called him the day after the Abbotts' party to say she'd love to see the lake in the daytime.

They'd taken a lunchtime stroll around the lake, then spent the afternoon in his bed before going their separate ways and having dinner with their families. And since then, he and Chandra had eaten lunch together at the café every day at one. On Tuesday and Thursday evenings, she'd ditched movie or game nights with her family, spending those evenings with him before returning to the winery later.

The more time they spent together, the more he realized that Chandra was someone he could imagine a future with.

But their time together was running out. The next day she would board a plane to San Diego. It was a reality Julian had been trying his damnedest not to dwell on.

"Is everything okay?" Chandra had stopped walking. "You're a million miles away. You nearly walked past your office."

He turned toward the redbrick building bearing the Abbott family's name. The medical building was only a few doors from the restaurant, so they'd parked in his reserved spot there and walked down. During dinner, he'd gotten a call from a patient. He needed to call in a new prescription for Mrs. Donaldson. But before calling in an alternate medication, he wanted to double-check the list of blood pressure medicines Doc Johnson had already tried and review the notes of her reaction to each.

"Sorry I'm a little distracted. I was running through the list of meds I might try with this patient. Let me get this prescription sorted out. Then you'll have my complete focus." He kissed her. "Promise."

They went up to his office and he logged on to his computer, while Chandra wandered the space. After he'd hung up with the pharmacy, she appeared in the doorway of his office. Her eyes glittered with mischief.

"Picture this…" Chandra held up her hands, as if she was framing him in a camera lens. "Me on an exam table with my feet in stirrups and you seated on that little red stool of yours." She laughed when his eyes went wide. "You asked about sexual fantasies." She shrugged. "This one just came to me."

"I will never, ever, be able to get the image of me feasting on you while you're spread out on an exam table out of my head." Julian adjusted himself before sitting on the front edge of the desk. "But truthfully, I have to conduct some pretty gross procedures in those exam rooms. So they're the least sexy places in the world to me."

"And now I'll never get *that* out of my head." Chandra frowned. "That just killed the fantasy."

Julian grasped Chandra's uninjured wrist and tugged her closer. "Or maybe we modify the fantasy. Like you seated on the edge of my desk instead. Or…" He closed his eyes, shuddering at the thought that entered his head.

"Or?" Chandra studied his face.

"I have the sudden urge to bend you over this desk and take you from behind." His voice was gruff, and a flash of heat crawled up his neck.

Chandra's smile widened. "I'll take what's behind Door #2, please." She locked the door, then stood between his open legs as he sat on the edge of his desk. He couldn't help marveling over how beautiful she was.

He captured her lips in a kiss, his arms encircling her waist. Julian molded Chandra's tempting curves against his body, aching to be buried inside her. Everything about this woman fueled his unquenchable desire for her.

The following afternoon she'd head back to San Diego, and they'd part ways as friends. He'd agreed to that, because it was all Chandra wanted. But the truth was *he* wanted more of her kiss. More of her touch. More time getting lost in those gorgeous brown eyes as they talked and laughed together.

His hands glided over her firm bottom as he tugged Chandra closer, their hunger for one another increasingly obvious.

Julian glided a hand up her outer thigh, beneath the flouncy little black skirt, as he devoured her mouth with a greedy kiss, relishing the sweet taste of her full lips.

"Please tell me you have a condom," she whispered against his lips.

He didn't carry any in his wallet, but he kept some in a bowl by the door for patients who needed them but were too embarrassed to ask. It was a tradition Doc Johnson had established two decades ago. Controversial at the time. But the Abbotts had backed Doc Johnson, and eventually, many of his loudest opposers grudgingly came to accept the wisdom of it.

"By the door." He trailed kisses down her neck.

Chandra glanced over her shoulder. "Those are...*colorful*."

Not his usual brand or size, but they'd do in a pinch.

Chandra sifted through the bowl filled with prophylactics in a range of rainbow colors. She picked a purple one and sashayed toward him, a smirk curving her sensuous lips.

He kissed her, his tongue gliding along hers as he palmed her full breast and grazed its pebbled tip with his thumb.

Chandra fumbled with his belt, unfastening it and then unzipping his jeans. She slipped her hand beneath the waistband of his boxers, her palm gliding along his fevered flesh as she stroked him with a loose grip. Then she tightened her grip and fisted him with a steady stroke.

"Fuck," he muttered against her lips.

Julian could barely think. Hell, he could barely breathe. His brain was capable of processing only two thoughts. One: he wanted to be buried so deeply inside Chandra that it would feel as if they were a single being. Two: he needed more moments like this with her.

Julian leaned into the first thought—the one over which he had control. He pushed the second thought from his head.

"Condom. On," he whispered roughly, his pulse racing.

It took three tries, but she ripped open the packet. She managed to inch the glaringly purple condom down his length, despite the snug fit.

"That seems...*uncomfortable*." Chandra frowned. "Maybe we should wait until we get back to your place."

Julian skimmed his palm up the inside of Chandra's thigh

and tugged aside the soaked panel of lace. She gasped softly when he glided his fingers back and forth over her sex.

"I'm willing to power through it, if you are," he murmured between kisses to her throat. He could barely hold back a smirk as she sighed softly, her hips moving against his hand as she gripped his shoulders and whispered *yes* again and again.

Julian plunged two fingers inside her, his thumb massaging the tight bundle of nerves. He swallowed her quiet gasp, his tongue searching hers as he slipped his fingers inside her, then retracted them, again and again, her legs wobbling. Chandra rode his hand until her body went stiff and she cried out his name so loudly he was glad no one else was working in the building on a Saturday afternoon.

In one swift move, he stood behind Chandra and lifted her skirt. He yanked the soaked fabric of her panties aside and slid into her. The sensation sent a shudder up his spine.

"Fuck, you feel incredible, Chandra." He kissed her neck and shoulder as he palmed her breast, teasing the tip with his thumb. His other hand braced her hip as he thrust into her from behind.

The sounds of their heavy breathing, his determined grunts, her quiet groans and their bodies meeting again and again filled the quiet office. Like an erotic symphony. The honeysuckle scent of her perfume mingled in the air with the scent of her arousal—a scent and taste he knew well.

Julian released her breast, now exposed by her disheveled blouse. He tipped Chandra's chin, drinking in the intoxicating expression on her gorgeous face. Julian captured her lips with his own, his tongue exploring the cavern of her mouth.

He pulled his hand from her hip and stroked her clit as he moved inside her, bringing her closer to the edge. Chandra flew apart, her body trembling as she whimpered his name. Julian kissed her neck, then her shoulder. His hips moving faster, urged on by the pulsing of her walls around his painfully hardened shaft. His body stiffened and his head felt light with the orgasm that seemed to slam into his chest, stealing his breath.

His heart raced as he quietly cursed and moaned, her name on his lips.

The sounds of their shallow breathing seemed to echo off the walls of the quiet space. But despite the euphoria of the moment, Julian couldn't help feeling a deep, aching sense of loss looming.

He'd fallen hard for Chandra. But tomorrow, she'd be gone.

Julian buried his face in Chandra's neck, inhaling the subtle scent he'd come to crave: a mingling of her honeysuckle perfume and the sweet coconut-and-vanilla scent of her dark hair. He kissed the shell of her ear.

"Don't go, Chandra," he whispered, then pressed another kiss to her ear. "Not yet. Please."

Chandra turned over her shoulder, her brown eyes glistening with unshed tears. She pressed her lips into a smile and cradled his cheek. "I wish we had more time, Julian. But we'd only be delaying the inevitable."

He'd known her answer before the plea had left his mouth. But he couldn't let her walk away without begging her to stay.

Julian nodded, then kissed her shoulder, their bodies still connected. "Of course. Let me take care of this. Then we can head out of here."

Before he could pull away completely, Chandra hooked an arm around him. "I have to return to work, but I could work remotely this week and head back to California next week. After that, if you're ever in San Diego and we're both free…"

"I'd really like that." Julian lifted Chandra's chin and

she twisted her body, meeting his lips in a soft, warm kiss that set his heart and his body on fire.

Julian didn't know what would happen with them beyond next week. But he was glad he wasn't the only one who wasn't ready for this to end.

# Fourteen

*One Month Later*

Chandra found a spot in the parking garage of the building that housed Phillips Athletic Wear. While she waited in the lobby for the elevator, she fired off a group text message to her sister, Naya, and her brother Alonzo. They'd spent the past few days brainstorming event ideas for the winery in a text message chain.

Only Naya and Nolan had accepted their father's invitation to join the winery. Naya was Valentine Vineyards' PR & events coordinator. Nolan would formally assume the role of CFO of Valentine Vineyards once he was done facilitating the sale of the textile firm.

But while Chandra, Sebastian, Alonzo and Nyles had declined to join the newly acquired family firm, they'd all been regularly consulted by their father, Nolan and Naya as they made plans for the official launch of the newly rebranded winery. During their time in Magnolia Lake, she, her dad and her siblings had worked with a graphic designer Max's wife, Quinn, had recommended. The woman created dynamic new branding for Valentine Vineyards, based on all of their input, including a logo, wine labels and signage.

It was exciting to be a part of shaping the new company from the start. In some ways, she envied Naya and Nolan being at the center of this exciting new family venture. But she'd been on a five-year-long mission, and she wouldn't let herself get derailed now. Not by her father's identity crisis, the discovery of mystery relatives or a sweet, handsome and far-too-young doctor who'd swept her off her feet.

Chandra stepped onto the elevator and punched the button for her floor. She scrolled through her phone, searching for Julian's latest text message.

Hey, beautiful. Hope you're doing well. Life around here just isn't the same without you. Miss you like crazy.

Chandra's heart fluttered. She could practically hear the words being uttered in Julian's deep, gravelly voice. His mouth pulled into a sexy grin that sent electricity down her spine.

She missed him, too. More than she could've imagined.

So much had changed since she'd boarded that plane to Magnolia Lake several weeks ago. She'd reconnected with her father and siblings, gotten to know her unknown relatives whom she really liked, discovered the beauty of the Smoky Mountains and the appeal of small-town living.

And she'd met, been rescued by, fake dated and screwed the brains out of the handsome young doctor.

Chandra couldn't stop thinking about Julian. They'd only met a couple of months ago. Yet the man had managed to turn her world upside down.

She'd finally met a man who seemed perfect. But in

the cosmic joke that was her life, he was nearly a decade younger and lived two thousand miles away.

Julian was unbothered by their age difference. But Chandra couldn't help worrying what other people would think. Besides, did she honestly want to spend the next four years dating someone she'd get to see maybe one weekend a month?

"Good morning, Ms. Valentine." The distressed look on the face of Evelyn Santos, assistant to Chandra's boss Ethan, caused uneasiness to creep up her spine.

Ethan and Evelyn were based in Nashville. What were they doing in San Diego unannounced?

"Good morning, Evelyn. I didn't realize Ethan was in town."

"Something came up. Ethan and Elliot are in the conference room waiting for you." Evelyn's eyes didn't meet Chandra's.

The uneasiness in her gut ratcheted up a notch. She was hit by a wave of nausea.

The Phillips brothers co-owned the firm. Ethan, the CEO based in Nashville, had hired her five years ago. She'd been sent to San Diego to turn things around and essentially babysit Elliot Phillips, whose title as COO was more of a wish than a job description.

For the past five years, she'd effectively been running the firm's San Diego operations. And while Elliot resented that his brother had sent her there, he seemed content to allow her to do the actual work while he took credit for it with board members and the media. Chandra had endured it because Elliot intended to retire next year, and she'd be the logical choice for his replacement.

The apprehension she felt was a heightened version of the unsettling feeling she'd had since her return one month ago.

Elliot Phillips's resentment was evident in the dead-eyed

smile he gave her each day. But since her return, his grin was different. Like he knew something she didn't.

"Let me stop at my office and—"

"Actually, Ethan asked that I bring you *straight* to the conference room." Evelyn's voice dripped with apology and her gaze landed somewhere over Chandra's left shoulder.

Chandra opened her mouth to demand to know what was going on, but Evelyn, whom she'd always liked, was simply doing her job. Chandra would take this up with Elliot and Ethan instead.

She stalked toward the glass conference room where the brothers were engaged in an argument, both of their faces red. She was undoubtedly the subject of their heated discussion.

Chandra shoved the glass door open. Both men stopped speaking and gave each other one last defiant look before turning to her.

"Good morning, Chandra. How was your trip to Seattle?" Ethan sounded exhausted. His usually bright blue eyes were dim.

"Productive, as always." Chandra set her bags on the table. "In fact, I was hoping to talk to you today about possible tech updates. But that clearly isn't what you're here to discuss."

She glared at Elliot, who had yet to speak and who looked like a cat who'd just had a bowl of cream with a hit of vodka and coffee liqueur. The man grinned, his dark eyes sparkling with malice.

"No, I'm afraid it isn't—" Ethan was saying.

"Come now, you act like this is a funeral or something." Elliot cut his brother off. "It isn't. This is good news, and a reason to celebrate."

"And why is that, Elliot?" The wave of nausea returned as Chandra anticipated his next words.

"My son has finally decided to join the firm." Elliot

beamed like a proud father whose little boy had just nailed his piano recital.

"That's wonderful," Chandra said, not meaning it.

Nothing she knew about Elliot Phillips Jr. made her think he'd be an asset to the firm. But that hadn't impacted Elliot Sr.'s tenure, had it? Having the surname on the letterhead had been his only necessary qualification.

A knot tightened in Chandra's gut. "What role will he be taking on at the company?"

Elliot's grin deepened and his dark eyes narrowed. "He'll take on my role—once I retire, of course. But for now, he'll take on a newly minted role—executive vice president of supply chain, logistics and workplace."

Chandra's throat went dry and she swallowed hard against the bile churning in her gut. Her fingernails dug into the palms of her hands, balled into trembling fists.

"You're firing me?"

"Of course not." Ethan's earnest tone was a deep contrast to his brother's amused grin. "Your work here has been stellar. Only a fool would let go of someone as brilliant as you."

"Then I'm being demoted?" She focused on Ethan but couldn't miss his brother's self-satisfied expression.

"Chandra, you're being a tad dramatic." Elliot sounded bored with the entire discussion. "You're the director of supply chain, logistics and workplace. Your role is unchanged. You'll simply report to EJ now instead of me." He shrugged. "It's all really quite simple." Elliot climbed to his feet and buttoned his tailored navy blue suit jacket. "Now, if you'll both excuse me, I have a meeting to attend."

Elliot strolled toward the door, then turned toward her with a sly grin. "Oh, by the way. There is *one* other change. Elliot Junior will be second in command now. His office space should reflect as much."

"You're giving your...*him*...my office?" Chandra tried her best not to let Elliot see just how infuriated she was.

"I had the movers make the switch over the weekend." Elliot's grin deepened. "Don't worry. Your things are all there and accounted for. Ms. Santos will show you to your new office. Welcome back, Ms. Valentine."

Chandra's cheeks and forehead were hot, her heart pounded in her chest and the sound of rushing blood filled her ears.

She could barely make out what Ethan was saying as he rushed to speak. "I can only imagine how disappointed you must be right now, Chandra. Please know I did *everything* in my power to block this move."

"Then why is Junior sitting in my office, the heir apparent to a title you'd all but promised *me*?"

Ethan flinched but didn't back down. "Because in the end, this is a family-run firm. My family voted to keep it that way. Even if it isn't in the best interest of the company." Ethan pressed a hand to his forehead. Chandra knew enough about the man to realize he was genuinely perturbed. "I'm sorry, Chandra. I honestly didn't see this coming. I would never have led you to believe you'd be appointed as our next COO if I hadn't believed it possible."

"So now what, Ethan?" Chandra studied him. "Am I supposed to babysit Elliot Senior *and* Junior for the rest of my career?"

"You are the backbone of this place. The increased profitability we've experienced these past few years... you deserve all of the credit for it," Ethan conceded. "So I'm asking you to keep making this company better and more profitable. Like Elliot said, your position here is unchanged."

"I didn't come here for this, Ethan," Chandra said calmly. "I came here because you said that if I proved myself, you'd recommend me for the COO position within five years. *That's* always been the brass ring for me. The reason I've put up with your brother's—"

"I know." Ethan held up a hand and sighed. "And I'm sorry I can't make that happen. But I can offer you a sizable salary increase to ease the blow."

"That won't be necessary," Chandra said coolly, enjoying the shock in Ethan's eyes.

"Are you saying you don't want the increase?" he said. "Or are you saying—"

"I resign, effective immediately." Chandra stood tall and tipped her chin, meeting Ethan's gaze.

Ethan's shoulders sank. He dragged a hand down his face, which suddenly looked more haggard. "You don't need to do this, Chandra. My nephew probably won't last in this job for an entire year. That'll buy me some time to show my family how valuable you are to this organization and why you're so deserving of the COO position."

"It won't change the fact that I'm not a Phillips. And if your family hasn't realized my value by now, Ethan, I doubt they ever will." Chandra lifted her purse and laptop bag onto her shoulder. "Now, should I call security to meet me at my desk? I just need to grab my family photos and a few plants."

"No, I trust you, Chandra," Ethan said wearily, shoving his hands in his pockets. "Go. Do whatever you need to do."

Chandra took a few steps toward the door, then turned back to the man who was now her former boss. "Thank you for all you've done, Ethan. Have a safe return to Nashville."

"I'll show you where your things were moved." Evelyn gave Chandra a subtle nod and smile, as if cheering on her decision.

Evelyn accompanied Chandra to the smaller, dimmer office where her things had been set up. Then the other woman wished her the best of luck and took her leave.

Chandra used one of the moving boxes left behind to box up her family photos, a few plants and the small personal items stored in her desk. She reset her phone to factory and left it and her work-issued laptop on the desk.

She held her head high as she strolled to the elevator and got on, watching the doors close on Phillips Athletic Wear for the last time.

On the lobby level, she barely made it into a bathroom stall before she threw up everything she'd eaten that morning. She washed her hands and popped a piece of gum in her mouth, hoping it would ease her nervous stomach. Then she made her way to the parking garage.

The words *I resign* had escaped her mouth before she had time to reconsider them. But Chandra knew she'd made the right decision.

If she was going to devote all her time and energy to minding the interests of someone's family, it would be her own. So if her father was willing to agree to her terms, she'd be back in Magnolia Lake with her dad and brother and sister and the good doctor whom she couldn't seem to get out of her head.

When Julian had asked her to stay, she'd desperately wanted to say yes. But she'd permitted her relationship fears, her hang-ups about the difference in their ages and her misguided need to prove her worth outside of her family to hold her back. It was a mistake she wouldn't make again.

# Fifteen

*Three Weeks Later*

Julian stepped out of his office and zipped his jacket against the chilly December air blowing down Main Street.

The new light posts, designed to look like antiques, were festively decorated with pine wreaths bound with red velvet bows. White fairy lights wound down each pole. Each shop on Main Street was decorated for the holidays. A towering Douglas fir was decked out over at the town square. By the time he left his office for the day, all the lights were twinkling, casting their ethereal glow over the town.

Julian had to admit that he'd enjoyed accompanying his mother to the official town lighting of the Christmas tree for the first time since his father's death. His father had loved Christmas, and the town's tree lighting had always been his dad's favorite event of the year. It hadn't seemed right to attend the event without him, so neither Julian nor his mother had.

He'd been stunned when his mother suggested they attend the event together. Julian had wanted to decline, but going to the tree lighting seemed really important to his mom. As it turned out, it was important for him, too.

Julian and his mother had stood on the festively decorated public square, surrounded by the people who comprised the town his father had adored. Attending the event that had always brought his father so much joy had been surprisingly cathartic.

She'd slipped her arm through his and it felt like they were finally grieving for his dad *together*. An essential part of the process if there was ever any hope of healing the rift between them. Neither one of them had talked about the past or the awkward nature of their current relationship. But they were both making an effort.

It wasn't always pretty, and sometimes it felt like he was pulling shards of glass from his skin. But things were slowly getting better between Julian and his mother.

His dad would've liked that. He would've liked Chandra, too.

Julian shoved a hand in his pocket and strolled across the street to the café that still held memories of Chandra.

He couldn't help thinking of Chandra's stunning smile. And the laugh that made him feel like he was floating in the balmy Caribbean Sea, his face warmed by the sun. The deep sense of happiness he felt whenever he was with Chandra. Despite the challenging logistics, Julian was convinced something genuine was happening between them.

He'd been hopeful when he'd asked if he could call her in San Diego, and she'd agreed. They'd chatted on the phone and exchanged text messages with increasing frequency during the first month after she left town. But three weeks ago, she'd sent him a cryptic message about something having come up and her being busy. Then suddenly, her line was no longer in service, and he felt like a complete ass.

Had she felt the need to change her number to get rid of him? Had she found someone else?

All Chandra had needed to do was say the word, and he would've respected her wishes. He hated to think that she'd felt it necessary to take such a drastic step to cut ties between them. And he couldn't bear her thinking poorly of him when he adored her and still wanted her in his life.

Julian pushed open the door to the café and greeted a few locals, including Mr. and Mrs. Donaldson—who was doing much better on her new blood pressure meds. Then he got in line.

"Hi, Julian."

Stunned, he turned his attention to the two women at the register. "Chandra? Naya?"

"It's really good to see you, Julian." Chandra tucked her hair behind her ear and smiled. She waved him forward. "I already added your pastrami sandwich to our order."

He joined Chandra and Naya at the head of the line, but when he tried to pay, she waved him off.

"My treat," Chandra insisted. "I was hoping we could talk."

"Of course." It felt surreal that she was there asking him to chat moments after he'd been wondering if he'd ever see her again.

"Actually, there's somewhere I need to be. Could you make my salad to go with the dressing on the side and have it ready in about an hour?" Naya asked the cashier before turning back to the two of them. "By then, you two should be done with lunch, right?" A mischievous smile lit Naya's face.

They both nodded in agreement.

Naya slid her expensive shades off her head and put them on. She ran her fingers through her purple bob and strutted out the door.

Julian and Chandra stepped aside to wait for their order. An awkward silence settled between them.

"So how have you been?" they asked at once. They both laughed, and it seemed to alleviate some of the awkwardness.

"You first." He gestured.

"Things have been…good." Chandra shifted her gaze around the space, then back to him. "How about you?"

"You know, still settling in." His gaze locked with hers. "Mostly missing you."

A shy smile curved her full lips. "Same."

"I'm really surprised to hear that." Julian rubbed his chin. "I mentioned that I'd like to fly out to San Diego to visit you after the New Year. Then suddenly you change your phone number. I assumed—"

"I didn't change my number because of you, Julian." Chandra placed a hand on his arm. "And I'm sorry you thought I was ghosting you. I wasn't."

"Then why did you change your number?" He studied the lovely face that he'd practically memorized in the three weeks she'd been in town.

"That wasn't my personal phone… It was a company phone. I returned it when I resigned from my position."

"You quit your job in San Diego? When? Why? How long have you been in town? And how long are you staying?" He rattled off the questions as quickly as they came to his mind.

"I quit three weeks ago because I realized they didn't deserve me and never would," she said. "It took me a couple of weeks to pack up my things and put my house up for sale. I've been here about a week, and I'll be here indefinitely because I've accepted my father's offer to be the CEO of Valentine Vineyards."

"That's amazing. Congrats." Julian hugged her. "Still doesn't explain why you didn't call."

"Me resigning...it all happened so suddenly. I didn't think to write down your number or anyone else's before I handed in my phone." Chandra lowered her gaze to her clasped hands. "Thankfully, after the accident, I saw the need to at least memorize my father's and sister's numbers."

"That explains why you didn't have my number," Julian acknowledged. "But there's this thing...it's called the internet. You could've looked up my office number. Or you could've come by the office or the cabin since you've been back. Why didn't you?"

"Well, this is the third time this week I've come here for lunch at one," she admitted with a shrug. "I didn't want to ambush you at your office or just show up at the cabin. And to be honest..." Chandra glanced around the café. Her gaze landed on the table where Deanna Jasper and a few of her friends sat watching them. "We agreed to a fling when I was in town for a couple weeks. Now that I'm here permanently... I didn't want you to feel pressured into making this something...more. After all, you are Magnolia Lake's hottest bachelor. Every unattached woman in town seems to be pursuing you." Chandra tipped her chin in Deanna's direction.

"I haven't thought about anyone but you since the moment I met you." Julian looped an arm around Chandra's waist and tipped her chin. His mouth met hers in a slow, lingering kiss.

"Same," she said again, when he forced himself to end the kiss. He could practically feel the heat radiating from her cheeks as Mr. and Mrs. Donaldson and a few of the other patrons grinned at them.

"There's something else bothering you, isn't there?" Julian threaded their fingers as he searched her face.

"I know I shouldn't care what other people think. But I also don't want everyone in town staring at me like they are now…thinking of me as some cougar who set her sights on the town's beloved prodigal son."

"I hate the term *cougar*. That's some sexist bullshit. Older men have been dating younger women since the beginning of time. And as for them…" He nodded toward the Donaldsons but lowered his voice. "They're staring because they're well-meaning but also nosy as hell. This is the equivalent of a Shonda Rhimes prime-time drama for most of them. But as much as they enjoy juicy drama, they're good people. And they're rooting for us, just like they're rooting for your family to make a success of Valentine Vineyards."

Julian breathed a small sigh of relief when Chandra smiled.

"When I'm with you, Chandra, the last thing in the world I'm thinking about is the difference in our ages. I'm thinking about how beautiful you are. How intelligent you are. How much I laugh when we're together. How my heart races whenever I see you. How much you've sacrificed for your family."

Julian cradled her face, grazing her cheek with his thumb. "And I'm envious of every person you've ever cared about."

Chandra's brown eyes shone. A smile crinkled the corners of her mouth. "You're very persuasive, Dr. Brandon. Anyone ever tell you that?"

Julian kissed her forehead. "And irresistible."

"And so very modest." Chandra giggled.

"True." Julian tightened his grip on her hand. "I don't care what anyone thinks about what we have. All I care about is being with you."

"Well, I *do* care about a few other things." A slow grin spread across her lips. "World peace. Global warming. Racial equality. This 'empire' my family is apparently building…"

"All right, point taken." Julian shook his head. "But I'm assuming I make the list."

"Oh, you definitely make the list." Chandra lifted onto her toes and kissed him.

Everyone behind the counter and several of the customers who'd been watching hooted and clapped.

"All right, you two lovebirds." Amina Lassiter, the owner of the café, grinned as she shoved a tray toward them. "Your order is ready."

Julian thanked the woman and grabbed their order. They slid into a booth near the back of the café.

"So what prompted you to accept your dad's offer?"

Chandra set her sandwich down after taking one bite, as if she'd suddenly lost her appetite.

"It became abundantly clear that no length of service or list of accomplishments would ever earn me a spot on the Phillips Athletic Wear executive team." Chandra sipped her soda thoughtfully before setting down the cup. "It was foolish of me to be obsessed with proving my worth outside of my family, only to end up working myself ragged to cement the legacy of someone else's family. If I'm shedding blood, sweat and tears, I want it to be for the people who matter most to *me*." She slapped a hand to her chest. "The people I know I can always count on, no matter what—my family."

"Good for you." Julian smiled. "Besides, you really seemed to enjoy helping your dad and sister with setting things up at the winery."

"I did." Her face lit up.

Julian's heart skipped a beat. It still didn't feel real that Chandra was there with him.

"Let's hope I'm still excited about all of this once I officially begin in my role as CEO at the beginning of the year." Chandra took another tentative nibble on her sandwich.

"Did you enjoy working with your family at the textile firm?" Julian asked between bites of his sandwich.

"I enjoyed working with my father and brothers. My grandmother? Not so much." Chandra frowned. "She was brilliant and focused, but very old-school. I think she believed that if we enjoyed our work, we must be doing it wrong."

Chandra set her sandwich down after a few bites and pressed a hand to her forehead.

"Are you all right?" he asked.

"I've been feeling a little run-down lately. Undoubtedly the stress of uprooting my life and taking a chance on my dad's dream. Plus, it's my dad's birthday this weekend. So all of my brothers are coming into town."

"You've been feeling run-down *how*?" Julian asked, the wheels turning in his head.

"Headaches, nausea, fatigue, insomnia, moodiness." She shrugged.

"Sweetheart, you don't think you could be...?"

Chandra's eyes widened with recognition. She mouthed the word *pregnant* and he nodded.

"That's impossible!" she said in a loud whisper. "We were careful. You wore a condom every single time."

"True. But they aren't infallible," he noted. "Few things in life are."

"No. No way. I had my *period*—" she mouthed the word "—soon after I returned to San Diego. It wasn't as heavy as usual. But I did have it."

"And since?" Julian tried not to sound like a doctor questioning his patient.

"I haven't..." Chandra paused. "But I'm thirty-nine. They've been irregular the past few months. I assumed I was entering—"

"Perimenopause," he offered.

Chandra covered her face and groaned. "Not a conversation you want to have with your much younger lover."

"Boyfriend," he corrected. This was about far more than

sex for either of them. "Who happens to be a doctor and is also mature enough to realize that it's a natural part of life." He squeezed her hand again, and she seemed relieved. "Your theory is possible, of course. But given the other symptoms you've described…"

"I'm not *that*." Chandra glanced around anxiously. "I haven't been with anyone else, and I just told you, I've had a period since we were together."

"Bleeding isn't as uncommon as you might think, especially in the first tri—"

"Stop talking like I'm…" Chandra couldn't seem to bring herself to say the word. "I think I'd know if I was."

"You'd be surprised how many women don't know they are." On the outside, Julian was calm and objective with his questions, as he was when speaking with a patient in the exam room. But inside, his heart beat wildly in his chest and his stomach did flips as he considered the very real possibility that he and Chandra had created more than just sparks during those steamy nights at his cabin.

"Well, I'm not," Chandra said with finality. She picked up her sandwich and bit into it. Suddenly, she looked like she was going to lose her lunch at any moment, much as she had the day they'd first met on the plane. But she continued to chew slowly, as if to prove a point.

Maybe Chandra was right. She would know her own body better than he, despite the fact that he'd committed every delicious curve and dimple to memory.

He was just glad she'd returned to Magnolia Lake and that she was willing to give them a chance. He wouldn't blow it by pressing the issue.

"I want to hear how things are going with you and your mom." She set down the sandwich.

"We've been spending more time together. Last weekend we actually went to the town Christmas tree lighting ceremony together. The event was a huge deal for my dad.

He'd transform into this oversize kid once they hit the lights on the town square." A sad smile curved Julian's mouth. "It was the first time Mom or I have attended the tree lighting since Dad died."

"Julian, that's amazing." Chandra grasped both his hands. "I'm really happy to hear that."

"Thanks." He kissed the back of her hand, his gaze locked with hers. "And I'm *really* glad you're here."

"Me, too." Her eyes danced and her skin practically glowed. "Now tell me how things are going with the new practice."

They talked about how the past few weeks had gone, and how he'd begun to win over a few of the diehards. Then Chandra told him what'd happened with the Phillips brothers back in San Diego and updated him on what was going on at the winery, her eyes sparkling with excitement as she shared the new branding and some of their plans.

"You have patients waiting back at the office." Chandra checked her watch, then shielded a yawn. "Go. We'll finish talking later."

"You're exhausted, aren't you?" Julian noted.

"I'm accustomed to living alone," Chandra said. "Now I'm staying with my dad, Nolan and Naya at the winery. Between my dad and brother, who are early risers, my sister—who talks incessantly and whose voice carries—all of the noises inherent in the wine-making process and the construction crew working on the house…getting any sleep in during the day is impossible. And I'm not getting the best sleep at night either." She yawned again. "My brothers are flying in for Dad's party and Nyles will probably stay through Christmas. So I doubt I'll get much sleep the next few nights either."

"Go to my cabin. You'll have the place to yourself for the next four hours. I'll text you a code to the door."

Chandra's eyebrows knitted together as she contemplated his offer. Finally, she nodded. "Thank you, Julian."

The woman he'd fallen head over heels for would be sleeping in his bed while he continued seeing patients.

*Not distracting at all.*

Chandra exhaled quietly and gripped his hand. "Julian, I haven't done this in a while, and if I'm being honest, I'm still a little gun-shy."

"It's okay." He squeezed Chandra's hand. "Like I said, we'll take this as fast or as slow as you'd like. I'm not going anywhere. All right?"

Chandra nodded. "Thanks for understanding."

Julian gave her a quick kiss goodbye. Then he made his way across the street, wondering how he'd gotten so damn lucky.

# Sixteen

Chandra paced the great room floor at Julian's cabin. Her heart thudded in her chest, her pulse raced and she felt light-headed.

When the front door swung open, Chandra nearly jumped out of her skin.

She should've heard Julian's SUV pull up or the turn of the front door lock. But apparently, she hadn't been able to hear anything over the thrum of the rushing blood that echoed in her ears.

"I'm sorry, sweetheart. I didn't mean to startle you." Julian set a bag on the counter.

The smell of the meal from the King's Finest Family Restaurant should have made her mouth water. Instead, she felt queasy. And now she knew why.

"Hey, you sure you're okay?" Julian placed the back of his hand to her forehead. Then he tipped her chin and studied her face. "I was hoping you'd get some rest. But you seem—"

*"Pregnant."* She cut him off. "Very, *very* pregnant. I don't know how you could've known when I didn't, but you were right. I had Naya stop at the drugstore before she dropped me here. I've taken two different pregnancy tests. They're both positive." Chandra could still hardly believe how her life, already in transition, had been turned upside down in a few hours.

"How are you—"

"I know this isn't what either of us expected from this relationship… But I do want this baby." Chandra placed a protective hand over her belly. "I realize fatherhood wasn't on the agenda, so I'll understand if you want to walk away. Keeping and raising the baby is my decision, and I'm prepared to deal with the consequences."

Julian blinked and seemed to come out of his momentary daze. He pulled her into his arms and kissed the top of her head. "I was going to ask how you're feeling."

"Oh." She'd been sure he was asking how she'd planned to deal with the pregnancy. "I'm fine. Just stunned. We were both so careful. I honestly didn't see this coming, and I swear I had no idea before I took that test this afternoon."

"Chandra, I believe you." Julian cupped her cheek, his reassuring gaze meeting hers. "And it's okay to be a little frightened and overwhelmed by this."

"Why would I be overwhelmed? I've managed business professionals most of my career, and I practically raised my brothers and sister. I'm more than capable of caring for this child."

Chandra didn't care that she sounded defensive. It was better than the alternative: being vulnerable and in a position to be hurt. Something she promised herself she'd never do again.

After all this time, the sting of Edward's rejection and the humiliation of his betrayal were still lodged beneath her skin, like the insidious cockleburs that stuck to her clothing and pricked her tender flesh when she and her brothers played in the field as kids.

"I've delivered my fair share of babies during my residency. Doesn't mean I'm not terrified at the thought of having a kid of my own. But we'll get through this. Together. Because I'll be there every step of the way."

Her heart swelled at Julian's heartfelt promise. Because despite her bravado, Chandra was definitely panicking. Julian recognized the vulnerability and fear in her eyes, and he'd stepped in to reassure her. Just as he'd done aboard the plane.

Julian was a genuinely good guy. Had he promised to be there for her and the baby strictly out of a sense of duty? If so, he'd undoubtedly come to resent that obligation. Eventually, he'd resent her and maybe even their child. And that was a thought she couldn't bear.

Chandra pulled free of Julian's embrace. A chill surrounded her immediately, despite the warm blaze of the fireplace.

"You're here because you have to be, Julian. We both know you're counting the days until you can return to Philadelphia. The last thing you want is a kid tying you to this place." Chandra slipped her hand in his. "Don't do this because you feel you have to, Julian. I can take care of this baby myself."

"I don't doubt it." Julian wrapped her in a hug and kissed her forehead. "Maybe parenthood wasn't part of either of our immediate plans, but I'm just as invested in this child as you are. So I'm not going anywhere, Chandra. If you're in, I'm in. Got it?"

Chandra nodded, tears gliding down her cheeks. She wiped at them, embarrassed. Less than twenty-four hours into parenthood and she'd already been reduced to tears.

"Everything will be fine, sweetheart. I promise."

When Julian's firm lips met hers in a kiss, Chandra melted into him. She gripped the lapels of his jacket.

What had begun as a source of comfort quickly blossomed into a heated embrace that set her skin on fire and made her belly flutter.

Julian shrugged his coat onto the floor, and she tugged the hem of his shirt from his waist and fumbled with the buttons as they continued their heated kiss. She dropped his shirt to the floor, followed by her own. Julian unzipped her skirt and it pooled at her feet. He gripped her bottom tight, his hardened length pinned between them, then lifted her. Chandra wrapped her legs around his waist as he transported her to his bedroom. The place where, perhaps, they'd conceived this child.

The thought sent a chill up her spine, her body tingling with desire for this man who'd come to mean so much to her.

She would never have imagined they'd end up here: about to be parents. But as Julian set her on her feet, and they fumbled to finish undressing one another amid their increasingly urgent kisses, she couldn't regret a single moment that had led them here.

They climbed into his bed, Julian's hands roaming her bare skin. Their kisses escalating as the heat built between them until she felt as if she would combust.

When Julian reached for the drawer beside his bed, Chandra grabbed his wrist. "If you really haven't been with anyone since we were together…"

"I haven't," he assured her.

"Then I don't think we'll be needing what's in that drawer for a while." She caressed his stubbled cheek and pressed a soft kiss to his lips.

Julian's eyes darkened, his mouth curving in a wicked grin. "No, I suppose we won't."

He made love to her. Worshipped the body that would

soon swell and sag and be marked with even more stretch marks as it nurtured the baby they'd made.

Chandra had no idea what the future would bring. Maybe Julian would never look at her again with the passion and hunger she saw in his eyes now. But she would enjoy these moments and commit them to memory. His taste. The weight of his body on hers. The sensation of him filling her. And the tender moments as he held her afterward and assured her everything would be all right.

# Seventeen

Julian held Chandra, her cheek pressed to his chest and her dark hair draped across his arm, as she slept. Being with Chandra was always incredible. But tonight, their impassioned connection—with no barrier between them, knowing they'd created life together—had been unlike anything he'd experienced. Intoxicating. Addictive. Soulbinding. Every kiss, every touch felt so much more consequential.

After they'd spent the evening getting reacquainted with each other's bodies and bringing each other intense pleasure, he'd reheated their abandoned meals from the King's Finest Family Restaurant. A Blake's Steak and a loaded baked potato for him. A Cole Slaw Burger and seasoned fries for her. They'd eaten in bed while watching TV, and soon afterward, Chandra had fallen asleep. She seemed absolutely exhausted.

Julian had let her sleep while he showered, unloaded the dishwasher and did laundry. Then he'd climbed back into bed, cradling her to him as he obsessed over his new reality.

*I'm going to be a father.*

All of his unspoken fears raced through his brain. Would Chandra be okay? Would the baby? How would this arrangement work? Was he prepared to be a father—a really good one, like his own?

But the longer he lay there, thoughts of the future churning in his head, he was crystal clear about the future he envisioned for himself and the little family they'd suddenly become.

"Julian, are you okay?" Chandra lifted her head and wiped the sleep from her beautiful brown eyes. "Your heart is racing."

"I'm fine," he said, despite his heart hammering in his chest. "I've just been thinking."

"About?" Chandra folded her arms on his chest, her chin propped on the back of her hand as she stared up at him looking more enticing than ever.

All of the eloquent words Julian had planned to say lodged in his parched throat, and his mind went blank.

Chandra's expression fell and her brows furrowed. But she mustered a smile and stroked his cheek. "It's okay, Julian. I know you feel the need to do right by this baby. But becoming a parent is my choice, not yours. So if you'd rather not be involved—"

"Marry me, Chandra." Julian blurted the words out as the sound of the blood rushing filled his ears.

"Did you just ask me to *marry* you?" Chandra sat up against the headboard, dragging the sheet up over her bare breasts.

Maybe he hadn't done this before, but he was pretty damn sure that wasn't the face of a woman who welcomed his marriage proposal. "Yes."

"Julian, you barely know me." She climbed out of the bed and slipped on her lacy black panties, then picked up the rest of her clothing and put it on—starting with her bra. "I'm some random chick you sat next to on the plane. The only reason we're here right now is because we're both apparently incompetent when it comes to birth control."

Julian climbed out of bed and slid his arms around Chandra's waist. He pulled her to him, halting her frantic attempts to get dressed.

"I need to be clear about something," he said. "No, I wasn't looking for a relationship when we met. But I agreed to a fling because that's all you were interested in. If you'd said you were only interested in a serious relationship that could lead to marriage and kids... I wouldn't have said no to that either." He dropped a kiss on her shoulder. "I was already too far gone."

Chandra's expression softened, but she still seemed anxious. "You're an amazing man, Julian. And I care very much for you. But marriage is the very opposite of taking this thing slowly."

"I know, but with the baby coming...it feels like we've vaulted past the taking-it-slow stage, right?" He gave her a small smile, and the tension in her back eased.

"Marriage is a serious commitment, Julian." Chandra seemed to be fighting a smile.

"It is," he agreed. "And even in the best of circumstances, marriage has a fifty-fifty shot of being successful. But I want to be a part of this child's life and yours. I wanna be the kind of dad who will *always* be there. The kind of dad I had and that you have. I'm ready to prove that. Right here. Right now."

"I'd never keep you from being a part of our child's life." She stroked his cheek. "But getting married just for the sake of the baby... That isn't necessary, Julian. My dad has *two* broken marriages that prove kids alone won't equate to an enduring union."

"I realize that."

The pain in Chandra's eyes broke Julian's heart. He

wasn't sure who'd had it worst: him because his father had been taken from him tragically, or her because her mother and stepmother had willingly walked away.

"We've both suffered irrevocably in the absence of a parent. I don't want that for our kid, Chandra. Do you?"

"Of course not. But I don't think we should get married just because I'm pregnant either." She placed a hand on her belly.

"Obviously, the timing is prompted by news of the baby. But I wouldn't ask you to marry me if I didn't genuinely *want* to be with you, Chandra."

"Julian, you don't need to pretend that—"

"That I haven't been able to get you out of my head since the day we met? That I've been in heaven with you these past few months? And you're the only woman I've ever considered a future with? Because every single word of that is true."

Chandra stared at him, blinking. "But we just met a few months ago." Her protest was weakening, her objection unsure.

"I know." Julian squeezed her hand, his eyes locked with hers. "But the moment you slipped your hand into mine on that plane... I swear I was a goner. It felt like I'd been waiting my entire life to meet you."

Chandra's eyes were suddenly glossy with unshed tears. She laughed nervously. "You really are persuasive, Dr. Brandon."

"Don't forget irresistible."

"And still modest." She shot a playful punch to his arm.

Julian chuckled. "Does that mean you're saying yes to my earnest, if slightly unconventional marriage proposal?"

"It means I'll give it serious consideration." Her sweet smile made his chest swell. "And that I feel the same about you."

Julian's smile widened. Maybe it wasn't a yes, but it

wasn't no, and Chandra had admitted to having feelings for him. It gave him hope. "That's all I ask."

"Now, I have a question for you," Chandra said.

"Shoot."

"Whatever our relationship turns out to be," she said tentatively, "this will be our first Christmas together. I'd like to get you something really special. So maybe give me a little hint about what you want?"

A wide grin spread across Julian's face. "Chandra Valentine, all I want for Christmas is you."

"How very Mariah Carey of you." Her sexy smile ignited something in his chest. Chandra glided a hand down his side, awakening every single nerve ending in his body.

"What about you?" he asked.

Her deep brown eyes swam with emotion. She settled a hand on her belly. "You've already given me more than I could've ever hoped for. I honestly didn't think I'd ever... Thank you, Julian. For everything."

Julian captured her soft lips with his own, losing himself in her kiss and in the swell of emotions he felt whenever he was with this incredible woman. He pulled her back into his bed and made love to her again.

Regardless of Chandra's answer to his proposal, because of her, his life would never ever be the same again. And for that, he was grateful.

# Eighteen

The following morning, Chandra stepped out of Julian's SUV, parked in the driveway of the Valentine Vineyards villa, as he held the door open for her. He leaned her against the back passenger door and gave her a dizzying kiss that evoked memories of the delicious, orgasm-inducing way he'd awakened her earlier that morning.

She clenched her thighs against the pulsing of her core.

"Meet me for lunch?" Julian nuzzled the side of her face with his scruffy cheek. His voice was gruff, much as it had been when he'd awakened that morning.

"I have a meeting with our winemaker, Maria, at one. But I'll make dinner at your place tonight. After all, you should know what you'd be getting yourself into." She grinned, then whimpered when he kissed the space behind her ear he knew drove her crazy. It sent a chill down her spine that had nothing to do with the frigid wind swirling down from the Smoky Mountains.

"Perfect. Just use the code to let yourself in." Julian kissed her temple. "This time, bring an overnight bag."

Chandra bit her lip and sighed. She hadn't intended to spend the night at Julian's. But she'd loved waking up to him, their limbs intertwined and him peppering her with kisses that began at her neck and ended with his head beneath the covers.

"I will." Her face and neck heated.

"Are you sure you don't want me to be there when you tell your family?" Julian's brows furrowed. "It only seems right that I be there."

*My God, you're precious.*

"I appreciate the offer." Chandra stroked his stubbled chin with her gloved hand. "But I'm a big girl. I can handle this. Besides, your first patient of the day is waiting."

"If you're sure." Julian tucked her arm into the crook of his elbow and walked her onto the back porch of the villa. He kissed her again, then jogged back to his running vehicle.

"God, that man is hot," Chandra whispered beneath her breath as she unlocked the back door and made her way inside.

"Well, look who decided to join us for breakfast after all." Her youngest brother stood from the breakfast table and gave her his signature bear hug.

Nolan, Sebastian and Alonzo were also at the table.

"I thought you all were coming in on Friday." Chandra tossed her coat on a nearby chair.

"We wanted to surprise you by coming in a couple days early." Sebastian's thick eyebrows lifted, his judgment face firmly in place.

*No time like the present.*

"Speaking of surprises…" Chandra glanced around the table. "I'm glad you're here early. There's something I need to tell you."

"All right." Her father's wiry gray brows knitted with concern. "Have a seat and tell us what's on your mind."

"Actually, I'd rather stand." Chandra tightened her grip on the back of the empty chair, suddenly needing its support. "It seems that I...uh...am...pregnant." She spread her hands, as if she'd just said... *Ta-da!*

They all stared in silence, as if awaiting the punch line of an ineptly told joke.

"Wait...you're serious?" Alonzo asked, finally. "Sis, you're like *the* most responsible person I have ever known. No offense, Pops."

"None taken," her father said. Though, by the furrow of his brow, there clearly was.

Alonzo didn't seem to notice. "How on earth did you—"

"We're good, Zo." Nolan held up a hand. "I'm pretty sure Dad gave everyone here the *where do babies come from* speech."

"Not me. If it was up to Dad, I'd still think we were all delivered by the stork." Naya narrowed her gaze at their father. "But I would like to take this time to say... *Yay!* I'm going to be an auntie. Also, you all were so sure *I* would be the one who'd get knocked up," Naya added gleefully. "Ha!"

"Not now, baby girl," her father warned.

"Fine," Naya muttered as their father and brothers glared.

Alonzo dragged a hand over his head, looking as stunned as he'd been when he'd discovered that their father was the real tooth fairy. "And you've obviously decided—"

"Yes," Chandra said firmly. She cupped a hand over her belly protectively. "This might be my only chance to have a child. I'm nearly forty, and I'm not involved with anyone—"

"With respect, sis, *clearly* you have been." Sebastian pointed his fork in her direction.

Her cheeks burned.

Chandra was a womanist and she certainly wasn't a

prude. Still, she couldn't help feeling a little embarrassed to have this conversation with her father and brothers. Talking about her sex life and the child now growing inside her... this was new territory for all of them. "Point taken, Bas."

"I didn't realize you wanted kids." Nolan's tone and expression softened. "You've never really talked about having children."

"I guess I didn't realize how much I wanted to be a mother until I discovered I was pregnant."

The range of emotions Chandra had gone through when one pregnancy test, then the other had turned positive replayed in her head. She'd gone from abject fear, to confusion, to the slow realization that she wanted to be a mother. A desire she'd carefully suppressed after her failed engagement.

"I've been so focused on my career the past few years. And prior to my engagement, I wasn't even sure I... I mean—"

"You didn't know if you wanted kids after having to practically raise all five of us." There was a hint of apology or maybe guilt in Alonzo's voice.

Chandra's gaze swept the room. Alonzo's sentiments were echoed in the expressions on Nolan's, Sebastian's, Nyles's and Naya's faces. As if they felt guilty for somehow derailing her life. But nothing could be further from the truth. They'd taught her so much: love and patience; empathy and kindness. And they needed to know that.

"I'm glad I was able to be there for all of you. And I'm proud of who you've become. Nurturing each of you taught me so much. It made me who I am today," Chandra said with a warm smile. "Maybe I was reluctant to have kids of my own because it sometimes felt like I'd raised all of you. Not that Dad wasn't there," she added.

"That's sweet of you, Chandra." Her father rubbed a hand over his thinning hair. "But we all know I wasn't. Not the way I should've been. I guess that was another reason I was anxious to wash my hands of Valentine Textiles. My blind commitment to the company is part of the reason my marriages failed. And it's why I missed out on so much of your lives. I wanted to make my parents proud. But that's no excuse. You kids deserved better, and I'm sorry I didn't give it to you." There was a sheen over her father's eyes. "I don't know that I've ever really thanked you for the sacrifices you made for this family, sweetheart."

He squeezed her hand, a soft smile lighting his eyes. "So if this is what you want, every last one of us will stand behind you and support you any way we can." He shot Nolan, Sebastian and Alonzo a warning glare. "Promise."

"Thanks, Dad." Warm tears slid down her cheeks. She leaned down to hug her father.

"You know we've got you, sis. No matter what." Alonzo offered her a crooked smile that reminded her of when he was a kid and wanted to make amends.

Her siblings nodded their agreement, and she felt a sense of relief.

"But what about the *good doctor*?" Sebastian said the words with a hint of derision. "What does he think of becoming a father?"

"I made it clear to him that this is my choice, and I have no expectations for him to be a part of this child's life or mine if that's not what he wants. Eighteen years of child-rearing certainly wasn't the expectation of our little fling," Chandra said carefully.

"Oh, you think raising kids is just an eighteen-year gig, huh?" Her dad chuckled dryly. "That's cute."

Nolan laughed. "Yeah. How old are you two again?" He gestured toward the twins. "Twenty-five?"

"Twenty-eight in a couple of months," Nyles corrected him.

"And we resent that." Naya directed one of her long,

pointy colorful fingernails at Nolan. "I'm an adult, and I take care of myself just fine, thank you."

"But you also ask Dad for shit…like all the time," Sebastian reminded her.

Naya's eyes narrowed. "Boy, mind yo' business—"

"Nolan and Sebastian, would you two please leave your sister alone?" Her father glared at them. "Besides, I like doing things for you kids. Makes me feel like you still need me. Can't blame an old man for wanting to feel needed."

"Dad, I will *always* need you. Clearly." Chandra pressed a hand to her belly. "More than ever once the baby is born."

Her father practically beamed. "You know I'll be there with anything you need."

"But will the baby's father be there? Or did he take the option to dip, which you so conveniently offered?" Sebastian Valentine was like a beagle with a bone. He never got off track and wasn't easily distracted, which had made him the perfect operations manager at Valentine Textiles. The trait was far less appealing in a sibling.

Chandra didn't owe any of them an explanation. And she didn't need to justify what she'd done or her plans for the future. But she couldn't bear her family thinking poorly of Julian when he'd been nothing but supportive.

"He's in, one hundred percent. He even…" Chandra drew in a shaky breath, not sure she should tell them everything. But the words rushed from her lips. "Julian asked me to marry him."

"You're kidding me!" Naya rushed over to Chandra. "You must've been completely shocked."

"I was. I still am stunned by all of this." Chandra felt like she was in a wildly vivid dream.

Her father rubbed his chin and nodded, seemingly pleased by Julian's act of chivalry.

"You hardly know each other," Alonzo noted. "Don't

get me wrong—you're an amazing catch, and he'd be damn lucky to have you. But I'm surprised he'd go straight for marriage."

"Me, too," she admitted. "I assured him I'd never come between him and our child, if he wants to be part of their life. But he doesn't want to be a part-time dad. And this isn't just about the baby for him." Chandra's cheeks warmed. "He seems genuinely excited about the prospect of us being together."

"Could Julian have a possible motive—besides the baby and wanting to be with you?" Sebastian pressed.

Chandra paced the floor, more than a little irritated.

Did her brother actually believe a man would have to have some ulterior motive in order to propose to her?

She was trying to be patient with her brothers. They only wanted to protect her; she realized that.

"I don't believe he has a motive other than wanting to be a fully present, full-time father to our child. We all know how devastating it is to have a parent walk away. Julian's experience wasn't the same as ours, but he lost a parent, too. He knows how much it hurts."

She'd never forget the trauma of her mother abandoning them. It affected her even now. And she knew it still impacted each of her siblings. Especially her brooding brother Sebastian, who seemed determined to view the world as a glass half empty, and Nyles, who pretended nothing really mattered.

"Not me." Nyles's vehement protest was punctuated by a bitter laugh. "We're better off without our mother. Didn't need her then, don't need her now."

A collective sadness seemed to wash over the room, but no one countered her youngest brother's claim.

"The general consensus around town seems to be that the young doc is a good, honorable man." Her father redirected the conversation. "And let's not forget that he genuinely seems to care for your sister."

"True." Nolan nodded thoughtfully. He sipped his mimosa. "He asks about you every time I see him in town."

"Same." Her father chuckled.

"Of course he does. Because he *clearly* has a thing for her." Naya wagged a finger at Alonzo and Sebastian. "I swear the man looks like he's about to die with happiness every time he looks in your eyes." Naya grinned. "It's fucking adorable."

"He said he was a goner the moment he met me on the plane. That it felt like he'd been waiting his entire life to meet me." A soft, dreamy smile turned up the corners of her mouth. Her cheeks burned and her chest tightened at the memory of the words spoken so sincerely. "I know it sounds corny to you and maybe you think it's foolish of me to believe him—"

"The young playa got game—I'll give him that," Sebastian muttered under his breath, and Nyles elbowed him.

"I don't think it's corny at all, and I believe him, too. Because that's exactly what I see in his eyes whenever he asks about you." Naya grinned, squeezing Chandra's hand. "The question is…did you accept his marriage proposal?"

"No. But I promised to give it serious consideration, and I will." Chandra rubbed the back of her neck. "Now, if you'll excuse me, I'm still a little tired. I'm going to take a nap. I'll see you all in a few hours."

Chandra left the room, her family silent until she closed the door behind her. Then they all seemed to speak at once.

She was tempted to press her ear to the door and eavesdrop on their conversation about her shocking revelation. But what they all thought of her decision was their business—not hers.

She'd decided to have this baby—with or without Julian and with or without the support of her family. But her heart felt full, and a deep sense of relief washed over her at having both.

That was enough for now.

# Nineteen

It wasn't quite five thirty in the evening, but the sun had already set when Julian pulled his SUV into his mother's driveway. He parked, then pulled out his phone, typing out a quick message to Chandra.

Made a quick stop at my mom's. Be home soon.

A flicker of joy bubbled in his chest at the thought of him and Chandra calling the same space *home*.

They hadn't discussed living together. That was his Plan B conversation if Chandra didn't accept his marriage proposal. Still, waking up with her in his arms that morning had been a slice of heaven. And knowing that the CEO-to-be mother of their child wanted to make him a meal and that she planned to spend another night in his bed made his usually cautious heart feel full in ways it hadn't before.

Julian had admittedly avoided making deep connections in his life, having learned early that the people he loved could be snatched away from him in a flash. And there was nothing he could do about it. But he'd felt an almost instant affinity for Chandra. And little by little, he'd been opening himself up to her and letting her in, and he was thankful that he had. Because being with her made him happier than he'd ever been.

When he knocked on the side door, his mother seemed pleasantly surprised to see him.

"I wasn't expecting you tonight." She opened the door to let him in. "I just made a gourmet grilled cheese sandwich for dinner, but I'd be happy to make you one."

"Thanks, Mom, but I'll only be a few minutes. Chandra is making dinner." He followed her into the kitchen, not missing the hitch in her step when he mentioned Chandra.

"So she's back in town." His mother pulled two bottles of water from the fridge and handed him one.

He opted to save his speech about the ecological dangers of bottled water and accepted it gratefully.

"Ray must be happy." She rubbed at her forehead and sighed quietly. A sure sign that she was carefully calculating how to phrase her next statement. "So I guess that means you two are back on?"

"We were never really off." Julian swigged water from the bottle. "It was more of a misunderstanding."

"Clear, frequent communication is vital in any relationship, son."

"Like ours?" Julian frowned, hiking an eyebrow.

His mother ignored the jab about their dysfunctional, though improving, relationship. She folded her arms and leaned against the edge of the counter. "I'm serious, Jules. It's difficult enough to keep the lines of communication open in a traditional relationship. But in a long-distance one—"

"Chandra accepted Ray's offer. She's going to be Valentine Vineyards' CEO." He tried, unsuccessfully, to strain the smugness from his tone. "She put her house in San Diego up for sale, and she's already moved here to Magnolia Lake. She's staying at the villa with her dad and sister."

"For now." It wasn't a question, so he didn't deny it.

"You just don't like Chandra." Julian set his water down. "You tolerated her because you thought she'd return to California and I'd move on."

"That isn't true." She set her bottle on the counter, then smoothed her hand over her shoulder-length salt-and-pepper gray hair, pinned up in a bun. "I like Chandra very much. She's sweet, thoughtful, accomplished. And my heart can't help but go out to a woman who's been through so much. Abandoned by her mother, stepmother and fiancé. Being tasked with practically raising her brothers and sister when she was only a kid herself."

"But—"

"But she is much older than you. Of course, there's no crime in that." She raised her palms to halt his objection. "But I think maybe you have different goals in life. You're a young man just beginning your career as a physician with an independent practice. Maybe you haven't given it much thought, but I'd imagine you'll eventually want to start a family. Chandra's nearly forty, right? So having kids might not be part of her trajectory, which is also fine. But that puts you two at—"

"Chandra's pregnant, Ma." Julian practically blurted out the words, punctuated by a nervous laugh.

He collapsed against the counter behind him after finally revealing the secret he'd carefully guarded all day. He hadn't intended to state it so bluntly without preamble. But he'd wanted to stop his mother's descent before she could dig herself any deeper with her *Chandra's too old to give me grandchildren* routine.

"I'm going to be a dad." Julian placed a palm over his

heart, then dragged his fingers through his hair and shook his head. "I can still hardly believe it."

"So the news came as a shock, but isn't necessarily unwelcome." His mother nodded; her arms folded. "Is that why Chandra came back?"

"Neither of us knew before yesterday." Julian drank more of his water. "Chandra moved here to be a part of her family's new venture at the vineyards and to give this relationship a legitimate shot."

"Well, it's good you were at least part of the reason Chandra chose to relocate here." His mother propped her chin on one fist. "With a baby on the way, it'll be tempting to hurry your relationship along. But there's no reason you two can't still take your time and—"

"I asked Chandra to marry me." Julian rubbed the back of his neck and tried to ignore his mother's shocked expression.

"I see. And what did she say?"

"She's considering it. But regardless of her answer, I need you to understand that I care deeply for this woman. And I want her to be part of my life."

"Congratulations is in order, then, I suppose." She squeezed his arm and gave him a soft smile. "If this is what you both *truly* want, then I'm happy for you."

Now wasn't the time to unpack his mother's conditional congratulations. Then again…maybe it was.

"I came here tonight because I wanted you to be the first person I told about the baby and about asking Chandra to marry me. But I also came to say this… I want to be a good dad. No, a great one. Like Dad was. But I can't do that if I'm drowning in guilt and resentment over the way things have been between us since Dad died." A knot clenched in Julian's gut. "So we need to stop pretending like everything is fine and talk about this."

"I've been thinking about that a lot lately." His mother's

brows furrowed, and her eyes were suddenly watery. She stared down at her clasped hands. "The state of our relationship… I realize it's my fault."

"I didn't come here to toss blame, Ma." He really hadn't. But he appreciated her acknowledging her role in all of this.

"You didn't toss blame, sweetheart. I'm just owning up to my mistakes. Something I should've done a long time ago." She sighed softly. "When you stopped coming home for the holidays, I said I didn't mind. But the truth was… I was devastated that my only child couldn't bear to endure Christmas with me. It forced me to reexamine my life and contemplate how royally I'd screwed up as a mother. I handled your father's death poorly. I was so consumed with my own grief and—"

"Blaming me for Dad's death?" Julian clutched the counter behind him, his forehead tensing.

"Yes," she whispered. The lines around her eyes seemed to age her a decade.

Julian had been ten and was running late for school and had missed the bus again. His mother insisted that he walk the two miles to school and endure detention for being late. But his dad had met him around the corner and given him a ride to school. Said it would be their little secret.

Julian had arrived at school just before the late bell rang, feeling smug because he'd outsmarted his mother. But the unplanned side trip made his father run late for work. His dad had been speeding when he hit an oil slick on the road and spun out, colliding with a logging truck. He'd been killed instantly.

Julian had revisited that day in his head again and again. Thought of all the things he would've done differently.

What if he'd heeded his mother's warning about staying up too late so he wouldn't oversleep? What if he'd laid his school clothes out the night before, as his mother had often admonished? What if he'd obeyed his mother and just walked to school that day?

Then his father would still be alive.

But he hadn't done any of those things. And though he hadn't caused his father's accident, had he been a more considerate, compliant son, his father would likely still be alive to celebrate the news of expecting his first grandchild.

"What happened to your father was an unfortunate accident." His mother's pained words broke into his thoughts. "I'm sorry for the irrational blame I laid at your feet. It was wrong of me. We were both grieving, and I should've been there for you instead of accusing you of…" She sucked in a deep breath, her lower lip wobbling. "I can't even imagine what a burden you must've been shouldering all this time. I'm so sorry, Jules."

"I appreciate that, Ma. But I didn't come here to revisit our painful history." He rubbed unconsciously at the ache in his chest. "I'm only interested in how we move forward from this."

"Maybe I can't make amends for the past. But if I don't at least try, we'll never break down this wall between us. And we'll never be able to build a bridge to a better future." His mother sniffled and swiped a knuckle beneath her glistening eyes. "When you didn't come home these past few years, it made me realize how much I've been missing out on your life. And I can't help thinking that if your father could see what's become of our relationship…it'd break his heart. This isn't what I want for us, sweetie."

"Me neither." Julian swallowed back the pain bubbling in his chest. "But after a while, I gave up." He shrugged. "It just seemed…hopeless."

She stepped forward and cupped his cheek, tears streaming down her face. "It isn't, I promise you. I didn't mention it before, but I started going to therapy a few months ago."

She squeezed his hand. "I'm trying *really* hard to change. Please, be patient with me."

"I will." Julian pulled his mother into a hug. This was the most optimistic he'd been about their relationship in twenty years. "Love you, Ma."

"Love you too, son."

Julian's cell phone dinged with a text message. He read the message from Chandra.

We really need groceries.

*True.* But he loved that she'd said *we*.

When the three dots, indicating that she was writing a reply, danced on his phone, Julian's smile broadened.

Think your mom can spare cucumbers and tomatoes?

He showed his mother the screen.

"For the woman who's made my baby so happy and who's finally going to make me a grandmother? Anything." She winked, then rummaged in the fridge and handed him the requested vegetables. "My future daughter-in-law is waiting. You'd better get on home."

Julian kissed his mother's cheek and headed for the SUV, hoping she was right and that Chandra Valentine would agree to be his wife.

# Twenty

Julian sang along to Mary J. Blige's "Family Affair" playing in the background as he stacked charcuterie trays in his refrigerator from the Magnolia Lake Bakery. He opened a case of imported beer and shoved the long-neck green glass bottles into a cooler on the floor. Then he unloaded the reusable grocery bags filled with chips, dip and other snacks onto the kitchen counter.

A few weeks ago, he'd mentioned to Cole Abbott how much he'd missed the monthly poker night he and his roommate had held back in Philly. Cole had grinned and asked if that was an invitation. Just like that, he'd been volunteered to host their first monthly poker night. He'd invited Cole and his brothers: Blake, Parker and Max; Cole's cousin Benji and brother-in-law Dallas; and Julian's cousins Elias and Ben from Gatlinburg.

Julian had been excited about hosting the game until Chandra returned to town a week and a half ago.

They'd been practically inseparable since then, and

Chandra had spent every single one of those nights in his bed.

Julian had been captivated by Chandra before. But now he was obsessed with discovering everything there was to know about this incredible woman who'd taken his breath away and turned his world upside down. The woman who would be the mother of his child. A connection they would always share.

He understood the science behind pregnancy glow: fluctuating hormones, increased blood flow, elevated oil production, etc. But seeing Chandra practically lit from within—like the holiday lanterns in the town square—and more beautiful than ever was mesmerizing. He could barely keep his hands off her.

But as addicted as he'd become to her taste, her sweet honeysuckle scent, the scintillating heat of her soft brown skin, and the growing passion between them, he enjoyed the quiet moments they spent together even more. Cooking a simple meal. Watching television together. Sharing stories—both funny and poignant—about their childhoods. Peeling back the layers to reveal a little more of themselves to each other as she lay in his arms each night.

Being with Chandra had been everything he'd imagined and more. Julian looked forward to waking up to her every morning, and he was sure she felt the same. Still, she hadn't mentioned his marriage proposal, and he hadn't wanted to push her. Her words that day at the café echoed in his head.

*Julian, I haven't done this in a while, and if I'm being honest, I'm still a little gun-shy.*

He needed to convince Chandra he was nothing like her former fiancé. That he'd never abandon or betray her and the baby. That their life together could be truly amazing, if she'd give them a chance.

The crunch of gravel in the driveway drew his attention. Julian glanced at his watch. The guests weren't scheduled to arrive for another forty minutes. But maybe his cousins had come down earlier to catch up before the other players arrived.

Julian unlocked the front door, then did a final straightening of the space.

Multiple footsteps climbed the front steps. Then there was a banging on the front door.

"Come in!" Julian poured some pretzels in a bowl. "And why the hell are you knocking on my front door like…?" Julian halted midsentence when his eyes met the steely, narrowed gaze of Sebastian Valentine.

Sebastian stood, legs wide, with his arms folded. He wore his usual scowl. Alonzo stood beside him, looking just as displeased. Nolan and Nyles completed the ragtag posse.

"Nolan, Sebastian, Alonzo, Nyles." Julian widened his stance and folded his arms as he acknowledged the four men. "Wasn't expecting you guys. What's up?"

"It's about our sister," Nolan said.

"Is she all right?" Julian's heart thumped, prompted by the worried look on Nolan's face.

He and Chandra hadn't spoken since they'd had lunch at the café earlier that day. She'd been tired and slightly nauseous but nothing that raised a red flag.

"Yes, she's fine. But she's—"

"Knocked up. Maybe you've heard?" Sebastian's hands curled into fists at his sides.

"Right." Julian nodded.

At Chandra's insistence, he hadn't spoken to her family since they'd discovered she was pregnant. She wanted to give Sebastian and Alonzo, her two hothead brothers, a chance to cool down. Clearly, that strategy hadn't worked.

"If this is the part where you show up at my house with a shotgun and insist I make an 'honest woman' of your sister, maybe you missed the part where I already asked her to marry me."

"We know about the proposal." The calmness in Alonzo's voice belied the anger evident in his narrowed gaze and flared nostrils. "But we also know about all your shady little side hustles—the gambling, the real estate *investment* schemes, and let's not forget your history of dating wealthy older women." Alonzo held up another finger as he ticked off each "offense."

Whomever the Valentines had hired to look into him had done their homework. But they'd sold the fellas a lot more sizzle than steak.

Unlike his trust fund buddies, he couldn't just make a sizable withdrawal or ask Daddy for a loan when he wanted to go into real estate investment. So he'd made the seed money for his earliest joint ventures by playing Texas Hold'em and Seven-Card Stud.

In the beginning, he'd lost more than he'd won. But he'd studied both games. Watched the pros. Practiced every chance he got. It hadn't taken him long to turn things around, and he'd made a lot of money. Money he'd used to buy into investments that had made him a lot more money and were a lot less risky.

"You haven't told your sister about any of this," Julian said, keeping his expression neutral.

"I just bet you would prefer we keep this from Chandra." Sebastian practically snarled. "But if you think—"

"That wasn't a request, Sebastian." Julian stared the other man down. "It was a statement. You clearly haven't mentioned any of this to Chandra. Because if you had, she would've told you she already knew all of this. I genuinely care for your sister." He scanned the faces of all four brothers. "And I have no secrets from her. Nor am I ashamed of my humble beginnings or the hustle and grind I put in to make a comfortable life for myself." He shrugged. "Chandra and I talked about all of this *before* we learned about the baby. So I'm sorry if you wasted your dime on your little private investigator. But if you'd just asked, I would've told you anything you wanted to know."

"If part of that 'hustle and grind'—" Sebastian used air quotes "—is trying to marry our sister to get your hands on her share of the sale of Valentine Textiles, just know you won't see a dime. There's no way in hell I'm letting my sister marry a virtual stranger without an ironclad prenup."

"I'm pretty sure your sister does whatever the hell she wants," Julian said. "And I don't want or need Chandra's money. If your sister asks me to sign a prenup, as I would expect someone in her position to do, I'll sign it without hesitation. End of story." Julian shoved his hands in his pockets. "Anything else?"

"We realize that you're doing well financially, Dr. Brandon." Nolan pushed his smudged glasses up the bridge of his nose. "I guess our concern is—"

"*How* you got that money," Alonzo interjected. "You have an affinity for wealthy older women."

"The kind that die and leave you a shitload of money," Sebastian added.

"So that's what this is about." Julian rubbed his jaw and sank onto a nearby bar stool.

As irritated as Julian was with the Valentine brothers for delving into his past, he admired how fiercely they were protecting their sister.

He tried to consider the situation from their perspective. Their sister meets a complete stranger on a plane—who happens to be a younger man. Within a few months of meeting her—and learning of her impending inheritance from the sale of their family's firm—she's pregnant and he's asking her to marry him. Then they discover he's inherited millions from an older woman before.

Maybe they were being a little melodramatic about it, but this was definitely beginning to sound like the setup to a murder mystery where he was the prime suspect.

"You want to know about my relationship with Meredith Valera and why she left me—"

"Four hundred million dollars," Sebastian and Alonzo said in stereo.

"Meredith Valera was determined to use her family's wealth to right wrongs and do some good in underserved communities. I volunteered at the rural and inner-city clinics her organization ran. We'd chat at the clinic and she'd sometimes consult me about different initiatives she planned to roll out."

Julian smiled at the memory of the kindhearted philanthropist who'd help him channel his pain and need for redemption into his volunteer work.

"When she became terminally ill, we talked about the legacy she wanted to leave and how her moneygrubbing children and grandchildren would squander her wealth. But I was as shocked as anyone that she left that money to me along with strict instructions on how it should be distributed. I've honored her wishes and will continue to do so. I've never used a cent of that money for myself, nor will I."

Sebastian and Alonzo didn't look convinced.

"As for the other wealthy older woman you're referring to, we met through mutual friends and dated for a few months. It didn't work out. We both moved on. End of story. Sorry to disappoint you, but there was nothing nefarious about my relationship with either of them."

"So just to be clear, there are no murdered wives whose insurance you collected?" Nyles added.

"You guys really need to lay off the true crime shows." Julian shook his head and chuckled.

Nolan and Alonzo laughed, and Julian was pretty sure Sebastian smiled for about a microsecond before resuming his usual scowl.

"Hey, that shit happens." Nyles folded his arms. "I need

to know what to look out for. I am not tryna end up with my face on an episode of *Snapped*."

Nolan shook his head. He shifted his gaze to Julian. "As you've probably determined, Chandra means a lot to us. She's been more than a sister. She's been like a mother to us."

"I know." Julian nodded. "She often talks about you all. I understand how much you all mean to her and why she must mean so much to you." Julian couldn't help smiling as he thought of Chandra's beautiful brown eyes and contagious laugh. Of the smile that made him feel like he was floating on air.

"Look, I'm by no means perfect. I've made a lot of mistakes in my life. Some of which I'm still trying to atone for. But I swear to you, I have no ulterior motives where your sister is concerned. Maybe I don't deserve her." Julian shrugged. "But I'm damn lucky she walked into my life, and I plan to spend the rest of it making her feel just as lucky she walked into mine."

The Valentine brothers stared at him, seemingly at a loss for words.

"Told you I liked this guy." Nyles nodded approvingly. "If you can't appreciate how beautiful that speech was, you're the Tin Man. You have no heart."

Sebastian elbowed his youngest brother in the ribs. "Whose side are you on, anyway?"

"Chandra's," Nyles, Alonzo and Nolan all answered simultaneously.

"C'mon, Bas. Chandra gave him every opportunity to walk away, and instead he asks her to *marry* him. Clearly, he's serious about her," Nolan said.

Sebastian frowned, still unconvinced. But the anger in his eyes dimmed, ceding to something softer: genuine love and concern for his sister.

"She's been through a lot. And she's sacrificed a lot.

For all of us. Now she's doing it again. This time for my dad's dream of building a wine empire." Sebastian sighed. "She's caring and self-sacrificing. She hasn't always gotten the same in her relationships. We just don't want to see her get hurt again."

The tension in Julian's shoulders eased. Maybe Sebastian could be kind of an asshole. But the man obviously loved his sister and wanted to protect her. Julian respected that, even if he didn't agree with his approach.

"Chandra and I sort of bonded over the pain of losing a parent when we were young. And I know about the broken engagement. I understand what's at stake here, Sebastian. Chandra is this unexpected ray of light in my life. Being with her makes me happy. I just want to do the same for her. But no matter what she chooses to do, I will *always* be there for her and for the baby."

The front door burst open and the room was filled with the raucous laughter of Julian's cousins Elias and Ben.

"What's up, Jules? Everything good?" Elias sized up the four men standing in Julian's great room. His cousin's face had gone from jovial to fight-ready in two seconds flat.

"Yeah. We're good." Julian introduced Chandra's brothers to his cousins.

"Hello." Ben smiled brightly as he shook hands with each of them, oblivious to the tension in the room.

Elias tipped his chin warily. "Y'all here for poker night?"

"Poker night?" Nyles rubbed his hands together. His dark eyes sparkled. "Oh, so you just weren't going to invite us? That's wrong, bro. We're practically family."

"None of you were in town when we made plans for tonight." Julian didn't want to spoil poker night with the tension between him and Chandra's brothers. But now that they were there, he couldn't not invite them. "You're welcome to stay, of course."

Nolan inched toward the door. "Thanks, but we should probably—"

"We'd love to stay. It'll give us a chance to get acquainted," Alonzo said. "Like Nyles said, we're practically family."

"Mind if I open the pita chips?" Nyles held up the bag.

"Help yourself. I was about to empty the bag into a bowl."

A mischievous smile slid across Nyles's face. "Thanks… *Jules*."

Julian narrowed his gaze at Chandra's youngest brother. *Just let it go.*

He remembered how Chandra had described the oldest twin. *A jokester who is doing his best to cope with the deep trauma inflicted by his mother's abandonment.*

Julian wasn't sure how the rest of the night would go, but he wanted to marry Chandra. And whether she said yes or not, they'd agreed to raise this child together. Things would go much smoother if he could win over Chandra's brothers.

Tonight seemed like a good place to start.

# Twenty-One

Chandra surveyed the driveway of Julian's cabin. Sebastian's car was there along with several others, including her cousin Cole's truck. Several other vehicles were parked along the road in front of the cabin.

Were her brothers clowning in front of half the town? Or had they enlisted their new cousins to intimidate Julian?

Either way, she was prepared to whip the entire lot of them. How dare they embarrass her like this?

"I need to find someplace to park," Naya said.

It was her sister who'd told her that while she was napping, her brothers had decided to go to the cabin and have a chat with Julian.

Chandra had tried calling him, but her calls had gone to voice mail. None of her brothers were answering their phones either. Chandra was so angry with Nolan, Sebastian, Alonzo and Nyles that her hands were shaking. So it was good her sister had insisted on driving her.

"Let me out here." Chandra released her seat belt and opened the door of her black Mercedes.

Naya grabbed her wrist. "Maybe take a deep breath before you go in."

"I will. Then I'll knock the four of their heads together if they've so much as breathed on Julian wrong."

"I think you're underestimating the man. He's more than capable of handling himself," Naya called to Chandra's back as she exited the car.

Chandra hurried up the drive and onto the porch. A crashing sound came from inside the cabin, followed by Sebastian shouting, "Take that! Now what you got to say?"

Her heart thundered and her pulse raced. She rang the bell, then banged on the front door. "Julian, are you all right?"

First, there was complete quiet. Then heavy footsteps plodded toward the door. The lock turned, and then the door opened. Nyles was standing there, his forehead beaded with perspiration and a pair of boxing gloves in his hand.

"Nyles, what have you done? And what on earth were the four of you thinking, coming here like this? I swear to God, if you've so much as—"

"Hey, sweetheart. Is everything okay?" Julian stepped out of the kitchen.

She leaped into his arms. "Are you all right? I'm sorry about my brothers. I had no idea they were coming here."

"I'm fine, babe. I promise." Julian rubbed a slow circle on her back and kissed her temple. "Were you expecting to find me beaten and tied to a chair?" He chuckled.

"No. *Maybe.*" She cradled his cheek and laughed, too. "I wasn't sure what to expect."

"Well, I appreciate the rescue attempt. But your brothers have been here awhile. They could've dumped my body in a back-road ditch by now." His chest rumbled with laughter.

"Hey, it's the thought that counts," she said.

"It is." Julian gazed down at her, his eyes filled with a warmth and affection that made her heart full and her tummy flutter. He lifted her chin. "You know what this means, right?"

"No, what?"

"It means…you care about me. A lot." A warm grin lit his dark eyes. "Like I love you."

"You…*love* me?"

"I do." Julian tucked her hair behind her ear. "My heart belongs to you, Chandra. Now and always."

Tears sprang to her eyes and her chest felt so full she thought it might explode. Chandra wanted to blame her raging hormones. But the truth was so much simpler.

She loved Julian, and she wanted to be with him, too.

Since her return from San Diego, Chandra's heart had been quietly whispering that what she felt for Julian was more than desire or infatuation. It was *love*. She'd just been too afraid to embrace it, fearful of being hurt again.

On the ride to Julian's cabin, she realized she was prepared to go to battle—even with her brothers—to protect the man she loved. The bighearted town doctor with a devastating smile who'd tended to her physical and emotional wounds and helped her mend the pieces of her once-broken heart.

Chandra's eyes filled with tears. "I love you, too."

Julian heaved a quiet sigh of relief and grinned. "You realize I was prepared to take an ass whipping from your brothers, if that's what it took to prove how serious I am about you, Chandra Valentine."

"You were gonna take on all four of my brothers for my hand in marriage?" Chandra couldn't help the euphoria she often felt in Julian's company.

"For you, girl, I would've fought a damn bear."

Julian captured her lips in a kiss that made her tummy flutter and sent heat down her spine.

"Dude, maybe we agreed to bury the hatchet…for now… but she's still my sister." Sebastian frowned, then sipped his imported beer. "I don't need to see this."

For a moment, she'd forgotten about her brothers and all the other cars in the driveway.

"Your poker night. I'm sorry. I completely forgot."

"It's okay." Julian squeezed her hand.

He stepped aside and she could see the two tables filled with familiar faces—many of whom shared her DNA.

"Hi." Chandra gave the roomful of men a small wave. Her cheeks heated with the realization that they'd been privy to their entire conversation. "Sorry to disturb your poker party."

"We needed a chance to regroup." Alonzo pulled out a different brand of imported beer from the cooler. "Your little boyfriend here is whipping our asses."

"Good. That'll save me the trouble." Chandra pointed a finger at her brother, indicating they'd talk more about this later. "And he's *not* my boyfriend."

Alonzo, Sebastian and Nyles shared puzzled looks while Julian looked wounded.

"He's my fiancé." Chandra's eyes searched Julian's as she squeezed his hand. "If your proposal is still on the table."

"*Yes.* Of course it is," Julian said. He wrapped her up in his arms, lifting her off her feet momentarily. He laughed nervously, fumbling to retrieve something from his pocket.

Julian produced a black ring box imprinted with the logo from Parker's wife Kayleigh's jewelry shop. It was a ring Chandra had admired at the store when she'd visited there several weeks ago. Only the ring had been enhanced since then. The setting and stone were much bigger, befitting an engagement ring.

"Have you been walking around with this ring in your pocket for a week?"

"No." He chuckled as he slid the ring onto her out-stretched finger. "Parker delivered it tonight." Julian nodded toward her cousin who was in the midst of cleaning his glasses. "I'd planned to ask you to marry me again in a few days, but this time, I wanted to do it right. Dinner, flowers, a night out, getting down on one knee. Because you deserve that and more."

"That's sweet, Julian. But I don't need any of that." She cupped his whiskered cheek. "I… No, *we*—" she pressed a hand to her belly "—just need you."

He kissed her again.

The sound of clapping and hooting reminded them they weren't alone, and she reluctantly pulled back from the kiss.

"Jeez, sis, get a room." Alonzo shuddered.

"Or like…*not*," Sebastian countered.

"What did I miss?" Naya huffed, her cheeks reddened by the cold air and her apparent jog. "Is everything okay?"

Julian gazed down at Chandra with a warm smile, his eyes not leaving hers. "Everything is perfect."

"Looks like the doc here will be our future brother-in-law." Nolan sank onto the sofa.

"Which makes him either hella brave or hella crazy." Nyles had strapped on the black-and-red boxing gloves along with a black virtual reality headset. He ducked a right jab from his on-screen opponent on the living room television. "Guess we'll find out which."

"And I guess we know who snitched." Sebastian narrowed his gaze at Naya.

Naya stuck out her tongue, revealing her tongue ring. She wrapped Chandra and Julian up in a hug.

"Congrats, you two." She kissed both of their cheeks. "Welcome to the family, Julian." Naya pressed a hand to Chandra's belly. "I can't wait to be this little muffin's aunt."

Her sister was quickly distracted by the scent of food. She sniffed the air. "Do I smell pastrami? What's the buy-in for this game, anyway? And where's the bathroom? I need to wash my hands before I eat. Never mind—I found it."

Naya was gone before either of them could answer a single one of her rapid-fire questions.

Chandra and Julian both laughed.

"Sorry about my siblings." She glanced around the room. "I feel like I'll be saying that a lot. Are you *sure* you want to do this?"

"I'm positive. They may be...*a lot*." Julian chuckled. "But they obviously care. I was an only kid." He shrugged. "It'll be cool to be part of a big family."

"In a couple of months, when they're all getting on your nerves, I'll remind you that you said that." Chandra pressed another quick kiss to Julian's lips, still slightly in disbelief that they were getting married and having a baby.

It all felt too perfect, just as her previous engagement and all of the perfect wedding plans that went along with it had. Because it was.

From Edward's meticulously orchestrated proposal at the lovely Cheekwood Estate and Gardens, to their elaborate plans for a wedding at The Parthenon in Centennial Park. For months, it had felt like she was floating in some incredible dream, until it'd turned into a nightmare. Just a few weeks shy of her wedding, she discovered her fiancé had rekindled his relationship with his ex.

Julian's proposal hadn't been carefully orchestrated or captured on film. But everything about it *felt* perfect. Like he was the missing piece of her heart that unlocked the fairy-tale love she'd once wanted so desperately. Would it all just blow up in her face again?

"Hey, come with me." Julian led her to his bedroom. They stepped inside and he closed the door. "You okay? Because you look a little..."

"Terrified?" Chandra sank onto the bed. "That's because I am. I know I said I wasn't afraid or overwhelmed by all of this, but that was me lying to myself, not deliberately being dishonest with you."

She was accustomed to walking into a room, taking charge and getting things done. Being in control and delegating. The vulnerability she was feeling now was hard to process.

"I meant what I said about being in love with you. I want to marry you, Julian," she said emphatically. "But you know I was engaged before. On paper, everything seemed picture-perfect. But I was betrayed and humiliated. My entire world imploded." Chandra wiped a finger beneath her eyes and sucked in a deep breath. "I don't know if I can handle another loss like that. You and I, we've already lost so much."

"We have." Julian sat on the bed beside her and threaded their fingers. He kissed the back of her hand. "Maybe that's why I've been afraid to really open up to anyone. But I wasn't expecting you, Chandra. I didn't expect to fall for you. I didn't expect to want a kid or to get married. But with you, I do. And I won't allow fear to make me miss out on the best thing that has ever happened to me."

How was this man so damn amazing?

Julian was an endless source of comfort. A compassionate confidant. A patient suitor. An unselfish lover who seemed to know her body, her needs and desires, even better than she did. He'd been completely open with her. She needed to do the same.

"I'm afraid something will go wrong with this pregnancy," she admitted. "I'm afraid I'll be a terrible mother because I haven't had an example of a good one. That our relationship won't last, and it'll be one more broken marriage in this family. That you'll look at me in a few months when I'm the size of a beached whale and regret this."

Julian's dark eyes seemed to glow with love and understanding. He tightened his grip on her hand. "I know this

feels scary, Chandra. But everything is going to be fine—
I promise."

She remembered when he'd uttered those very words to
her on the plane. Just like then, she realized it was a promise
he couldn't keep—even if he wanted to. Still, it felt damn
good to hear. "I want to believe that. I *really* do."

"We both know there are lots of things in this life we
can't control. But whatever happens, we'll get through it.
*Together.* But you should know that I don't have a single
doubt about what a great mom you'll be. Because I know
you'll be the kind of mother you wished you had. And
you're wrong about not having a good example of moth-
ering. From what your brothers have been telling me, you
were incredibly nurturing and self-sacrificing. That's why
every one of them would run through a brick wall for you.
So would I." He stroked her cheek. "Because I love you."

Warm tears slid down Chandra's cheeks. Her heart
swelled with affection for this incredible man whom fate
seemed to have gift wrapped and hand delivered to her. "I
love you too, Julian."

She pressed her lips to his, and his tongue glided against
hers.

There was a tap at the bedroom door.

"You realize I was joking when I said get a room?"

"Go away, Alonzo!" they said, simultaneously.

"Y'all got folks out here waiting for y'all. Seems a little
rude." Alonzo's voice grew quieter as his footsteps receded.

"Your brother's right." Julian kissed the shell of her ear.
"Can we finish this later?"

"We'd better." Chandra giggled when he kissed the space
where her neck and shoulder met.

Julian stood, pulling her into a hug that lifted her off her
feet. He set her back down and they returned to the great
room, where their family and friends awaited.

Chandra's feet may have been on solid ground, but her heart was soaring.

Maybe this hadn't been the happy ending she'd imagined for herself. But she was excited to begin the next chapter of her life with Julian by her side.

# Epilogue

"I now pronounce you husband and wife." The wedding officiant beamed at Julian and Chandra as she placed a hand over her heart. "You may now kiss your bride."

Julian's heart thundered in his chest as the moment settled over him.

Chandra Yvonne Valentine had agreed to be his, and he had promised to be hers. For as long as they both should live.

Julian choked back the tears that clogged his throat. His heart swelled with emotions as he met the gaze of his stunning bride. Her eyes also shone with unshed tears and her almost shy smile made his heart expand uncomfortably in his chest.

Three months ago, Julian couldn't possibly have imagined that he'd be standing here on New Year's Day, newly married, expecting his first child and planning a long-term future in Magnolia Lake with the woman of his dreams.

But here he was. He'd fallen head over heels for Chandra. And now he couldn't imagine life without her.

Julian slipped his arms around Chandra's waist. His lips glided over hers in a kiss that was passionate but sweet.

No matter how many times he kissed Chandra, he could never quite get his fill of those soft, full lips. But this was their wedding, so he'd show some restraint.

"I love you, baby," he whispered so only she could hear him, as the hooting and applause of their friends and family slowly died down.

"I love you, too." Chandra's broad smile made his heart reel.

Julian took her hand. They'd only taken a few steps up the aisle when they were surrounded by their families. First, Julian's mother, looking stunning in her floor-length tan mother-of-the-bride dress, hugged him, then her new daughter-in-law. Next, Chandra's father and sister hugged them both, while her brothers kissed her cheek and shook his hand.

Joe Abbott approached them with a big grin. Julian and Chandra gave the old man a big hug, knowing none of this would've happened if not for him.

Julian glanced around the space that had been a dusty, unused wine-tasting room just two weeks ago. Soon after Chandra had accepted his proposal, they'd planned to get married on New Year's Day in a simple, informal ceremony. She'd wanted to get married at the vineyard, as a symbol of all the good things to come there.

Parker's wife, Kayleigh, had made the engagement ring and their wedding rings.

Naya, Zora, Savannah, Quinn, Julian's mother, and Duke's wife, Iris, had jumped in and helped Chandra find an incredible wedding dress on short notice, arranged the flowers with a local vendor and sourced every other item they'd need. Cole, Julian, Chandra's brothers, Blake, Max,

Dallas, and Julian's cousins Elias and Ben helped paint the old place inside and out.

Iris and Savannah had tables, chairs, fairy lights and a host of other decorations brought over from the King's Finest wedding venue barn. Iris and Quinn had baked and decorated the three-tier wedding cake.

Julian couldn't be more grateful for the outpouring of love and support from their friends and family and all the effort they'd put into making their hastily planned wedding both beautiful and memorable.

"I can't believe our families did all this." Chandra smoothed down the skirt of her dress.

The sheer fabric was dotted with crystals that resembled a starry night, especially in the darkened room. A reminder of that first walk around the lake beneath the stars. The V-neck and low-cut back flattered Chandra's curvy frame. And the nude slip beneath the skirt prevented the dress from being too sheer while adding to the ethereal, bohemian aesthetic.

Chandra's wavy sable-brown hair was pulled back in a low, loose chignon, framed by a beautiful halo headpiece Kayleigh created for her. Crystals and freshwater pearls were twisted in a design reminiscent of the grapevines that grew in the vineyards the Valentine family now owned. Her simple makeup enhanced her natural glow.

Julian could barely take his eyes off his wife long enough to survey the room and the people who filled it. He smiled. "I can't believe they were able to make this happen so quickly. You Abbotts are a fierce lot. I pity the soul foolish enough to cross any of you."

"And don't you forget it." Chandra poked a finger in his sternum. Her laugh and soft gaze, filled with love, warmed his chest. She glanced up at him. "I still can't believe this is real."

He understood how she felt. He'd awakened that morn-

ing feeling like he was floating on a cloud of bliss. Missing
Chandra, since she'd spent the night at the vineyard with
her family. But he'd been grateful, knowing her face would
be the first one he'd see for the rest of his life.

"Believe it, sweetheart." Julian placed the hand that bore
her wedding ring over his heart. He cupped her cheek. "Because I love you, Chandra Valentine-Brandon. And I am
so damn lucky to be starting a life and a family with you."

Chandra blinked back the tears that filled her brown
eyes. She lifted onto her toes and kissed him.

For a moment, he was lost in her kiss and in the sweet
scent of honeysuckle that reminded him of summers when
he was a kid and all was right with the world. Before he'd
known the pain of grief and loss.

"I wish my dad could've met you. That he'd get to hold
his first grandchild." Julian forced a pained smile. "He
would've loved you."

"Your dad will always be right here." Chandra pressed
a hand to his heart. "And so will I. I can't wait to make
memories of our own here."

Julian gathered his wife in a tight embrace. And for the
first time in a very long time, all *was* right with his world
again.

\* \* \* \* \*

# WORK-LOVE BALANCE

## NICKI NIGHT

# One

The Money Maven. That's what they called her now. Ivy Blackwell was still trying the moniker on for size. Sometimes she loved it. Other times it felt pretentious. Both times, it still made sense to her.

What didn't make sense was how fast the persona took off. It was startling, propelling her into the life of a social media influencer within one short year. And, with that, came the deals. Big deals. Of course, the Blackwell name had an impact but the hard work that it took keeping up with the demands of this lifestyle was all on Ivy. This was all new to her. It was exhilarating…yet it was also exhausting.

Ivy twirled, checking out her reflection in the mirrored wall in her walk-in closet. The black strapless gown couldn't have fit more perfectly. The large ruffle that ran down the side from her breast to the hem of her gown was almost obnoxious. It was way more flamboyant than she would have ever chosen for herself but she knew it was absolutely stunning and would certainly get lots of attention on the red carpet.

The thought of being in the spotlight made her a bit nervous. It's not like it was her first time. Her cousins were in the entertainment business. They practically ran Hollywood, producing shows and marrying A-listers. She'd gone to plenty of star-studded events with them but was always in the background. She wasn't an attention hog. In fact, too much attention made her uncomfortable. However, tonight, she wasn't going to be in the background. This was work. It was her job to be seen.

Ivy had been styled by an up-and-coming designer. This young woman hit the fashion scene with a vengeance, commanding the attention of popular celebrities. When the network invited Ivy to the launch party for *The Real Deal*, a reality show featuring female venture capitalists negotiating high-stakes business deals, this designer reached out and asked if she could style her for the big event. Ivy did her research on the young woman, fell in love with her work and responded with a "Hell, yeah!"

Jade, the makeup artist she hired for the evening, walked up to Ivy and dabbed her face with one of those fancy sponges.

"Take this with you so you can freshen up throughout the evening." She put a tube of lipstick in a small pouch and handed it to Ivy. "I also put a sponge in there so you can dab away the shine if you need to."

"Thanks, Jade." Ivy took a deep breath.

"Still nervous?" the woman asked.

"A little. This is—" she tried to find the right words "—just a lot. Look at me—a face full of makeup. This dress." Ivy ran her hand down the front of her body as if she were presenting herself. "This is way more than what I usually do. Actually, this is more my mother's speed."

"Girl! You're a Blackwell. You should be used to this."

"Don't get me wrong, I like to look fabulous just like any other gal, but this is different. This is my cousins' lifestyle. I never envied them for always being in the spotlight. We have our flashy few, but generally, people in finance are nothing like the entertainment industry."

"You've got a point," Jade said, sliding her brushes into the holder. "It *is* different. But you're made for this."

Ivy tilted her head. "You think so?"

"Of course." Jade stopped putting her makeup tools away and placed one hand on her hip. "You're the most stylish person I know in finance. Most of those women are ultraconservative in their suits and sheath dresses with their smart-looking selves. That's why you became popular so fast. You've got financial savvy, and pizzazz. With your chic style, you make learning about money seem cool. Smart and savvy is the new sexy, honey. That's why you're the Money Maven. You're the full package."

"Aww. Thanks."

"Seriously. Own it! Enjoy it. Think of times like these as a girl playing dress-up. Doesn't everyone like to play dress-up every now and then?" Jade asked as if the idea of not doing so was ridiculous.

Ivy twisted her lips thoughtfully. "I like that." She looked at herself in the mirror one more time, spun around and walked off like she'd just hit the runway. After a few steps, she took a dramatic pivot, tossed her hair over her shoulders and shot Jade a smoldering gaze as if she were posing on the red carpet.

"That's what I'm talking about!" The makeup artist threw her head back and laughed.

Ivy laughed with her.

"Ivy!" A male's baritone voice carried itself up her stairs.

"Ty!" She lifted her dress and shuffled as fast as she could. The gown hugged her legs. "Coming!"

Ivy made her way down the stairs swiftly and carefully,

stepping into Tyson's waiting arms at the bottom. "What's up, cousin?"

He kissed her cheek, then held her at arm's length. With an approving smile, he took her in from head to toe. "Wow. You look stunning."

With a hand placed gently over her heart, Ivy said, "Thank you." She looked around. "Where's Kendall?" she asked as Jade made her way down the steps with her makeup kit the size of a carry-on bag.

Jade halted on the bottom step. "Wait! Tyson Blackwell is your cousin?"

"Yes, this big head is my cousin." Ivy swatted him on the back of his head, then nestled into his arm.

"Whoa!" Jade's eyes stretched wide. "I didn't even put that together. How cool!" She turned her attention to Tyson. "Pleasure to meet you. You're married to Kendall Chandler, right?"

"Yes, that's my lady."

"I love her music." Jade turned back to Ivy. "Have a great night and remember what I told you. Call me when you come back to LA."

"I will." Ivy gave her an air kiss on both sides.

As Jade was walking out, Kendall came in the door. Jade stopped abruptly and just stared at Ty's wife. A second later, everyone laughed. They were used to that happening when Kendall was around.

"Hi!" Kendall held out her hand to Jade.

"Oh…um…my goodness. Kendall Chandler." Jade grabbed her hand and shook it hard. "This is so cool. It's a pleasure to meet you." Jade was still shaking Kendall's hand. "I'd love to do your makeup one day."

Kendall looked down at her hand still in Jade's grasp, then looked back up at Jade.

"Oh." Jade dropped Kendall's hand and nervously rubbed her hands along the sides of her legs. "Sorry."

Kendall laughed. "No problem. I'll get your information from Ivy."

"Wow! Okay. I should go. Wow. Um. Thanks. Have a great night, you all." Jade stepped through the door. When it closed behind her. Ivy heard her squeal. The three of them laughed again.

Kendall shook her head. "I don't know if I'll ever truly get used to that."

"I'm going to tell you like Jade just told me. *Own it!*" Ivy and Kendall laughed together. "Thanks for agreeing to join me tonight. They told me I could bring a plus one, but when I told them Tyson would be joining me, they said, 'And Kendall Chandler too, of course.' I told them you absolutely would. I'm just glad you were available so I wouldn't seem like a liar."

Tyson looked at his watch and said, "Time to go."

Ivy sucked in a heaping breath and let it out with a rush. "Well…" She held up her hands and let them fall to her sides. "Let's go."

The three headed out to the car. Their driver held the doors open until they were safely inside.

The next hour went by in a blur. Within minutes, they were on the red carpet. The popping sounds of camera flashes sparked in the air. Journalists, bloggers and entertainment commentators from every kind of media outlet captured the guests. Some held cameras with long fancy lenses, others had cell phones and everything in between.

"That's the Money Maven! Hey, Money Maven!" Ivy heard someone call out to her, but she could hardly see from all the flashing cameras.

Ivy smiled and posed. Pop, pop, pop went the cameras.

"Thank you!" one of the journalists yelled.

Ivy grinned again, waved and continued toward the door. She was surprised that person had noticed her. Because, truth be told, she wasn't sure how popular influencers were

in the world of entertainment. She looked back to see that
Tyson and Kendall were moving slowly down the carpet,
posing and answering questions. They seemed so at ease
to Ivy. She was still blinking from all the flashing lights.

Inside, they were ushered to a reception area. Waiters
carried trays of wine and hors d'oeuvres. Ivy took a flute
and sipped. Someone bumped her hard, causing the champagne to spill over the rim. She jumped back just in time
to avoid splashing the liquid all over her dress.

Annoyed, Ivy turned toward the culprit holding her
elbow to help steady her. She looked up into his face and
the sharp words on the tip of her tongue stayed put as she
snatched her arm from his grasp. She'd been ready to lash
out but his drop-dead gorgeous looks had rendered her momentarily speechless. Besides, she also remembered that
she was there on assignment. She couldn't cause a scene.
Ivy was being paid the big bucks to appear at this event. Her
job was to shoot short videos and take tons of pictures so
she could chat it up on social media and influence people
to want to download the network's app and watch the show
when it aired. Cameras were everywhere. With all that in
mind, she shoved her spicy response down her throat and
nodded stiffly at his apology.

"I'm so sorry. I was in a rush and didn't see you. Did it
get on your dress?" He looked down at her gown and she
felt heat rise on her legs.

Ivy huffed. She remembered that this man had almost
ruined her dress. "No!" she said sharply. She couldn't help
the eye roll.

"Thank goodness. Again, my apologies."

Ivy only responded with a glare. She didn't trust her
words. It didn't matter how handsome and poised this man
was. She still felt the spot on the back of her shoulder where
he'd bumped her, knocking her off balance. Had he been
running?

After a few awkward seconds he bid her a good night, apologized one final time and walked off. Ivy couldn't help but watch him stride away. His swift gait was mesmerizing. She couldn't see under his tux, but something about his back let her know that it was strong and sturdy. His posture was regal. His pace purposeful. It was obvious that he had somewhere to be. He wasn't lingering, sipping champagne, greeting guests with a plastered smile while he nibbled bites like everyone else. Ivy watched him until he disappeared behind a set of double doors.

"You okay?"

Ivy was startled by Tyson's voice.

"Oh. Yeah. I'm fine."

"Ms. Blackwell?" A lean gentleman with a camera in one hand and cell phone in another stepped up to her. Ivy nodded. "I'm Dillon from the agency. I'll be working with you tonight to capture footage." His tone made his comment sound more like a question.

"Hello, Dillon. It's good to meet you."

"Likewise. All you need to do is interact and enjoy yourself. I'll capture as much footage as possible. Let us know how you feel, and how much you're enjoying the event. Okay?"

Ivy took a deep breath. "Okay."

"You'll be fine, Ms. Blackwell."

"Thank you, and please, call me Ivy."

"Okay. Let's get started."

Ivy sipped the remainder of the champagne in her glass and exhaled. She turned to Tyson and Kendall. "Might as well start with this fabulous couple." She stepped between her cousins so Dillon could snap several shots with a camera and then with his cell phone.

It took another glass of champagne for Ivy to get used to the fact that Dillon was following her around. But after a while, she felt herself loosening up and finally started to enjoy herself. Taking pictures with celebrities, the ladies from the show and then sitting down to watch the first episode of the new season were the highlights of her night. After the viewing, they were ushered into a ballroom to partake in the after-party.

Several times, she caught the guy who made her spill her drink looking at her. She ignored him, yet watched him discreetly in return. He'd interacted with Tyson at one point. They seemed quite familiar with one another. She refused to ask Tyson who he was. She wasn't there to meet men. Though she pretended to not see him, she couldn't get him off her mind.

# Two

"We need something fresh," Jordan Chambers said, sitting back in the chair at the head of the executive boardroom and rubbing his chin. He knew the pressure was on. The competition in the television industry was fierce, forcing his production company to constantly keep good content in their pipeline. Some of the best options had recently been snatched up by other production companies and networks. "Our current shows are doing well, but at the same time, we need something new, different and binge worthy."

"You know Hollywood loves more of the same, but you're absolutely right," Anderson Parks, Jordan's vice president of programming, said. He stood and paced the glass conference room. "I know some networks are looking at the publishing industry for book-to-film options. There are a few authors that I've been watching…"

"That's good. Let's consider that, but we could use another reality smash hit," Jordan told Anderson. The others on his small team sat around the white marble table as well, looking pensive as they thought.

After a while, Jordan spoke up. "Let's take a look at the book lists."

"Don't forget social media. Flix TV just signed an influencer and her show has really taken off."

Jordan stood, walked to the whiteboard and made four columns: books, reality, dramas, influencers. "Okay," he said, turning back to his programming team of five. "Let's throw some ideas on the wall."

The crew called out suggestions for each category.

"I have some friends in the big six," Jordan said, referring to the largest publishing houses. "I can check what books are on the schedule to drop in the next few months and we can see if there's something there. We can do some more book-to-film deals."

"What about that money woman?" Anderson asked. "She's an influencer that talks about finances, investing and all that. I just read an article about her. They call her the Money Maven. She's got a book coming out soon. Not to mention, she's hot!" Anderson picked up his cell phone and thumbed through it. "This is her," he said, turning his phone so his team members could see. "She's got over a million followers now. We can do a reality show with her."

"Let me see that." Jordan took the VP's phone and looked through her profile. He tilted his head.

There was something familiar about her. Then he realized where he'd seen her. It was the same woman he'd bumped into at *The Real Deal* event. Immediately he remembered the fire in her eyes when he made her spill her drink. Luckily her dress wasn't ruined. Jordan also remembered how beautiful she was…

"You know her?" Anderson asked, bringing Jordan's attention back to the present.

"No. I ran into her at the event the other night." He

paused there and handed the phone back to Anderson. Jordan remembered what she was like based on the way she glared at him. Despite being in Hollywood, huge egos were a turnoff. He'd dealt with them because it was part of his world but he didn't always like it.

Furrowing his brow, Jordan recalled more about that event. He'd taken her in a few times that evening despite being busy. He was there to rub elbows for a few upcoming deals. But something about her pulled him in throughout the night. He kept finding her. Each time, he'd watch her for a moment, mindful not to stare too long. Once or twice, she caught him, but her expression seemed blank. He couldn't tell what she was thinking. Jordan figured she was annoyed about the near miss with her dress. "Women," he'd whispered to himself and left it alone.

"You know what?" Something came to Jordan's mind at that very moment. "I think I remember seeing her with Tyler Blackwell."

"Actually, I think they might be related," Anderson said. "Look." He walked his phone over to Jordan and scrolled through her profile. "She was there on business. Look at all these posts about the event." Anderson squinted as he read through a short bio on her Instagram profile. "Her name is Ivy Blackwell. And she has a bunch of pictures with Tyler and his wife, Kendall Chandler."

"Let's see if she has something in the works with Tyler's media company," another programming team member said.

"Possibly, but BMG is into movies and dramatic series. They don't really touch reality," Jordan mused. "Let's put her on the list," he announced.

He spun on his heels and wrote Tyler's name on the board next to hers in parentheses.

"Good call," Anderson said. "And I'll do some research on her new book and find out who's on her team."

"Perfect." Jordan smiled. Despite their inauspicious

start, he wouldn't mind working with the woman. It looked like her social media following could be a win for their company. And he couldn't help but acknowledge how stunning she was. Jordan just hoped that his first impression of her was wrong. She didn't seem very nice and the last thing he needed was one more entitled, egotistical, celebrity brat to deal with. "Let's get some more names on this board."

Jordan's phone rang. When his mother's number flashed across his phone, he paused, wondering if he should answer, send her to voice mail or shoot her a text letting her know he'd call her right back. Charisse Lane didn't often call during business hours.

"Excuse me." He put up a finger dismissing himself and stepped out of the conference room as he answered. "How's my favorite lady?"

"Hey, sweetie. Your mama's…fine."

Jordan noticed the hesitation. He looked toward his team still brainstorming and walked farther down the hall to avoid being heard. "Everything okay, Mom?"

"Well. Not exactly…"

Jordan's heart leaped in his chest. "What's wrong? What do you need?"

"Well…" After another pregnant pause Charisse continued. "It's Timothy."

Jordan let out the breath he'd been holding. His mother was okay, but her husband, Timothy, was a different situation. He remained cordial with his stepfather for his mother's sake. "What's wrong with him?" Jordan's words came out sharper than he'd intended.

"He needs a little help."

"With all due respect, Mom, you're calling me to help that man?"

"Honey. I know how you feel about Timmy, but this impacts both of us."

Jordan huffed. He wanted to immediately say no to whatever it was but this was his mother asking and he had to hear her out. There wasn't anything he wouldn't do for her.

"Can you call us right after work, please?"

"What's…" Jordan stopped himself from asking what this was all about. It didn't matter. He wasn't going to like it.

"Please, Jordan," his mother pleaded after his abrupt pause.

Several more beats of silence passed. "Okay. I'll call at five thirty. Okay?" That would give him time to get to his condo and it wouldn't be too late for his mom, considering the three-hour time difference between LA and New York.

"That's perfect. Thank you, sweetie."

"See you later, Mom." He wanted to say more but decided to leave it for now.

After ending the call, he paced a bit before going back into the conference room. He needed to get his mind in check. What did his stepfather want with him? They hadn't been on good terms since he'd married his mother when he and his brother, Dorian, were teens. In fact, he was the reason that Jordan and Dorian vowed not to return home after college. They refused to continue living with that man. Yet, somehow, he seemed to make their mother's life better at a time where she was at her lowest. Despite their feelings for Timothy, seeing their mother happy made it easier for them to tolerate their stepfather's existence. They worked hard to be cordial to the man for Charisse's sake.

Jordan took a deep breath, held it in for a moment and let it out slowly before heading back into the conference room. He'd spent the next fifteen minutes trying to concentrate on the meeting but couldn't stay focused.

"Let's pick this back up tomorrow. That will give us some time to come up with some more fresh ideas."

Anderson tilted his head and eyed Jordan. He sensed the questions behind the other man's eyes. Jordan may have been able to fool the rest of his team, but Anderson was a different story. They were close friends and had been working together too long for Anderson not to sense when something was off with Jordan.

"Sure. Let's leave all of that up for tomorrow," Anderson said, pointing to the board they used to post their ideas.

Jordan was the first to leave the conference room. Anderson was on his heels but said nothing until they were behind closed doors in Jordan's palatial office. The glass walls overseeing Wilshire Boulevard flooded the space with natural light.

Jordan walked in past his desk and chair and looked out at the view. He watched the people mill about on the pavement below him. Anderson sat back on the navy tufted sofa and crossed one leg over the other. Neither spoke for several moments.

"My mother called," Jordan finally said.

"Is she okay?"

He shrugged. "She seems fine."

"Say no more. I just knew something was off."

"It's *him*."

Anderson sighed hard. Jordan heard his huff from behind but continued focusing on the movement down on Wilshire Boulevard. Anderson knew his history. He got how much he disliked his stepfather. And knew how much the man got under his skin.

"Is he okay?"

"Don't know yet." Jordan finally turned to face his friend. "I guess I'll find out tonight. My mom asked that I call later to talk. I don't know what it's about, but it can't be good."

Anderson shook his head and then stood. "Let me know if you need me, man."

"I'm sure Dorian will be there. I'll be fine."

Anderson tugged on the sleeves of his tailored button-down shirt. "Call me if you want to grab a drink after."

"Will do."

Anderson exited Jordan's office, and Jordan went back to looking out the window. He needed to prepare his mind for tonight. He was either going to need a drink or coffee before talking to his mother and stepfather. He opted for coffee before and a drink after.

Jordan put in a few more hours before leaving the office. He headed to his favorite coffee shop, owned by a friend. They had filmed a few scenes from different shows at this place. With his eyes lowered to the phone in his hand, he opened the door to the coffee shop and collided with a woman on her way out.

The cup gave, the lid tumbled off and the steaming hot beverage lifted into the air and came crashing down on both of them. It all seemed to happen in slow motion until he felt the heat from the liquid on his chest. The woman gasped and jumped back to avoid more of the coffee hitting her. She pulled at her blouse, moving it away from her skin. Jordan glanced over at her angry face and couldn't believe this was happening again.

"I'm so sorry, miss."

The woman looked back at him with wide eyes and huffed. Recognition set in for both of them at the same time. It was the same woman from the other night.

"You have to be kidding me," she said, glaring at him.

Jordan didn't know what was hotter, the coffee singeing his skin or the heat from her glare. He shook his head. "Man, I'm *really* sorry. Please. Let me help you." Jordan stepped past her and reached for napkins at the stand next to the door.

"No." The woman held both hands up. "No. Thank you! I don't want your help." Her words were harsh. She went back inside and headed for the bathroom.

Jordan pulled napkins from the dispenser, wiped his shirt and ordered an Americano for him and another of whatever it was that the woman was drinking. Though his friend, the owner, wasn't there, he waited a while for the woman to come out of the bathroom. When the barista handed her a fresh cup, she pointed in Jordan's direction. Jordan lifted his cup in acknowledgment. The woman took the cup from the barista, smiled tightly, turned toward Jordan and glared one last time before marching out of the coffee shop.

What were the chances of him spilling a drink on the same woman twice? Jordan hoped his day wouldn't get any worse.

# Three

Ivy couldn't believe her luck. How did she have two drinks spilled on her by the same person in a matter of days? This time, there was no getting away. No matter how much scrubbing she did in the bathroom, she couldn't get the brown stains out of her white shirt. She'd definitely have to go back to her hotel room before meeting up with Tyler. She was exhausted. Adding another stop to her busy day was the last thing she wanted to do. Between the lack of sleep and today's crazy schedule, she wasn't sure how she would get through the next few hours.

She tapped out a text to her cousin to let him know she needed to push their dinner back a bit. Irritation had her fingers moving across her phone screen at lightning speed. After texting Tyler, she exited the bathroom, retrieved her replacement drink from the barista and only half nodded a sentiment of appreciation to the gentleman after the barista told her he'd paid for it. At least he'd bought her another drink. That was a decent enough gesture. She got an Uber and headed back to the hotel. Within an hour she entered the restaurant where Tyler and Kendall had been waiting for her.

"I'm so sorry I'm late," she said in rush as she flopped into the chair. "You won't believe what happened."

"It's fine." Kendall dismissed Ivy's concern with a wave of her hand. "We ordered for you. I know you need to get back to make your red-eye tonight. This good?" she asked, pointing to what she'd ordered for Ivy.

"Yep. That's perfect."

"Good. So, what happened?" Tyler prodded, bringing them back to what Ivy had just said.

Ivy told them about her second run-in with the man and her ruined shirt.

"Are you kidding me?" Kendall said. "What are the chances?"

Tyler shook his head.

"I know, right? If I didn't know better, I'd think that guy had it out for me," Ivy huffed.

"Well, in any event, I'm glad we get to see you once more before you head back home," Kendall said. "The next time you come back to LA, we won't be here."

"I know. Are you excited about the tour? How long will you be away?" Ivy asked as Tyler flagged down their waiter.

"Tyler and I will be in Scotland for a few weeks shooting the new movie. The tour starts after that. I'll have a short break between the US dates and the ones overseas."

"That album really took off. I'm proud of you. How do you do it all?" Ivy asked.

"I really take advantage of my downtime. After the tour, I'll have about two solid months of rest before having to do anything else."

"Yes. We plan to be off the grid for at least one of those months," Tyler said and kissed Kendall's forehead. "I'll have my wife all to myself."

"We're going to take a trip." Kendall sang the last word. Her face lit up with excitement. Then she turned to Tyler, flashed a tender smile and gently touched the back of his hand. Her husband winked at her.

"I've been promising to take her on an excursion. We're going to stay at the house in Montana for a few weeks and then head overseas."

"That's sweet," Ivy said, leaning her head sideways. "Two months off the grid is great, but until then, things are nonstop. Really...how do you do it?"

Ivy wasn't just being curious. She really wanted to know. This new life of hers had become so demanding. Several times in the past year, she entertained fleeting thoughts of walking away from it all.

Ivy thought starting and running that women's group at Blackwell the year before was a lot. There, she'd spent countless hours planning events, facilitating workshops and teaching women about finance and wealth building. These efforts extended her workday and filled up her calendar on the weekends. It was so empowering, and her father was ecstatic about the company's growth with the surge of female clients. But then, her popularity grew among women's organizations, which is what led to Ivy's current situation and the angst between her and her parents, Bill and Lydia.

One conference appearance led to Ivy becoming an influencer. That paved the way for the book deal and now she was completely exhausted all of the time. But Ivy wasn't a quitter.

After the waitress placed their orders on the table, Ivy asked Kendall one more time, "Please, help me with this. How do you do it all? I'm not doing half as much as you and I'm exhausted. This influencer life is not what I expected and I see no end in sight. I'm grateful for all the opportunities, but I don't know how long I will be able to keep this up *and* keep my job."

Kendall and Tyler looked at each other and then back at Ivy.

"Quit!" Kendall and Tyler both said that with such ease Ivy's heart sank.

But in all honesty, that thought had crossed her mind over the past few months as well. Her position at Blackwell made this life possible for her. Even though she was often drained, she really did enjoy reaching women all over the country and felt as though this was her way to give back to the world for all she'd been able to gain. She was proud of what she'd accomplished at Blackwell in a short period of time and becoming an influencer gave her the ability to increase her impact exponentially. Ivy also thought about how her parents would feel if she quit. Another Blackwell, walking away from everything they worked so hard to build for them. How would she even break that news to her father?

"Ivy!"

"Huh?" Ivy looked up at Kendall and Tyler, realizing she'd been lost in her thoughts. "I'm sorry."

"You don't want to walk away from the family business, do you?" Tyler asked.

Ivy sighed. "I don't."

"Is it that *you* don't want to walk away or you don't want to disappoint Uncle Bill and Aunt Lydia?"

Ivy's shoulder slumped and she groaned. "Both."

"How do they feel about everything you're doing outside of your work at Blackwell?"

Ivy frowned. "They're not impressed. They think I'm cheapening my image—i.e., the *Blackwell* image."

"Yeah," Tyler said. He and Kendall nodded knowingly.

"I get it, Ivy. My family is very similar to yours, but for your sanity, one day you'll be forced to choose. A lot can come out of this for you. In fact, a lot has. This new book deal, you've made a name for yourself."

"Yeah," Ivy said. "That's part of the problem according

to Dad. I already had a name to be proud of. Mom said the Money Maven sounds like I run a brothel." She laughed. She'd gotten used to the jab but deep down it still stung.

"Want my advice?" Kendall asked.

"Yeah! That's what I've been asking for."

"Give yourself time to think about what you really want. You'll learn how to manage your demanding life just like we did. It's still new to you. Just remember to take the time you need to unplug and refresh yourself. Most importantly, every important decision you make for yourself has the potential to make someone unhappy. Who will it be? You or them?"

Kendall's last statement hit hard. Ivy had some thinking to do. Questions raced through her mind. Whose happiness would she have to sacrifice in order to have the life she wanted most? What did she really want? What was missing in her life? Could she make room for love?

# Four

Jordan tried hard to concentrate but his mind kept wandering to last night's conversation with his mother and stepfather. He hadn't been able to get Dorian on the phone yet, which meant he'd been holding in all of his thoughts about his stepfather's request. When he finally got a text back from Dorian, his brother promised to call later that evening.

Anderson tapped on Jordan's office door before peeking in. "You're in early."

"Yeah." Jordan released a slow breath. "I wanted to get an early start. Couldn't sleep anyway, so I decided to come in." He glanced at his watch. "Why are you here so early?"

"One of my contacts came through big-time!" Anderson stepped all the way into Jordan's office and clasped his hands together. He smiled. "I think we picked a winner but of course we'll have to act fast. I wanted to get some stuff together in time for our meeting this morning so I can share my findings with everyone!"

"I could use some good news." Jordan waved Anderson all the way in and gestured toward the chair in front of his desk.

Anderson danced a two-step, shuffling his way toward Jordan's desk, and sat down. His smile widened. "Are you ready for this?"

"Yep. Spill it." Jordan learned forward, ready to take in whatever it was that his VP of programming had for him.

"As I said, my contact at the publishing house came through big-time. They're dropping a book by the Money Maven in a couple of weeks. Ivy Blackwell's really hot right now. I told him we're looking for something new for the networks and how I thought maybe a reality show with her helping people get rich or fix money problems would be great! We could work together with the book launch— maybe even promote the launch as part of the promotion for the show. This book could hit the *New York Times* list and be a huge win for both of us." He cleared his throat. "He loved the idea —said he'll speak with his executive team today so they can hop on this ASAP since they have TV and film rights for the book. We can meet with them while we're in New York next week."

Jordan tilted his head. "I think she lives here. We should try to meet with her before we head to New York. See if you can get her contact information."

"I'm on it!"

Jordan loved the idea. It was timely and he knew it could work. They needed fresh content to present to the networks. Jordan wondered how well that Ivy Blackwell woman would take to an offer from his company. Surely a little spilled wine and coffee wouldn't be enough for her to walk away from a great deal. If Jordan was completely honest, he'd admit that he really wanted to see Ivy again. He could still feel the remnants of the spark he felt when his body touched hers. Her eyes, though they sparkled with a bit of feistiness, still drew him in.

Anderson shot up from his seat, promising to reach out to her publisher, and Jordan gave him a thumbs-up before the other man headed out. This new development energized him and made him forget about his family situation for a moment. When thoughts of the previous evening came back, Jordan brushed them away and tried to focus.

Excited about the prospect of the new show, Jordan jotted down a few ideas for a pilot. Then he picked up his cell phone and searched through the Money Maven's social media profiles. From his unfortunate and limited interaction with the woman, he didn't know much about her. He knew social media only told half the story but he wanted to find out as much about her as possible. She came from a family of finance kings and queens in New York. Hailing from New York with most of his family still residing there, he knew that her family affiliation alone spoke volumes. He'd seen Tyler Blackwell with her at the event. Now he understood their connection. They were cousins.

Ivy's online presence was well curated and polished. It exuded wealth and luxury, yet she still managed to come across as professional and down to earth. She had short videos offering financial tips that also showed her sense of humor. He could see why her followers loved her. They wanted to be like her.

Jordan found what he'd been looking for, but continued scrolling through her profiles. The more he discovered about Ivy, the more he liked the idea of working with her. With competition in the industry becoming stiffer by the day, he needed to keep his pipeline of new show ideas full. His team had never worked harder.

Jordan scrolled across pictures from the event. She was just as beautiful as he remembered. One thing he did notice was that she didn't seem to have a significant other in her life. Perhaps she kept her personal business on a separate profile.

Jordan came across one private account and assumed it had to be her but couldn't tell by the profile picture because she wasn't showing her full face. This made him even more curious about her. What was she like behind her public façade? He was intrigued by the fact that there wasn't much personal information about her on social media.

Jordan's last girlfriend, Mya, was a social media fiend, constantly posting pictures, checking her DMs and inbox messages and looking for new comments and likes on her posts. He was always in competition with her phone when it came to getting her attention. They couldn't even go out for dinner without her taking tons of pictures to post throughout the evening. She ate up the attention she received from her fans. It was all too much for a humble guy like Jordan.

Sadly, they'd reached an impasse in their relationship. She complained about the long hours he put into his production company and he complained about how much time she spent focusing on her social media. One day he came home to the sprawling house they shared and found it empty. He knew they'd had their problems, but he'd loved her and considered her the one that got away. Eventually, he blocked her on social media. He couldn't bear to see her constant posts and yet have no access to her. She belonged to her friends and followers, not to him anymore.

Almost a year later, he ran into her and was shocked to see an engagement ring and her swollen belly. A pang shot through his heart. Their brief, awkward encounter gave him closure. She'd run from his house straight into the arms of another man. Jordan wondered if he was around while they were still together.

Looking at his watch, Jordan realized more than a half hour had passed. He put the phone down and turned his attention to his laptop. He continued doing research on Ivy Blackwell online. Pictures of her with a microphone in her hand came up. He read about the successful women's initiative she launched at Blackwell. Several interviews gave him the chance to hear her voice. This woman was brilliant. He got new ideas about a show after checking her out. Her voice was full and mellow like that of a jazz singer. Jordan could listen to her all day.

After switching his focus to other business matters, his stepfather's request came back to mind again. Jordan reached for the phone again. He dialed Dorian's number. His brother didn't answer but he sent a text saying he'd call him later that evening. Jordan huffed.

His phone rang a half hour later. He reached for it quickly, hoping it was Dorian calling earlier than he'd mentioned. It was his mother.

"Hey, Mom." He tried not to sound like all the cheer had been siphoned from his tone.

"I was checking on you."

"I'm fine, Ma. How about you?"

"I'm good. I just wanted you to know that I appreciate you hearing your stepfather out last night."

Jordan held his breath a moment before answering. "Sure. You're welcome."

"I was thinking, honey. It's been a while since I've seen you. When are you coming home for a visit?"

"Me and my team are actually planning to be in NYC for a few meetings next week."

"Oh, great!" His mother's voice rose, her enthusiasm evident. "When are you coming in?"

"I was planning on arriving Sunday but I can come a day earlier."

"That would be great! We can do brunch on Sunday."

"I'd be happy to take my favorite lady to brunch." Jordan hoped she wouldn't ask for that husband of hers to join them.

"Great, honey. It will be my treat."

"Not on my watch, Ma. I'll pick you up at noon on Sunday."

"That would be perfect. I can't wait to see you."

"I can't wait to see you either." Jordan felt a smile spread across his face. After more small talk, he said goodbye to his mother.

Putting his phone down, he thought about the day Tim Lane came into their lives. It was two years after they'd lost their father. Jordan, Dorian and his mother were buried in grief. Tim seemed like a knight in shining armor and Jordan was sure he would fill the gaping void that their father's sudden death had left. That didn't happen. Tim doted on their mom, but Jordan and Dorian seemed nothing more than a burden to him. They were in Tim's way. Now this man wanted his help.

# Five

"Wait! *What?*" Ivy stood abruptly, almost knocking over her office chair. Her mouth dropped open. "A television show!" Ivy ran to close her office door. She didn't want anyone to hear this. "Oh, my goodness." She covered her gaping mouth.

"Yes!" her agent, Jamie, said. "This. Is. Huge."

"Wow!" Slowly, Ivy sat down on the white couch inside her office. She took a deep breath. "I never imagined."

"Well, it's happening. The producers will be in town next week. They want to meet with you."

"What day?" A short wave of anxiety squiggled through Ivy's stomach. Her schedule was already booked solid but she had to make time for this. Ivy thought about how limited her time was already. She couldn't say no to a TV show, but how could she possibly fit filming a show into her schedule too?

"Tuesday at ten thirty. Will that work?" Jamie asked, breaking into Ivy's thoughts,

"Um…hold on." She flipped thorough the calendar on her phone. "Unfortunately, I have a meeting at that time."

"Oh, man," Jamie said. "They need to meet with us before their meeting with the network. I don't think we have another option. Is there anything you can do? Meanwhile I can try to see if another time would be possible."

Ivy rubbed her temple. "Okay. Please ask. If they can't meet any other time, then book it. I'll work things out on my side."

"Good. I'll get all of the details to you and meet you there."

"Wow! My own show," Ivy whispered.

"Yep. Your very own show. I'll call you back when I have some updates."

"Thanks, Jamie. Bye."

When the call ended, Ivy sat on the couch staring at nothing in particular. She was shocked. Being an influencer had garnered so much attention and time. It was starting to challenge her ability to continue her work at Blackwell. Speaking of Blackwell, Ivy's meeting on Tuesday was with Dale Billington, an heiress to a huge portfolio of businesses and real estate in New York. If she landed this account, Dale would be the largest client Ivy ever secured. It took months to pin her down. Dale was extremely particular and didn't want to meet with anyone else besides Ivy after seeing her in an article.

Ivy flopped back on the couch. Again, her influencer life was running interference with work. She'd promised her dad, Bill, that it wouldn't. She'd sold him on this idea of Blackwell Wealth needing a woman in a high-profile position to bring in more females. It worked. She told her idea to her brother's wife, Zoe. She also loved the idea and agreed to come back to Blackwell to help Ivy run the women's division. With Ivy in the lead, she and Zoe attracted an impressive clientele of wealthy women, growing the company's visibility and customer base exponentially. Ivy was proud of their accomplishments, but increasingly, her burgeoning fame had caused conflict both within the company and her family.

Ivy dialed Zoe.

When Zoe answered she stood and started pacing again.

"Uh…you're calling me from down the hall?"

"I need you to come to my office right this moment." Ivy spoke slowly and steadily, making every effort to control the tone of her voice. But deep down she felt like screaming.

Moments later, Zoe poked her head in. She looked at Ivy pacing and stepped into the office cautiously. Her eyes on Ivy and full of questions. "Okay, sister. Spill it!"

"Come!" Ivy grabbed her sister in-law's hand and dragged her to the couch. "Sit." Ivy sat and pulled Zoe down next to her."

"What's going on?" the other woman asked.

"I was offered a television show!"

"What?" Zoe shrieked.

Ivy covered Zoe's mouth. "Shhh!" She looked at her office door before continuing. Ivy got up and led Zoe to the chair in front of her desk. Zoe's hand was still over her opened mouth.

"A television show?" Zoe whispered.

Ivy laughed. She wasn't ready for Zoe to tell the world but she didn't have to whisper. "Yes. I can't believe it." Ivy put her hand on her heart and walked over to the windowed wall. She looked down at the traffic rushing along Sixth Avenue. The people looked miniscule. She turned back to Zoe.

"Well!" Zoe said impatiently. "Tell me all about it!"

Ivy trotted over and sat on the edge of her desk facing the other woman. "This is all I know." She told Zoe about her conversation with Jamie and the conflict with the meeting times.

"Oh, no!" Zoe sat back, sucked in a deep breath and released it slowly. "We have to figure something out. It took forever to get this appointment with Dale." She stood up and paced Ivy's office. "I'm assuming you haven't spoken to Pop yet?" That's what Zoe called Mr. Blackwell.

"Of course not! I need to sort everything out first. I know rescheduling with Dale is not an option, so I'm hoping Jamie can get the time switched of this meeting with these producers."

"Oh, my goodness, Ivy!" Zoe lifted her eyes to the ceiling and shook her head. She laughed. "A freaking television show. Unbelievable! How are you going to keep up with everything?"

"I have no idea but this is too good to pass up. As a kid I used to imagine myself doing talk shows like *The View*. I saw myself sitting at a table with a few fabulous women talking about all kinds of topics, interviewing celebrities. That aspiration faded away when I went for my MBA and ended up working for Dad. So, yeah, this is like a dream come true. I would never have imagined."

Zoe crossed her arms and shook her head.

"And!" Ivy raised a finger at Zoe. "We have to keep this to ourselves. You have to promise."

"He won't—"

*"Zoe!"* Ivy scolded. "Promise me you won't say anything to Ethan. I can't have this get back to Dad until I know for sure what's going to happen."

"Fine." Zoe dropped her shoulders. "I promise."

Ivy stared at her, doubting she wasn't going to share this news with her husband, which was also Ivy's brother Ethan. The two were spouses and the best of friends. They kept nothing from each other.

"Okay. Stop looking at me like that. I won't say a thing. But as soon as it's okay to tell, you have to let me know," Zoe said. "Ethan is going to lose his mind."

"Ugh. You're a mess. I will."

"In the meantime—" Zoe headed for the door as she spoke "—we need to figure out how to make both meetings happen. Let me know as soon as you hear back from your agent."

"I will!" Ivy huffed. She had to make this work.

Her sister-in-law opened the door and stepped through. She turned back. "You're in town next week, right?"

"Yes. I have that awards dinner, remember?"

"Oh, yes! The Forty Under Forty Awards. So, you're definitely joining us for Ethan's birthday dinner Tuesday evening?"

"Sure will."

"And I'll be forced to keep this a secret the whole time."

"You sure will!" Ivy raised a brow.

Zoe raised her hand to her lips and pretended to turn a key. Then she whispered, "You're going to be a star!" She giggled her way out the door.

Ivy threw her head back and laughed, but that joy didn't last long. She dragged herself behind her desk and plopped into her chair. She looked at her reflection in the mirror that sat on her desk. Her eyes had bags under them. The light makeup did little to hide the weariness. How was she going to do it all? And what would this mean for her position at Blackwell?

# Six

Up until the time Jordan picked up his mother from her house in Jamaica Estates, Queens, thoughts of Ivy Blackwell had been wandering through his mind. She would be perfect for the show he had in mind. He watched her zany Instagram reels revealing snippets of her personality and explored some of the sound financial advice she'd doled out across the internet. He even called his broker and snagged a couple hundred shares of a stock she'd added to her "ones to watch" after doing some research. He loved the fact that she was a strong advocate for community service and helped women build wealth. His mother could have used someone like her in her life after his father passed.

That said, her level of interaction on social media alarmed him just a bit, because of his previous girlfriend Mya's obsession with it. How much of her online presence did she actually manage herself and how much was done by her team? More and more, he wanted to know the woman behind the public persona of the Money Maven.

A smile spread across his face as he pulled into his mother's driveway. Charisse had been waiting on his arrival. She came running out the front door with arms wide open. Jordan got out of the car and stepped right into her waiting embrace.

"Oh! My baby is home!" Charisse squeezed him tight. In turn, Jordan wrapped his arms around his mother and lifted her in the air.

"How are you, pretty lady?" He lowered her gently until her feet hit the ground.

"So much better now that my baby boy is here."

Jordan chuckled and rolled his eyes toward the sky.

Charisse reached up and placed her palm on his cheek. "I don't care how old you are, you're always going to be my baby boy." She stepped back from him, took both his hands in hers and looked up at him. With the inheritance of their father's height, he and Dorian towered over their mom. She came no higher than their strong pecs. "You're getting too skinny. We've got to find you nice lady. Not another tricky one that's going to run out on you."

"Ma!" Jordan scolded and laughed. To Charisse, every issue with him and Dorian lead back to them not having a "nice lady" in their lives. If they lost weight, or gained weight. If they came down with a head cold or pulled a muscle at the gym, it was because they needed a good woman. She took every chance she could to remind them about their bachelor status whether it made sense or not. It became a running joke in their family.

"Okay!" She waved him off before he could continue. "Let's go eat!" She walked back to the house to lock the door and climbed in the passenger side of the car. "They've got a great new place in Long Beach that's right on the water. I want to go there." Charisse reached over and tapped her way through the on-screen navigation and put in the address.

"Have you ever seen that…" His mother paused. Jordan cringed and held his breath. "That…woman…since that day?"

Jordan released the breath he'd been holding and laughed before pulling out of the driveway. He was sure she was going to come out with a more insulting word than *woman*. She'd done it several times before. It was obvious that Charisse was trying to be nicer about her inquiries, despite the fact that she was still clearly upset by Mya's abrupt departure.

"No, Ma. I haven't seen her since then."

"Does it still bother you, honey?"

"Not anymore."

"Good, because it still bothers me. Is that why you haven't started dating again yet?"

"Ma!"

"Well, have you at least met any nice women lately? No prospects?"

Jordan shook his head at this mother's insistence, but the image of Ivy in that beautiful gown at the wrap party popped into his mind. He felt that same magnetic feeling he had that night as he watched her. Even after he upset her with his clumsiness. What if? Jordan chided himself, rolling his eyes discreetly before chuckling quietly.

"Ma!" He laughed. "No prospects yet, okay?" Even as he said these words to his mother, he wondered about Ivy.

"Okay! I'll drop it. I just want you and your brother happy. That bachelor life will get you in big trouble these days. You two need to find yourselves a good woman and settle down. I keep telling y'all. I worry."

"Ma!" Jordan scolded her with his tone again. "There's nothing to worry about."

"Okay! Okay!" Charisse broke out in joyful laughter. "I'm just so glad to see you. You have to come home more often. Or stay longer when you do come. I miss you," she whined as she said those last words.

Charisse patted his arm and then snuggled into her seat. She chatted all the way to the restaurant, barely allowing Jordan to get a word in. In fact, his mom was so preoccupied with catching him up on everything that had happened since his last visit that she never noticed Dorian enter the restaurant until he was standing right next to their table.

"Oh!" Charisse shrieked and hopped to her feet. "You mean to tell me I get to spend time with *both* my babies today?" She wrapped her arms around Dorian, laying the side of her face against his chest.

"Hey, Ma!" Dorian hugged his mother back and kissed the top of her head.

"What a nice surprise. We'll need more mimosas!" She threw her hands in the air. All three laughed.

Dorian greeted his brother with a hug, took his seat at the table and ordered his meal. For a while they ate and simply enjoyed each other's company. But eventually they had to breech the subject of why Jordan invited Dorian to their brunch. Yes, they hadn't seen their mother in a while and were incredibly close to her, but neither of the boys made big business decisions without the other since both were heavily invested in each other's companies.

Dorian, though he didn't make it to the pros, was a staunch sports fan. His athletic physique was evidence that he'd kept up his workout regimen. After college he launched a company that manufactured a sports energy drink that garnered endorsements by many of his athlete friends who did make it to the pros. Over a year later, their support turned the drink into a billion-dollar brand.

After her meal, Charisse delicately wiped her mouth with her napkin and placed it on the table. She sat back and sighed. "That was delicious."

"It was," Dorian agreed. Jordan, still chewing, shook his head.

"Now let's get this out of the way before I have my dessert," the older woman said. She'd never been one to dance around important subjects. She was always ready and willing to face situations head-on. "Let me explain why we're asking for your help with Tim's business."

Jordan and Dorian shared a quick glance.

Charisse looked at Jordan and then Dorian before spreading her lips into a loving smile. "I know you're not fond of him. And you never seem to believe me when I say he really cares about you boys."

This time, Jordan and Dorian exchanged doubtful glances.

"I know you said you'll think about it and discuss it with each other, but I need you to not say no to him," Charisse said.

"Why?" Jordan said.

"Because the reason his business is in trouble is because of me. He would never come to you two to bail him out. Like you, he has too much pride. But he also wouldn't reveal the fact that I caused this issue."

Jordan looked at Charisse, waiting for more. Dorian's expression showed he was questioning what their mother could have possibly done as well.

Their mom's eyes suddenly looked sullen.

Dorian put down his fork. "What is it, Ma?"

Charisse heaved a huge sigh. "I had this idea to start a company. Tim has taken wonderful care of me all these years, but I felt like I needed something for myself."

"What kind of company?" Dorian asked.

Charisse shrugged. "A trucking business."

Both Dorian's and Jordan's brows furrowed, and they looked at one another and then back at their mother.

"A *trucking* business?" Jordan asked. Though that

seemed odd, Jordan had always credited their mother for passing down her entrepreneurial spirit to them. Charisse had always found ways to reinvent herself.

"I can't wait to hear this," Dorian said dryly.

"I wanted to do something different. Bold. We used some of our savings and Tim took money from his company to invest in the business. We got a small fleet of trucks, set up our offices, hired drivers and got things going. I loved it, but shortly after, Tim was diagnosed with prostate cancer." She blew out a breath. "The doctor said if we treated it aggressively, we could get him out of the woods. We didn't tell anyone because we believed in what the doctors said. We focused on getting Tim the best, most aggressive treatment so he would be back on his feet and all would be well. It should have taken no more than a few short months. That didn't happen as quickly as we anticipated. His care was so costly." Charisse went on to explain how the trucking business and Tim's treatment was the catalyst for a perfect storm of financial turmoil. In a short period of time, they accrued astronomical debt.

"Why didn't you tell us?" Jordan was baffled. He and Dorian were self-made men, determined to be wealthy to avoid living like they did after their father's passing. Either of them had more than enough to bail them out. Despite their strained relationship with Timothy, his construction management firm had helped pull their family out of grief and debt.

"We were managing it all until recently. Tim's major clients got wind of his condition and started excluding him from bids. With the possibility of him not being around, clients didn't want to chance their new contracts not knowing who would take over. Revenues plummeted. He didn't want me to ask you, but I told him we had no choice. He's a proud man—like you boys. Tim didn't want to burden you or mention the fact that I had anything to do with it.

I invited Jordan to brunch so I could tell him the whole story. It's a bonus that you were able to join us, Dorian. I was going to you next."

"Wow!" Dorian said. "How's Tim doing?"

Charisse took a deep breath. Her posture slumped. "He's getting better."

Jordan didn't say anything but was relieved. Tim may not have been his favorite person, but he was good to his mother.

"How much do you need?" Dorian asked.

Charisse held her hands up. "I don't want a bailout. I want to make you an offer, part ownership for your investment."

"Does Tim know this?" Jordan sat back. "Does he want to be in business with his stepsons?" He couldn't read the expression on Dorian's face and wondered what he was thinking. He wasn't fond of the man but never wanted to see him suffer. He couldn't imagine his mother dealing with all of this on her own.

"Not yet. It took so much for him to agree to ask for a loan when we spoke to you the other night. I thought this would be a better idea. As of right now, the business is solely in Tim's name. I want to make sure that once you helped us out, you were able to get some kind of return on your investment if something happened to Tim. I'm trying to protect your interest and ours. I wanted to see what you had to say before telling him my plan."

Charisse looked between her boys. Jordan imagined his expression looked as pensive as Dorian's.

"How do you know that he'll agree to this?" Dorian asked.

"Because we really have no other options, and now that he's healthy again, I couldn't stand it if he lost the business he spent so many years building. This partnership would be much more beneficial than just a loan."

Jordan sat back and instinctively messaged his temples. He had no choice. He'd have to help his stepfather's business. Helping him was helping his mother. Despite his feelings for the man, he'd always been good to his mother. They were poor when he'd come around. As a business owner, his earnings afforded Charisse a much better life. And until now, their mother hadn't wanted for anything since Tim came into her life. However, the lives Jordan and Dorian created for themselves far exceeded what Tim had made possible. Their investment into his business wouldn't create a dent in their financial portfolios.

"Let's figure out the terms and get the attorneys to draw up the paperwork," Jordan said and turned to Dorian for his approval. His brother nodded.

Charisse exhaled so hard her chest heaved. She clasped her hands together with a clap. "Looks like we're going to be in business together. Now I just have to get Tim to agree to the new partnership. I'll need a little time."

Jordan's mother was a smart woman. He appreciated her desire to protect all of their interests. Jordan wondered if Tim's pride would get in the way.

# Seven

Ivy wiped her clammy hands down the sides of her slacks again. She took three deep breaths and let them out slowly. Then she checked her reflection one more time. The smart, blue tailored suit fit perfectly. And she was happy with how her hair turned out—a full head of crinkly coils framed her head. She tugged on one in the front and it bounced right back into place. She felt excited, nervous and stressed. Each emotion fought to take the lead.

After grabbing her tote from the velvet bench in her bedroom, she headed down to the first floor. She paced, checked her smart watch and paced some more as she awaited her car service. She was too anxious to take the railroad or drive herself into the city.

Zoe had tried to get the meeting with Dale Billington moved to later in the day while Jamie tried to get the producers to give them an earlier time. Dale wouldn't budge and was still adamant about making sure she met with Ivy specifically. The producers said their schedule was already very tight. At the last minute, they told her they could only meet a half hour earlier. This meant their meetings would still overlap. The distance between the offices was fifteen minutes so, no matter what, she would get back to her office after the meeting with Dale started.

She looked at her watch again and tried not to worry. Zoe promised to take good care of Dale but had urged Ivy to get to the office as soon as she possibly could.

Ivy's smart watch vibrated. The driver texted her letting her know he was outside. She grabbed her phone and designer tote bag and headed to the car. Inside the luxury vehicle, she laid her head against the seat headrest and closed her eyes, thankful that she wasn't at the wheel about to navigate New York.

The moment she arrived, Ivy spotted Jamie at the curbside. She opened the window and waved her hand as they pulled up. Jamie leaped and headed toward the car.

"You ready for this?" Jamie asked once the driver helped Ivy out.

"As ready as I'm ever going to be. I still can't believe it's happening." Ivy turned to the driver. "Thank you." He nodded and tipped his hat.

"Oh. It's happening, my dear," Jamie said.

Ivy struggled to keep up with Jamie's long-legged stride. She barely remembered entering the building and riding the elevator. Before she knew it, they were following a slim blonde woman inside a modern, all-white conference room. Even with white walls, table and chairs, the room managed to not look sterile. Her chest swelled with anticipation and her cheeks hurt because she couldn't keep herself from smiling. Yet she got nervous every time she glanced at her watch. She couldn't wait for the meeting to happen and wondered how soon it could be over.

"Mr. Chambers and Mr. Parks will be right in. Would you like water, coffee or tea?" the woman asked.

"Water will be fine," Ivy said.

"I'll take water too. Thank you," Jamie added.

The woman bought over two bottled waters and clear plastic cups.

Ivy didn't bother with the cups. She took the water bottle straight to her mouth, drank half and twisted the cap back on. Then she untwisted it again, not knowing what to do what her hands.

Ivy and Jamie turned their heads toward the door when they heard voices. A tall, fair-skinned gentleman walked in first, holding out his hand. They stood.

"Hello! I'm Anderson Parks." He shook Jamie's hand first, nodding as she said her name. Then he turned to Ivy and held out both hands. "And you're the Money Maven!" He took her hand between both of his and shook vigorously. "It's a pleasure to meet you."

"Pleasure to meet you too," she replied.

"Jordan Chambers."

Ivy heard the second man introduce himself to Jamie. She turned to see who the sultry voice belonged to, assuming he was as handsome as his baritone sound suggested. Smiling, she looked up and halted. She couldn't believe her eyes. It was the same man that had spilled wine and coffee on her just last week while she was in LA. She knew it was him. She'd never forget that gorgeous face belonging to such a clumsy man. She wondered if this was some kind of joke.

"Ivy," she heard Jamie whisper.

Jordan stood before her with his hand outstretched, waiting for her to shake it.

"Oh...um...sorry." She finally shook his hand. "Ivy Blackwell." Despite her memory of the ruined outfit, something sparked when his hand touched hers. She removed her hand from his quickly.

"Also known as the Money Maven," Jordan added.

"Please, sit." He gestured toward the seat and sat in a chair across from Ivy.

Ivy thought she might have been mistaken about Jordan and brushed off what she thought she remembered. What were the chances it would be the same man? Who was she kidding? She remembered him being gorgeous. Tall, dark and handsome was an understatement. She took him in, attempting to be discreet as her gaze roved over his piercing hazel eyes, smooth brown skin, lightly shaved beard…and dimples. The man had *dimples*! Deep ones that she could get lost in. From the way his casual button-down shirt fit, she knew he was well acquainted with a gym somewhere. She felt Jamie tap her under the table.

"I believe Ms. Blackwell is just trying to figure out where she knows me from."

Jamie looked confused.

"Unfortunately, I caused a bit of a spill. Twice. One of those times, I'm sure I ruined Ms. Blackwell's attire. Again, my apologies. I hope you'll forgive me."

That voice. She almost moaned it sounded so sexy. Ivy cocked her head sideways. Yep. It *was* him! "Is this some kind of joke, because I don't find it funny at all."

"What's going on here?" Jamie asked, looking around the room in confusion. It was apparent she was the only one who wasn't aware of what had happened.

"I assure you it isn't, Ms. Blackwell. I wanted to get that part out of the way so we could get on to business. Believe me, it's all pure coincidence."

Ivy looked from Jordan to Anderson. Anderson nodded—his attempt at confirming what Jordan had just said.

Anderson stood. "Ms. Blackwell. If I may?"

Ivy turned toward Anderson. She still wasn't sure how to feel. She had to get herself together. Jordan's good looks were distracting. She remembered the spark and knew she felt drawn to him despite the accident. Yet part of her wanted to be angry at Jordan. She felt as if she were being toyed with, but focused on keeping her composure in case this whole television opportunity was real.

Anderson cleared his throat before speaking again. He picked up the remote on the conference table and pointed it toward the flat screen on the wall. The television sprung to live. After another series of clicks, their logo was on the screen. Anderson started his presentation with a history of their company and a list of popular shows they'd produced. She knew many of them, some making her list of favorite shows to binge-watch whenever she found time.

"You've managed quite an impressive résumé." Images from her social media, speaking engagements and a few articles that she was featured in flashed across the screen as Anderson spoke. "Your social media presence is great. Your followers love you. We see you're representing major brands and have built a reputation as an authority in finance among women." He cleared his throat. "And, of course, we've been made aware that you have a new book coming out in a few weeks. We'd like to work with you to produce a television show featuring you helping people with poor financial management skills navigate large financial windfalls.

"And due to your expertise, we're happy to offer you producer credits as you help us streamline the content for the pilot. We have a few ideas for the title of the show and welcome your input there as well. As for now, here's our idea of how this will work…"

This *was* real. Ivy was so astonished she was having a hard time sitting still. Jordan and Anderson tag-teamed their presentation of show ideas for the first season and what they planned to present to the networks they were meeting with during the week. The more they shared, the more excited she became. By the time they asked her if she had any questions, she'd almost completely shaken off the angst she felt when she realized who Jordan was. However, she still felt drawn to Jordan. Ivy needed to get it together. She was never one to mix business with pleasure.

"We know this is short notice, but we'd like to propose something a bit unprecedented," Jordan said. "Due to the timing of the release of your book and our upcoming meetings with the networks this week, we'd like to expedite your contract with a contingency plan, giving us the okay to shop your ideas with the network while the agreement is being reviewed. If one of our networks is interested, we would then immediately get this show ready for the upcoming season so we can capitalize on the release of your book within the first few months. We're of course happy to consider any inconveniences in your compensation."

"We'll have to revisit what's in her publishing contract as it pertains to television rights," Jamie added.

"Wow. This is…a lot," Ivy murmured. "There's so much to consider. I need to speak to my team. When are your meetings with the networks?"

"Thursday and Friday," Jordan replied. "We can give you until noon on Thursday to respond and get this first part of the agreement to us so we can shop it at our meeting that afternoon." He paused. "And we've already outlined a treatment and series bible."

"What's that?" Ivy asked.

"Basically, a synopsis of the show with an outline of what each episode will be about," Anderson explained.

"Oh. Okay. Wow!"

"Any other questions?" Jordan paused while Jamie and Ivy looked at each other, then back at him.

Ivy's mind flooded with questions. "I need to absorb all of this. I'm sure I'll have plenty of questions after that."

"Great!" Jordan said. "Feel free to reach out to Anderson or me." Both men passed their business cards across the table.

"Thanks!" Ivy glanced at her watch as she reached for the business cards. More than an hour had passed. *Dale!* Ivy stood abruptly. All eyes shifted to her. She planned to be out of this meeting within the hour. "I'm sorry. I have to get to another meeting. I look forward to reviewing the agreement that you send." She turned to Jamie. "Do you mind closing this out alone? I really have to go."

"Sure. You go ahead."

"Thanks!" she said, giving Jamie a quick hug. She shook Anderson's hand and then Jordan's. She left feeling his touch linger on her hand.

Ivy still wasn't sure what to think of all of this. Jordan...the show...the quick turnaround. But right now, she couldn't focus any more of her time or attention on that. She needed to get to Blackwell to catch whatever was left of the meeting with Dale.

Ivy called the driver to let him know she was on her way down. Maneuvering quickly, she exited the elevator and practically ran outside. As usual, New York City traffic was unforgiving. After ten minutes, she'd only traveled three blocks. Sirens blared and Ivy was sure she wasn't going to get to Blackwell in time.

Unable to sit still, she fidgeted until they arrived at the Blackwell offices twenty minutes later. The meeting was slated for an hour and had started an hour and twenty minutes ago. The second her driver stopped outside of the Blackwell building, she bolted out of the car, ran into the building and jabbed at the elevator call button until it came.

By the time she got upstairs the office was unusually quiet. She peeked into the conference room. It was empty. She headed for Zoe's office but she wasn't there. Ivy went to her office to drop her things. She plopped down into her office chair and twisted her head from side to side. Stress caused kinks to settle into her neck.

"Come in," Ivy responded to the soft knocks on her door.

Her father's secretary stuck her head in. "Mr. Blackwell would like to see you."

"I'll be right in," she said. When she heard the door close, she groaned. With the eerie silence of the office and the formal way in which her father's secretary had spoken, Ivy knew that this meeting wasn't going to be good. She felt a weight in the pit of her stomach as if a brick had settled there. Ivy stood. Placing one foot in front of the other, she made her way to her father's office.

Ivy tapped on his door but didn't wait for him to respond before cautiously stepping inside. She walked into another eerily silent atmosphere. Bill's narrowed eyes settled on her and stayed until she'd come all the way in. Zoe was already in the office and didn't look happy either. They exchanged knowing glances.

"Please. Sit!" Bill's tone was sharp. Ivy sat down slowly. "Now do you want to explain to me why we just lost one of the biggest possible accounts of the year?"

Ivy wished she could disappear.

# Eight

Jordan's mind and body hadn't reconciled with the time difference. His body was still operating on West Coast time. This East Coast schedule was getting the best of him. With all the appointments that he and Anderson had on their calendars, including dinner meetings each night, Jordan felt exhausted.

Jordan dragged himself through the door of his Manhattan condominium, dropped his light jacket on the couch and headed to his en suite. For a moment, he stood at the entrance to his room and just stared at his custom bed. It was larger than the average king and looked inviting with the crisp, white down comforter and sheets. Jordan wanted to jump right in and wrap himself in the cocoon of comfort but that would have to wait.

Despite his fatigue, Jordan had to keep going. His mind, on the other hand, wouldn't stop. He went over the meeting with Ivy in his head a thousand times. He remembered how beautiful she looked today and the first day he'd laid eyes on her. He'd felt something when they shook hands. Had Ivy felt it too? He'd handle business first but at some point he would find a way to get to know Ivy on a more personal level.

Tonight, he was scheduled to attend an event that he was invited to by one of the network executives. Christopher Yates, a friend and colleague from film school, was being honored as one of the youngest, most successful network executives in the industry. When he found out Jordan would still be in town, he had urged him to join him that evening as his guest—an invitation Jordan couldn't dare decline. The Forty Under Forty Awards event honored successful trailblazing professionals. Chris wasn't even thirty and had made a huge splash in the television and film industry.

Jordan trudged into the bathroom and turned on the water in the shower. Despite his age, he put on music from the nineties. His mother called him an old soul. Jordan adjusted the volume and R&B soul flowed from the speakers embedded throughout the master suite. The music energized him just enough. He bobbed his head as he dressed, wondering how long this second wind of his would last.

Dabbing on a bit of cologne, Jordan was ready to go. The car he ordered was waiting for him by the time he reached the lobby of his luxury building on Central Park West. Jordan loved the hustle and bustle of midtown, but appreciated the less busy, more residential atmosphere of the Upper West Side.

The event was taking place at one of the iconic hotels in Times Square. Jordan's driver pulled up and deposited him into the hands of one of the attendants, who greeted Jordan with a warm smile. Jordan pulled on the lapels of his black tux. There was a chill in the air. Perhaps he was no longer used to the autumn air in New York City. He made it a point to spend the cooler months in Los Angeles.

The elevator doors opened on the sixth floor of the hotel.

Jordan stepped right into a bustling cocktail reception. High tables, three bars and tables full of delightful hors d'oeuvres were positioned around the space. Jordan headed to the bar, ordered himself a neat snifter of scotch and started looking for Chris. Texting him while he waited for his drink, Jordan let Chris know that he'd arrived.

Chris responded, letting him know to hang tight. He was in a room with the other honorees taking pictures and would be out as soon as he could. His friend gave him their table number to let him know where they would be seated. Soon after, Chris found him.

"Jordan!" Chris walked over to him, decked out in a well-fitting tux. "I'm glad you were able to make it." They shook hands.

"Wow. You're looking like quite the dapper guest of honor," Jordan teased, pointing at the rose tucked in Chris's breast pocket.

"Listen. I don't know what made them pick me for this honor," Chris grumbled, "but I'm going to make the best of it before anyone notices they made a mistake."

"Aw, you're too humble."

Out of the corner of his eye, Jordan thought he saw Ivy Blackwell.

Jordan continued talking to Chris but scanned the room to make sure his eyes weren't playing tricks on him. He looked down at the drink in his hand and made a note to himself to keep his distance and then laughed to himself. There would be *no* way to recover from spilling his drink on her a third time.

Jordan heard the unmistakable sound of Ivy's voice. The warm, soothing tone was familiar to him. It flowed through him. Whatever that feeling was, it felt good. Jordan furrowed his eyebrows at his body's response. What was that? Why had her voice sounded that way? Jordan shook his head as if it would rid him of the effects of this beautiful, unnerving woman.

Turning toward the voice, Jordan spotted her before she spotted him. His eyes narrowed a bit as he took her in. Like the first time he saw her at the premiere, she looked stunning. Her black sequin dress dropped off her shoulder, hugged every curve of her beautiful body and flared around her feet, cascading in a waterfall of delicate shimmering fabric. Her hair, loaded with full beautiful natural coils, was pulled up on one side. She was flawless. Jordan felt some kind of butterfly action in his stomach. He couldn't remember ever feeling that before.

Ivy's beauty was undeniable, but if all went well, they would be entering into a business agreement. There was no room for whatever this was he was feeling. Besides, the only thing he knew about this woman was what he'd read online. Jordan recalled her expression when she realized he was the same guy that spilled drinks on her twice. The excited smile that she entered the meeting with fell faster than a shooting star.

Jordan took her in for several long moments and noticed she was wearing a corsage. Ivy was an honoree like Chris. Jordan found himself walking toward her and wondered what he would say. The internal question caught him off guard. Despite the fact that he hadn't dated in a while, Jordan had never been at a loss for words when it came to women. He wasn't the player he used to be but he certainly wasn't shy around the opposite sex.

The closer Jordan got, the more he noticed her smooth brown skin. He wondered how soft her shoulders must have felt. The curve of her neck enticed him. He continued to survey Ivy. Full ruby red lips spread into a cordial smile lifting up lovely high cheekbones toward her doe eyes. This woman was absolutely gorgeous. Her looks would certainly help boost the show. Hollywood and viewers loved beautiful women.

Jordan had been studying her so closely he saw the sudden shift in her posture go from graceful to rigid. Ivy's sculptured back stiffened. Her chin lifted. And from her profile, he could see her smile melt and the set of her jaw tighten. Someone must have said something to upset her. For the first time since he started in her direction, he took notice of the people around him. He noticed two women and one man. Who was that man? Could he have been her significant other? Jordan rolled his eyes toward the ceiling. He shouldn't care who the man was.

He had second thoughts about continuing his approach now that she seemed bothered but he kept heading in her direction. Just when he'd made it to her, Ivy lifted the bottom of her dress and turned abruptly. He halted, leaving a short distance between them. Their eyes met briefly, fire in hers, questioning in his. She blinked twice and recognition seemed to set in. She inhaled a slight gasp.

"Oh. Hello, Jordan." Ivy's tone was clipped. She looked at his hand at the drink he was holding and then back at his face.

Jordan raised a brow. "Miss Blackwell," he greeted smoothly. He drew his drink back as if to let her know she didn't have to worry about it landing on her beautiful gown.

"I'm sorry but now is not a good time." She turned to a young man holding a camera next to her. "Come on, Radcliffe." She stepped around Jordan. "Enjoy the event, Mr. Chambers." Then Ivy walked away, leaving Jordan to wonder what has just happened.

One thing was for sure…her icy greeting had definitely given him pause. It was obvious that something had just happened that had the potential to ruin an evening that was supposed to be all about her. Then Jordan remembered that since he'd met Ivy, every encounter they'd shared had been far from cheerful. Granted, she had reason to be annoyed with him the first two times. He wondered if the woman ever flashed a genuine smile. Was she generally grumpy? Still, none of that kept his body from involuntarily responding to her presence. He needed to get a grip on all those unexpected reactions. It was clear that Ivy wasn't interested in him in any way. Now he wondered if she was even a nice person.

# Nine

This week wasn't going well *at all*. Ivy was exhausted. Her dad was upset with her because he blamed her for losing a huge client. And now on a night that was supposed to be a great celebration, Ivy was trying to keep her composure. This Forty Under Forty Awards event sure wasn't turning out to be as festive as she'd looked forward to.

Ivy couldn't believe what had just happened. Her feet couldn't carry her away fast enough. Her branding assistant, Jess, and sister-in-law, Zoe, were fast on her heels. Ivy's anger made her eyes sting but she wouldn't dare allow one tear to drop in front of all those people at the reception. Thankful that she'd reserved a room in that hotel for the night, she jabbed the elevator button and immediately felt like the elevator took too long to arrive. Jess remained silent but Zoe rubbed her back.

The reception was just getting started and she and the other honorees should have been mingling with guests, but Ivy had to get away. She'd ordered Radcliff to stop taking

pictures and filming. Her anger flared way too hot to be on
camera. A fellow influencer and honoree had just insulted
her, literally calling her a pretentious bitch in the middle of
the reception. It caused a slight commotion when Ivy tried
her best to respond without stooping to that woman's level.
Ivy didn't understand why but this woman, Kenya Brown,
seemed to have it out for her. Although this was the first
time she'd seen her in person, it wasn't the first snide re-
mark she'd slid in Ivy's direction. Ivy's social media team
had to delete comments from her in the past. However, she
had never resorted to name-calling.

Ivy had swallowed, bringing herself back to the present before directing a glare toward Kenya and saying,
"It's obvious that my existence offends you. It's certainly
not my fault that you don't believe you measure up. How
unfortunate." It was then that she turned abruptly and
looked right into the eyes of Jordan Chambers. His presence surprised her. Ivy hadn't known how long he'd been
there or how much he'd overheard. She'd hoped he hadn't
heard much. Ivy was never condescending but this woman
had gone too far and in public. Ivy had done nothing to
her personally.

Turning and looking into Jordan's handsome face had
sliced through her anger for a quick moment. Instantly she
had been fully aware of how gorgeous he was. His timing was always horrible, yet something inside of her was
happy to see him.

After greeting him, she'd looked around and saw that
several people had cell phones turned in her direction. She
needed to get away. She was a Blackwell. She was also a
public figure and wasn't about to give people a show for
them to post and get likes at her expense. Her parents would
have never let her live that down.

"I need a minute," she had said to Zoe, who was standing by her side when all of this had gone down.

Zoe and Jess headed up with her to her room. Ivy was glad she'd booked a suite when she found out about the event. She knew going upstairs at the end of the night would be much more convenient than traveling back to Long Island after all of the festivities. Plus, she had a meeting with Dale in the morning and wanted to be fresh for that. A short commute would definitely help.

"What was that woman's problem?" Zoe asked in the elevator.

"I really don't know. I recognized her from her Instagram page. She's another influencer but I have no idea why she's so fixated on me."

"These things happen on social media sometimes," Jess mused. "It's a way for a lesser-known influencer to gain popularity."

"We need to block her completely," Ivy said as she held her key card up to her hotel room door.

"Please do," Zoe said. "Take a moment to gather yourself and let's head back down." She flopped down on the couch.

Jess disappeared momentarily and came back with bottles of water for Zoe and Ivy.

"And who was that guy that came up to you?" Zoe asked, taking a sip from her bottle.

"Oh!" Ivy sighed and dropped her shoulders. "That was Jordan Chambers, the producer that wants to do the show with me."

"Oh!" Zoe said. "He's a good-looking man. Did you know he would be here?"

"I didn't. Seeing him was a complete surprise."

"I'm glad you managed to keep your cool. We don't want you getting the wrong kind of press." Zoe parked her hands on her hips. "I should have socked her right in the mouth for you. Then it wouldn't have reflected negatively on you!" Zoe and Jess laughed.

Ivy smiled at Zoe's comment but her focus was now on Jordan Chambers. Saying his name bought his handsome face back to the forefront of her mind. He was the last person she expected to see, as usual. He just kept showing up in the most interesting ways. Ivy wondered if he'd caught her gasp when she saw him. She hadn't expected her breath to catch at the sight of his gorgeous face. Now that she thought about it, she hadn't been very friendly toward him. Hopefully she'd have a chance to make up for her cold greeting and swift departure. Plus, she didn't want to jeopardize her chances at working with him on the show.

She'd been thinking about the show proposal. Actually, if she was being honest, she'd been thinking about much more than that. And right now, thoughts of Jordan made her less angry. She remembered his smooth dark skin, piercing brown eyes, full luscious lips and tall, athletic stance. Their first two encounters were less than desirable, but she couldn't deny even then that the man was a majestic work of art.

"Ivy!"

"Huh?" She turned toward Zoe, who exchanged a raised-brow glance with Jess.

"I just asked if you were okay to go back down now. It's almost time to line up with the rest of the awardees."

Ivy hadn't heard a word. "Oh...yeah." Thinking about Jordan had stolen all of her senses. She stood, finished the remnants of her water and huffed. "Okay. Let's go."

"It's your night, sissy! We won't let anything or anyone ruin this for you," Zoe said. "Ready?" She stepped to Ivy and held out her elbow toward her.

"You're right." Ivy linked her arm in Zoe's.

"And I meant what I said earlier. If she says one more nasty word, I'll punch her right in that overly bronzed nose of hers."

All three women laughed.

When they stepped off the elevator on the same floor as the ballroom, one of the event managers rushed to Ivy.

"Ms. Blackwell!" a slender woman said urgently. "We've addressed Ms. Brown and advised that her behavior was both unacceptable and unbecoming of an honoree. You shouldn't have any more issues tonight. We sincerely apologize for her behavior and please let us know if you have any further issues with her tonight."

"Thank you," Ivy murmured politely. She was glad she held her composure.

Ivy smiled, held her head up and waltzed toward the waiting area where the rest of the honorees were now standing. Despite how the publicist took care of the situation, something told Ivy she'd still have to keep an eye on Kenya Brown.

From the corner of her eye, Ivy spotted Jordan.

"Give me one second," she said to Jess and Zoe.

Ivy walked over to Jordan, who was talking to one of the other honorees. She believed his name was Chris. "Jordan?" Ivy got his attention.

"Ivy." Jordan smiled. Ivy's stomach fluttered. Most would consider that bright-toothed smile to be professional, but for some reason, it looked incredibly sexy to her.

"Sorry to interrupt. Can I speak to you for a quick moment?" She nodded politely, acknowledging Chris.

"Sure. Excuse me, Chris." Jordan followed Ivy a few feet, placing distance between them, the network executive and the rest of the honorees.

"I just wanted to apologize. My greeting earlier was less than cordial. I had a situation…arise that I had to address immediately."

Jordan held up both hands. "No need to apologize. I understand."

"Thanks. Maybe I'll buy you dinner or something to

make up for it if things get started with the show you've proposed."

"You mean *when*, not if," Jordan said.

"Yes. When we get started with the show."

Silence expanded between them for a moment. Just when it started to get uncomfortable, Jordan asked, "Why wait? How about a celebratory drink after the event tonight? That would suffice."

"Oh. Um…" Ivy paused. His question was unexpected. She would love to have a drink with him, but wondered if she should.

"It's okay if you're not available. I was just…thinking…"

Ivy *was* available. She was staying at the hotel. Alone. Zoe and the rest of the family were heading back to their respective homes after the event. "I guess that would be fine. I'm actually staying here tonight so I wouldn't have to travel back home after this was over. I knew I'd be tired. So…sure."

"Great!" Jordan said. "We can meet at the bar, or one of the local places nearby. See you later." He tipped an imaginary hat and flashed that gorgeous smile of his.

"Yes. See you then." Her stomach fluttered at his smile. "I'm really a nice person." For some reason, Ivy felt a need to add that statement.

A bemused look spread across Jordan's face but he didn't respond. After a simple nod he started off before turning back to say, "And congratulations."

"Thank you," Ivy said, smiling back at him. She didn't move right away. Instead, she just stood there, watching Jordan leave. His gait was masculine and confident, just the way she liked. Rolling her eyes at her inner thoughts, Ivy snickered and made her way to the line moments before being called to make her entrance. Sporting a narrowed glare, Kenya watched her the whole time. Ivy ignored her. She'd deal with that pest later. This was *her* night and Zoe was right. She couldn't let Kenya ruin it. As excited as she was about this honor, she felt even more excitement growing inside her belly in anticipation of having a drink with Jordan later that evening.

# Ten

Jordan didn't expect to enjoy himself as much in Ivy's company. He'd pegged her as cordial but also rigid.

As they sat in a set of posh lounge chairs near the bar in the hotel lobby, Ivy told him about the encounter with the woman, Kenya, just before he had approached her. She also apologized for not being so nice when she greeted him. That really seemed to bother her, especially the fact that the woman called her pretentious. Ivy insisted that she was anything *but* pretentious. Jordan made note to keep his preconceived notion about her to himself forever.

Several times, as she recounted the story, Jordan found himself getting lost in studying her smooth brown skin, beautiful full lips and perfectly sculptured cheekbones. The rise of her neck was regal, almost majestic. He felt like he was in the presence of a queen. And that raspy voice of hers made her conversation sound like a song. Her hair, full and unruly, blossomed from her head in a perfect spray of curls that framed her face.

"Enough about me. Tell me more about yourself, Mr. Chambers. How did you get into television?"

Jordan picked up his snifter of scotch. "I've always been fascinated by movies and shows. I thought about being an actor but quickly realized that being in front of the camera wasn't for me."

"As handsome as you are, I'm sure you would have done well," Ivy said but then her smile dropped immediately as if she hadn't meant to say that. "I'm sorry. I wasn't trying to…"

Her embarrassment tickled him. He watched her shift in her seat and take sip of her own scotch. That intrigued him too. A woman that wasn't afraid of whiskey.

"Thank you," he said. "I just enjoyed being behind the camera much more. I like making up stories and decided to go to film school." Jordan sipped. "NYU."

"That's fantastic!"

"I wanted to go to UCLA, but I didn't want to be that far from my mom. Plus, NYU was doling out some really good scholarships at the time."

"So, you live in LA now?"

"Both. I have a place there and one here. My mom is still here."

"Got it."

"And you? What's your story?" Jordan asked. "At least the part you're willing to tell." He'd meant to be flirty… was testing the waters.

Ivy's smile gave him the response he had been looking for. She shared some of her background and talked about the new initiatives at Blackwell, which ended up being the catalyst for speaking and becoming an influencer. This woman was all kinds of intriguing, Jordan thought to himself. She was smart, innovative, ambitious and insanely sexy. Why didn't she have someone special in her life?

"Wow!" Jordan whispered when she finished speaking. "I have to ask. Are you single?"

Ivy sniffed out a laugh and playfully rolled her eyes toward the ceiling. "Yep."

"Why?" He really wanted to understand why someone hadn't tried to make her their wife yet.

Ivy side-eyed him. With her glass to her lips she asked, "You've been talking with my mother?"

That made him laugh. "You know what?" He held both arms up in surrender. "I'm sorry. Now I sound like my own mother, and yours too, I'm sure. Forgive me. I didn't mean to pry."

"Just busy." She answered him anyway. "That's all. No time for dating. I take it you're riding the single train too?"

"Yep." He raised his glass and took a sip.

"Why?" Ivy mocked and chuckled.

"Touché. Busy. Like you." Jordan looked directly into her eyes. For a moment, they were suspended in each other's gaze.

After a few seconds, both looked away and focused on the drinks in their hand. Silenced settled between them. Ivy looked around the bar like she was avoiding his gaze.

Maybe her being single made her even more attractive. Jordan cleared his throat, took one last sip and put his empty tumbler down on the table between them. Then he sat back in his chair and cuffed his chin in his hand. He felt warmth spread inside of him. It could have been the whiskey. More likely, it was probably his body's response to Ivy. The longer he sat with her, the more drawn he was to her.

Jordan summed Ivy up. Beyond the curves, beauty, melodic voice and strong presence, he liked her cool demeanor and could tell she had a take-charge kind of attitude. She wasn't exactly a girlie-girl, but a feminine power emanated from her. He didn't expect that from her after doing his research. But then again, he had just seen the glamorous highlight reel posted on social media. He realized he didn't know much about the real Ivy Blackwell at all.

Seeing her wrap her pretty red lips around that glass of whiskey created a feeling in his core that Jordan had never experienced but truly enjoyed. Most of the women in his life happened to enjoy wine or mixed drinks. None were ever bourbon or whiskey connoisseurs. If it hadn't been for the fact that they may be working together soon, he'd ask her out. Like Ivy, he had no time for dating, but wanted to get to know more about this fascinating woman.

Ivy leaned toward him to speak over the crowd that was growing louder. "It's getting pretty packed in here," she said, placing her empty glass down on the table as well.

Jordan took that as his cue. The night was ending even though he didn't want it to. "Yeah." He noticed there were lots more people in the lounge now than there was when they first arrived.

He'd been so into Ivy he hadn't realized the place had filled up. It seemed that someone turned up the volume. He noticed the background noise now, though. Blended languages and conversations created a buzzing backdrop.

Jordan waited to see what Ivy would do next. He wasn't going to be the first to stand. That would mark their time together as done and he refused to be the one to end their evening.

"Maybe there's someplace quieter?" he suggested huskily, leaning to her so she could hear him.

"I'd invite you to my room, Mr. Chambers, if I could trust you to behave…"

At first Jordan wasn't sure if she was joking or not. He questioned her statement with his furrowed brows and a squint.

"Easy, cowboy. I'm teasing. You're welcome to join me for another drink if you're not ready to head home. I have a great single malt up there that my sister-in-law bought me tonight. I'd like to try it out and I usually don't drink alone." Ivy looked around. "At least we will be able to hear each other talk."

Jordan smiled. She was witty and direct. He liked that about her. "I'd be happy to join you," he said, thrilled that she wasn't ready to end the night either.

Inside of Ivy's penthouse, he got comfortable in the living room, while she retreated to the bedroom to change out of her fancy dress. She returned in leggings and an Ivy League hoodie and looked just as alluring as before. Jordan had never considered a woman in a hoodie sexy until now.

"Neat or on the rocks?" she asked, approaching the mini-bar. She picked up the bottle and looked over the label.

"Neat works for me."

"I noticed that about you," Ivy said, taking two glasses to the sink at the wet bar to rinse them out. "And I agree. Especially with a single malt. I don't want to water down the flavor." She poured about an inch of the amber liquid into each glass and handed one to Jordan. "Wanna sit on the balcony? It's cool but still really nice out."

Jordan stood from his seated position on the couch and held out his hand, gesturing for her to go first. He followed closely behind.

Outside, they sat watching the stars that lit up the velvet sky while letting the autumn breeze wash over them. Moments passed without either of them speaking. There was nothing uncomfortable about the silence. Jordan basked in it as well as the breeze and his extended time with Ivy.

Taking another sip, he held out his glass and looked at it. He swirled the liquid around. "This is good."

"Isn't it." Ivy's voice was relaxed.

To Jordan her voice seemed deeper. Sexier. "So why

don't you have a significant other…?" Yep. He went there again.

Jordan watched a smile spread across her pretty face in the moonlight. Ivy chuckled.

"According to my last boyfriend, I'm not a good girl-friend."

Jordan hissed. "That was harsh."

"Humph. I agreed with him at the time."

"Seriously?" Jordan reared his head back. A sense of alarm shot through him.

"I really wasn't a good girlfriend—for *him*. Why do you ask?"

"I want to know. You're beautiful, smart, you like single malts." He shrugged and tilted his head matter-of-factly. Both of them laughed.

"Ha! Cute. I didn't meet his idea of what a girlfriend was supposed to be. I guess I'm…different. Oh. And I was way too busy for him. He complained that I never spent enough time with him. That was before I started doing all of this social media stuff and became an author. Now I may be doing a television show."

"*Will* be doing one. Not may be," Jordan corrected her.

"Yes. Okay. Will! Now that I'll also be doing a television show." She looked over at Jordan and smiled. "We never would have made it work. This would all be too much for him."

Jordan shook his head and sighed. "I never understood men who had issues with ambitious women."

"I'm okay with being single." Ivy sat back in her chair.

"Me too," he said. At least he was until now. Unraveling all that Ivy Blackwell represented made him want to know more. She was soft and strong. Elegant and grounded. The dichotomy of her fascinated him.

"What will your next boyfriend be like?" Jordan continued to push the issue. He wanted know.

"Whenever that happens," Ivy said with a wry laugh. Then, growing serious, she tilted her head to the side, seeming to think about Jordan's question. After a while she continued. "A friend," she said quietly, looking past him. "I want my next boyfriend to be my friend."

Jordan felt something heavy in her response. It made him want to hug her.

"What about you? What will your next one be like?" She spun the inquisition back to him.

Jordan thought for a moment. "Present," he said, following her lead on heavy responses. He thought about his ex. Even when they were together, she was never truly present with him. Maybe that's what was so intriguing about being with Ivy. In their short time together, she was fully there with him.

"Hmm. Nice." She sipped from her glass and looked out over the skyline.

The two sat silently for several moments. Then Ivy turned to him and stared directly into his eyes. Her voice was soft. "Maybe the next ones won't leave these voids."

The weight of her response settled between them. The acknowledgment of both of them being unfulfilled linked them in that moment. Ivy hadn't taken her eyes off him. Returning her gaze, he summed things up again. That's why they both worked hard. They had voids to fill.

Desire for Ivy rose in his chest, nearly choking him. He looked at her pretty lips and wanted to kiss away the sadness in her eyes. There was something else in her eyes. It resembled yearning. The same that was in his soul. He hadn't noticed it until that moment.

Compelled by all that he was feeling, Jordan put his glass down, stepped over to Ivy and closed the distance between them. He knelt down and touched her chin. She continued looking straight into his eyes. He studied her. Jordan wanted to press his lips against hers but not without permission. Something about this beautiful, captivating woman drew him in. He leaned closer but knew he couldn't be the one to initiate a kiss. Blinking, he tried to tamp down the craving swirling inside of him. Then Ivy lifted her chin. Her lips were mere inches from his. Jordan willed himself to be still. They were caught in each other's gaze. Ivy's lips parted slightly. She closed her eyes and came closer, inch by inch, until her lips touched his.

When their lips finally connected, a hot trail blazed through his belly. Taking her face in his hands, Jordan kissed Ivy with a hunger he didn't realize he'd possessed. Before he knew it, they were standing, and Jordan slid his arms around her waist. Ivy's hands rubbed up and down his torso as they devoured one another in the kiss. Breathless, they continued. Jordan felt himself grow hard inside his slacks and then pressed intimately against her. He had to stop. If not, he would drown in his own desire. It took all of his strength for him to pull away. When he did, they just stared at each other again. He wanted more and could tell she did too.

"Thank you," he whispered.

She returned a breathy, "No. Thank you."

"I better go."

Ivy pressed her lips together and nodded in agreement.

Slowly, Jordan removed his hands from around her waist. The moment he released her, he was reminded of the coolness of the night. He backed away to keep himself from reaching for her again. Ivy touched her lips, cleared her throat and then walked past him. He followed her to the door. She opened it, swallowed and gave him a small smile. Jordan ran his thumb across her cheek and touched her lip. He couldn't help it. Just one more touch of that supple skin was all he needed to take with him.

This time, Jordan was the one who swallowed and cleared his throat. His eyes were on hers. Finally, he nodded and willed himself out of her hotel room. The door connected behind him slowly. He stood still and took a long, deep breath and pondered all that could have happened.

# Eleven

"**Y**ou *what*?" Zoe screamed and immediately covered her mouth.

"Zoe! Shhh." Ivy looked around the restaurant at all the eyes staring back at them. It was just before nine in the morning.

"You kissed him?" This time Zoe whispered. "Who initiated the kiss?"

"Me. Well, both of us," Ivy admitted. "He came over to me and leaned in but stopped. I took that as him asking permission and by then I wanted to kiss him too, so I sealed the deal."

"Then what happened?" Zoe asked.

Ivy looked at her watch. Dale would be arriving any minute.

"Nothing. He left after that and boy am I glad he did. I'm not sure what would have happened. There was so much chemistry between us!"

"So, are you going to see him again?" her sister-in-law asked.

"Here's the crazy part, Zoe. I don't even have a number for him. I'd have to call my agent to get in touch with him."

"You have got to be kidding me." Zoe covered her sharp bark of laughter with her hand. She shook her head. "Do you *want* to see him again?"

"I'd like to but I don't think it will make sense to bother. He has a place here in the city but spends most of his time in LA. His schedule is crazy busy and so is mine. Not to mention mine is about to get busier with this book coming out and I can't forget about the show. He's convinced that it's going to happen. If we hook up, that will probably make things more awkward."

"You're right. But it's been forever since you dated."

"That's probably why I kissed him. I forgot what it was like to kiss a man." Ivy threw her head back and laughed.

"I'm sure!" Zoe said sarcastically and laughed too. "If he called you, *would* you see him again?"

"I doubt it. I don't like mixing business with pleasure..."

"That's fair! Okay. Let's talk about Dale." Zoe clasped her hands together and changed the subject.

The two of them had a half hour to prepare for their meeting with Dale. Ivy wanted to smooth things over with her and try to recover the deal.

"You know I don't get nervous, but I'm anxious about this meeting."

"I know. Dale was pretty upset about what happened. She felt slighted. I did everything I could to convince her that it was okay that you weren't there. But she wasn't buying it. Dale wants to deal with you, not me. She's not like our other clients."

"I know. Dad still seems angry with me. I also think working with Dale will be good for so many reasons. First of all, her investment portfolio is huge. Also, I'd love to pull her in on some of my speaking engagements."

"Maybe that will win her over," Zoe said. "I believe that's why she was adamant about working with you. She loves the spotlight. Does she know about the book?"

"No," Ivy said. "Let's go over what we want to say. We'll tag team on these items." She pointed to the bulleted points in her notes.

Ivy and Zoe went over their game plan until Dale made her entrance. She walked in, dressed in sky blue from head to toe—a fedora, light jacket to ward off the autumn breeze, blouse, trousers and pumps. Dale stepped in and looked around as if waiting for one of the waiters to come take her jacket. Ivy waved her over. She lifted her chin acknowledging Ivy before prancing in their direction. Ivy and Zoe shared a quick glance and stifled a laugh. If anyone was pretentious, it was certainly Dale Billington.

"Ladies!" Dale nodded at both of them as they stood.

"Good morning, Dale," Zoe said.

"I'm so glad you could make it," Ivy added.

Dale looked behind her as if someone was going to pull out her chair. She huffed and slid it back and sat down. "I squeezed you in. I don't have much time. I have another meeting downtown after this."

"These busy schedules are a killer, right?" Zoe sympathized. "Will you have something to eat?"

"Yes, but something quick. I'm starving."

Zoe waved the waiter over. Ivy and Zoe ordered something simple from the menu. But Dale, on the other hand, required avocado toast and rearranged everything else that came with it to fit to her liking. "I only want the eggs if they're cage free. Please put my seasoning on the side. I'd like extra tomatoes, and orange juice only if it's freshly squeezed. And please bring me a steaming cup of coffee

ASAP." She practically shooed the waiter away before turning her attention back to Ivy and Zoe.

"I'm going to cut to the chase, Dale. I'll start by apologizing for being late for the meeting. I'll have to let you in on a secret to explain why but you have to promise not to say a word to anyone."

The woman raised both brows and sat up straighter. "Hmm. Confidentiality. I can handle that."

Ivy explained everything. The more she talked, the wider Dale smiled. By the time she was done talking about the book and the television show, Dale was smiling from ear to ear.

Ivy ended by saying, "With that said, I think we will be able to work together in more ways than one. I see it being mutually beneficial."

Dale leaned aside while the waiter placed their breakfast in front of them. "I knew you were a gem. Congratulations and I forgive you." After chewing a bit of avocado, Dale asked a few more questions about Ivy's new endeavors. She seemed genuinely interested. "This all sounds so wonderful."

"I'm really excited." Ivy glanced over at Zoe, who looked like she'd released a breath she'd been holding in for hours.

She was getting ready to dig into her meal when she heard Dale say, "But I'll have to think about transferring my portfolio to Blackwell…"

Ivy and Zoe exchanged glances once again.

"Can I ask why?" Zoe asked.

"Sure. I completely support you in all of these wonderful opportunities. However, my concern is this— with all that Ivy will have on her plate, leaving you, Zoe, to do most of the managing of my portfolio, which is quite significant, I wonder how much attention you will be able to pay to my investments. It's your combined brilliance that attracted me to Blackwell and without you—" Dale looked at Zoe and then Ivy "—managing my assets as a team, then who will? You sold me on your financial savvy. With you out of the picture, I'm not so sure about this." Dale cut her knife into a slice of her avocado toast as if what she had just said didn't make Ivy's heart drop into her stomach.

For a quick moment, Ivy was at a loss for words. Her plan backfired. Instead of using her opportunities to secure the business, it seemed to be the one thing that could drive the woman's business away.

"Rest assured, Dale, that our savvy is still very much part of the strategy for our women's investment initiatives and will especially be integral to managing your portfolio."

"I'm sure you believe that."

Ivy kept her composure as she watched Dale enjoy her breakfast. She'd lost her own appetite.

"Dale, I will always be part of the Blackwell team. My book tour will only be a few weeks and my understanding about the show is that it will require only a couple of weeks of filming. I can assure you that your investments will be safe with us as it is for all of our amazing clients."

Dale shopped chewing and sat back.

No one spoke for several moments. Ivy hoped a "yes" was brewing.

"I'll have to give this some thought," Dale finally said.

"Of course! I know you're busy. But how about we give you a moment to think about it. In the meantime, we'll provide you with a few details about our recommendations for your portfolio and we can schedule to meet in about three weeks," Ivy suggested.

"I'll have my assistant connect yours to get something on our calendars," Zoe added.

Dale inhaled and exhaled with a groan. "I'll take a look at the information." She didn't commit to anything else. "By far these people have the best avocado toast in the city." Dale closed her eyes and savored the flavor.

"Yes. Their food is pretty good," Ivy said, forcing a smile but feeling deflated.

Dale looked at her cell phone. "Oh! I need to get going." She wiped her mouth, put her napkin down and pushed back from the table.

Zoe and Ivy stood with her. "It's always a pleasure spending time with you," Ivy said.

Dale held out her arms and Ivy stepped into her embrace. Then she hugged Zoe and gave them both air kisses.

"Thanks for breakfast, ladies. I'll be in touch." Dale dialed someone on her cell phone. "I'll be right there," she told them and pranced out of the restaurant the same way she'd pranced in.

Once again, Zoe and Ivy looked at each other. Zoe shook her head as they sat back down. Neither of them had touched their food. Ivy grunted.

"We're not giving up," Zoe declared.

"No. We're not," Ivy agreed but Dale's words stuck with her. Her concern was valid. How was Ivy supposed to manage it all? She had been so sure they were going to close this deal with Dale over breakfast, but now who knew? Ivy sighed. Dale Billington would have become their biggest female client. Her business would have led to other big clients. Her dad, Bill, was expecting them to come back with a sealed deal as well.

The scariest thought was, what if other clients started to feel the same way? She'd promised her father that taking on this extra stuff wouldn't affect her work at Blackwell. But it did—more and more each day.

Ivy heard Zoe ask the waitress to wrap their food. She then said that she was ordering a car to take them back to the office. Thoughts about losing clients continued to plague Ivy as they paid the bill and headed out of the restaurant.

While they were waiting for the car to arrive, Ivy's phone

vibrated. She checked her text messages and then opened her Instagram app. Her largest number of followers were on Instagram. Checking it regularly had become a habit. In a heap of direct messages, she spotted one that had just come in from Jordan. Ivy remembered their kiss. She felt his lips on hers. He'd taken her breath away. Although she hadn't planned to see him again, she smiled.

# Twelve

After kissing Ivy, Jordan headed back to his apartment in Manhattan. He'd slept better that night than he had in days. Is that what a woman did for a man who hadn't dated in a while? Yet early the next morning, as he prepared for his flight back to LA, he scolded himself for succumbing to his desires. He'd left at just the right time. Any longer and who knows what could have happened.

Jordan didn't want things to get awkward between the two of them. He really wanted this show to work. Networks were hungry for content and he needed to make sure he could continuously supply them with innovative show ideas. Since the explosion of all of the subscription television services, business had been wild. Things moved fast, and to stay on top of the game, his company had to keep up with the frenzied pace or get left behind.

As he packed, he wondered if he should tell Anderson about what had happened. He was never a man who would kiss and tell, but this could interfere with business, and if it did, Anderson would need to know. Jordan decided to keep his colleague on a need-to-know basis.

Thoughts of Ivy invaded his mind all the way to the airport. He wanted to call her. Jordan didn't expect to start a whole relationship based on one kiss, but he also didn't want to seem like a jerk either. He wasn't the type to kiss and disappear. If nothing ever happened between them again, he needed to at least make sure things between them were going to be okay moving forward.

Picking up his phone, Jordan realized he didn't have a telephone number for Ivy. Anderson had been in contact with her publisher and agent. Neither of them had called the Money Maven directly. Jordan tapped his Instagram icon and left a direct message.

Good morning, Ivy. Congratulations again on your award. It was great hanging with you last night. Please know that I don't have any weird expectations after yesterday. I look forward to working with you. Let's do lunch the next time you're in LA or the next time I'm in New York. Take care.

Jordan hoped his message would be received the way he intended. Simple and direct was what he was going for. He'd love to kiss her again and do so much more, but didn't want to assume too much or cause any issues while they worked together. All the same, Jordan was going to cherish that kiss in case he never got to feel Ivy's lips on his again.

Jordan pulled out his laptop in the airport lounge to get some work done while he waited for his plane to board. He checked his phone a few times to see if Ivy had responded. The last time, he laughed at himself. How had she gotten to him so quickly that he was checking his phone for her to reply? Sighing, he picked up his phone one last time. There was still no reply to his direct message. More than two hours had passed.

Jordan sent one last message. I realized we never exchanged numbers. I figured it would make sense since we will be working together soon. Take care.

Jordan was done—allegedly. No more messages and no more checking to see if she messaged him back. It was time to move on. All they shared was a kiss. It was an incredible kiss but it was just one. It didn't mean anything. She may never respond and that was okay with Jordan. He needed to get back to work. There were tons of emails awaiting his attention.

Despite his attempt to focus, his mind kept wandering to thoughts of Ivy. Flashes of her in her beautiful gown played in his mind's eye. Then he saw her curled up in the chair on her balcony dressed in a hoodie and leggings, nursing a glass of scotch. The last image enticed him as much as her in the gorgeous gown. Thoughts and visuals accompanied him all the way back to LA.

"Over here!" Jordan heard Anderson say when he exited the terminal at LAX.

He shielded his eyes from the beaming West Coast sun. Spotting Anderson, he lifted his chin and headed toward him. "What's up, man?" They shook hands.

Jordan tapped the trunk. Anderson popped it open with his key fob. After dumping his bag inside, Jordan jumped into the passenger seat of Anderson's Aston Martin.

"How was the rest of your trip? The family is all good?" his friend asked as he pulled into the line of cars heading toward the airport exit.

"They're all good," Jordan said, looking out the window. He loved New York but really missed LA whenever he left.

"The stepfather too?" Anderson asked.

Jordan raised a brow. He referred to that man as his mother's husband, not his stepdad. "He's fine, I guess."

"You decided not to help?"

"I actually never spoke to him about it. Dorian and I

met with my mother. She wanted a little time to speak to Timothy."

"So, you've decided to help him out."

"I'm going to help my *mother* out."

"Got it."

For a while Jordan sat quietly, taking in the California landscape. "So. Guess who I saw last night?"

"Who?"

"Ivy Blackwell. She was at the same awards ceremony as Chris. She was getting an award too."

"Cool! See I told you. She's hot right now. All of this will help with the show. I hope the network moves fast on this. We need to lock it in ASAP to take advantage of her publishing timelines."

"Yeah. I know." Jordan grew quiet again. Apparently, his silence appeared suspicious to Anderson. He could feel him looking at him through his periphery.

"And?" his friend asked.

"What?" Jordan said.

"Man. I've known you way too long. What's going on?"

"Nah. Nothing. It's just that…you know." Jordan was purposely beating around the bush.

"Spit it out!"

Jordan laughed. "We had a few drinks after the awards dinner. Then she invited me up to her penthouse."

"What!" Anderson's eyes widened. His foot hit the brake and the car behind them blared its horn. "Sorry." Anderson held up his hand to the driver. "Don't tell me you…"

"No!"

"Whoa! I was going to say that's not even like you. That's something *I* would have done," he admitted. Both Anderson and Jordan laughed.

"So, what happened?"

"None of that. We talked, exchanged a few kisses. Then I left. Now I'm home."

"What the—" Anderson shook his head. "You're trying to make me crash! So, what's next?"

"Nothing!"

"Nothing! You're losing your touch, man."

"I don't even have her number. I had to DM her to let her know it was cool hanging with her."

"You've been out of the game way too long, dude. Do you need a refresher course on women?"

"From you? Ha! Hell, no. I'm just chilling. I don't want her to feel pressured while we're trying to work out this deal. I'd hate for her to think she'd have to sleep with me to move things forward. We have to be careful."

"Okay, okay. You're right. So, wait until after everything is done and go for it after that." Anderson shook his head. "I have to admit…that girl is gorgeous!"

"She definitely is. And she seems cool, but I've seen sides of her that I'm still not so sure about."

"I get that," Anderson said as he maneuvered the car into a parking lot on Ventura Boulevard. "Let's go make this next deal happen, bruh!"

"Yeah, let's do it," Jordan said. They exited the car and headed to a lunch meeting with another network.

As a team, they handled business as usual but Jordan still couldn't keep his mind from traveling to thoughts of Ivy. Parts of her were still a mystery that he wanted to unravel.

# Thirteen

Ivy was startled awake by the banging at her front door. Yawning, she sat up and blinked at her cell phone until the numbers came into focus. She'd missed several calls and texts.

"Oh, no!" Ivy threw the covers back and jumped out of the bed. She was late. No. She was *more* than late. Ivy was supposed to meet her mother, Lydia, and her sisters-in-law—Zoe, as well as Phoenix and Lincoln's wife, Britney—for brunch over two hours ago. She'd overslept again. Their monthly outing was Lydia's idea to keep the women of the Blackwell family connected. No husbands, brothers or children allowed. It was their time to eat and shop.

Lydia was going to have a few choice words for Ivy. Last month, Ivy hadn't made it because she was traveling for a conference. Her mom wasn't happy about that but understood that it was business. Ivy put one leg into her lounge pants and hopped to the door. She could hear Phoenix and

Zoe on the other side. She pulled the door open and slapped her hand across her forehead.

"I'm so sorry!"

Zoe and Phoenix looked at Ivy, before looking at each other, shaking their heads and laughing. It wasn't them she had to worry about. Ivy stepped aside and waved Zoe and Phoenix into her sunlit foyer. Ivy looked past them and caught the irritated look in her mother's eye as she marched up the walk with Britney at her side.

"We brought you brunch. You'll want to eat fast so we can get to the stores. You know shopping calms your mother's nerves." Zoe held up a bag from the restaurant, kissed Ivy's cheek and then made her way to the kitchen to set the bag down.

Phoenix hugged Ivy. "How are you doing?"

Ivy huffed and shrugged.

"I know," Phoenix said. She headed to the kitchen behind Zoe. That was the designated meeting spot in Ivy's home when the girls got together.

"You haven't even showered?" Lydia's voice rang through Ivy's two-story foyer, laced with irritation.

"Hi, Mom."

Lydia stood planted in the doorway blinking at her daughter.

"Hey, Ivy," Britney said as she hugged Ivy and went off to the kitchen with the other girls.

Ivy knew they were getting out of the way of Lydia's annoyance. Despite the scowl she sported, Lydia looked stunning as always. Several weeks ago, she shocked everyone by shaving one side of her hair and cutting her long hair into a stylish one-sided bob. No one ever guessed that Lydia was in her sixties. Now with her new hairstyle, designer bag, mocha sweater dress and matching boots, Lydia looked even younger, despite her salt-and-pepper tresses. It almost looked as if she'd colored her hair that way.

With arms folded across her chest, Lydia glared at Ivy. She felt herself shrinking inside her mother's glare, but she shook that off with a groan.

"I'm sorry, Ma! I overslept."

Lydia finally stepped all the way in and pushed the door hard behind her. "And you look like you just dragged yourself from under your bed. Your eyes are dark and baggy. You're overextending yourself, and for the life of me, I can't understand why. You want for nothing!"

"That's not the point, Mom!" Ivy locked the door behind them.

"Then what is?" Lydia folded her arms again. She cocked her head to the side and demanded a response with her stern expression.

Ivy closed her eyes and inhaled.

"I like what I do, Ma. Not to mention it's benefitting the company."

"Oh, yeah? What about Dale Billington?"

Ivy looked away, trying to contain her frustration. Her parents wouldn't let her live that down. "I'm working on that," she said. Lydia raised her brow but held her rigid stance. "Wine?" Ivy asked but didn't stick around for an answer. She walked off toward the kitchen, got a bottle of her mother's favorite red. She poured her a glass, then set it on the massive marble island. "Let me go freshen up before I eat my breakfast."

"Go right ahead," Britney said.

"Yes! 'Cause I can smell you from here," Zoe said and laughed. Phoenix and Britney snickered. Lydia's face was stoic. The girls looked at the older woman and then each other before stifling their laughs.

It was obvious that Ivy and Zoe were closer than the others. They were similar in so many ways and they worked together daily at Blackwell since Ivy joined the team after Carter left to start his business.

Ivy playfully rolled her eyes and dismissed Zoe's jest with a wave. "Maybe I won't brush my teeth and then I can sit next to you in the car and talk all the way."

Phoenix and Britney fell out laughing.

"Don't encourage her," Zoe said, laughing too. "She just might do that."

"Oh! Hurry. We're already late," Lydia huffed, taking a place at the island before sipping her wine. "And put some cream under those eyes. You look like a raccoon."

"Oh, thanks, Ma!" Ivy said in a feigned cheerfulness. Arguing with her mother wouldn't be worth it. They were already on rocky terms.

Ivy dressed in record time and returned to the kitchen with the rest of the ladies. She was glad to hear her mother laughing along with the others when she stepped back in the room. Hopefully Lydia's annoyed state had dissipated.

"It took you long enough," Lydia said but complimented her on the cashmere sweater, jeans and knee-high boots she'd changed into. "Your eyes still look tired."

"Because I *am* tired, Mom." Ivy was becoming exasperated.

"I told you that you need to slow down. I don't know how else to say it."

"And, Mother, I told you I can handle it."

"Really? This is the third time this week you overslept. That's not like you. What time did you get to the office yesterday?" Lydia stood from the stool at the island and parked her hands on her hips.

Ivy simply averted her eyes.

"Exactly. Lately you're either late or missing stuff altogether. We called you at least ten times while we were at the restaurant. Did you even hear your phone ring? You fell asleep in church last Sunday. In fact, any time we sit still for more than five minutes you start yawning. Those bags around your eyes are becoming relentless. And don't think it's just me that notices all of this." Lydia looked from Phoenix to Zoe to Britney.

The girls tilted their heads, each giving a look showing their confirmation and compassion. Lydia was right.

"Every one of us has expressed concern about your well-being these past few weeks. Every time someone says something to you, you brush us off or get irritated. Next thing you know, we'll be visiting you in the hospital because of the toll this is taking on you." Lydia shook her head in frustration.

"I'm fine. I just have to get past a few deadlines. That's all."

"Listen." Her mother stepped over to Ivy and gently lifted her chin. "We're worried about you. We can get over missed brunches and your apparent lack of focus at times, but you've taken on too much and refuse to listen to anyone when we try to tell you to take a break. By all means, enjoy life, live your dreams, but don't let them take you out."

Ivy felt a tear threaten to trickle down her face. She blinked fast, moved away from the girls and headed to the fridge to grab a bottle of water. "I said I'll be fine."

"Oh, honey!" Lydia wrapped her arms around Ivy. "I'd recognize that stubbornness anywhere. You got it from me."

Ivy received her mother's embrace. It had been a long time since she felt it. She pulled back from her mother, looked at the others, then spoke. "Can we be done with the 'Let's pick on Ivy' session and just go shopping now?"

"See. That's the irritability we were talking about. Come on, Groucho, let's go buy something nice," Zoe said, which made everyone chuckle.

"Maybe we can find her a nice man while we're out shopping," Lydia smarted.

"Mom!"

"Well, if you would settle down I wouldn't have to worry

about you so much. Live a little. You plan on being single all your life?"

"Don't start that again, Mom. Please!" Ivy's singleness wasn't by choice. She didn't have the strength needed for this conversation with her mother.

"All right! Okay!" Lydia waved dismissively and then winked at Zoe, Phoenix and Britney.

Ivy narrowed her eyes at Zoe and all the girls laughed.

"I'm not driving either," Ivy said. "I'm too tired." Her commend dripped with sarcasm.

Lydia furrowed her brow at Ivy. The others snickered.

The women stepped down from their stools at the kitchen island and started toward the door. Lydia led the line. Zoe hung back waiting for Ivy to lock up while the others headed to Britney's luxury SUV.

"Ivy," Zoe called her name quietly. "Did you see this?" Her sister-in-law held her phone up so Ivy could see. One of the social media gossip sites posted side-by-side images of Ivy and Kenya Brown with the headline about Kenya calling her a pretentious bitch.

Ivy drew in a sharp breath and blew it out with a groan. She felt her face grow warm. "How did this get out?"

"I'm sure she's responsible. This is probably why she picked a fight with you in the first place. I think what Jess said is true. This woman is using you to gain fame."

Ivy held her hands up. "What does she think? We're in some reality show?"

"Let's have the agency deal with it," Zoe suggested. "I just wanted to make sure you saw it before anyone came asking about it. Let's go enjoy what's left of our Blackwell ladies day out."

"Thanks. I hope no one comes asking. This is embarrassing." Most of all, Ivy hoped no one else in her family would see the post.

Britney tooted the horn.

"We're coming!" Ivy yelled as she and Zoe picked up their pace toward the car.

Inside the car, the conversation between the women was lively. Ivy would occasionally nod absently, smile or fling a quick comment into the conversation. Her mind was far away from what was going on as she settled into her own thoughts while watching the leaves begin to change on the trees as they drove by. She noticed Zoe watching her a few times. She probably figured Ivy was concerned about the social media post she'd just shown her but so much more weighed heavily on her mind, including her mother's words.

Despite "having it all," Ivy had goals she wanted to accomplish on her own. Yes. She was tired a lot. But it wouldn't always be that way. She'd be able to take a break soon enough and promised to schedule some time off right after the first leg of her book tour.

But if she was completely honest, the emotional toll was also part of the cause of her irritability. Her family was close. They were her anchor. But now her father was angry with her. Her mother was always on her back about slowing down and doing better at work. Whenever Ivy did slow down, she was reminded that despite the love of her family, she was lonely. She blamed herself for always pushing her boyfriends away with her ambition.

Lydia constantly reminded Ivy of her single status. Did she think Ivy chose to be single? She was the only one left out of her brothers that couldn't seem to manage a relationship for more than a few months. She wasn't trying to be the ultimate bachelorette. Even Carter was married now. He was the brother they all thought would be single forever.

Ivy desperately wanted to have success beyond what her parents had laid out for her. She needed to have something of her own, like her brothers. That didn't make her less proud to be a Blackwell. Why couldn't she have had love and success at the same time? Wasn't that possible?

Ivy's mind drifted to all the texts, emails and callbacks that were piling up. She still hadn't responded to Jordan's direct message because, to be frank, she wasn't sure what to say. That kiss still had her reeling. Dating him wouldn't be a good look since they could end up working together. Never could she have been accused of dating her way into an opportunity, or worse, sleeping her way to the top. And the show…

This would be a reality show. Would it bring more negative attention like the kind she was getting because of Kenya Brown? If so, she didn't want to be associated with anything like that.

But there was something about Jordan that she liked. Yes. He was smart and successful but something about his presence heightened all of her senses. She felt him in the room before she saw him enter. He was more than sexy. Something undeniable and combustible resided between them.

Ivy welcomed the idea of getting to know Jordan better despite a rocky start. She wanted to find out what made him tick. Jordan didn't seem put off by her busy schedule. He had one himself. It's just that the timing wasn't right at all. How could she fit him into her life? She'd probably push Jordan away like she had with other men she dated. With all that she had going on, Ivy didn't even have the emotional capacity to deal with a man. She wanted to respond to Jordan. Ivy thought of him often—especially the kiss they shared—but she needed more time.

After the tour, she promised to take a little time off. And after she found out about the show, maybe she would consider kissing Jordan Chambers again.

# Fourteen

Jordan arrived at his office earlier than usual in preparation for the meeting with his team, Ivy's and the network that had accepted his pitch for the show. From this point forward, he'd wanted to keep all communications between him and the Money Maven professional and cordial. But that didn't stop him from looking forward to seeing her at their upcoming meeting.

Jordan had gotten the message loud and clear that she wasn't interested in anything more. Weeks had passed since he'd last seen or heard from Ivy. To date, she'd never responded to his DM. All communication between them went through their teams. Contracts had been reviewed on all sides and now it was time to talk about their production schedule. If he wanted to pursue anything further with Ivy, it would have to wait.

Jordan took special care in preparing for the meeting, not just professionally, but personally. He was meticulous in choosing his outfit, a stylish sweater, dress pants and designer shoes. This was way dressier that he'd normally wear to the office but he was going to see Ivy today. Jordan couldn't half-step. He added a light spray of his favorite cologne. The scent was fresh and clean. Jordan wanted the fact that he would be around Ivy to be no big deal. Yet he anticipated her arrival with every part of his being. The truth was, before he ever put his lips on Ivy, she'd already intrigued him. If anything, he would follow her lead. There was more to know about Ivy Blackwell. Their time together in New York had only allowed him to touch the surface.

Jordan looked at his watch once more. The meeting was scheduled to start soon, though not soon enough as far as he was concerned. He wondered how Ivy would respond to seeing him. Just then, he thought about how large her following was. It was possible that she'd never even seen his message. Perhaps it was buried in a sea of hundreds of other DMs? In that moment a wave of hoped passed through him. He'd rather she had not seen the message at all than to see it and ignore it.

Burying himself in his work, Jordan was startled when the office assistant knocked and then peeked her head inside his office.

"Ms. Blackwell and her team have arrived and the network will be up shortly."

"Thank you, Kayla."

Ivy was in the building. A smile spread across his face as he closed out the programs on his laptop and shut it down.

He caught up with Anderson on the way to the conference room. He spotted Ivy through the glass wall and felt a tightening in his stomach. Once inside, it was all business. Jordan and his team greeting everyone with a firm handshake and a professional demeanor.

"Ms. Blackwell." Jordan nodded cordially when he greeted her.

"Great to see you again, Mr. Chambers," she responded

with a tight smile, receiving his firm handshake and returning just the right amount of firmness.

Jordan tried to be discreet. His gaze swept over Ivy
quickly. He never imagined a woman could look so sexy
in a suit. His eyes made their way to her lips. He remembered how soft they felt when they kissed. He remembered
the fire that ignited in his belly when her lips met his. He
pulled himself together.

"Let's get started." Jordan clasped his hands together
before sitting at the head of the conference table.

They got right down to business. Within the hour, they'd
determined a full schedule of dates for picking show participants, studios, filming, postproduction and promos. Input
from the network included having all show participants be
celebrities with terrible spending habits. The show, titled
*Fix My Finances*, would be filmed in LA over a four-week
period. The pilot season would consist of six episodes. Ivy
asked plenty of good questions. It was obvious she wasn't
privy to the world of television. All they needed now was
confirmation from the studio and other partners to make
sure the schedule would work with everyone involved.

By the end of the meeting, Ivy smiled, but that smile
didn't reach her eyes. Jordan wasn't sure what had happened since he'd last spoken to her after that awards ceremony. He thought she was excited about the show. What
changed?

As everyone filed out of the conference room, Jordan
called Ivy's name.

At first, he studied her when she turned to him. He
couldn't read her expression. Again, he wondered if she'd
seen his message.

"Just wondering about your thoughts after today. Are
you still excited?" he asked.

"Of course," Ivy said, but didn't sound convincing. Her
demeanor seemed rigid.

Jordan studied her another moment. She averted her eyes.

"Who wouldn't be excited?" she reiterated, looking toward the door.

"Am I...holding you up?" Jordan scrunched his brows as he asked.

"Um. No! I do have to get ready for a book signing this evening. I just got in early this morning and I'm a bit tired. Jet lag setting in already. That's all." Ivy shifted her weight from one foot to the other. "My schedule is booked solid while I'm here in LA. But...as for the show—yes, I'm excited. I just have to work out some things on my end schedule-wise. Know what I mean?"

He narrowed his eyes at Ivy. Something was off with her. She didn't seem the same. The spark was gone. Perhaps she didn't want to be bothered with him. Or maybe now that it was confirmed that they would be working together, she felt awkward about the kiss they shared. Maybe she was fighting her feelings just like he was.

Jordan looked around to make sure no one was in earshot before speaking. He spoke softly. "I hope you don't feel awkward about—"

"No!" she interrupted. Her tone was sharp and louder than expected. She looked around before saying in a lower tone, "I'm fine. This is a professional relationship now."

Jordan held his hands up. "Yes, it is. I look forward to working with you." He straightened his back. He felt coolness emanating from her but nevertheless he had to feel her out.

Ivy offered another tight smile and nodded. "Me too."

"Is everything okay with us?" he asked outright.

"Yes. It's fine. Really. I just have a lot going on." Ivy seemed sincere when she said that.

Jordan felt a bit relieved.

"Your signing this evening. Where is it? Maybe some

of us can come support you—perhaps get a few photos of you signing books. We could use it for the show."

"Oh. Sure. Good idea! It's a great bookstore that's been around for years. They get a lot of bookings for big signings. My publicist thought it would be a good place to do a signing while I was here. I'll send you the address."

"Good. Text it to me," Jordan said.

Ivy hesitated for a moment. "Sure." She pulled out her phone. "What's your number?"

Once he gave it to her, she sent the link.

Jordan tapped on it and studied the information. "I know this store. We've filmed there a few times."

"Great." Ivy covered an elongated yawn.

"Sorry to be such a bore," Jordan teased.

That got a chuckle out of her. "I'm sorry. I'd better get going."

"Good luck with the signing. I'll see you there. Maybe…" Jordan was about to say they could go for a drink after but decided to keep his suggestion to himself. "I'll get a copy for my mother."

"I'll make sure to put in a special message for her." Her smile seemed genuine to Jordan for the first time since the meeting started.

"That would be nice. Thanks."

"See you later," Ivy said and turned to leave without waiting for his response.

Jordan wasn't sure what has just happened but he was glad that he'd get to see her again at the bookstore.

Back in his office, he put his head down and got deep into his work. Later he shared the fact that Ivy would be signing at the bookstore. Unfortunately, Anderson couldn't make it. His assistant, Kayla, had a family dinner. Jordan decided to attend alone and take a few pictures on his cell phone. They'd have more chances to get footage of Ivy for the show promos.

He went home to freshen up before going over to the book signing. Again, he took meticulous care in his attire and chosen scent. He arrived right on time. The line was snaked outside the store and down the block. He hadn't expected so many people. How was she going to sign books for all these people in an hour? He pressed his way inside and searched for the owner. There was no way he was standing in that line. There had to be at least a hundred people waiting to see her. Jordan was impressed.

The owner, a short, gray-haired woman named Pat, greeted him with a big hug and warm smile.

"You here to see the Money Maven?" She let out a big laugh. "She's a looker. Isn't she?"

"Actually, yes. And she is quite beautiful. We're working with her."

"Oh, good! How exciting!" She clapped her hands together. "Follow me. I'll take you to her."

Pat grabbed Jordan's hand and navigated through the crowd until she was at Ivy's side. "Ms. Blackwell. You have company."

Ivy looked up at the older woman. "Thanks, Pat."

"No problem. And I'll have someone bring you some more water."

She nodded appreciatively, then turned toward Jordan after Pat hurried off. "Hi," Ivy said. She smiled, but again, it didn't reach her tired eyes.

Jordan empathized with her. He knew what it was like to feel as though he were running on fumes.

"Hey!" he said back. "Nice crowd." He looked around again, seeing nothing but heads over the shelves. "Do your thing. Mind if I take a few pictures while you're signing?"

"No problem," Ivy said.

Jordan stepped out of the way. He took pictures of Ivy scribbling her signature in each book and caught a few shots of the enthused crowd.

Ivy's agent and publisher flanked her on both sides, opening books to the title pages and placing sticky notes with people's names inside. Jordan captured all of that. Then he stuck around until the end of the signing, which was well beyond an hour by the time they cut the line off. Had they allowed people to keep coming, Ivy would have been in the bookstore beyond closing.

When she was done, Pat had her sign a few extra copies and told her she would put stickers on those books to let people know they had been autographed by her.

Once they cleared out all the people, Ivy stood, stretched and yawned.

"I'll get us a car," she told her female companions.

"How far are you going?" Jordan asked.

"The Four Seasons," Ivy said.

"No need to get a car. I'll take you."

"You have room for all three of us?" Ivy asked in surprise.

"Yep."

"That's awesome. Thanks so much, Jordan!" Ivy said. "I can't wait to get to my bed."

Ivy's mention of her bed made him chuckle on the inside. Jordan knew she was tired but wished he could share a few moments with her like they had before. He really wanted to know what was going on with her and make sure she wasn't feeling awkward about what had happened between them.

"It would be my pleasure. You ladies look like you can't get to your hotel fast enough. I know how those New York to LA flights get to you."

"You're right," one of the girls said. "I know you're tired, Ivy, but we want to hang out at the hotel bar. If you feel up to it after getting some rest, join us."

"I'll probably see you ladies in the morning," Ivy said. "Before we adjust to this time difference, we'll be in another time zone. I'm going to get my rest."

Jordan drove them the short distance to the hotel. Though it took no more than a few minutes, Jordan had to nudge Ivy awake once they arrived.

Jordan exited the car. The hotel attendants helped the ladies out. They said their goodbyes and headed inside. Ivy took her time getting out of the car. Jordan took her by the arm to help steady her.

"I'm going to go ahead and walk her to the room," he said to the attendant. He nodded in return.

"No, Jordan. You don't have to do that. I'll be fine," Ivy insisted, yawning yet again.

"I want to make sure you're okay," Jordan said.

Ivy let her hands flop to her sides and sighed. "Fine." She'd given up her resistance.

Jordan walked Ivy through the lavish lobby toward the elevators.

She stopped abruptly and turned to him. "Listen. Don't think you're going to come to my room and try to pick up where you left off in New York. I should never have kissed you."

Jordan's jaw clenched. He couldn't believe she was accusing him of having ulterior motives. He was just genuinely concerned about her well-being. "That wasn't my intention."

"I just wanted to be clear." Ivy's hands were on her hips.

Jordan reared his head back. "What kind of person… You know what? Never mind! I was just trying to be nice. Have a good night." Jordan's words were curt. He backed away.

"Whatever!" Ivy said and folded her arms across her chest.

Jordan glowered at her. He was going to say more, like tell her she was being unreasonable. But then thought better of it. Maybe he'd sent mixed messages. Perhaps Hollywood's bad rap on the treatment of women was to blame.

He wasn't sure, but it didn't take much for him to recognize when his presence wasn't welcomed.

At one last gesture prompted by his chivalrous nature, Jordan put distance between them but waited until the elevator came. At least he would know she made it onto the elevator safely. As the doors opened, Ivy looked back at him. Her irritated glare melted. Her eyes lost the rest of their spark and she seemed to look past him. Then Ivy swooned, and a moment later she crumpled to the floor. Jordan's heart fell into his stomach and he heard himself yell Ivy's name.

# Fifteen

Ivy blinked. Blinding brightness caused her to shut her eyes immediately. She squeezed them tight and tried to open them again. This time, she lifted her heavy lids slowly. For a moment she wondered where she was. Beeping machines grounded her. Was this a hospital? Ivy blinked a few times again. Faded memories tried to come to her but only showed flashes.

Why was she here? she wondered. Was she in New York? Where was her family?

"Ivy," someone said her name. They sounded relieved.

The person sounded familiar but she couldn't figure out who it was. She lifted herself up in the bed, trying to focus on the bright room around her. Her sight was blurry but her ears seem to hear more keenly. Those beeping sounds came in loudest. She heard voices in the distance. There were footsteps.

"Nurse! She's awake," the familiar voice said. After a

few padded steps, someone stood before her. "Ivy. Can you hear me?"

Ivy looked up. Clarity rolled in pushing the haze away. "Jordan?" Her voice was hoarse. She cleared her throat. "W-what are you doing here?" She looked around again, taking in the emergency room. "Why am *I* here?"

"You fainted," Jordan said and gently touched her hand. His hand felt good on hers. She needed to feel his warmth. Ivy looked down at it. He followed her eyes and moved his hand away. "Sorry," he said before asking, "How are you feeling?"

"I'm okay. You said I fainted? Where?"

"At the hotel, just before getting into the elevator," he told her. "I tried to get in touch with your agent and the other woman you were with, but couldn't get into your phone. I called 911 and got you here ASAP."

She asked anxiously, "Did you tell anyone else?"

"I didn't know who else to call. I reached out to your cousin Tyler through his Instagram, but I haven't heard anything back. I don't have his phone number."

Ivy tried to sit up fast. Her head hurt. Slowly she sat back. "What did you say to him?"

"I didn't want to alarm him, so I just said to call me and left my number."

"How long have I been in here?" She looked at the IV connected to her arm.

"About two hours. The doctors ran some tests. I didn't want you to wake up alone." Jordan walked over to the chair he was sitting in. "Here's your phone. I was hoping someone would call that could get me closer to one of your family members."

*"No!"* Ivy held both hands up. Jordan's brows furrowed. "I mean…thanks. I don't want to alarm anyone without knowing what's happening."

"Okay. I'll let the nurse know you're awake." He handed

her cell phone to her. "Now you can call who you need to." Jordan stepped out, giving her space to think about what was happening.

Everything was getting clearer. She remembered being in the hotel, exchanging words with Jordan. Ivy cringed. She recalled that they may not have been nice words. But what caused her to faint?

She laid back on the cool pillows. Now that she thought about it, she had a pretty good idea of what caused her to faint. Ivy had been going nonstop all week. Today was by far the most taxing day of them all. Starting with an extremely early flight, the meeting with Jordan's production company, followed by an interview at a radio station. A mini–photo session to capture pictures and footage of what was happening behind the scenes on her trip to LA and the book tour in general. The last thing was her book signing. She hadn't had a solid meal and was tired beyond any kind of fatigue she'd ever felt.

Ivy closed her eyes and a tear spilled from her eye down the side of her face. She was glad Jordan wasn't able to get into her phone to call anyone. Especially Lydia. The last thing she needed to hear from her mom was "I told you so." She needed to find out what exactly was wrong with her before she spoke with her family.

Jordan stuck around so someone could be here when she opened her eyes. If she remembered correctly, she had been pretty awful to him, which made his gesture to be there for her even more admirable. Ivy sighed. She'd clearly bitten off way more than she could chew, but what could she do about it now?

"Ms. Blackwell!" An older distinguished-looking gentleman pushed the curtain aside and stepped in closer to her bed. "It's good to see you awake. How are you feeling?"

"Okay, I guess. Slight headache." Ivy narrowed her

eyes to see the name written across the doctor's white coat. "Dr..."

"Brighton," he said for her.

Ivy pulled herself into a sitting position and rested her back against the bed. "What happened to me?"

"The good news is that it doesn't look like anything major such as a heart attack." He flipped through a chart he had secured on a clipboard. "Your EKG came out fine." He ran down a list of other tests. "I believe your passing out was your body's response to unchecked stress."

"How would you know that?"

"Well, the body gives lots of clues when we're stressed. The problem is that we often overlook the symptoms or consider them to be signs of other things."

"Like what?"

"Well, things as simple as hair shedding or loss."

"Hair loss?"

"That's right. You may notice more hair coming out in your combs than usual. Other symptoms include irritability, loss of focus, headaches, fatigue, muscle stiffness in the back or neck, sleeplessness... The list goes on. Right now, all signs are pointing to stress. But if you don't slow down, you're going to have some bigger issues to contend with. I'm prescribing rest and would suggest you clear your calendar for the next few days."

"The next few days!" Ivy sat up straighter and her posture became rigid. "Doctor, I'm in the middle of a book tour. I have to be in San Francisco by..." She looked at her wrist. Her watch wasn't there. "What day is it?"

"It's still Wednesday for another few minutes."

"Tomorrow evening. I have a signing tomorrow and another one the day after that." Ivy didn't mention all the media opportunities she'd committed to in each city, including radio interviews, news segments and talk show appearances that were scheduled for each city. Not to mention all the mini shoots to get B-roll footage at major landmarks in each location.

"For the sake of your health, I strongly suggest you re-schedule. I don't think those bookstores are going any-where. Now," Dr. Brighton said with finality as if he were her father. "We're waiting on one last test but would like to keep you overnight for observation."

"Overnight! I can't do that." Ivy slumped down and groaned.

Dr. Brighton sighed and pressed his lips together. "And I can't make you, but I'd hate to see you hospitalized again with more serious issues, but that's exactly what is going to happen if you don't take care of yourself now. Your body needs this, Ms. Blackwell. Please think about it seriously." The doctor raised a brow and looked at her as if he were waiting on her to make the right decision. "I'll go check on that other test."

The moment Dr. Brighton stepped out of her bay, Ivy put her face in her hands and cried. She knew he was right. Over the past few weeks, she'd exhibited every single symp-tom that he'd mentioned as signs of stress. Her life had be-come a runaway train that she couldn't seem to slow down. And now that she had the show, everything was taking off at the same time. She was tired but so happy with all of her progress. The key words were *her progress*. She had made all of this happen. These were *her* accomplishments.

Ivy sighed. She just needed to pace herself and then things would fall into place. The other thing she had to do was keep this little mishap away from her family. They couldn't know about her hospitalization. Because if they got wind of it, all hell would break loose. She released a re-lieved breath. She hated ending up in the ER, but she was thankful this hadn't happened when she was in New York.

"You're okay?" Jordan said softly, coming back into the room.

"Yeah." Her quick response was a whisper. "I'm fine." Ivy swatted her tears away. She didn't want to cry in front of Jordan. "Look, um, I think I remember not being very nice to you before all of this."

"Don't worry about it."

She held one hand up, making him pause. "I need to apologize and ask you two questions."

"Sure. Anything."

Ivy swallowed. "I know this is a lot to ask." She paused.

"It's okay. Ask me whatever you need."

Ivy shut her eyes for a moment. She lifted her head toward the ceiling before looking straight at Jordan. She took another breath before asking, "Can you keep this little situation between the two of us?" She sank into her shoulders and pleaded with a puppy dog look. Ivy could summarize the questions behind Jordan's surprised expression. Eventually she'd explain to him why, but not now.

"And the other question?" Jordan looked as if he wasn't sure he wanted to hear the second one.

"Can you stay?"

# Sixteen

Jordan was exhausted. He'd stayed with Ivy until the hospital placed her in a room, and refused to leave until he was sure that she was resting peacefully. That relaxed sleep finally came after four in the morning with the help of a sleeping aid. That gave him and Ivy plenty of time to talk.

When she felt more comfortable, she explained why she didn't want anyone to contact her family. A chorus of "I told you so" from them was the last thing she needed. Jordan insisted that she had to tell them at some point and finally she promised once the tour was over.

He had left the hospital, promising Ivy that he'd return that afternoon and then texted Anderson to let him know that he'd be in the office late. Jordan needed time to rest his body, and wrestle with the burgeoning feelings that were coming up for Ivy. She apologized for her attitude several times throughout the night.

Fortunately, it was a light day at the office. Jordan visited the set to check one of the shows in production. Things were looking up for his company. Not only did the network approve Ivy's show, a few other ideas were also in the works. Content was in demand so they had to stay on their toes, keep fresh ideas coming and keep delivering.

Jordan's phone vibrated while he was in the studio. He looked at the caller, excused himself and headed outside to answer so he wouldn't disturb the actors.

"Hey! How are you feeling?" he asked Ivy.

"Better now that I got some rest."

Jordan looked at his watch—it was almost quitting time. "How long have you been up?"

"A few hours. I made some calls, had my agent reschedule my signings for the next few days." Ivy quieted a moment. "They're letting me out of here."

"Do you need me to come and get you?"

Jordan heard her sigh. "I really don't want to be a burden."

"So, what are you going to do, call a ride share company? Give me a half hour." Jordan didn't hesitate. Back inside, he let the crew know he was heading out.

When he arrived at the hospital, Ivy was dressed and ready to go. He could tell that she'd tried to finger comb her disheveled hair. Her eyes still looked tired. Jordan had now seen her in several states—formal gowns with a face full of makeup, leggings and hoodies and now a worn post-hospital-stay look. And each and every time, she was simply beautiful in his eyes.

Trying to be a gentleman, Jordan escorted her from the hospital to her hotel suite. She'd extended her stay until her next signing in two days. The rest of the crew flew back to New York and would meet her at the East Coast book tour dates. He made sure she was comfortable before attempting to leave. Even though a huge part of him wanted to stay. But in any event, it became important to him to make sure she was all right.

"So…" Jordan stuffed a hand in his jeans pocket. "You're all good?"

"Yes. Thanks." Ivy still moved a bit slow. She walked over to the refrigerator, opened a bottled water and took a long sip. "I just need a long, hot shower."

"Okay. Let me know if you need anything." He looked into her eyes. Suddenly he wanted to be needed by her.

"I will." She smiled. It was the sweetest smile he'd ever seen on a woman. "Thanks again…for everything." She put her bottle of water aside and leaned against the wall, arms folded, with her eyes on him.

"Do you have something to eat for later so you don't have to go out?" He was finding reasons to stay or have to come back. Right or wrong, Jordan wanted to be by her side.

"I'll probably order room service. I won't bother you again, I promise."

"No. It's no bother at all," he insisted, wondering yet again why he was so drawn to Ivy. They shared totally different backgrounds but had so much in common. Both worked too hard and spent too much time alone. Despite not knowing Ivy for very long, he found comfort in her presence, even when she was being irritable most of that time. Jordan stepped toward the door. He was close enough to reach for the knob. He remembered their kiss and instinctively licked his lips. "Okay, but if you need anything, I'm only a phone call away." He lifted his cell. Jordan was mastering the art of procrastination. He didn't move any closer to the door. Ivy hadn't moved either. They watched each other for a few moments.

"You're a good guy, Jordan Chambers, but don't worry about me. I just need rest. I can manage feeding myself and walking around this room."

"Just trying to be helpful." Jordan shrugged and tilted his head to the side.

"And I appreciate you." Her voice was soft. It flowed through him like a melody in the air.

They locked eyes again. The unspoken connection spoke volumes compared to what they had said with their mouths. Jordan didn't believe she wanted him to go.

"You want me to go now?" His voice was a bit huskier than he intended. He wanted her to tell him to stay.

Ivy didn't say anything.

*Say no*, Jordan said in his head. His body felt warm as if a sudden fever rose in him. He couldn't deny his wild attraction to Ivy. He noticed that she still hadn't said for him to go or stay. He knew she needed rest. Maybe he should go before she became irritable again. That would have reminded him to keep his distance. Who wanted to be with someone who was insufferable?

Ivy said that she wasn't usually the incessantly irritable type. Something inside him believed her. Even the doctor admitted that her attitude could have been a sign of her exhaustion. Besides, despite her delivery, he understood her position about drawing a line between them that night.

If they were going to be working together, getting intimate wouldn't necessarily be a good look for her. The double standardized world they lived in would give him credit and ridicule her. Having a relationship with the talent could *really* complicate things. Jordan had been there before. He knew he liked Ivy but was willing to wait until they could explore each other without the complexities that came with a working relationship.

Jordan worked out all the scenarios in his head. What if the show was a hit and they were asked to film additional seasons after the pilot? Maybe he would have to wait a little longer, but at some point, he wanted to explore more with Ivy Blackwell. Somehow, he knew she'd be worth the wait.

"Jordan." She called his name softly, pulling him from

his thoughts. "I really wouldn't mind if you stayed. That's if you can. I don't want to impose."

"I can stay." Jordan wanted to pull her into his arms, but kept his composure. He looked at his watch as if he had someplace else he needed to be.

"If you did leave, I'd be all alone again." Ivy cast her eyes downward. When she looked back up at him, he felt his core tighten. For a brief moment, he saw the glimmer of loneliness in her eyes. It dissipated.

Jordan stepped farther into the room. "What about Tyler?"

"Tyler and Kendall are out of town. My team went back to New York. I'm here by myself and could use the company."

"At least I can make sure you have a good meal before you fall asleep tonight."

The smile that spread across Ivy's face seemed sweet but had a hint of spice in it.

"Great! Why don't you go and get it while I freshen up? I need to get the scent of the hospital off me."

"Preferences?"

"No hospital food." Both of them laughed.

"Allergies?" he asked.

"None. I really enjoy sushi, seafood, Italian…"

"Perfect! I'll be right back."

Jordan called into one of his favorite Italian restaurants and ordered an array of dishes. He also stopped for a bottle of scotch. By the time, he returned, Ivy was out of the shower and had slipped into another comfortable pair of leggings, a T-shirt and fluffy slippers. Again, she was absolutely beautiful. Jordan looked forward to spending the next few hours with her. For some reason, he couldn't get enough of her.

# Seventeen

This was the second time Ivy had invited Jordan to her hotel room within a few short weeks. Why did she feel so comfortable around him? She did know. Yes, their first impressions were rocky as heck, but Jordan Chambers had certainly redeemed himself.

Ivy couldn't say she didn't think about their kiss often. Jordan's good looks had captured her attention from day one. She regretted that she hadn't been nice to him on more than on occasion, especially the times he hadn't spilled his drinks on her. Now she realized why she'd been so irritable all the time. That wasn't really her. The exhaustion made her insufferable.

She knew she was asking a lot when she asked him to stay with her at the hospital but she had absolutely no one else she could call on. She didn't have a personal relationship with her agent and publicists and the only other person that she was really close to within LA was out of town. She could have trusted Tyler to keep her secret had he been home.

Ivy felt incredibly alone but now Jordan was by her side.

Finding herself curled up on the couch again, she looked over at the half-eaten dishes strewn across the coffee table in her hotel suite. They had paused the comedy show they were watching because Jordan's phone rang. He had stepped away to take the call. At first, Ivy couldn't help wondering if it was another woman but then she remembered their conversation about being single. Relief washed over her. She definitely wasn't the type to deal with married men. Nor was she interested in being anyone's side chick. Heck! If she could be someone's chick, period, she might applaud herself. Her last three relationships were short-lived failures, mostly on her part. She was convinced that men just didn't understand her. Perhaps growing up as the only girl in a household full of boys impacted her more than she realized. She never felt like she needed a man, but she sure liked having one around.

What would it be like to date Jordan? Ivy entertained that thought for a moment. The first strike against them would be the fact that both of them traveled a lot. Second, they lived far from one another. She'd tried the long-distance thing before and it sucked horribly.

"Okay. I'll send you all the details when I book," she heard Jordan say as he walked back into the suite. He'd left the door cracked so he could get back in. "Love you too. Good night."

Ivy turned to him just as he ended the call. "Everything okay?"

"It will be." Jordan huffed. "Family stuff. That was my mom."

"Oh! Cool." She was glad to hear it was his mom. "I'm going to get this stuff out of our way." Ivy unfolded her legs from under her and put the leftover scraps in the trash. "A drink?"

"Sure."

"I want to taste this scotch you bought. Neat?"

"You know me," Jordan joked.

"I guess we both know more about each other than we would have imagined at this point," Ivy said softly.

"After that call, I could use something to take the edge off," he added.

"Coming right up!" Ivy took the bottle from the coffee table, grabbed two glasses and poured about an inch of scotch into each. The truth was she could also use something to help her unwind as well. Having Jordan around was great, but she couldn't keep her eyes off him. It wasn't like she hadn't caught him staring a few times either.

The sensual tension between them was extremely apparent. Being around him was like playing with matches. She'd already felt a spark inside her belly a time or two, like when he touched her hand at the hospital. She felt the warmth of care, but also something hotter. And then again, she remembered the feel of his lips on hers.

Ivy brought both glasses back to the living room area and placed them on the table. She sat back down, picked up the remote and pointed it at the television. The paused comedian came back to life, right in the middle of a joke. Ivy was seated on one side of the sofa and Jordan on the other. Both of them guffawed hard at the man's jokes.

"You have no idea how much I love to laugh," Ivy said after catching her breath.

Jordan turned and looked at her. She felt as if he was looking into her soul. "Me too." He turned back to the television. That gave Ivy a moment to study his profile. His jawline was strong and sculptured. Smooth brown skin reminded her of warm, melted milk chocolate. And that dimple. Have mercy! Whenever he smiled or laughed, it played peekaboo, making her want to kiss the crevice. And his eyes radiated a sexy laziness and were framed by lush lashes most women would pay to have.

More laughter. The show was over too soon. "Let's watch something else," Ivy said quickly. She didn't want Jordan to leave. Yet she also didn't want too much idle time to pass between them. Otherwise, they'd be forced to reckon with the chemistry that sat in the room like a large pink elephant.

Jordan looked at his watch. "I'm up for it if you are."

"Do you have to go?" Ivy hoped he could stay.

"No. I just don't want to wear out my welcome. If you get tired, just let me know."

"Are you going to tuck me in?" Ivy froze after those words left her lips. She didn't mean to be so flirtatious. And she couldn't even blame it on the scotch since she'd barely touched her drink. Ivy felt Jordan looking at her. She could see him through her peripheral but couldn't tell if he was smiling or not. To distract herself, she picked up her glass and took a small sip. The liquid strolled down her throat like lava, leaving a savory burn in its wake. Finally, she heard him laughing.

"Are you flirting with me?"

With her glass to her lips, she turned toward him. "Maybe."

Jordan was definitely smiling. "Interesting," he said through perfect teeth.

Ivy put the glass down. "I read a room well and I'm pretty…how should I say this? Direct. I'm grateful for you keeping me company and being kind enough to be here for me, but I won't deny the fact that I find you attractive." She cleared her throat. "I just don't think it would be a good idea for us to become…entangled. Dating or sleeping with people that you do business with usually doesn't turn out well. At least, it hasn't worked out for me in the past. However, I'm glad you're here."

"Well, since we're being frank..." Jordan sat up and looked directly into Ivy's eyes. His expression was serious. "I thought you were stunning since the day I spilled wine on your beautiful dress at the wrap party. If I hadn't been working that night and didn't almost ruin your outfit, I would have asked for your number then. After the next spill, I figured I'd ruined my chances." He blew out a breath. "So, imagine my surprise when Anderson suggested we contact you regarding a show idea. I thought you were going to get up from the table and leave during that first meeting."

"Really?" She flashed him a teasing look. "Well, to be honest, the thought did cross my mind!"

"I bet. Well, in any event, I've wanted to know more about you ever since that first night. Needless to say, I find you extremely attractive whether you're wearing a gown, suit, leggings, hoodies, coffee or wine."

Ivy's laugher spilled from her mouth like a faucet. "Remind me to send you my cleaning bill."

Jordan chuckled too. Several moments ticked by with them simply taking each other in. Jordan moved closer to her on the couch. "Well, where does that put us, Ms. Blackwell?"

Ivy grinned. She tilted her head and asked seriously, "Where would you like it to?"

Jordan drew in a breath. "Right where we are. Exploring."

Ivy's expression turned serious. She looked down at her glass and placed it back on the table, wanting Jordan to understand that this was all her speaking, not the scotch. "I have an idea where I'd like for it to go, but I'm concerned about what happens next. I've never been good at casual dating and I'm not exactly fling material. Plus, I have a busy life. I just don't have the time to dedicate to giving situations like this what it needs."

"I get that. It's a risk I'm willing to take." Jordan moved even closer to her. "But tell me what you'd like." His voice was like a caress. "Be honest with me."

A sprig of warmth started in Ivy's belly and made goose bumps rise on her skin. She covered her lips with her hand and thought about how to muster the words. "Brutally honest?"

"Brutally," he repeated. "I promise you. I can take it."

"I want what's brewing here," Ivy said. She felt her voice grow hoarse with the weight of longing.

"Me too." Jordan was so close now that Ivy could feel his breath on her cheek.

"But what happens after that?" She felt deflated by the reality of her words.

Jordan gently touched her cheek, turning her face toward him. "I like you. I'm willing to take the chance and see how far this could go. I don't believe either of us got to where we are in our lives by playing it safe."

Jordan got that right. Everything about him made her want more. His words. His deep, husky voice. The heat emanating from him that seemed to transfer to her. Finally, her lips said, "One day at a time. No commitments." Her mind caught up only after the words were out. What had she just agreed to? An *anything goes* arrangement? Those could be just as dangerous.

"Just two consenting adults, with busy lives, enjoying each other's company," Jordan said. Ivy stared as each word fell from his full, luscious lips.

Giving in, she shrugged. "Having fun until it's no longer feeling like fun. Then a clean break. Nothing awkward or complicated. Deal?"

"Deal."

Ivy held up her pinkie. "Pinkie swear?"

Jordan threw his head back and laughed.

Ivy shrugged again. "It's less formal than a handshake but still binding."

"Fine." He linked his pinkie with hers. After, he looked into her eyes again, and Ivy felt his gaze penetrate her soul once again.

"Kiss me, Jordan," she whispered.

Without hesitation, Jordan pulled Ivy into his embrace and unleashed a passion so complete she was breathless within seconds. Ivy hugged him back, groping hungrily at his sweater. The kiss was frantic, urgent even. They ravished each other as if they were water quenching one another's thirst.

"I've been wanting to kiss you again since the day you left my room in New York," Ivy panted.

"And not one day has gone by without me thinking about kissing you again," Jordan admitted gruffly.

Ivy pulled him in for more. They kissed and kissed and kissed until both their bodies were on fire. Then they broke apart just long enough to breathe and start right back up again. Jordan's hands roamed Ivy's body and she explored all of his. Jordan's skin felt feverish under Ivy's touch. Soon she wouldn't be able to control her cravings. She had to make a decision. Either send him home or take him to her bedroom.

"You have protection?" she managed to gasp a whisper.

Jordan returned a breathy, "Yes." He pulled back for a moment and searched her face. "You sure about this?"

Instead of answering, Ivy stood, took him by the hand and led him to her room. She couldn't remember ever being this impulsive but was enjoying every moment of it.

Inside the room, Jordan took his time slowly peeling off each item of clothing and kissing the places the garments used to cover. He started with her T-shirt. Lifting it and kissing her belly. He unhooked her bra and took her pebbled nipples into his mouth. Ivy's back arched. She moaned. Then he removed her leggings and kissed from her ankles to her panties. Running his finger along her moist center, he slipped the material aside and circled her slickness. Ivy moaned again. Jordan slid her panties down her legs and tossed them. Ivy lay naked, giggling at his touch and enjoying how the coolness of the room licked against the heat emanating from her hot skin.

Ivy turned him over. Now she was on top. Returning the favor, she pulled Jordan's sweater over his head. Kissed his pecs. She slid her tongue down his torso over the ripples of his six-pack. His breathing quickened. Next, she loosened his belt. Tossed it aside. Ivy opened his jeans, shimmying them down the sides of his legs, then pulled them off and let them drop to the floor. She stood and looked at Jordan. Chest heaving and erection straining against his gray boxer briefs. Her eyes widened a bit at his girth. She pulled on the front of his underwear, releasing him and watching it spring to attention. A groan rose in her throat. She liked what she saw.

Jordan sat up. He reached for Ivy. Using his index finger, he outlined her body from the lips to her pelvic center and then slid his finger between her wet folds. He found her swollen bud and massaged it. Ivy's legs grew week and wobbled. Jordan stood, lifted her and gently placed her back on the bed. He showed adoration for every inch of her body, kissing, caressing, gently massaging, until Ivy felt like she would combust into a million fiery pieces.

"You're so beautiful," he rasped in her ear.

"Please," she pleaded with him breathlessly.

"Anything for you."

Jordan seemed to disappear for a quick moment. When he returned, he crawled over her, kissed her one more time and then carefully penetrated her with just the sheathed tip. Ivy's breath caught. A delicious pain shot through her and then a ravenous hunger set in. She wanted all of him inside of her. Slick with the moisture of her own juices, Jordan entered easily. He was a snug and perfect fit. His rhythm enticed her. She matched him beat by delectable beat. They rode that rhythm to a thunderous and urgent tempo.

Ivy felt herself getting ready to explode. Jordan's thrusts became more urgent. Fastening her eyes shut, she held on so they could ride their climactic wave together. His moans turned to grunts and Ivy stifled a scream. Then it happened. The dam broke. A guttural groan rose in Jordan's throat. He panted out frantic thrusts until his back arched hard. He lost his composure completely. Ivy's back arched too as her orgasm rippled through her. Together they cried out. Ivy reached a sensual height she couldn't remember reaching before. Spent, they both laid on their backs trying to catch their breaths.

Once her breathing returned to normal, Ivy felt a peace she hadn't felt in long time. With a smile on her face, she allowed herself to drift off to sleep.

That sleep was broken by the morning sun glaring through her hotel room window. Ivy blinked a few times. As the haze dissipated, she realized she was still in her hotel room. Beside her was Jordan's beautifully sculpted and naked body. His chest rose and fell steadily in sync with his light snore. It wasn't a dream. Ivy looked at the clock on the nightstand beside her bed. It was after eleven in the morning. She hadn't slept more than a full eight hours in months. It was the most peaceful sleep she'd ever remembered. Ivy chuckled, pulled the sheet over her and laid back down. It had been a good night. Careful not to wake Jordan, Ivy murmured in a low voice, "This was all that I needed."

# Eighteen

Jordan woke up alone in Ivy's hotel bed. He picked up his phone and shot off a text to Anderson, who had been looking for him. Jordan was taking the day off.

He heard the faint sounds of hip-hop music and the shower running. In his full naked glory, Jordan stretched, got up from of the bed and headed to the bathroom. He knocked and waited for Ivy to respond. There was nothing. He knocked louder to make sure she heard of him over the sound of water and her own rapping. Still nothing.

Jordan turned the knob, peeked inside the steamy bath and called Ivy's name over the music. She stopped singing and pulled the curtain back.

"Hey, you," she said. "There's room for two."

Jordan grinned. "Thanks for the invitation. I'd be happy to join you. But how about I order us some breakfast before I get in? I'm starving. That way it will arrive around the time we are done getting dressed."

"Good idea." Ivy let the curtain fall back into place and started singing again.

Jordan shook his head and laughed.

Not being sure what she wanted, Jordan ordered an array of options including fruit, eggs, waffles, coffee and juice. When he returned to the bathroom, Ivy was loudly rapping a song from one of his favorite artists. Jordan joined her in the shower and sang along. Being careful not to fall, they faced each other singing the chorus and then melted into laughter as water from the shower cascaded over them.

"I didn't peg you for a rap lover."

"There's a lot you still don't know about me, Mr. Chambers."

"I can't wait to find out more."

For several beats, no words passed between them. They stood before each other, naked, admiring one another. Ivy pulled in her bottom lip and bit it seductively. She tilted her head sweetly. Jordan instinctively licked his lips.

"Can you help me wash my back?" Ivy's voice was low and husky. She turned, giving Jordan a full view off her soft back and round bottom.

"I'm happy to help." Jordan took the cloth from her and gently rubbed soapy circles on her back.

Ivy looked over her shoulder at him. Her smile made his core tighten. When Jordan was done with her back, he wrapped his arms around her and kissed her shoulders.

"Anything else I can help you wash?" he whispered in Ivy's ear.

Ivy turned back to him, lifted onto her toes and kissed him. She guided his hand with the soapy cloth along her neck on both sides and then down her torso.

Jordan was certain that the temperature in the bathroom shot up at least ten more degrees. For the next several moments they washed each other and kissed. Jordan's erection grew rigid. He lifted Ivy into his arms. Her firm breasts pressed against his chest. Their tongues connected, entangled into a fierce passionate battle. Ivy lifted her chin. Jordan kissed her neck and rested her back against the shower wall. He wanted to enter her, but restrained his desire since he didn't have protection. Their kisses cause more steam to rise in the room.

"I want…"

Before Ivy could finish, Jordan interrupted. "I want you too."

Ivy pushed back the shower curtain. Jordan continued to hold her in his arms while carefully stepping over the side of the tub. She pushed the bathroom door open wider with her foot as he carried her back to her room. Then Jordan gingerly laid Ivy on bed and fished his last condom from his wallet. He handed it to her. She ripped the package, and rolled the protection over his stiff erection. Lifting Ivy's legs, he carefully entered, talking his time and relishing the snug, moist fit. Jordan hissed. The feel of her was too much for him to stand.

Jordan took his time. He didn't know when they would have a chance to be together like this again. He savored her, taking her with long rhythmic strokes. Unlike the night before, they took things slow. Jordan felt like he would soon lose control. He pulled out. Ivy pleaded for him to continue. Instead, he kissed her up and down her legs. He entered her again. His strokes were steady and long. Again, he felt himself slipping away. Jordan didn't want this to end. Pulling out, he took turns suckling each nipple, then he lost himself inside her again. After a few strokes, his eyes started to roll back in his head.

Jordan removed himself from Ivy one last time. She beat the sheet with her fist. Jordan buried his face between her legs, flicked, then suckled her swollen bud. Ivy gasped and sweet moans rumbled in her throat. The sounds of her pleasure made Jordan work harder to please her. Ivy panted, bellowed a luscious and guttural melody. She grabbed a pillow and squeezed it against her chest. Jordan continued to lick until she trembled, moved back into position and entered while her orgasm claimed her body in waves.

Ivy tossed the pillow, dug her fingers into Jordan's back and pulled him to her with each thrust. A guttural moan rose from her throat, which made Jordan lose complete control. He quickened his pace from steady intentional strokes to wild bucking. Together, they convulsed over and over again. His face contorted as euphoric pleasure rippled through him like violent waves crashing against the shore. He groaned one last time before collapsing over Ivy, feeling her chest heave up and down. She wrapped her arms around him. They stayed that way for several blissful moments.

There was a knock on the door. He lifted himself high enough to look at her. The sated smile on her face let him know that she enjoyed herself as much as he did.

"Coming!" Ivy yelled. Both of them laughed.

Their room service had arrived and the timing couldn't have been better.

"I'll get it." Jordan jumped out of bed, quickly cleaned himself with a towel and slipped into his jeans.

Grabbing his wallet, he jogged to the door and welcomed their breakfast spread. Giving the gentleman who delivered the food a healthy tip, he closed the door behind him and pushed the serving tray into the bedroom. Jordan removed his jeans and climbed back into the bed beside Ivy. She had given him so much satisfaction he was barely hungry. But that didn't stop them from feeding each other the entire hearty breakfast, bite by delicious bite between kisses.

Once they finished eating, Jordan pulled back the covers to get out of bed.

"Leaving so soon," Ivy said and pouted.

Jordan picked up his briefs and jeans. He leaned over and kissed her lips.

"You're supposed to be resting. As long as I'm around you won't get much rest."

"You've got a point." She placed her hands on the top of her head. "To be honest, I haven't felt more relaxed in months. I believe I have you to thank for that."

"You're welcome," Jordan said, grabbing his shirt.

Ivy got out of the bed and wrapped the sheet around her naked body. She walked to Jordan and placed her hand on his chest. She looked up into his eyes. "I've enjoyed your company."

He slid his arms around her waist. "I wish I didn't have to go, but you need rest." He kissed her nose.

"You're right. With you here, we haven't rested at all."

"When do you leave?" Jordan asked.

"Tomorrow. I'm heading back home for a few days. My publisher pushed some of my tour dates back so I can recuperate a little longer."

He wished she didn't have to go.

"Get some rest today and tonight. I have a few errands to run. I can come pick you up tomorrow and take you to the airport."

"That would be nice," Ivy said. She tilted her head pensively. "I think I'll book some spa treatments."

Jordan nodded. "Good idea." They kissed again. He never tired of kissing Ivy. "I have some business in New York over the next few weeks. I hope I can see you while I'm there."

"Okay. Let's work it out."

Still wrapped in her sheet, Ivy followed Jordan to the shower. They continued chatting while he dressed. At the door, they kissed one more time. They held one another like they didn't want to ever let go. Finally releasing Ivy,

Jordan backed out. He winked before turning and strolling down the hallway, feeling lighter than he had in months.

Jordan had agreed to her condition about no commitments, but after spending this past day and a half with Jordan, he needed to find a way to work around that rule.

# Nineteen

Ivy didn't know if it was the time she'd spent with Jordan in Los Angeles, or the days she spent at home just resting, but she felt better than she had in months. She wasn't being ushered from one place to the other, signing books, getting made up so she could look perfect as she smiled for the cameras or rushing through the airport. And she'd hardly looked at her social media profiles, which was something she usually monitored daily. She was free and that freedom felt amazing. But sadly, that didn't last long. She was now back to the grind.

Her family still didn't know about her brief visit to the hospital. If anyone asked them, she was on tour, visiting one city after the other. She'd definitely tell them eventually. The timing had to be right. However, she did miss speaking to her family. Especially Zoe. She couldn't believe she still hadn't told her anything. But Ivy couldn't risk it. Her sister-in-law had also warned her about her demanding schedule. But Ivy was sure she had this covered. She just needed a little break. Now she understood why Kendall and Tyler took long vacations where they went off the grid. But as long as she still worked for Blackwell, she couldn't get away with that. Her dad wouldn't have it.

She got ready for a team meeting over video conference. Several days a week, she'd work remotely despite being on tour. Ivy didn't want to be totally out of the loop or have a ton of worked piled up and waiting for her when she returned. She ran the women's division, so fortunately she had control over the meeting schedule unless the meeting was being planned by the company's other executives. They took her schedule into consideration.

"Hey, everybody!" Ivy waved into the camera as faces were popping up on the screen.

"Hey, Ivy," her assistant, Jess, said. "What time is it, and where are you today?"

"It's like that show *Where in the World Is Carmen* somebody. What's her name?" Zoe said.

"Sandiego," Ivy said.

"You're in San Diego?" Jess asked with a scrunched face. She helped manage some parts of Ivy's schedule, but the team at the publishing house dominated her scheduling during the tour.

"No! The girl's last name in the show is Sandiego. *Where in the World Is Carmen Sandiego?*" Zoe said.

Everyone laughed. "Gotcha!" Jess said.

"I'm in San Francisco today and will be in Seattle tomorrow evening. I'll see you back there on Monday. I'll be home for a few days before heading out again," Ivy said.

"That's great because Dale wants to meet again. Can I put her on the schedule for next week?"

Yes! Ivy pumped her fist. She hadn't heard anything from Dale and all the waiting was making her anxious. "Hold on." She flipped through the calendar on her phone.

"I'm available Wednesday or Thursday morning. Zoe, does that work for you?" Zoe checked her schedule and agreed.

"Perfect!"

Bill, Ethan and the rest of the executive team popped up on the screen.

"Looks like everyone is here," Zoe said.

"Let's get this meeting started," Bill said.

The next half hour was filled with reports on how well each region performed. The continued success with acquiring more women clients despite Dale's potential loss of business was gratifying.

"The more your face is out there, the more women we get, Ivy. Great job," Ivy's brother Ethan said. Several others joined in congratulating her.

"Thanks, Ethan. It's really empowering." Ivy was grateful for her brother's praise, but she could tell her father wasn't impressed by the stoic look on his face. He was the only one that didn't compliment her on what her presence brought to Blackwell.

Bill was old-fashioned. Despite the fact that business was thriving, he wanted Ivy to be in the office way more than she was capable of showing up. Yet her work got done. Work that she was super proud of. Work that filled that part of her that desired to make a contribution to the world that was all her own.

Another half hour passed with a few more reports and plans for the upcoming quarter. They'd had one hundred percent of Ivy's attention during the first half of the meeting, but the second half—not so much.

In the middle of the meeting, Jordan sent her a text reminding her that he'd be in New York next week and if she was in town he'd love to see her. After that, she couldn't keep her mind from conjuring up steamy thoughts about him. They'd spoken every day since she left Los Angeles, and each time she heard his voice or saw his name on her phone, he dominated her focus for a while. She was still on the fence about pursuing this "thing" with Jordan, though she could never deny that she both liked and appreciated him a lot.

Their chemistry had all the right ingredients. They enjoyed each other's company. Their conversation was stimulating and could easily flow from one subject to another. Whether they were together or on the phone, they could talk for hours. They loved the same music and some of the same favorite artists. It seemed he understood her ambition, which was a different experience for her. Ivy certainly wanted to explore more about Jordan. He seemed perfect, which was scary.

And in bed? Whew! Jordan was *amazing*. He'd make love to her body and soul. He was a patient lover—something she didn't realize she loved. She could easily see herself becoming addicted to Jordan but that wouldn't be good. Would it?

What was going to happen once they started filming the show? Hollywood was funny place. She already started to get more attention from social media. Her following increased significantly after the incident with Kenya at the awards show. They spiked again once the book was released and now Ivy spent more time monitoring her social media. More brands wanted to work with her. However, not all of the attention she received on social media was good. Kenya had been blocked so she didn't see much from her, but there was other "haters" out there. Trolls were coming at her left and right. Her team tried to delete their negative comments before they stirred any trouble. They didn't like Ivy seeing those comments because she hadn't learned how to ignore them yet. That was just something influencers had to deal with. Still, Ivy couldn't understand why people were so mean.

Jordan texted her again. This time, he mentioned some

special place he'd like to take her. Ivy waited until the meeting ended. Instead of texting him back, she called just to hear his voice.

"Hey!" Jordan's deep voice flowed through the phone making her wish he wasn't over three hundred miles away. "How are you feeling?"

Ivy felt her lips ease into a smile. It happened every time she heard his voice. "Great. Thanks for asking."

"Did you get my text?"

"I did. What's this special place you're talking about?"

"Nope! No details for you. That's a secret. Just let me know when you're available so I can make the arrangements. One night with you will do."

"Hmm. Top secret. And just one night, huh? Sounds like the makings of a steamy romance novel."

"Ha! I hope you enjoy it just the same."

"I have a feeling I will. Let me check my calendar." Ivy reviewed her availability and let Jordan know that Friday would work best. As a single hardworking woman with a ridiculously busy schedule, Friday nights tended to be uneventful unless she was traveling. She hardly had time to hang with the girls.

"This is perfect. I'll be in on Wednesday evening," Jordan said.

"Let me know what time. Maybe I can pick you up at the airport."

"I'll text the times. If not, I have a service that I use."

"Cool. Gotta run but I look forward to seeing you next week."

Just as Ivy ended the call with Jordan, her phone rang again. It was her dad.

"Hi, Dad."

"Hi, honey." He called her *honey*, but his voice was void of any sweetness. "We need to talk."

# Twenty

Jordan shut down his laptop, stuffed it in the carrying case and stood. There was no point in trying to concentrate on work any longer. He was heading to New York and the thought of being in the same city as Ivy had stolen his focus all morning. Thinking about her made him smile. Remembering their conversation and her words *fun while it lasted* made him wonder if the fun could ever run out. He'd enjoyed every minute of every conversation with Ivy since she'd left.

He looked at his watch, realizing he had just an hour to get to the airport. There was no need for luggage when he had a penthouse in New York that was just as packed as his luxury condo in LA. His laptop was his travel companion. Maybe he'd manage to get some work done in the airport lounge or on the plane.

Suddenly, Anderson burst through Jordan's office door. "Did you see the email?"

"What email?" Jordan asked.

Anderson stepped all the way in "They literally just sent it—the production schedule. They want to start filming next month. They're ready to move on this one."

*"Fix My Money?"* Jordan asked. They had other shows in the works but were most excited about their show with Ivy.

"We've got some details to work out. Call me when you get through airport security. I don't want this to wait until you land."

"No problem."

"In the meantime," Anderson continued, "I'll compile some of the things they asked about in the email. I'll run it by you when we talk. We've got great contestants lined up ready to go."

"This is going to be great! I'll check out the email on the way to the airport. My car should be here any minute."

The fast pace of the industry had always excited the two of them. Recently, things had changed drastically. It used to take months or longer to get a deal done on a show and get a production schedule in place. Now, with such a high demand for content and so many channels and streaming options, decisions were being made in record time. Everyone wanted to grab the most compelling content as soon as possible.

The show was being produced in Los Angeles, which meant that Jordan would see a lot more of Ivy. Being on set would require them to make sure they kept their composure and remained professional. Jordan had no problem with that.

Instead of waiting until he got to the airport, Jordan called Anderson while he was in the car. They went over details and next steps. Once Jordan got through security, he settled in the airline's lounge, ordered a glass of scotch and phoned Ivy.

"We've got something to celebrate but first, how are you feeling?" Jordan asked.

"Not bad. I managed to sleep off my jet lag after my trip to San Francisco. What are we celebrating?" Jordan could hear the excitement in Ivy's voice and was glad he was the one that could share the news with her.

"You'll get a call from your team, but I wanted to be the first to let you know that the network is ready to move forward. They sent a production schedule and would like to start shooting next month!" Jordan was expecting Ivy to laugh, shout, scream—something.

After a few moments of silence, Ivy finally said, "Wow."

"Shocked, huh?"

"Well, yes. Shocked and a bit nervous. This is so new to me. What if I mess up? What if I forget my lines? I have to clear my schedule. What—"

"Whoa! Take a breath," Jordan soothed. "And don't worry…this is a reality show. There aren't really any lines to remember. You're the expert, Ivy. You'll do what you normally do, tell people how to build wealth. It's just that your 'clients' will be rather…interesting since most of them are celebrities or celebrity adjacent. They won't be anything like your regular clientele."

Ivy snorted. "Yeah. Spoiled rich brats who go through money like water. This *is* going to be interesting. Wow. I can't wait. I have to run. See you when you get here?"

"Yes. And thanks for offering to pick me up at the airport, but don't worry about it," he told her. "I'm arriving early to take care of some family business. But I'd love to see you after that. Think you'll be up for a late dinner?"

"Around what time?" Jordan sensed the hesitancy in Ivy's tone. He knew her schedule had been packed, and while he really wanted to see her, he didn't want to burden her knowing she still needed to rest as much as possible between tour dates, speaking engagements and work.

"Is eight too late? I'll come to you. You pick the place."

"Works for me. Maybe you can help me relax a bit more." Ivy snickered.

"Ha! I can definitely do that." Jordan laughed knowing that Ivy was talking about being intimate. They joked about how relaxed they felt after being together at her hotel previously. Whether they made love or not, being with Ivy calmed him.

Jordan's phone vibrated. It was a text letting him know his flight was boarding. Finishing off his drink, he headed to the gate. Either he was tired or his first-class seat was comfortable because Jordan didn't remember taking off. He'd woken up at the rumble caused by the airplane's wheels making contact with the runway.

Jordan's brother, Dorian, picked him up at the airport and they headed to his mother's house.

"My boys!" Charisse came running out of the house when they pulled up.

Their mom looked stunning in smart-looking navy slacks and a matching blouse with a large bow at the top. She embraced them tight as she always did.

"Come on in. Are you hungry? I have some leftovers in the fridge. I've been busy all day and didn't have time to make anything. How about a drink? You boys want a drink?"

"That would be nice," Dorian said, heading to the refrigerator and retrieving two bottles of water. He tossed one to Jordan.

Jordan twisted the cap and downed half the bottle. "Ah! I didn't realize I was that thirsty."

Charisse pulled a bottle of scotch and three glasses from the spirits cabinet and placed them on the table in the living room. She was responsible for Jordan and Dorian's appreciation of top-shelf scotch. Their mom taught them things that fathers usually taught their boys. Things like how to drive and how to drink properly, explaining to them the difference between the finer selections and the cheap stuff. She also taught them to sip casually and not gulp, which she considered classless. Their mom insisted that would only get them drunk prematurely. Jordan poured an inch of scotch in each glass and handed them out. They followed Charisse into the living room.

"Come." She patted the sofa beside her. "Sit. It will be a few minutes before Tim gets here."

"So, what did he have to say about our proposal?" Jordan asked.

Charisse smiled at him. "Looks like we're getting right down to business."

Jordan raised his glass as a response. His mom and Dorian touched glasses with his and the three of them sipped.

"Here's the deal," Charisse said and placed her glass down on the coffee table.

Jordan held his sigh in, bracing himself for what his mother was about to say. He glanced at Dorian, who was already looking his way. The way their mother started made him think they may not like the answer.

"Tim most certainly needs your help, but doesn't feel like the arrangement we proposed is in his best interest."

"What? I thought—"

"Hold on." Charisse held up her hand. "He's a prideful man. I don't have to remind you boys that your relationship with him has always been a bit…strained."

"But this is a solid business offer, Ma." Dorian said the very words that Jordan wanted to say. "Did you tell him this proposal was your idea?"

"I did." Charisse sighed. "It's just hard for him. Asking you two for help isn't easy. And I think that he just wants to make sure he has some say in how this proposal is finalized. He doesn't want to feel bulldozed just because he needs help."

"What's that supposed to mean?" Dorian snapped, looking between Jordan and his mother.

Door locks clicked. Jordan, Dorian and Charisse's focus shifted to Tim stepping in. He was a tall, strapping man whose only hint of his years was a neatly shaven salt-and-pepper beard. Tension rose in the room immediately.

"Hello, honey." Tim's long strides swept across the floor, taking him to Charisse's side quickly. He kissed her lips.

"Hello, sweetie," she said, touching his cheek and wiping her lipstick from his lips.

"Jordan. Dorian." Tim nodded at both of them. They nodded back. The greeting was devoid of any warmth.

Jordan noticed Tim's eyes dart between their drinks on the table.

"Give me a moment and I'll join you."

Jordan sat back in his chair and hoped this interaction would be painless.

Tim poured his own drink and joined them in the living room, sitting next to his wife. Charisse took his free hand in hers.

"I'll assume you've been chatting about this arrangement."

"Yes. It appears you have an issue with the proposal?" Jordan asked. He had no time for small talk.

"It's a good deal," Dorian added.

"I didn't say it wasn't." Tim huffed. "But it's my company and I'm not signing anything without having my input and interest fully represented."

"What?" Dorian said. "Mom!"

"You guys made this arrangement with her. Not me. This company supports her but it's not hers."

Both boys looked at their mom.

"So, what do you propose?" Jordan asked, feeling himself becoming irritated. "What specific aspects of the contract do you have a problem with?"

"All of it!" Tim yelled.

"Timothy," Charisse admonished.

Jordan knew where this was going. Tim felt emasculated because he had nothing to do with the terms. While he understood that, they had no time to engage in pissing matches with this man while his company quickly went under.

"I don't want you as partners. I just need a loan. I'll pay it back. I've been in business for over twenty-five years." Tim stabbed the air with his index finger as he spoke. "I know what I'm doing, and I'm not selling off my stakes in a business I built because of one rough spot. I've been in rough spots before and never folded." Tim stood and paced. "I know you guys don't think that well of me, but despite that, I took good care of you boys and gave your mother the best life I could possibly provide for her. But no matter what I did, it was never good enough for you guys. I asked for help. I don't need your pity and I won't be taken advantage of. And I won't let you stand by and take my business from me."

"Timothy!" Charisse cried. "No one is trying to take advantage of you!"

"Or take your business," Jordan said. "This was supposed to help."

"Help who?" Tim shouted. He then proceeded to rant on about their intentions, ending with, "Just forget about it. I don't want any help from either of you." He glared at Jordan and then Dorian.

Jordan couldn't believe what was he was hearing. Tim had said things that angered him but they hurt as well. What made him believe that Dorian and Jordan would take advantage of him or try to take his business? Despite not getting along, they never acted without integrity.

Dorian stood and popped his collar. "I'm out of here."

He walked over to Charisse. "Ma, I love you, but I've got to go." He hugged Charisse and kissed her cheek.

Their mom stood now too. Her shoulders slumped. "Wait. We have to talk this out." She turned to Timothy. "Listen, honey, that's not what we intended here. This is to help and protect all of our interests."

"Not mine!" he barked.

Jordan hugged his mother. He was on the same page as Dorian. "Love you, Mom." He kissed her cheek too. "But there doesn't look like there's much to talk about."

"I don't need to bow to your boys. I'll get through this myself."

"Timothy!"

Jordan heard the man continue to protest as he and his brother exited. Leaving was the best thing for them to do. Things would have gotten ugly. Jordan was sure Dorian wouldn't have had a problem issuing Tim a loan, but his words cut, accusing them of trying to take advantage of him, steal his business. Never. Jordan would rather not deal with Tim at all than to be accused of being underhanded.

In spite of his hurt and anger, Jordan was torn. Tim definitely needed their help but was too stubborn to take it. And their mom was caught in the middle.

Outside, Dorian stalked from the front of the car to the back with his hands on his hips. "Can you believe the nerve of this man?"

Jordan massaged his throbbing temples. "No. I can't."

"I need another drink. Want to join me?" Dorian said once he finally got in the car and slammed the door.

"Sure," Jordan agreed. He huffed. Somehow, he knew he would have to be the one to fix this situation. Another drink would help but being with Ivy would be even better. Nothing would take the edge off like time alone with her.

# Twenty-One

"Oh, no!" Ivy yelled. She threw back the comforter, moved Jordan's arm from around her waist and jumped out of bed. "I can't be late."

Ivy felt Jordan's eyes on her bare bottom as she ran to the master bathroom. She turned on the shower and held her hand under the flow of water for a few moments. That was a habit of hers. After a quick shower, she covered herself in a towel and rummaged through her walk-in closet to find something that didn't require ironing. Normally, Ivy would take out her clothes the night before, but once Jordan got to her home, she'd forgotten all about that.

Ivy had been excited to see Jordan, but when he arrived in a sullen mood, she turned her focus on putting a smile on his face. She'd been stressed about work and he'd been stressed about the situation with his parents. Their lovemaking was slow and deep as if they were filling all the gaps in each other's lives. They soothed one another's woes and fell asleep wrapped in each other's arms. Between the news that Jordan shared about her new television show and the way he held her, Ivy's stress all but melted away.

Until now.

Ivy needed to get to work on time today. She had a meeting with her dad and was due to connect with Dale. She grabbed a light sweater dress, undergarments and boots and headed back to the bedroom. Jordan had made his way into her shower. Ivy almost wished she could take the day and spend it in his arms. However, both of them had full schedules. She'd get to spend more quality time with him during the evening Jordan had planned for them. He still wouldn't tell her anything about it.

Ivy peeked into the bathroom. "Morning! I'm heading down. Want coffee to go?"

"Sure! Thanks," Jordan said over the water. "I have a car coming. He can drop you off and take me to my meeting."

Ivy looked at her watch. "Really? That would be great!" This ride into the city was going to save her time. She should get to work on time so she could face her father.

An hour later, Ivy was kissing Jordan goodbye. She jumped out of the car in front of Blackwell's headquarters. Inside she made it to her office without running into her dad. Ivy sat, turned to the window and took in the view of the city's skyline. With a deep breath in and a long breath out, she closed her eyes and calmed herself. She dreaded this meeting with her dad. He had questions for her. She had answers for some of them, but they weren't the ones he was looking for. She couldn't understand why he couldn't just be proud of her.

When her phone buzzed, she didn't even bother to look at her text messages. She stood, tugged on the front of her suit jacket and straightened her back. It was time to face Bill.

Ivy passed Zoe's office. She could hear her on the phone. She waved. Then she passed Ethan's office. Peeking in, she saw that he was on the phone as well. She greeted him with a nod and a smile, then stepped out and closed his door. Ivy sighed. She was procrastinating. Squaring her shoulders, she headed straight for Bill's office.

The door was ajar. Ivy lifted her hand to knock but before her knuckles connected with the wood, Bill said, "Come on in."

"Hey... Dad." Ivy wrung her hands. Her anxiety flowed from her stomach to the extremities. Sinking down into the leather tufted seat in front of his desk, she tapped her foot and toyed with her freshly manicured nails.

It took several moments for Bill to glance up from his laptop. When he did, he pulled off his glasses and held them loosely. He looked at her and sat back in his massive leather chair. "Good morning, my daughter."

Outside of work, Bill often called her "baby girl." He'd called her daughter when he wanted to make a statement.

"Father." She was being as formal as he was.

"Let's start with the state of the deal with Dale," Bill said, placing his glasses down and folding his hands.

"I'm meeting with her today. We're a step closer to closing the deal. She loves the fact that we've been getting so much exposure regarding our women's initiatives, but she really wanted to make sure her investments were getting the best attention." She swallowed. "I assured her that they would be and gave her some insight into how our executive team is vital in making sure the investment strategies attempt to get us the best possible returns."

"Let's cut to the chase here, Ivy," Bill said, sitting back in his chair. "The bottom line is that this new initiative has been quite successful. You deserve full credit for that. But this isn't going to be successful without you. You asked for this position. I gave it you. You've proved yourself, but it can't continue to grow if you're not focused or you're not here. The exposure is good, but people want to know that you're part of the deal when they transfer their assets over to Blackwell. And lately, you just haven't been around."

Ivy sighed. "Dad." Bill tilted his head. He was listening. But all she could think about was how he'd respond to the fact that she got this show and it would require her to be in Los Angeles to shoot for several weeks. "Zoe is just as capable as me. She's my partner on this initiative."

"But Zoe's public image is not tied to Blackwell the way yours is. You're selling these people something that when they come to Blackwell they're not seeing. Do you know a client reached out because she was unable to connect with you for days while you were on tour? You're usually much more responsive. What happened?" Bill shook his head. "I'm excited for you and your book, but, Ivy, this is affecting business."

Ivy felt deflated. Her posture matched how she felt on the inside. There was so much she wanted to say to her father. Things like, what about what *she* wanted? That customer had been looking for her while she was in the hospital. She couldn't tell Bill about that yet. It would prove his point that things were falling through the cracks because she had too much on her plate.

"My book tour will be over soon and my schedule won't be as busy," she said.

"Honey. If it's not the tour, it's a conference, a speaking engagement or something else."

Ivy thought about the show when he said that. She had to be in LA in thirty days. She wanted to tell him, but couldn't bring herself do it just yet.

"I just need a little more time." Ivy didn't want to disappoint him. "The tour will be done in two more weeks. I'm sure you realize the conferences and speaking engagements will continue but that's how we've gotten so many of our new women clients. Those engagements have been great for business." She was proud of what she'd started at

Blackwell. Bill was right, she'd asked for this. But she also didn't want to disappoint herself.

Despite being exhausted, she deserved to enjoy all the amazing opportunities heading her way. It was new, different and exciting. Being the Money Maven pulled her entirely out of her comfort zone in the most dynamic ways. It was a life she created outside of the Blackwell name. The publisher, Jordan, the networks and her audience were less concerned about her being a Blackwell. They loved the profile she'd created with the help of her branding and social media team. Ivy never imagined she'd have her own show. How could she say no to that?

Ivy swallowed a lump in her throat. She remembered Kendall and Tyson's advice when they suggested she may have to quit Blackwell. It was looking more and more like having her position at Blackwell and her life as the Money Maven was becoming impossible to maintain simultaneously.

"I need to see some significant changes…" she heard Bill say. Ivy had gotten lost in her thoughts. "After this whole—" Bill waved his hand dismissively "—*book tour* thing is over, I need you to focus on your department. Your objectives. I built this company for my children. First Lincoln left. Then Carter. Looks like you're on your way out too. And for what? Your mother and I have broken our backs to give you everything. What more do you need?" And there it was, the "after all we've done for you" speech.

It was true. In the past few years, all but Ethan had walked away from Blackwell to pursue other opportunities. Each of them seemed to be walking away from the legacy Bill and Lydia worked so hard to create for them. Again, guilt and anger swirled in her chest, feeling like a bad case of heartburn. Ivy swallowed. She understood Bill's desire to create a legacy. It was notable. But had he even once asked her what she wanted?

# Twenty-Two

Jordan kissed Ivy's lips. He took his forefinger and gently touched the tip of her nose, where the light of the morning sun had settled. He wanted to wake up next to her every day. Ivy giggled under his touch.

"Today's your big day. How do you feel?" he asked, facing her as he lay on his side. Crisp white sheets covered their naked bodies.

"I can't even put my feelings into words," Ivy said. "I still can't believe I have my own television show. Oh, my goodness!" She laid on her back, squeezed her eyes shut and squealed. "I have a television show!"

Jordan chuckled, happy about his role in making her smile. At one point he thought this deal was never going to happen. Their production schedule was delayed by almost six additional weeks. Even the season had changed. Ivy was glad to be in Los Angeles because Old Man Winter had a heck of a grip on New York. She hadn't bothered to book a hotel for her stay in LA. Jordan's condo had become their regular hangout. The only benefit to the frustrating delays was the fact that Jordan and Ivy got to spend so much time together before the show started shooting.

"We need to get dressed so we can get down to the studio. We've got a long day ahead of us," Ivy said, turning back toward Jordan.

"Yeah. Right after this." He wrapped his arms around Ivy and pulled her on top of him. "Do you see what you do to me?"

Ivy showered his face with kisses. Tenderness spread through Jordan. Being with Ivy, feeling her touch, seeing her smile, being the subject of her undivided attention—all of these things made his chest warm on the inside. He couldn't ever remember a woman's attention making him feel this way.

Jordan drew Ivy even closer to him. Skin to skin, they stared deep into each other's eyes. There was something about this woman. Something that Jordan couldn't put into words. Her presence in his life over the past few months felt right in every way.

Staring up at her, he searched Ivy's eyes. He hoped she was as enamored with him as he was with her. Jordan felt his erection growing, standing at attention between them. He wanted to feel her. He wanted to be inside of her. However, he didn't want to stop admiring Ivy. He ran his finger through her hair. Kissed her nose. Then ran his thumb across her lips and claimed her mouth with his. Ivy looked back at him and blinked. Pulling back, he watched her pretty lashes flutter and gently kissed each lid.

As he continued basking in her, Ivy reached down and wrapped her hand around his erection. Jordan's core tightened. Instinctively, his eyes closed briefly. He felt Ivy's lips on his. Their kiss was passionate. Deep. Hungry. Jordan licked a scorching trail from Ivy's lips to her navel. He spread her legs, circled his tongue along her love canal before gently nibbling on her bud. She hissed. Jordan smiled. Ivy's excitement excited him. He couldn't get enough of her.

Jordan continued nibbling until Ivy's moans grew louder and louder, compelling Jordan to please her more. He wrapped his hand around her hips and worked her bud until she beat the sheets with her fists and howled. Lifting himself, he entered her slickness. All the while, Ivy gasped and groped at Jordan. His sweat-covered body wouldn't allow her to get a good grip.

Jordan drove himself inside of Ivy, burying his shaft deep within her. Her walls tightened around him, giving him pleasure so profound he could feel himself slipping into euphoria.

"Ivy!" Her name slipped from his lips in a whisper.

"Jordan." She said his name and the sound was so wondrous to his ears that his heart clenched.

Together they found a glorious rhythm and rode each other until Jordan's skin prickled with sweet, sweltering heat and the pain of too much pleasure.

"Ivy. Ivy." He called her name with each downstroke. His body bucked, making his rhythm staccato. "Ivy," Jordan grunted.

"Jordan!" Ivy was breathless. She dug her fingernails into his backside, pushing him deeper inside of her. "Oh, Jordan!"

"Ivy." Jordan pumped faster. He could feel the quickened pace of his heart. Another second inside of her and he was going to blow. "Ivy... I..." Jordan's eyes popped open. He looked down at her moving under him and blinked. Her eyes were closed and the look of pure pleasure was plastered across her face. She was caught up in the moment. Blissfully unaware of what almost came out of his mouth. Jordan tried not to lose his rhythm. Closing his eyes, he found a new tempo and hung on to it until Ivy cried out and shuddered. His peak ripped through him with the fire and force of a shooting star. Jordan groaned. His abdomen tightened. His strokes became short, urgent and fast until the dam broke inside of him. Jordan removed himself and felt the life flow from him in back-shattering waves. Together their bodies went limp.

With eyes closed, Ivy snuggled against his damp chest. She snaked her arms around his torso and squeezed him to her. Jordan's eyes were fixed on the sunlight glowing orange outside the window. They had to get going but he didn't want to move. His heart was still pumping rapidly. Not because he'd just had the best sex of his life, but because he'd almost shouted that he loved Ivy in the middle of it.

Jordan didn't move. He just let Ivy stay there in his arms, sated, as his mind analyzed what had just happened. He replayed all that had transpired between the evening he'd first seen Ivy at the wrap event right up to her being in his arms tonight.

Over the last few weeks, they had spent every possible moment together. He visited New York and she visited Los Angeles often. They commuted to each other as if they were a mere subway ride away. Jordan would also meet her in other cities when she traveled.

They were doing more than having fun. Jordan and Ivy were having the time of their lives. He made note of all the things that brought her joy and made a sport of spoiling Ivy. He hadn't met her family, but from their long conversations and all of the pillow talk, he felt like he already knew them. They hadn't actually labeled their commitment, but Jordan certainly hadn't thought of entertaining any other women. Despite a lack of definition, what they shared was special to Jordan. They hadn't set out to keep their dating a secret, but very few people knew about them.

Jordan had only just mentioned Ivy to Dorian. He couldn't keep anything from Anderson, so he hadn't tried, knowing he could trust him implicitly. Jordan knew that Ivy's sister-in-law Zoe knew about them. But she was Ivy's keeper of secrets. Both Jordan and Ivy preferred to keep their love lives low-key for two reasons. First, because they valued their privacy, and second, because they wanted to keep their work interactions professional.

They were usually successful in keeping their connection under wraps but sometimes the intense chemistry between them would ooze into the atmosphere. They'd laugh about it later over dinner or in bed.

"Jordan," Ivy called his name, bringing him back to the present. Her sultry voice made him want to make love to her again but they were running out of time.

He kissed her forehead. "Yeah?"

"We have to go," she said.

"I know."

Instead of getting out of the bed, Ivy straddled him, wrapped her palm around his limpness and massaged him back to life. It didn't take long at all. She guided him inside of her and rode him until a cacophony of groans and moans created a sultry chorus.

Finally, they dressed and headed to the studio. Jordan's thoughts keep slipping back to what he'd almost said in the sizzling heat of the moment. Had he meant what he was about to say or was it a case of temporary incredible sexual insanity?

# Twenty-Three

Ivy went to the studio by car service. Jordan drove. It was her idea. Neither wanted to leave the bed they'd come to share regularly. Ivy wasn't necessarily hiding the fact that she was dating Jordan; she was simply keeping her business to herself. Jordan was her delicious little secret. More importantly, they wanted to keep things professional for the sake of the show. Being the Money Maven was her public profile, but Ivy Blackwell appreciated her privacy. Which was becoming more and more difficult to manage.

She had been wondering where things were going with them for a while now but didn't want to be the one to bring it up. They could revisit that after shooting the show. Jordan had become like a balm. Being with him soothed Ivy. Just hearing his voice helped to ease real pressures of her busy life whether he was in person or over the phone. He'd become a confidant, a voice of reason and the person she bounced ideas off of.

Jordan encouraged her to fly Dale Billington out to the

studio to watch the filming of the show. He helped her convince Dale that all the opportunities that Ivy enjoyed helped to raise the profile for Ivy, Blackwell and her clients, bringing Dale another step closer to signing with them. Jordan was brilliant when it came to working with picky clientele.

Ivy's car pulled up to the studio. She opened her window to take it all in. The driver rolled through the studio arriving at a trailer with Ivy's name on it. Giggles bubbled out of her. She couldn't contain herself!

Exiting the car, Ivy took in the trailer, covered her mouth and shook her head. Both her names were on the trailer, Ivy Blackwell and the Money Maven. A young woman with a clipboard walked up to her.

"Morning, Money Maven." She held out her small hand. Her petite stature didn't match her booming voice. Ivy like her immediately.

"Good morning…" Ivy paused.

"Hailey," the woman said and they shook hands.

"Good morning, Hailey."

"Let's get you settled in and ready to start."

Ivy smiled. She was never at a loss for words, but didn't know what else to say. She followed Hailey to her trailer so she could put her things down and then they toured the set. More people arrived, including Jordan and Anderson. Ivy was carried off to wardrobe to pick out a few outfits and meet some of the celebs she would be working with to fix their finances. After hours of prep, they were finally ready to shoot a few scenes.

Ivy's excitement managed to help keep her mind off Jordan. Yet, several times, she'd catch a glimpse of him in action. Ivy was impressed at how he navigated the set, gave orders or interacted with the crew. When she thought no one was looking, she'd allow herself a moment to study his handsome face, broad shoulders and taut chest. His smile made her swoon even from a distance. What Ivy hadn't expected was the twinge of jealousy that squiggled through her when she realized that she wasn't the only woman on the set eyeing him.

That unexpected envy had thrown her when the crew was trying to capture a few video clips of her around the set that were going be used in the show's opening. She was supposed to be posing for videos and photos but her eyes kept wandering toward Jordan on the other side of the studio. He was speaking to a woman who kept rubbing this arm.

Ivy shook it off but watching the woman dote on him put a damper on her excitement. At one point the director, Carly, followed Ivy's line of sight to Jordan all the way on the other side of the set. She looked away, hoping the woman didn't realize she had been watching Jordan. During a break, she grabbed a granola bar, and her stomach lurched when the director came over to examine the snacks at the food table.

"Doing okay?" Carly asked.

"Me?" Ivy asked.

"Yes. First day going okay?"

"Yes. This is very thrilling."

"Good," Carly said and fell silent for a moment while she studied Ivy. "Just be careful."

"Careful of what?"

"You're not the only woman around here with their eyes on Jordan Chambers. Every eligible chick wants a piece of him. He doesn't exactly wear himself thin like most of the other producers out here, which is why he's in demand. Competition is stiff around here." Carly chuckled. "Vicious and relentless too," she said before walking off.

Ivy wanted to ask Carly what she meant by that but bit her tongue. That would let the director know she was interested in Jordan, and what they had was their secret. However, Carly's words did fire off a bunch more questions in Ivy's mind. They also planted some seeds of worry and doubt. How many women on the set were after Jordan? Had anyone else noticed how she'd studied him? Would they make things difficult on the set?

By the time the day ended, Ivy convinced herself that dating Jordan while the show was in production wasn't a good idea. She found herself wondering about who he was likely to spend time with while she was back in New York.

Ivy groaned aloud as she paced her trailer during another break. Why was she even worried about women crushing on Jordan? What did she care about who he was spending his time with when she was in New York? Ivy had never been the jealous type. And she and Jordan has intentionally avoided labeling what they had together. None of this stuff should have mattered to Ivy. Yet all of it did.

Ivy popped open one of the sparkling waters stored in her refrigerator. Sat down and pulled out her cell phone. She hadn't noticed her parents' and brothers' messages in their family chat. They were asking about the first day of shooting. Her father still wasn't 100 percent on board, but her brothers had convinced him that good things would come from this. The delays to the start of the shooting schedule did give Ivy the time she needed to prepare him for the fact that she would need a six-week leave to be in LA to film the show. Only Zoe knew that she was staying with Jordan instead of renting a place of her own. It was his idea. They'd agreed that she could check into the hotel whenever she felt like she needed space.

Ivy sent them a few pictures of the set that she'd taken throughout the day. She uploaded a fun selfie of her pointing to her name on the side of the trailer to her social media profiles.

There were two short hard knocks on Ivy's door. She looked at the time on her cell to make sure she hadn't overstayed her break time.

"Coming!" she said, assuming it was one of the production assistants coming to get her.

Ivy opened the door to find Jordan standing on the other side.

"Hey. Come on in." Ivy nervously scanned the area outside of her trailer. Had someone seen him come inside? Did it matter?

Jordan stepped in and looked around. Ivy glanced around one more time before closing the door behind him.

"You happy with the trailer? I told them to take good care of you," he murmured, stepping closer to her.

Ivy turned, walked over to grab her bottle of sparkling water and took a sip. "It's great. Why did you tell them to do that?"

"We do that for all of our major talent."

"Oh…okay. Thanks. It's fine," Ivy said.

Jordan narrowed his eyes at her. "Are you okay?"

"Yeah. I'm fine."

He tilted his head and studied her for a moment. "You sure?"

Ivy chuckled and waved away his concern. "I'm sure."

"Still excited?"

"Absolutely!"

Jordan closed the space between them and slid his arms around her waist. "We will celebrate your first full day when we get home."

*Home.* Jordan had said the word as if his home was also her home. Everything that Carly said about other women pursuing Jordan flooded Ivy's mind. Was she doing the right thing?

Before she could protest, Jordan put his lips on hers. She closed her eyes and melted in his embrace.

Ivy wiped her lipstick from Jordan's lips when they finished kissing. "Maybe we shouldn't be doing this here."

"Who's going to know?" Jordan asked, shrugging.

"I'm just saying." Ivy pulled away. "We said we would keep it professional on set."

Jordan held his hand up. "You're right. I just wanted to check on you. I have to run. Meet you back at my house later?"

"Sure."

Jordan kissed her before leaving her trailer. His kiss, as passionate as all the others, seemed to lift her off her feet. The second he left, the reality of how close they were cutting things came crashing down on her again. What was she doing?

She sat down and gathered her emotions. They were all over the place. If they needed her on the set, they'd send a production assistant to get her. She checked in with Dale, who was supposed to arrive that day. The next day, she would come to visit the set like Jordan suggested.

Ivy's phone buzzed indicating that she had another text message. It was an image and link from Zoe with a text that said, Have you seen this?

What came up shocked Ivy. The link took her to a gossip site's media profile displaying several pictures of her and Jordan at different times over the past week. The caption said, "Is the Money Maven 'fixing' more than just celebrity's finances while in LA?"

Ivy covered her mouth. Where had this come from?

# Twenty-Four

Jordan sat with his head in his hands. The day couldn't have started better. He'd woken up beside Ivy, relished her excitement of the first day of her show and made sweet love to her. What the heck happened to get them to where they were now?

He watched Ivy stuff her belongings in her suitcase and frantically explain why she had to go.

"This doesn't make sense to me, Ivy." He was exasperated.

"I don't know how else to say this, Jordan. This—" she looked around and then pointed to him and then her "—wasn't a good idea. We just got carried away. I mean, it was fun while it lasted but this is proof that it was a bad idea!" Ivy held up her phone displaying the social media post speculating about their involvement. "My family has seen this, and now they're concerned about some kind of viral scandal blowing up and making us look bad." Ivy flopped down on the chaise across from Jordan's massive king-size bed. Her head hung low and she closed her eyes.

"This is all part of being a public figure. You can't let this kind of stuff affect you!"

"Well, I haven't learned how to do that yet. It's bothering the heck out of me. I don't want to be the subject of anybody's attention-seeking headline to get some likes and clicks."

"You gave up that option when you became the Money Maven," Jordan said, and Ivy's head snapped in his direction. She looked like she would burst into tears at any moment.

"I'm sorry but it's the truth. Ugh!" Jordan stood and paced. After a few moments, he huffed and turned to Ivy. "Just let your family know that this kind of stuff is part of the process. Explain that to your parents. I'm pretty sure your brothers get it."

"You don't understand, Jordan." Ivy's shoulders slumped.

"So, what are you going to do? Stop being the Money Maven? No social media, no speaking events, no more workshops and no show?" Jordan asked. Ivy rubbed her temples. "Because that's what it's going to take for the gossip sites and internet trolls to back off. You'd have to be insignificant to them. Stop reading that crap and keep doing all the amazing things you've been doing."

Her hands flopped into her lap. "It's one thing to see this happen to others. But it's me. This doesn't feel good. Look what happened at the awards and now this. My parents are furious, asking me all kinds of crazy questions that I can't answer. It's too much! How am I supposed to just ignore it all?"

"By continuing to be you. You love helping women. Keep doing that." Jordan pivoted like he had a great idea. "We could get in front of this, you know."

"How?"

"We put something out on our own social media," he proposed. "Let people know we're seeing each other. It's no big deal."

Ivy took a deep breath. She finally stood. "That's not going to work, Jordan. It will look like I got this opportunity because I was sleeping with you. That's the last thing I want."

Jordan grunted. "It doesn't have to be that way."

Ivy threw her hands up. "Stop. I need to go."

"Why?"

"If I'm going to be any good on set. I need to keep a clear head, and with all that's going on, it's becoming harder to do."

Jordan clenched his jaw. "You're talking about us, aren't you?" He stepped closer to her. Ivy took a step back as he approached. "What happened today?" He reached out for Ivy. She moved out of his reach. "Did I do something?" Jordan asked incredulously. He was hurt and confused.

"No." Her voice was just above a whisper. "I just…we took this too far, too soon. I…don't want this to look the wrong way." She started pacing again. "We need to put space between us at least until after we're done with filming."

"Where are you going to go?" Jordan folded his arms, unfolded them and put his thumb and index finger on his forehead.

"I'll stay at a hotel." She flipped her hand as if it were no big deal.

"You don't have to do this." Frustration rose in him. He didn't mean to sound harsh. Jordan was just having a hard time keeping his emotions in check. This was the woman that he almost admitted his love for less than twenty-four hours ago. Everything was great then. Now, things were drastically different and he couldn't understand why. "What about our plans for tonight? What about this weekend? Dale is coming to the set tomorrow."

"I'm sorry, Jordan."

"This social media stuff will die down. All we—"

"I'm dealing with it the best way I know how," Ivy interjected.

"By running away from everything? By running away from *me*?" Jordan jabbed his chest.

"Especially you."

Jordan felt as if he'd been kicked in the chest. He reared his head back.

"This is my profession. It's an amazing opportunity. I can't have it tainted with some kind of crazy scandal. I'm sorry but I have to do this."

Jordan stood, shaking his head. He wasn't a scandal. He loved this woman. She just didn't know it. Maybe he should have told her but that window of opportunity had passed. Saying it now wouldn't change anything. If Ivy wanted to go, he'd have to let her no matter how bad he wanted her to stay. He would never be the one to keep company that didn't want to be kept.

He lifted his hands up in defeat. Biting his lip, he fought to reel in his emotions. He turned, stepped into the walk-in closet in the en suite and came back with keys.

"Here." He handed them to Ivy, who was facing the window with her arms folded.

"What is this?"

"Keys to my company's corporate apartment. We keep it for special guests. If you have to leave here, stay there. You don't have to go to a hotel. Plus, you'll have much more privacy."

Ivy looked at the keys a moment before taking them. "What's the address?"

Jordan looked at her. After several moments ticked by, he said, "It's the other penthouse across the hall."

Ivy blinked a few times. Jordan thought she was about to hand him back the keys. Instead, she swallowed hard, put the keys in her jean pocket and gathered her bags. He watched her pack the rest of her things and pile them by the door. He tried to help, but she refused any assistance from him. No words passed between them but the tension in the air was stifling.

Finally, Ivy opened the door and looked back at him. "Thank you." Putting everything on the other side of the door, she looked at Jordan. The sadness in her eyes made his chest tighten. He wondered if this hurt her as much as it was hurting him.

The sounds of the door shutting and connecting with the locks felt as if the door of his heart had also been slammed shut. What was he supposed to do without Ivy?

# Twenty-Five

"Are you ready?" Ivy asked Zoe.

"I've *been* ready. I got up super early, worked out, ate, and now I'm here sitting on my thumbs waiting for you. I'm so excited I don't know what to do with myself. I already spoke to my mom twice and your mom once. Ethan and the baby probably won't answer any more of my calls." Zoe cackled.

"Okay. I'm on my way to get you now." Ivy was so happy to see Zoe. It would be several weeks before she got to see any other family members. She grabbed her purse and headed to the door. "And I can't wait until dinner. You're going to love this place."

Ivy stepped out the door at the same time Jordan walked out of his. Her heart skipped. A few awkward seconds passed.

"Hey, Zoe. Hold on one sec," Ivy said and muted her phone.

"Good morning," Jordan said. His usual bright smile appeared dull.

"Morning," Ivy said and spread her lips into a cordial smile.

Another few seconds passed. Jordan wasn't apologetic at all about his desire for Ivy. She could see it in his eyes. No matter what, she needed to keep her distance.

"Have a good shoot today. I may stop by."

"Thanks," Ivy said.

More seconds ticked by. "Okay. See you later." Jordan walked to the elevator.

"I'm back," Ivy said, taking the other woman off mute. She continued chatting with Zoe but waited for Jordan to get on the elevator before walking down the hall and pressing the call button herself. "I'm getting on the elevator. I might lose you. I'll see you in a few." She ended their call.

Downstairs, she headed to the car that waited on her. Despite keeping his distance, Jordan made sure she had a ride to work every day even if he no longer rode with her. The time alone gave her the space to think.

Ivy's days on the set had grown increasingly awkward since she left Jordan's penthouse. When he was around, she spent all of her energy trying to act like his presence didn't affect her. On the days he wasn't there, Ivy longed to see him. At the penthouse, listening to him come and go sent her mind wandering. Who was he spending his time with? How long would he be gone? When would he get back? Less than a week had passed but it felt like she'd been missing Jordan forever.

Ivy made the right choice. Didn't she? She couldn't tell Jordan that she needed to leave because she was falling for him harder and faster than she could have ever imagined. Her feelings for him started to affect everything. She found herself acting out of character, getting jealous when other women were around him on the set, losing her focus. Ivy loved being the Money Maven, but behind the scenes, she valued her privacy. Those gossip posts about her and Jordan really upset her and she didn't want them to negatively impact either of their careers.

Getting out of his house and separating herself from him was supposed to help her figure things out. It didn't work. Being away from Jordan was hard to bear. Ivy thought about him constantly. She missed him terribly.

Dale's visit to the set that week went extremely well. She was elated about being at the studio, and squealed in delight when they asked her to join Ivy in one of the scenes at a local restaurant. After spending time with Ivy both on and off the set, Dale told her that she understood Ivy's mission to help women become financially savvy. She'd added that Ivy's goal went beyond telling women what to do what money; she helped women understand the importance of building a legacy of wealth. It was empowering. And despite some of the ridiculous antics of the celebrity clients she worked with on the show, this came through.

When Dale returned to New York, she told Ivy that she was looking forward to transferring her assets to Blackwell. That fifty-million-dollar portfolio would be the largest of all her women customers. Bill was ecstatic. Ivy invited Dale to come back to LA with her family for the show's upcoming wrap party.

Ivy was so glad that it all went well. She'd never worked so hard to close a deal with a client before in her life. When Dale left to go back to New York there was nothing to distract Ivy from missing Jordan. Now Zoe had arrived and would help to keep Ivy's mind off him—at least for the two days that she would be there. Zoe needed a break and Ivy encouraged her to come for a visit. Only, Zoe stayed at a hotel. She didn't want to invite her to the penthouse. She never would have been able to hide all the tension between her and Jordan in such close proximity.

The driver pulled up to Zoe's hotel. Ivy dialed her and let her know she was downstairs. Minutes later, Zoe came bursting through front entrance of the hotel. Ivy jumped out of the car and met her with open arms. The two hugged, swaying like long-lost friends who hadn't seen each other in years. It had only been weeks and they usually spoke daily.

"I'm so happy to see you!" Ivy gushed to Zoe as they slid into the car.

"I'm glad to see you too. And I can't wait to see you in action. I still can't believe you have a show. Ethan told me to take plenty of pictures."

At the studio, Ivy gave her a tour of her trailer. Zoe took a selfie next to her name on the outside. Ivy went to wardrobe and makeup, came out and modeled for Zoe.

"OMG! You look amazing!"

"Ha! It's like playing dress-up every day. It's crazy."

One of the production assistants told Ivy they were ready for her to shoot her wrap-up from the day before. It took a few takes, but Ivy was able to get through it without stumbling over her words. She was getting better at this part every day.

Through her peripheral, Ivy caught a glimpse of Jordan. She didn't have to see him fully to know it was him. Her body responded to his presence before she ever set eyes on him. Butterflies would take flight in her stomach if she heard his voice or witnessed his sexy gait. She stiffened just a little. She looked for Zoe, who had walked to the other side of the set. Ivy was glad her sister-in-law wasn't there to witness her body's response to Jordan's arrival. Zoe noticed nuances like that all the time.

Ivy pushed through for the rest of the day. Once they let her go, she couldn't wait to leave the set.

"Dinnertime!" she announced to Zoe, trying to sound cheerful.

"Great! I'm starving and that food they have over there is a bit too fancy to get me full."

"Good evening. You must be Zoe?" The sound of Jordan's voice made Ivy's heart pause. "Ivy." He nodded and turned his attention back to Zoe.

"Yes, and I believe you're Jordan Chambers."

"I am. It's great to have you here. I hope you're enjoying your trip so far. Ivy is amazing in front of the camera, isn't she?"

Jordan's glance made air swirl in Ivy's chest. Why did he have to be so handsome, even when he was being dry and cordial?

"Yes, she was. I'm so proud of her."

"Me too. I think this show is going to be a hit with the viewers."

"Oh, for sure! It's got everything. Glitz, glam, spoiled celebrity brats with ridiculously bad financial habits and some heartfelt lessons. Plus, my sister here is absolutely beautiful. We know TV land loves a pretty face."

"I have to agree with you on all those points—especially that last one," Jordan said, glancing at Ivy.

Her cheeks warmed. "Thanks." Ivy smiled. "Well, we have some really exciting dinner plans…" She grabbed her bag.

"Sure. Don't let me stand in the way of a great meal." His eyes lingered on her face for a moment. "Have a good evening, Ivy." He turned to Zoe. "It was nice meeting you. Enjoy your stay."

"That man is a work of freaking art!" Zoe said once Jordan was out of earshot. "I thought things were going well between you two. Did I sense some tension?"

Ivy sighed. "I'll tell you over dinner." She texted the driver. "Let's go." She and Zoe headed out of the hotel and jumped in the car the moment her driver arrived.

Within fifteen minutes, they arrived at the Mexican

restaurant Ivy had grown to love since she'd been in Los Angeles.

"Before you order, let me tell you all about my favorites," Ivy said once they were seated.

"All of it sounds delicious. Let's order different meals and share."

"Perfect idea." Ivy waved over their server and they put in their orders.

"Now, what's up with you and that gorgeous man?"

She told her sister-in-law everything. When she was done speaking, she expected Zoe to agree with her side and offer her some moral support. When Zoe didn't speak right away, she furrowed her brow and stared at her.

"What is it? Just spit it out already," she demanded, growing uncomfortable under Zoe's narrowed gaze.

"Are you kidding me? You're walking away from this man, who has been nothing short of amazing, because you can't control your hormones?"

"Zoe!" Ivy looked around to see if anyone else in the restaurant had heard her. "You're oversimplifying this as usual."

"Okay. Maybe I am, but listen to yourself and admit the man was right. You can't control people—especially social media trolls. Who cares if you fell into his bed before, after or during the production of this show? You are two grown, consenting adults. As long as you weren't taken advantage of, you have the right to do whatever you wish. Do you like him?"

"I…" Ivy huffed, buying time.

"Yes! You do. It's written all over your face. So, if you like him, screw what anyone else has to say and go for it." Zoe sat back. "You've been out of the dating game for so long you forgot how to play."

"Zoe, he lives clear across the country."

"So what! And he has an apartment in Manhattan.

Somehow the two of you have found a way to consistently see each other until now."

Ivy lifted her chin. "Once the show is over, that will change."

"Does he have a girlfriend, fiancée, wife?"

"No."

"Neither do you," Zoe reminded her. "So, what's stopping you from being with Jordan?"

Ivy groaned, and fluffed her full hair. "I really don't have the time to nurture a relationship right now. I've been offered a second book by my publisher. And this show will air soon. That's going to lead to more engagements and Dad is only temporarily happy because of this big win from Dale." She blew out a breath. "My schedule is filling up by the minute. And in all honesty, I don't know how much longer I'll be able to stay at Blackwell. I may need to go part-time or stay on in name only to help you out with the women's initiative. You know that." Ivy sat back hard.

"And all of that means you can't date? I'm confused."

"*What?* I'm not saying that."

Zoe folded her arms, making her statement. Ivy looked at her and rolled her eyes. "Ivy, none of that means that you have to walk away from a man that you obviously care about. Stop making excuses. I know you want to be with this man, so be with him. You don't owe anyone any explanations but you do owe it to yourself to be happy, and if being with Jordan makes you happy, go get your man even if it scares you to pieces!"

Zoe had summed it all up. But the truth was, Ivy *was* scared. She'd messed up so many relationships before. What if she messed this up with Jordan too?

# Twenty-Six

Jordan's day started out well but quickly went sour. Running into Ivy on and off the set had become taxing. As much as he wanted to pull her aside and kiss her breathless, he had to keep his distance. He gave her the space she needed and hoped that things would come together after their shooting schedule was over. Once the show went into postproduction, she'd head back to New York and Jordan could figure out his next step. As for now, seeing her without being able to take her into his arms was like torture.

He'd stopped by the set to check in with the crew. When he laid eyes on Ivy, the tempo of his pulse increased. Jordan started from her feet and slowly swept his gaze upward. Sexy pumps gave her foot the perfect lift. An off-white pantsuit bestowed her with an air of elegance, yet didn't hide a single luscious curve, and the tapered jacket accentuated her waist. The silk blouse underneath was unbuttoned just enough to make his mind wander, her red kissable lips were edgy and seductive, and Ivy's beautiful full head of crinkly curls was pulled stylishly to one side. Plus, the makeup was *flawless*. She looked hot and all business at the same time.

Ivy stood next to one of the celebrities from the show but completely outshined them. Jordan knew she was right about one thing. It was easier for him to focus at work when she wasn't around. He could never seem to keep his eyes off her.

She glanced up. Jordan and her locked eyes. Longing shot through him like a lightning bolt. She blinked and her lashes fluttered. She was absolutely exquisite. Anderson had to call his name twice before his voice registered in Jordan's ear.

Tearing himself away from that perfect vision, Jordan headed to over to Anderson to discuss scheduling. Then his phone rang. His stepfather's number came up. Jordan looked at the number, felt the phone vibrate and contemplated whether or not he should let it go to voice mail. Their last exchange wasn't good. Tim said some pretty sharp words the last time Jordan was in New York. Jordan finally answered. Tim asked for him to call him back later that evening so they could talk.

Jordan ended the call wondering what the man had to say this time. He assumed he'd get a call from his mother by the time Tim called him back. She was still upset about how things went when her husband blew up.

Next, Jordan heard a scream followed by a huge commotion. Two of the contestants got into a fight and knocked over a bookshelf. Ivy fell trying to avoid getting toppled by the shelf and ended up twisting her ankle. Jordan helped her up and tended to her before addressing the incident.

For the next few hours, he and the crew spent their energy on settling the disagreement between the two spoiled-rich contestants and dealing with the damage from their altercation. One threatened to sue everyone on set until

Jordan reminded him that he could be found in violation of his contract. Money wasn't the issue. The contestants could buy the whole studio. It was the fame they desired. They weren't well-known actors themselves. They were the grown children of entertainers and celebrities who relished getting fifteen minutes in the spotlight whenever possible. Jordan told him that this wasn't that kind of reality show.

By the time he got home, it was too late to call his stepfather back. Entering his penthouse, Jordan tossed his car keys on the marble-topped table near the door, headed straight to his wine cabinet and poured half a glass of scotch. He was mentally and physically drained. Flopping down on the couch, he sat in darkness. Only the light of the full moon illuminated the room. Jordan wondered if that moon had anything to do with the odd happenings of the day—the call from Timothy and the fight on the set.

Jordan sipped and rested his head against the back of the couch. He thought about his conversation with his stepfather. They would have to work something out for the sake of his mother. Tim was most likely asleep, but with the tension that resided between them, Jordan took his chances and called Tim back.

"I was waiting up. Thought you weren't going to call," the older man said.

"I just got in. What's up, Tim?"

"I wanted to apologize and talk to you. Last week my doctor thought my cancer had returned. After running tests, it hadn't. But that got me thinking. Life is fragile and I wanted to make things right with you boys."

"I'm glad you're okay."

"I never had kids," Tim said.

Jordan wondered where Tim was going with his statement. It seemed random.

"But I loved your mother from the first day I met her. I could see the pain in her eyes. I could *feel* it. And I wanted to make her happy. I knew nothing about raising kids, let alone teenage boys. I tried. But I couldn't break through your and your brother's grief."

Tim fell silent for a few moments. "Maybe I should have tried harder." He huffed. "Asking you boys for help was hard. My pride got the best of me. Honestly, I would never think that you guys would try to take advantage of me. And with my health challenges, your proposal makes sense. As I said, I realize how fragile life is. And though I know you boys will always be there for your mother, I want to do my part to make sure she's well taken care of if something happens to me." There was a long pause. "So, I'm signing the proposal and wanted to make sure you and Dorian were still interested in doing business with me."

"Wow!" Jordan was taken aback by Tim's admission. "We didn't make it very easy on you, did we?"

"You guys were young," Tim acknowledged. "I get why you resisted letting me into your life."

"We didn't know what to do with you when you came around. We just wanted our dad. I guess all of us could have done more to make things work better," Jordan admitted.

Silence expanded between them. After a while, Tim said, "If you'll have me, I'd love to do business with you guys."

"I'm okay with that. I'll reach out to Dorian. How about we review the terms together one more time and make sure we're all okay with everything. I'll be out there in a few weeks after this show wraps and we can tie up all the loose ends then. Deal?"

"Deal!" Tim said. After another long pause, Tim said, "Thanks."

They ended the call and Jordan placed his phone beside him on the couch. He rested his head against the back of the couch again. Moments later, there was a soft knock at his door. *"What now,"* he grumbled aloud. He just wanted to rest.

Jordan didn't feel like answering and thought about staying put right on the couch. The knock came again. He heard a voice call his name.

"Jordan." Ivy's sultry voice was muffled through the door but he knew it was her by the way his body responded with a tightening in his core.

Jordan sat up. He put his drink on the coffee table. He wondered what Ivy could want at this time of night and then remembered her ankle. Maybe she needed something. Was she in pain? Jordan shot up and headed to the door.

"Coming." He looked through the peephole to confirm. It was Ivy. She was gorgeous as usual. Clicking the locks, Jordan opened the door. He took a breath. She was no longer wearing the sexy white suit, but she looked just as alluring in her leggings and sweatshirt.

"Hi," Ivy said softly.

"Hi," Jordan murmured. He noticed she didn't move. "Want to come in?"

"Sure."

Jordan stepped aside to let Ivy pass. "I'm sorry. I meant to call and check on you. How's your ankle? Do you need anything?"

"It's fine. That's part of the reason I'm here. I wanted to thank you for helping me earlier. I can't believe what happened."

"Oh. No problem. Of course."

Ivy wrung her hands. Both stood awkwardly by the door. Several moments of silence wavered between them.

Jordan averted his eyes from her face. He couldn't stand to look at her lips. Because it just made him want to pull her into his arms and feast on her. He sighed. Ivy was in his system. She affected him. Despite the short amount of time, they had known one another, those words he'd almost uttered were true. He loved Ivy. He knew it then, but really knew it now after having to live without her. Jordan went to bed at night wishing she was beside him. He woke up reaching for her only to find the bed empty. It pained him to see her on the set, in meetings, in the building or around the neighborhood and not be with her, holding her hand or lying beside her. Jordan had incredible dates planned that they never had the opportunity to go on.

However, Ivy had to want him too. He'd always heard a saying about letting things you love go. If it was meant to be she'd come back. He understood her position and was willing to wait until the show was out of the way. He hoped she'd still be interested in finishing what they started or at least seeing where things would go from there.

It had been years since a woman had a grip on Jordan's heart like Ivy had. He'd wait on her if he had to.

"Was there something else?" Jordan asked stiffly.

"Pardon?"

"You said you stopped by to thank me. Was there something else you wanted to say?"

"Yes." Ivy tilted her head. "Jordan, I'm sorry." She shook her head.

Realizing he still hadn't shut the door, Jordan closed it, turned and gave Ivy his full attention. "Sorry for what?"

Ivy looked to the ceiling, shut her eyes and sighed. Then she looked directly into Jordan's eyes. "For acting crazy. I was scared. You were right about everything. I didn't expect things between us to…ugh… This social media life, books, television, the trolls… This is all new to me. I know finance. It's pretty calm in this industry. What I'm trying to say is that… Jordan…" She called his name with urgency.

"Yes, Ivy?"

Her mouth opened but nothing came out. She closed it and tried again. "I miss you." Her voice was low.

"You…"

"I. Miss. You," Ivy pronounced louder. "It's been so hard

staying this close to you and not being able to be with you. I don't know what you did to me!"

"Whatever it was, I think you did the same to me. I haven't stopped thinking about you."

"Really?" Ivy looked as if she would cry.

"Really. I've missed you too." Jordan took a step closer to her.

"Do you forgive me?" Ivy moved closer to him, lessening the space between them.

"No need to forgive you. I understand you."

Jordan didn't know what it was about what he said, but Ivy pulled him into her, held his face in her hands and kissed him. Overcome with emotion, Jordan lifted her into his arms, then placed her gently back on her feet. They kissed as if their lips were water in a dry desert. Jordan's heart beat hard in his chest as if it were just coming back to life. Ivy squeezed him tightly. They kissed until they ran out of breath.

Ivy looked into Jordan's eyes again. No words passed between them for several moments, yet he believed she understood what was in his heart and mind.

"I don't want to be with you just until the wheels fall off. I don't want casual sex or to just have some fun. I want you, Ivy. All of you. I want you to be my lady."

"I've never perfected this girlfriend thing but if you'll have me…" Ivy admitted softly.

"I don't expect perfection from you. We can figure this out together."

"There's so much to figure out," Ivy said, then threw her head back and giggled.

"So, let's have fun figuring it out." Jordan laughed too.

They kissed again. Long, lovingly and hungrily. Jordan finally tore himself away from her and smiled. She traced a finger along his chest.

"So. We're a…thing?"

"As long as you don't get mad if someone posts a picture of us on social media with a caption that says I'm your boyfriend," he teased.

Ivy playfully slapped his chest. "Silly. It will take some getting used to but I'm willing to deal with it." Ivy winked, eliciting a chuckle from him.

His expression changed abruptly when a thought came to mind. "Go get dressed. Put on something nice." He ushered Ivy to the door.

"For what? Where are we going?"

"On the date we were supposed to go on when you left."

"Seriously?"

"Yes. Put on something pretty and meet me back here in an hour."

Ivy took Jordan's wrist in her hand and looked at her watch. "It's late."

"A half hour. We still have time. Hurry."

Ivy scrunched her brow. "If you say so. Be right back."

In exactly a half hour, Jordan knocked on Ivy's door dressed in slacks and a stylish printed button-down shirt. She opened the door and all the air left Jordan's body. In that short amount of time, Ivy transformed into a stunning vision of sexiness. Her little black dress stopped midthigh revealing beautiful toned legs. Her hair, though perfectly styled, looked wilder and hotter than ever. Unable to help himself, Jordan pulled her in for a kiss.

"Let's go." Jordan grabbed Ivy's hand and led her laughing down the hall.

Twenty minutes later they were dining solo on a rooftop with a breathtaking view of downtown Los Angeles, while a world-renowned chef served them lobster, chateaubriand and sautéed veggies. Next, he took her to an exclusive club owned by an A-list entertainer. The average person had no idea places like this existed. Only the "who's who" of Hollywood and the entertainment scene were allowed inside.

Jordan and Ivy enjoyed the band and sang the lyrics from popular songs along with the crowd. Afterward they walked along the beach, hand in hand, as the moonlight rippled along the water. Ivy held her shoes in her hand.

"Ready to go home?" Jordan asked as they embraced under the moonlight.

"Home?" Ivy teased.

"Yes. My home."

"Why? You're tired?" she asked with a salacious smile. Jordan gave her a seductive wink. "Not at all."

"Then let's go!" Ivy giggled all the way back to the car.

They started kissing in the elevator. His hands touched her everywhere. Ivy slid her hands under his shirt and caressed his skin. Jordan body grew hot and his erection strained against his pants. They kissed and laughed and kissed some more.

At the door, Jordan fumbled with the keys. Finally getting them in the lock, he swung the door open. Their lips connected again. Jordan kicked the door closed with his foot and locked it. They kissed their way to his room.

Ivy slid the arms of her little black dress down and shimmied out of it. Jordan tossed off his shirt and pants. When they were fully naked, he pulled her to him and lifted her. Ivy wrapped her legs around his waist. Backing her up to the wall, Jordan entered Ivy. She moaned in ecstasy. Jordan's thrusts were full. Every stroke was intentional. Ivy scratched at his back, urging him to go deeper. He did. Soon after, his legs grew weak. He stood strong, keeping his stride until Ivy started to shiver. She whimpered, held him tighter and cried out when her climax claimed her. Jordan's release came immediately after. He grunted with each thrust until he felt life flowing through him. Then he pulled out. Ivy massaged the flow from his erection while Jordan bucked, holding the wall to keep from crumpling to the floor.

Afterward, Jordan carried her to the bed. Ivy snuggled in his arms as they talked about nothing and everything. Then they kissed until their bodies were set ablaze all over again by one another's touch. As Jordan entered her for the second time that night, he looked straight into her eyes. They didn't hold back this time.

"I love you, Ivy."

"I love you too, Jordan."

# Twenty-Seven

"We're here!" Ivy announced and jumped out of the party bus, careful not to rip her formfitting dress. She waved her family out. It was important to her that they traveled to the wrap party together.

"This is so exciting!" Phoenix said, exiting the party bus that Ivy rented.

"I can't wait for you all to meet the cast and crew." she replied. "And I'm so glad you were able to join us," she said, turning to Dale as the woman cautiously stepped out of the bus.

"I wouldn't have missed it for the world," Dale said.

One by one, her parents, siblings and sisters-in-law pooled onto the sidewalk.

Standing tall, Bill looked around—a big grin on his face. His smile made Ivy smile. It wasn't often that Bill showed how proud he was of his children.

"When do we get to meet the dude?" her brother Carter teased.

His wife, Phoenix, swatted him playfully. "Leave her alone."

"Yeah. That's what I want to know," the oldest brother, Lincoln, said.

"Me too," Ethan echoed. "Zoe has already met him. So, I know he must be kind of normal."

"Really, Ethan?" Ivy gave him a sideways glance.

"Yeah. He's dating you, right? That begs a few questions." Ethan laughed. Ivy's brothers Carter and Lincoln joined in. Lydia shook her head.

"Grow up!" Ivy rolled her eyes and laughed.

"Okay. Let's get this party started!" Zoe raised one hand in the air.

Ivy led her family into the chic office building, up the elevator and to the top floor. The wrap party was being held at a penthouse venue with a rooftop that boasted stunning views of Los Angeles.

Ivy checked in at the table separating the venue from the private party room that cost twenty-five thousand dollars to secure. A red carpet led the path to where the festivities would be held. Cameras flashed nonstop as photographers snapped countless pictures of Ivy with her family. They took several pictures before changing up their poses. Bill and Lydia with Ivy. Ivy with her sisters and then her brothers. They made funny faces.

"Ivy!" Her assistant from her branding agency called her name. "Want me to take some photos of you with your family?"

Ivy paused for a moment. She tried not to mix her public life with her family life. She thought a moment longer. "Yes. Take a few, please." Ivy pulled her family back together while her assistant took a few more shots.

"Hey, Ivy!" Someone else called her name.

"Hi, Nadia." After saying hello, Ivy introduced the daughter of one of Hollywood's biggest directors to her family.

A chorus of "Nice to meet you" was exchanged between Nadia and Ivy's family.

The door opened to the rooftop and Ivy turned around. She was hoping it was Jordan. It was Tyson and Kendall. She ran to them, hugged and kissed them both. They joined the rest of the family. Tyson kissed his aunt and uncle before loudly greeting his cousins. The women circled around one another, admiring each other's stylish outfits.

The door opened again. Ivy's eyes went straight to it. It wasn't Jordan. The longer she waited for him, the more anxious she became. Wringing her hands, she fought a mix of nervousness and excitement. Jordan was going to meet the rest of her family. How would Bill and Lydia respond? She wasn't really worried about her brothers. They were mostly bark.

Several other reporters called Ivy. She excused herself from her family, leaving them to get comfortable and enjoy themselves. She smiled for pictures, took selfies and mingled with the crew and cast as they arrived.

Despite being anxious, Ivy sighed. She looked around the wrap party and realized how far she'd come in the past few months. The women's initiative at Blackwell was wildly successful and had grown even more once Dale signed and started sharing with her network of very wealthy woman. Ivy's book made the *New York Times* bestseller list. She was the star of a reality show. It was a lot to take in but she was working at becoming more comfortable with her newfound fame every day. Even the social media trolls didn't bother her the way they used to. She'd done it. She made a name for herself outside of being a Blackwell. The best part about all of this was the most unexpected—she'd found love.

A hand slid around her waist from the back. Without turning around, she knew exactly who it was. Ivy knew his scent. She could feel his presence. Immediately she'd relax whenever he was around. Ivy finally turned around and put her arms around Jordan's neck. He kissed her lips. It was a peck but he'd done it slow and sweet.

"This is your night," he said, holding the small of her back.

"It's your night too."

"Okay. It's *our* night. Are you okay?"

"Yes. I'm fine. I'm excited."

"Good. If you feel like you need to get out of here at some point and go put on some leggings and a hoodie, just give me a signal."

Ivy chuckled. "I'll be fine. Come meet my family."

"Oh, boy!" Jordan let Ivy lead her to them.

"Mom. Dad," Ivy called out as she moved across the room. She waved at her siblings. When they were all together, Ivy said, "This is the executive producer, Jordan Chambers."

"Hello, Jordan," Bill said and shook his hand.

"You must be Mr. Blackwell," Jordan murmured. "And this must be your lovely wife." Jordan nodded and shook Lydia's hand as well.

"Nice to meet you. So, you're that gentleman that's trying to make my baby girl a star." Tight-lipped. Lydia looked him up and down before finally releasing a smile.

"Oh, no, ma'am. She's a star all on her own."

"I'm glad you recognize that."

Jordan greeted Ivy's brothers and sisters.

"And!" Ivy said, getting everyone's attention. "FYI he's also my boyfriend."

"Mmm," Zoe moaned and burst out laughing. The other ladies joined her.

"I see…" Bill said.

"Well, now," Lydia murmured. "I guess dinner is in order so we can get to know you a little better. Tomorrow evening at a place of your choice?" She looked at Jordan as if she dared him to say no.

"Absolutely."

"Good answer!" Ethan said and everyone fell out laughing again. "This calls for another drink. What do you say, fellows?" The men agreed. Jordan walked to the bar with Ivy's brothers and cousin.

Jordan looked back and winked at Ivy, letting her know he was going to be fine.

Ivy breathed in and let out a long exhale. She was glad that this part was over. So far, they all seemed to embrace Jordan. That made her happy because he was her peace.

Someone clinked a glass, gathering the attention of everyone in the room. They welcomed everyone and called Jordan and Anderson to the center of the room. Anderson told everyone how they came to the idea of this show. His energy lit up the room. When they were done, everyone applauded. The music became louder and people filled the room dancing.

Jordan found his way over to Ivy. Somehow, they became the center of attention. A circle formed around them. The DJ put on the rap song they'd sung together in the shower. Ivy's eyes grew as wide as her smile. She looked at Jordan, daring him to sing with her.

"Somebody, give me a mic," he said.

Her assistant ran to the DJ and brought a mic back to her. In one hand she gathered the bottom of her shimmering dress. In the other, she held the mic to her mouth and started reciting the lyrics. Jordan pumped his fist in the air. The crowd around them became hyped, cheering her on as she sang. Ivy and Jordan sang the chorus together. She handed him the microphone and he performed the second verse.

While he sang, Ivy danced and swayed, pumping her fist and cheering him on. People were snapping pictures. She didn't care. Joy filled her heart, making her giddy. Jordan finished his verse. Ivy thought he was going to hand the microphone back to her. She reached for it but the artist who sang the song stepped into their circle and took over.

Ivy froze. Her mouth dropped open. Her eyes were as wide as saucers. She covered her mouth and laughed as the rap artist D Murphy sang to her.

Ivy looked at Jordan and pointed to the guy as he performed. Ivy couldn't believe it. She was having the time of her life. D. Murphy waved her over. She joined him and Jordan, singing the rest of the lyrics with him. When they were done, everyone cheered. What a surprise! She hadn't expected him show up. Ivy thought they would all go back to dancing but that didn't happen.

"Ivy," D Murphy said her name. "I have a special message for you."

"For me?" Ivy reared her head back. She looked over at Jordan. He shrugged his shoulders. She looked at Anderson. He held both hands up as if to say he didn't know what was going on either. "For me?" she asked again.

"Yes. You see my man here—" he put his hands on Jordan's shoulders "—has a question for you."

Butterflies took flight in Ivy's stomach. "Wait! *What?*" Ivy looked around. No one else seemed surprised by any of this, not even her parents.

The artist proceeded to rap about her and Jordan's first encounter and then the second. Everyone laughed. Ivy blushed. The rest of his lyrics had her stunned. Tears flowed from her eyes. He sang about how she came into Jordan's life like a force and knocked him off his feet. Then she'd put him on ice. Everyone laughed. But then, when she agreed to come back to him, it made him the happiest man alive. He reached out to her family, got her father's and brothers' blessing and got interrogated.

Her brothers walked out onto the floor. Ethan took a ring box out of his pocket. He handed it to Carter, who handed it to Lincoln. Lincoln looked at Jordan and raised a brow. More laughter. He handed the box to Jordan, but pulled it back and wagged his finger at Jordan. Jordan gave him the thumbs-up and took the velvet box.

He opened it and dropped to one knee. Both hands flew to Ivy's mouth. Tears sprang in her eyes and she gasped for air. Ivy stood frozen in her shock. Phoenix, Zoe and Britney, who had made their way beside Ivy, nudged her forward.

D Murphy handed the microphone to Jordan.

"Ivy Blackwell. It doesn't take long to realize when you've got a good thing. You make me a better man. Now, I'd love if you'd make me the happiest man. Will you marry me?"

"Jordan! Yes. Yes, I'll marry you."

Jordan stood and Ivy wrapped her arms around his neck.

The room burst into applause. The DJ threw on another song by D Murphy. The crowd sang with him.

Despite the frenzy around them, Ivy and Jordan swayed in each other's arms as if a love song were playing instead of an up-tempo rap song.

"When did you contact my family?"

"The day after you said you loved me back."

"Wow!" she said breathlessly. "You sure didn't waste any time."

"Those days without you showed me how much I wanted to be with you. I was going to wait on you no matter how long it took, even though I was hoping you'd come around after the show wrapped. Thank goodness you came to your senses before that."

Giggles bubbled out of Ivy. "I'm glad too."

Jordan kissed her lips again "I could kiss you all night," he said.

"I can't get enough of you either," Ivy whispered.

"Good, because I plan to be around for a long, long time." Jordan pulled her in and kissed her like no one else was in the room.

\* \* \* \* \*

# COMING SOON!

We really hope you enjoyed reading this book.
If you're looking for more romance, be sure to
head to the shops when new books are
available on

# Thursday 8th
December

# MILLS & BOON

## THE HEART OF ROMANCE

---

## A ROMANCE FOR EVERY READER

---

**MODERN**

Prepare to be swept off your feet by sophisticated, sexy and seductive heroes, in some of the world's most glamourous and romantic locations, where power and passion collide.

**HISTORICAL**

Escape with historical heroes from time gone by. Whether your passion is for wicked Regency Rakes, muscled Vikings or rugged Highlanders, awaken the romance of the past.

**MEDICAL**

Set your pulse racing with dedicated, delectable doctors in the high-pressure world of medicine, where emotions run high and passion, comfort and love are the best medicine.

**True Love**

Celebrate true love with tender stories of heartfelt romance, from the rush of falling in love to the joy a new baby can bring, and a focus on the emotional heart of a relationship.

**Desire**

Indulge in secrets and scandal, intense drama and plenty of sizzling hot action with powerful and passionate heroes who have it all: wealth, status, good looks...everything but the right woman.

**HEROES**

Experience all the excitement of a gripping thriller, with an intense romance at its heart. Resourceful, true-to-life women and strong, fearless men face danger and desire - a killer combination!

---

To see which titles are coming soon, please visit

## millsandboon.co.uk/nextmonth